DOSTOEVSKY'S
GREATEST CHARACTERS

Also by Bernard J. Paris

Experiments in Life: George Eliot's Quest for Values (1965)

A Psychological Approach to Fiction: Studies in Thackeray, Stendhal, George Eliot, Dostoevsky, and Conrad (1974)

Character and Conflict in Jane Austen's Novels: A Psychological Approach (1978)

Third Force Psychology and the Study of Literature, Ed. (1986)

Shakespeare's Personality, Ed. with Norman Holland and Sidney Homan (1989)

Bargains with Fate: Psychological Crises and Conflicts in Shakespeare and His Plays (1991)

Character as a Subversive Force in Shakespeare: The History and the Roman Plays (1991)

Karen Horney: A Psychoanalyst's Search for Self-Understanding (1994)

Imagined Human Beings: A Psychological Approach to Character and Conflict in Literature (1997)

The Therapeutic Process: Essays and Lectures by Karen Horney, Ed. (1999)

The Unknown Karen Horney: Essays on Gender, Culture, and Psychoanalysis, Ed. (2000)

Rereading George Eliot: Changing Responses to Her Experiments in Life (2003)

Conrad's Charlie Marlow: A New Approach to "Heart of Darkness" and Lord Jim (2005)

Dostoevsky's Greatest Characters:
A New Approach to "Notes from Underground," *Crime and Punishment*, and *The Brothers Karamazov*

Bernard J. Paris

DOSTOEVSKY'S GREATEST CHARACTERS
Copyright © Bernard J. Paris, 2008.
All rights reserved. No part of this book may be used or reproduced in any manner whatsoever without written permission except in the case of brief quotations embodied in critical articles or reviews.

First published in 2008 by
PALGRAVE MACMILLAN™
175 Fifth Avenue, New York, N.Y. 10010 and
Houndmills, Basingstoke, Hampshire, England RG21 6XS.
Companies and representatives throughout the world.

PALGRAVE MACMILLAN is the global academic imprint of the Palgrave Macmillan division of St. Martin's Press, LLC and of Palgrave Macmillan Ltd. Macmillan® is a registered trademark in the United States, United Kingdom and other countries. Palgrave is a registered trademark in the European Union and other countries.

ISBN-13: 978-0-230-60293-9
ISBN-10: 0-230-60293-2

Library of Congress Cataloging-in-Publication Data is available from the Library of Congress.

A catalogue record of the book is available from the British Library.

Design by Scribe Inc.

First edition: February 2008

10 9 8 7 6 5 4 3 2 1

Printed in the United States of America

For
Jeffrey Berman
Franz Epting
Phyllis Grosskurth
Norman Holland
Celia Hunt
Peter Rudnytsky
Cherished friends, esteemed colleagues

And in memory of Andrew and Tania Tershakovec

Contents

Preface · xi

I "Notes from Underground"

1 History and Personality · 3
   i My Approach versus Frank's and Bakhtin's · 3
   ii Oppression and Suffering · 6
   iii Inner Conflicts · 9
   iv A Spiteful Official · 13

2 Zverkov and Liza · 17
   i Daydreams, the Visit to Simonov, and the Dinner for Zverkov · 17
   ii Liza in the Brothel · 23
   iii Liza's Visit · 27

3 The Diarist · 33
   i Introduction · 33
   ii Why Can't He Act? · 35
   iii "That Strange Enjoyment" · 38
   iv The Most Advantageous Advantage · 42

II *Crime and Punishment*

4 Rhetoric in *Crime and Punishment* · 51
   i Introduction · 51
   ii My Approach versus Bakhtin's · 52
   iii Dostoevsky's Rhetorical Techniques · 56
   iv Fashionable Modern Unbelief · 58
   v The Right-minded Characters · 63
   vi Dostoevsky's Perspective · 71

5	History and Inner Conflicts	73
	i Introduction	73
	ii Raskolnikov and His Family	74
	iii Inner Conflicts	82
	iv An Extraordinary Man	86
	v After the Murder	89
6	Sonya, Svidrigaylov, and Raskolnikov's Conversion	95
	i Introduction	95
	ii Raskolnikov and Sonya	96
	iii Raskolnikov and Svidrigaylov	105
	iv Raskolnikov's Conversion	108
	v The Happy Ending of *Crime and Punishment*	112

III *The Brothers Karamazov*

7	Thematic Analysis of *The Brothers Karamazov*	117
	i Introduction	117
	ii Ivan's Challenge	119
	iii Contradiction in Ivan's Position	124
	iv Responses to Ivan	126
	v Seeds That Bear Much Fruit	128
	vi We Are Responsible for All	131
	vii Freedom versus Happiness	133
8	Ivan: Character Structure and Beliefs	135
	i Introduction	135
	ii Detachment	136
	iii Anger and Aggression	139
	iv Search for Glory	143
	v The Grand Inquisitor	146
9	Ivan: Before the Murder	155
	i The Emergence of Ivan's Inner Conflicts	155
	ii Ivan and Smerdyakov	159
	iii Temptation and Fall	163
10	Ivan: After the Murder	169
	i Introduction	169
	ii The First Meeting with Smerdyakov	170

	iii	The Second Interview	173
	iv	The Final Visit to Smerdyakov	176
	v.	Continued Inner Conflicts	180
11	Alyosha: History, Personality, and Relationship with Zossima		189
	i	Introduction	189
	ii	Alyosha and His Mother	192
	iii	Alyosha's Defenses	194
	iv	Alyosha and Father Zossima	199
	v	Zossima's Teachings	201
12	Alyosha: Trials and Resolutions		207
	i	Alyosha in the World	207
	ii	Comforts and Complications	212
	iii	Rebellion: The Death of Zossima	216
	iv	Raised from the Depths	218
	v	One of the Elect	220
	vi	Conclusion	222
References			225
Index			229

Preface

One of the supreme achievements of realistic writers is the creation of what E. M. Forster calls "round" characters—complex, multifaceted, inwardly motivated beings who resemble people like ourselves. Shakespeare and Dostoevsky are the two greatest creators of such characters. I have discussed Shakespeare's characters in two previous studies (Paris 1991a, 1991b); I shall focus on Dostoevsky's here.

Not all round characters are created equal. As Shlomith Rimmon-Kenan points out, there is a continuum from lesser to greater degrees of "complexity, development," and "penetration into the inner life" (1996, 41). In my view, Dostoevsky's greatest character creations are the underground man, Raskolnikov, and Ivan and Alyosha Karamazov; and I shall concentrate on them in this book.

It is a curious phenomenon that, although criticism abounds with tributes to Dostoevsky's remarkable insight into human nature, sufficient justice has not yet been done to his genius in characterization. One of the chief reasons for this is that Dostoevsky is a great philosophical novelist, and his characters have such a rich and absorbing ideological interest that attention tends to be focused on their thematic significance rather than on their motivations, personalities, and relationships. Ernest Simmons observes that "we never seem to think of Dostoevsky's characters absolutely in terms of themselves" but "rather in terms of the ideas which they personify" (1940, 267). The ideas they personify are important, but to appreciate Dostoevsky's achievement, we must look at his characters as beings of interest in themselves and not just *through* them to what we think the author is using them to say.

Another reason why Dostoevsky's skill in characterization has not been fully explored is that critics who are sympathetic to his ideology tend to feel, with Eliseo Vivas, that in his fiction the metaphysical level "informs" or is "below" the psychological level (1955, 58, 64). As Vivas suggests, Dostoevsky's object was to present portrayals of life that would show spiritual forces at work in the world and demonstrate the inadequacy of naturalistic explanations to account for the mysteries of the human soul. This produces a paradoxical situation: Dostoevsky created great psychological portraits, but he did not want us to understand them psychologically. If we try to account for his characters' behavior as products of their personalities and experiences, we are going against his fundamental assumption that humans are spiritual beings who cannot be adequately comprehended from an empirical point of view.

Nonetheless, I argue that the behavior of Dostoevsky's greatest characters is intelligible in psychological terms. Dostoevsky was not only a philosophical novelist committed to reaffirming man's spiritual nature and destiny in the face of contemporary secular thought, he was also a realistic novelist who created characters of such depth and complexity that they can be understood independently of their illustrative function. That is one reason why his novels appeal not only to those who subscribe to his beliefs but also to those who disagree. Although I often quarrel with Dostoevsky's interpretations of his characters, I am awestruck by the subtlety and depth of his psychological portraiture. It may be one of the ironies of criticism that this aspect of Dostoevsky's art cannot be properly appreciated by those who share his assumptions about human nature and the human condition, but only by those who have a different perspective.

I shall reverse the order of priorities Vivas has proposed. That is, I shall argue that the psychological level "informs" or underlies the metaphysical—that the behavior and beliefs of Dostoevsky's greatest characters flow from their personalities and experiences and from the strategies of defense these have led them to develop. I shall also reverse Joseph Frank's derivation of the characters' personalities from their ideas, which he tends to ascribe to the intellectual climate of their times (1986, 1995, 2002). I shall argue that the characters are so responsive to certain currents of thought because they are psychologically predisposed toward them to begin with.

Although most commentators discuss Dostoevsky's characters in thematic terms, often treating them as coded messages from the author that it is the critic's job to decipher, not everyone has done this. Two major exceptions have been psychoanalytic critics and Mikhail Bakhtin. The approach I shall employ here has something in common with both, but it will also be different in many ways.

There is a substantial body of psychoanalytic criticism that discusses Dostoevsky's characters in motivational terms. I shall do the same thing, but not in the same way. Whereas most psychoanalytic criticism employs a diachronic approach that explains the present in terms of very early experience, I shall draw on the predominantly synchronic theory of Karen Horney, which explains a person's thoughts, feelings, and behaviors in terms of their function within the present structure of the psyche. The psychology of the adult is still seen as being influenced by childhood, and information about formative experience can be used when it is available; but the adult personality can be understood in terms of its current dynamics even when there is little information about the person's early life.

A predominantly synchronic approach is especially well suited to the analysis of literary characters (of the round variety), for although their childhoods are often but sketchily portrayed, their current personality traits, defenses, and inner conflicts are depicted in great detail (see Paris 1974, 1997). In the case of Dostoevsky's greatest characters, the information we are given about their formative years is highly revealing and helps us to see why their personalities developed as they did. I shall not have to speculate about infantile origins but shall stick closely to the details Dostoevsky provides.

I shall introduce specific aspects of Horney's theory where appropriate as I try to understand Dostoevsky's extraordinarily complex creations, with the fullest discussion occurring in my chapters on "Notes from Underground" (for a comprehensive account, see Paris 1994a). Horney's ideas do not work equally well with all aspects of Dostoevsky's fiction, but they are remarkably congruent with the characters I shall discuss.

Through the use of a present-oriented approach, I hope to recover many of Dostoevsky's hitherto unrecognized psychological intuitions and to enhance our appreciation of his mimetic portraiture. I shall pay close attention to aspects of characterization that are crucial to his art but that have been largely ignored in the criticism. W. J. Harvey has observed that in the creation of "imagined human beings" (his term for highly rounded characters), there is "a surplus margin of gratuitous life, a sheer excess of material, a fecundity of detail and invention" that "often overflows the strict necessities of form" (1965, 188). It is this fecundity of detail that brings characters to life and enables them to transcend the author's time and place and his own conscious understanding of them. The approach I employ will enable us to see the significance of such detail and its contribution to the enduring interest of Dostoevsky's imagined human beings.

As I examine the details of Dostoevsky's psychological portraiture, it may seem at times that I am retelling the story (a practice I dislike in other critics), but usually the story I am telling has not yet been clearly seen, though it may appear obvious once it has been pointed out. What we see depends on the questions we ask and the interpretive tools we employ. My questions and my tools are different than those that have been in play so far, and the Dostoevsky I see is also different as a consequence. When I shared some drafts of my chapters with a colleague who teaches Dostoevsky and is intimately familiar with *The Brothers Karamazov*, I received the following response: "I'm reading BK with the Paris glasses. Makes a *big* difference." I hope that readers of this book will feel the same.

I have mentioned Bakhtin as an exception to the usual practice of seeing Dostoevsky's characters as embodiments of ideas, and in the chapters that follow I shall have several occasions to compare my approach with his. I share his view of Dostoevsky's characters as autonomous beings who are capable of standing alongside their creator and even rebelling against him. And I think he is right that there is a conflict in Dostoevsky's novels between the "internal open-endedness of the characters" and the "compositional and thematic *completeness*" of the larger structures in which they participate (Bahktin 1984, 39). He sees this conflict being resolved in a transcendent harmony, an overall artistic unity, but I do not.

Indeed, one of my major theses is that there is a tension between Dostoevsky's most fully developed characters and the roles they are supposed to play in the works in which they appear. This tension is minimal in "Notes from Underground" because of the first person narration; but *Crime and Punishment* and *The Brothers Karamazov* are novels with elaborate thematic structures from which the main characters tend to escape when they are understood in motivational terms. In his insistence on the absence of a fixed ideological framework, Bakhtin ignores the rhetorical component of these works, but I shall begin my discussion of each with a thematic analysis, within which I shall then situate my discussion of the characters as imagined human beings who do, indeed, have the "independence and freedom" Bakhtin ascribes to them (1984, 13). They also have histories and undergo processes of development that Bakhtin denies but which are the source of much of their fascination. While I greatly admire Bakhtin's subtle analysis of the dialogues that go on within and between characters, there are aspects of his version of Dostoevsky with which I cannot agree. Ernest Simmons contends that "nothing in human experience as we know it will satisfactorily explain the exaggerated motives and actions of old Karamazov, Dmitry, Ivan, Alyosha, Smerdyakov, Zossima, Grushenka, and Katerina Ivanovna" (1940, 31). That depends, I would say, on how closely we study these characters and on the conceptions of human experience we bring to the fiction. But I think that even the most psychologically sophisticated of us will be challenged by Dostoevsky because however much we may know beforehand, he has a great deal to teach us. His mimetic portrayal of his great characters conveys an intuitive grasp of human behavior which is far richer than that contained in any conceptual understanding, including his—and also including mine.

* * *

I taught Dostoevsky for over thirty years, first in Comparative Fiction courses at Michigan State University and then in Psychological Approaches to Literature courses at the University of Florida. I am deeply indebted to my students for their patience as I struggled with difficult texts and for their probing questions and astute observations. I could not have developed my interpretations without the stimulus they provided.

In my chapters on "Notes from Underground" and *Crime and Punishment*, I have drawn on earlier publications; and I am grateful to those who assisted me with my previous work. "'Notes from Underground': A Horneyan Analysis," published in *PMLA* in 1973, became, with some revisions, a chapter in *A Psychological Approach to Fiction: Studies in Thackeray, Stendhal, George Eliot, Dostoevsky, and Conrad* (1974). That chapter has been much expanded here. I again thank those whose help has been acknowledged in the preface to *A Psychological Approach to Fiction*. My first study of *Crime and Punishment* ("The Two Selves of Rodion Raskolnikov") appeared in *Gradiva* in 1978, and a revised version was incorporated in "A Horneyan Approach to Literature," published in *The American Journal of Psychoanalysis* in 1991. I developed a fuller account of Raskolnikov's relationship with his mother in "Pulkheria Alexandrovna and Raskolnikov, My Mother and Me," which was published in *Self-Analysis in Literary Study*, edited by Daniel Rancour-Lafferiere (1994). This essay shows how my analysis of my relationship with *my* mother helped me to understand Raskolnikov's relationship with his. The essay is posted on my Web site: http://grove.ufl.edu/~bjparis. As with my chapters on "Notes from Underground," my chapters on *Crime and Punishment* go well beyond the earlier work that was their starting point. My chapters on *The Brothers Karamazov* are entirely new.

    I wish to thank Paul Brachhold of Sound Ideas for help in repairing a tape of one of my classes on Alyosha Karamazov and John Van Hook for his assistance in utilizing the resources of the University of Florida library. Joe Barnhart, who is working on a sequel to *The Brothers Karamazov*, read my chapters on that novel as they were being written and gave me helpful and encouraging feedback. It has meant a great deal to me to have such an interested and knowledgeable reader in mind as I was working on those chapters. Celia Hunt has been urging me for years to pay more attention to Bakhtin and has given me thoughtful responses to almost all of this study. As always, my first reader has been my dear wife, Shirley, who has pondered Dostoevsky with me over a number of decades. Her initial skepticism about my reading of Ivan made me strengthen my argument, and her enthusiasm for this project carried me through many a dry spell. I have been sustained also by the friendship of those to whom I have dedicated this book. They have been an important part of the audience I imagined as I wrote.

Note on Citations

I am using the Garnett translations of "Notes from Underground" and *The Brothers Karamazov* and the Coulson translation of *Crime and Punishment*. I give the chapter number after the first quotation in each paragraph and each time the chapter number changes. If all quotations in a paragraph are from the same chapter, there is only the initial citation.

PART I

"NOTES FROM UNDERGROUND"

CHAPTER 1

HISTORY AND PERSONALITY

I. MY APPROACH VERSUS FRANK'S AND BAKHTIN'S

AS ALBERT GUERARD HAS OBSERVED, "NOTES FROM UNDERGROUND" is "the most intense and most authentic rendering in Dostoevsky, perhaps in all of novelistic literature, of neurotic suffering seen from within," but "it is also a document of major philosophical interest" (1976, 166). In his celebrated discussion of the novella, Joseph Frank remarks that although most critics emphasize "one or the other of the work's two main aspects," the "text cannot be properly understood" unless we grasp the intimate interconnection between the underground man's psychology and his ideas (1986, 310). I agree with Frank's premise but not with his approach, which is in many ways opposite to mine.

Frank's approach is predominantly thematic. He acknowledges that the first person narration "makes it difficult to see *through*" the underground man to Dostoevsky's satiric intentions and that "the parodistic function of his character" tends to be "obscured by the immense vitality of its artistic embodiment" (1986, 315, emphasis mine). Dostoevsky's "very genius for the creation of character" has "interfered with the proper understanding" of his work. The opening footnote of "Notes from Underground" indicates that Dostoevsky meant us to see the protagonist as a "social-cultural type" who was the inevitable outcome of the conditions of Russian society (331). Dostoevsky's objective was to create a "Swiftian satire" that "dramatizes the dilemmas of a representative Russian personality attempting to live" by two European philosophies, the social romanticism of the

1840s and the utilitarian philosophy of rational egoism set forth in Nikolai Chernyshevsky's *What Is To Be Done?* (316). For Frank, "Notes from Underground" is "above all a diptych depicting two episodes of a symbolic history of the Russian intelligentsia," with Part I focusing on the 1860s and Part II on the 1840s.

Frank may be right about Dostoevsky's intentions, although the first person narration makes it difficult to determine where the author stands in this work. Aside from the footnote, there is little overt authorial rhetoric; but Frank has made a strong case for the novella's parodistic characteristics and satiric and ideological import, as have other critics as well. These are important features of the work, and I am grateful to those who have enriched our comprehension of them. However, I see "Notes from Underground" as above all a masterful psychological portrait in which the complexity of the underground man's motivations cannot be adequately accounted for in thematic terms. Even if Frank is correct about the author's intentions, Dostoevsky's character-creating impulse led him to fashion a protagonist who cannot—or, at least, should not—be reduced to his illustrative roles. As Frank himself observes, in "Notes from Underground" Dostoevsky the novelist tends "to overpower Dostoevsky the satirist" (1986, 315).

Frank's objective is to rescue the thematic components of the novella from the remarkably rich characterization by which he feels readers have been distracted. My objective is to rescue Dostoevsky's portrait of his protagonist from the emphasis on satire, parody, and ideology that has prevented many critics from paying close attention to the underground man's personality. Frank wants "to see *through* the character" to the satire (1986, 315, emphasis mine); I want to look *at* the underground man, to see the imagined human being that a focus on thematic elements tends to obscure.

As I have said, I agree with Frank that discussions of "Notes from Underground" have tended to be one-sided and that the work "cannot be properly understood without grasping the interaction" between the protagonist's psychology and his ideological stance (1986, 310). Frank connects these aspects of the novella by seeing psychology as a product of ideology and "strictly subordinated" to it (346). He derives the underground man's beliefs from his culture, particularly his reading, and his psychology from his beliefs. The narrator's vanity, his inner chaos, and his self-derision are all related to his "intellectual culture" (335) and his often rebellious responses to it.

The same is true of his masochism, which has a "positive significance," according to Frank (337). "For the first time," says Frank, Dostoevsky "motivates an action *entirely* in terms of a psychology shaped by a radical ideology; every feature of the text serves to bring out the consequences in personal behavior of certain ideas" (346).

Whereas Frank derives the underground man's psychology from his beliefs, I see his ideological stance as in large part a product of his history and personality. I am not alone in doing so, of course. Mark Spilka asks, "what forces" the underground man to "carry ideologies to extremes"? (1966, 239). Ralph Matlaw observes that "through a complex series of psychological and social motivations," the narrator is "actually driven to the philosophical position" he enunciates in Part I (1958, 108). James Lethcoe formulates "the problem" of "the relationship between the psychological and the philosophical levels" of the novella in the following way: "Is the paradoxical character of the underground man to be evaluated in light of his philosophical theories about the nature of man, i.e., that man is free, arbitrary, many-sided, and irrational; or are we to see such theories as the kind of theories such a character as the underground man would naturally hold in order to rationalize his existence?" (1966, 17).

Possibly in response to Frank's original essay on "Notes from Underground" (1961), Lethcoe proposes a shift in critical perspective: "Instead of emphasizing the underground man's personality as exemplifying his theories, we should perhaps see his views as the expression of his personality" (1966, 17). Lethcoe does not provide the analysis he calls for; nor, with the exception of my own earlier work (Paris 1973, 1974), do the numerous psychological studies of "Notes from Underground." I shall try to supply here a fuller account of the characterological sources of the protagonist's philosophic stance than has been proffered so far.

Before we look at the underground man's attitudes and beliefs, we must try to understand his character structure; and in order to do this, we must pay closer attention to his history than has usually been done. Mikhail Bakhtin contends that "there is no causality in Dostoevsky's novels, no genesis, no explanations based on the past, on the influences of the environment or of upbringing" (1984, 29). A consciousness in Dostoevsky's world is not presented historically, "on the path of its own evolution," but rather "*alongside* other consciousnesses" (32). Dostoevsky's people do not "live a biographical life in biographical time" (169). Their acts are "not predetermined" but are "conceived of and represented by the author as free." I do not think that Bakhtin's observations are true for the underground man—nor for the other characters I shall discuss.

I subscribe to the consensus of psychologically oriented critics that the underground man's ostensibly "capricious behavior" is "compulsive" (Bouson 1989, 39), that "he cannot help himself" (Guerard 1976, 169), that "the protagonist of 'freedom' is himself unfree" (Goodheart, 1968, 97). As Mark Spilka observes, "the narrator claims to choose perversity," but "clearly . . . perversity has chosen him" (1966, 239–40). Spilka sees the narrator's adult personality as resulting in part from "early victimization" (239), and so do I. The underground man has been profoundly influenced by his life in biographical time.

Our knowledge of the protagonist's life is uneven. We are given information about his existence as a child, a schoolboy, a government clerk, and a diarist. We know something about his circumstances before he leaves for school, more about his schooldays, and much more about his midtwenties, when he is working as a clerk and has the experiences he describes in Part II. He writes his "notes" when he is forty, having retired at the midlevel rank of collegiate assessor the previous year, when a relative leaves him 6000 roubles in his will (I, i). He describes the wretched conditions in which he lives, which have been much the same for the past twenty years; but his outer existence is uneventful, and his main activity seems to be writing in his diary, which reveals a great deal about his inner world.

In this chapter I shall examine the underground man's character structure as a product of his history and his behavior as a product of his character structure. In the next, I shall look at how his character structure manifests itself in the sequence of events that begins with his visit to Simonov and concludes with Liza's appearance at his lodging. In my final chapter on the novella, I shall explore the underground man's motivations for writing his "notes" and the relationship between his psychology and his attitudes and beliefs.

II. OPPRESSION AND SUFFERING

Perhaps because of his desire to explain the protagonist's behavior in ideological terms, Frank denies that the underground man has been victimized: "Dostoevsky is a master at portraying the psychology of pride and humiliation, and when the humiliation springs from some genuine oppression or suffering, he knows how to make it intensely moving; but it would be a flagrant misreading to take the underground man as such a victim" (1986, 335–36). I think that the misreading is Frank's.

The underground man is an orphan raised by "distant relations" who resented having to care for him and treated him badly (II, iii). When he is in his teens, they send him away to school "a forlorn, silent boy, already crushed by their reproaches . . . and looking with savage distrust at every one." He never hears from them again. He tells Liza that if he "had had a home from childhood," he wouldn't be what he is now (II, vi), but that he "grew up without a home": "However bad it may be at home, anyway they are your father and mother, and not enemies, strangers. Once a year at least, they'll show their love of you."

As a child, the underground man was so starved for affection (and still is, as an adult) that a show of love once a year looks good to him. He longed for more than that, of course, as the picture of family life he paints for Liza indicates. He is trying to manipulate her to be sure, but the images he conjures up express some of his own deepest longings. He wishes he had had parents who felt joy in denying themselves for him, who served an "an example" and "a support," who felt that having children was not "a trial" but "heavenly happiness"(II, vi). He asks Liza if she is "fond of little children" and says that he is "awfully fond of them." We see no evidence of such fondness elsewhere in his narration, but he is probably expressing sympathy toward his own earlier self and a wish that someone had been fond of him.

It should be noted that the narrator offers explanations of his behavior based on his past, on the influence of his upbringing and environment. It is because he grew up without a home, he tells Liza, that he has "turned so . . . unfeeling" (II, vi); and he sees his behavior at school and his fate there as emanating from his childhood experience.

* * *

The underground man's years at school are no less wretched than his earlier life. Odd, defensive, radiating hostility and distrust, he is mercilessly tormented by his schoolmates, who take no trouble to "conceal their aversion" (II, iii). They laugh not only at his behavior but also at his "face" and "clumsy figure." He is made to feel repulsive in every way. He "hate[s] them horribly," and they hate him in return. On leaving school, he wants "to cut off all connection with [his] hateful childhood. Curses on that school and all those terrible years of penal servitude!" (II, ii). After he invites himself to the dinner for Zverkov, he is "oppressed by memories of [his] miserable days at school" and has "the most hideous dreams" (II, iii).

The underground man experiences genuine oppression and suffering in his early years, and I, for one, am deeply moved by his humiliations. They shape his character profoundly, generating inconsistencies and inner conflicts at every stage of his life.

In the opening pages of his notes, for instance, when he is describing his government service, he tells us that he was a spiteful official who was rude to petitioners and enjoyed making them unhappy but that there was something that kept him from being wholeheartedly sadistic: "even in the moment of acutest spleen, I was inwardly conscious with shame that I was not only not a spiteful but not even an embittered man" (I, i). He "might foam at the mouth," but he could be easily "appeased" or "touched," though he would "grind [his] teeth at [himself] afterwards and lie awake at night with shame for months after." "In reality," he says, he "could never become spiteful" because he was "conscious every moment" of many elements in himself "absolutely opposite to that." These elements had always been "swarming" in him, craving an outlet, but he "would not let them come out." They tormented him until he was "ashamed," drove him to "convulsions," and "sickened" him. He concludes this part of his account by asking his imagined readers if they are fancying that he is "expressing remorse for something" or seeking their "forgiveness," and assuring them that he does "not care" if they are.

What is going on here? Why is the underground man so sadistic? Why does he believe that he is not spiteful and embittered when clearly he is? Why does this belief cause him shame? Why is he so easily appeased? Why does being appeased make him so angry with himself that for months afterward he lies awake with shame? What are the elements within him that have been craving an outlet and that he has suppressed? Why do they drive him to convulsions and make him ill? Why does he say that he doesn't care if anyone thinks he is expressing remorse or asking forgiveness when it is evident that he does?

To my knowledge, no other critic has grappled with such questions about the underground man's psychology in a sustained way. In his effort to understand his lack of a stable identity, the underground man attributes his condition to the "fundamental laws of over-acute consciousness" (I, i), but this explanation, which I shall examine in chapter 3, seems inadequate to the complexity of his behavior. His oscillations can be traced, I believe, to the effects of his early life.

III. INNER CONFLICTS

As we have seen, the underground man has a singularly bleak and loveless childhood. He lives with abusive relatives who make him feel unwanted and insignificant. He regards his relations as "enemies" (II, iv) who are not to be trusted and against whom he must defend himself. This is not an environment in which he can experience his spontaneous thoughts, feelings, wishes, and interests. As a result, he loses touch with his own center and lacks a stable sense of identity. He is motivated primarily by his defenses, which are often at odds with each other.

The psychoanalyst Karen Horney has provided a good description of people who feel unsafe, unloved, and unvalued like the underground man and of the coping devices they employ. They tend to move toward, against, or away from other people, adopting self-effacing, aggressive, or detached strategies of defense. Each of these solutions generates its own character traits, values, behaviors, and beliefs as well as a set of inner dictates that cannot be violated without exacerbating feelings of anxiety and self-contempt.

The object of the self-effacing strategy is to gain affection, approval, and protection through compliance, humility, and devotion. In this solution, goodness and love are valued above all else, and suffering and sacrifice are glorified. Self-assertive and self-protective activities are severely inhibited, and there are powerful taboos against "all that is presumptuous, selfish, and aggressive" (Horney 1950, 219). There is a belief in turning the other cheek, and the world is seen as displaying a providential order in which virtue is rewarded.

In the expansive solution, the highest value is not love but mastery. Considerateness, compassion, and loyalty are scorned as signs of weakness, as are all manifestations of softer feelings. Strength, efficiency, and toughness are admired, as is the ruthless pursuit of power. The world is perceived as a jungle in which might makes right, the fittest survive, and all are out for themselves. There is an abhorrence of the dependency, helplessness, and suffering on which the self-effacing solution relies.

The detached solution involves dealing with a threatening world by removing oneself from its power and shutting others out of one's inner life. Those employing this solution seek privacy, find it a great strain to associate with people, and may go to pieces if their magic circle is entered and they are thrown into intimate contact with others. The primary goals of this solution are not love or mastery but freedom and independence. There is a desire to be left alone, to have nothing expected of one, and to be subject to no restrictions. Intelligence, imagination, and individuality are highly prized, as are willpower and psychological insight. Ambitious pursuits are avoided because they make one vulnerable—better not to try than to fail. Needs for superiority or triumph are realized in imagination rather than through actual accomplishments. Resignation is an important part of the detached solution. In order to avoid being dependent on others, those who employ this defensive strategy try to relinquish expectations, subdue inner cravings, and be content with little. They cultivate a "don't care" attitude and protect themselves against frustration by feeling that "nothing matters."

The movements toward, against, or away from others are incompatible with each other, but people whose basic emotional needs have been thwarted will make all three of the moves compulsively and will be torn by inner conflicts. To gain some sense of wholeness, they will emphasize one move more than the others and will become mainly self-effacing, aggressive, or detached. Which move they emphasize will depend on a combination of temperamental and environmental factors, and the relationship between the solutions within their character structure will vary from person to person and from time to time. The subordinate trends will manifest themselves in every configuration, and one of them may become dominant if the primary solution fails.

* * *

The underground man longs for approval, for protection, for the warmth of family life. But there is no point in seeking them by moving toward the "strangers" with whom he lives; they view him as a burden and have nothing to give. The only thing to do with his need for love is to stifle it. Instead of receiving affection, he is severely reproached for failing to meet the demands of people whom he hates. His demeanor at school suggests that he probably expressed his resentment through a haughty attitude and surly behavior, but he feels too weak and fearful to stand up for himself. Full of repressed rage, he leaves home a forlorn and silent figure who is subject to recurrent depression.

Unable either to fight or to obtain love, the underground man seeks to protect himself by means of detachment. He leads a solitary existence at almost every stage of his life. At school he shuts himself "away from everyone" in response to being persecuted (II, iii), and when he leaves school he takes an inferior position in order to avoid further contact with his classmates. By the age of twenty-four, he tells us, his life was "gloomy, ill-regulated, and as solitary as that of a savage." He finds it "loathsome sometimes to go to the office" and "often [comes] home ill" (II, i). As soon as he receives a small inheritance, he retires from service and retreats almost entirely into his underground world: "my lodging was my private solitude, my shell, my cave, in which I concealed myself from all mankind" (II, viii). When his privacy is invaded or emotional demands are made on him, as in the episode with Liza, he becomes hysterical: "I was . . . insufferably oppressed by her being here. I wanted her to disappear. I wanted 'peace,' to be left alone in my underground world" (II, x). The consequences of the underground man's withdrawal from life force him to withdraw even more. He scorns worldly success, but he is deeply humiliated by his poverty and the insignificance of his position, and he feels terribly inferior to his more prosperous schoolmates. His contact with other people is so painful in part because it reminds him of his lowly status, which fills him with shame and is very much at odds with his claims for himself. He is sickened by the wretchedness of his life; but he "grew used to" it, he tells us, "or rather I voluntarily resigned myself to enduring it" (II, ii). He defends himself against his feelings of failure by protestations of indifference and by escaping into dreams of glory: "I would dream for three months on end, tucked away in my corner. . . . I suddenly became a hero."

* * *

Although detachment is the underground man's predominant defense, his conflicting needs make him unable to employ this strategy consistently. He has cravings for vindictive triumphs and for human companionship that propel him into the adventures he describes in Part II. In both his school years and his life as a clerk, he moves not only away from but also against and toward other people.

At school, the other boys meet him "with spiteful and merciless jibes" because he is "not like any of them" (II, iii). Already hypersensitive to rejection because of his treatment at home, he is terribly pained by this reception. He despises the appeasing behavior that he sees some of the boys employing (to deal with bullying, no doubt) and adopts the only strategy that has worked for him: he shuts himself away from his fellow students and looks down on them with scorn.

But he cannot detach himself enough to become indifferent to their derision, and consumed by hatred, he longs "for their humiliation" (II, iii). More intelligent than his schoolmates and far better read, he seeks to turn the tables on them and to vindicate himself by applying himself to his studies. He now has an outlet for his aggression that he did not have at home. When he forces his way to the top of the class, the boys are impressed and the mockery stops; however, the "hostility remain[s]," and his relations with others are cold and distant.

In the end the underground man cannot bear his alienation. He develops "a craving for society" and tries "to get on friendly terms" with some of his schoolfellows, but his relationships are "always strained" and do not last very long (II, iii). He wants friendship but still harbors much resentment, as do his classmates. His fear of closeness makes him aloof and distrustful; in his experience, other people have always caused him pain.

The underground man's one friendship in his school days is destroyed by his contradictory needs. He frightens his friend with his "passionate affection," reducing him "to hysterics" by his demands. When his friend "devote[s] himself to [him] entirely," however, the underground man immediately begins to drive him away (II, iii). His hunger for love and validation is so intense that he craves an absolute response. He needs his friend to become his unquestioning ally and requires of him a "complete break" with the "surroundings" for which he himself feels so much "contempt." But when his friend gives him the devotion he seeks, the underground man despises him for allowing himself to be dominated.

I believe that the underground man's contempt for his friend is an externalization of what he feels toward the side of himself that is tempted to seek safety, love, and approval by being submissive. This is a strategy that has never worked for him and which he fears. Not only would it weaken him, but he would detest himself if he should employ it. Having been subjected to so much abuse, he is afraid of being vulnerable and needs to be hard and tough.

Having a compliant friend gives the underground man a chance to be in a position of ascendancy for the first time in his life, and he exercises his power in a tyrannical manner. But once he attains dominance, he loses interest in a person whose submissiveness is contemptible and whose devotion cannot be worth very much if he is such a weakling. At the same time, however, the side of him that craves and values love is critical of his desire for dominance and his heartless rejection of his companion. He accuses himself of being a tyrant and is uncomfortable because it seems he only wanted to subjugate his friend. He did want something else, of course, but his craving for love is weaker than his other needs. Because of his inner conflicts, the underground man can pursue neither love nor mastery without blaming himself. After the collapse of his friendship, he makes his most characteristic move, which is to shrink away from other people.

IV. A Spiteful Official

The underground man's inner conflicts continue to manifest themselves during his years as a government clerk. He is now even more isolated than he had been at school. He "never looks at anyone," has no friends, and feels that his fellow workers regard him with "loathing" and "aversion" (II, i). Joseph Frank sees him as a social-cultural type, but he himself believes that he is "unlike anyone else." "I am alone," he laments, "and they are *every one*" (author's emphasis). From his perspective, others are typical figures who regard him as a "queer fellow."

As at school, he cannot not bear his isolation indefinitely and develops a craving for society. He shifts from being unwilling to speak to his fellow workers to "contemplating making friends with them" (II, i). He tells us that during one period he even "visited their homes, played preference, drank vodka, talked of promotions." But again, as at school, he cannot "maintain friendly relations" and reverts to being alone. His renewed withdrawal does not work, however, for he becomes "overwhelmed with depression" and longs "for movement in spite of everything." In his social and sexual frustration, he engages in "dark, underground, loathsome vice," furtively visiting houses of prostitution. This allows him to have human contact without becoming emotionally involved with anyone. His dissipations are followed by shame and remorse, from which he seeks refuge in dreams of the good and the beautiful; but after some months of dreaming, he always feels a renewed need for society.

Now that we have some understanding of the underground man's inner conflicts, we are in a position to consider his treatment of petitioners and his ambivalent attitude toward his behavior. He tells us that he was "a spiteful official" who "felt intense enjoyment when [he] succeeded in making anybody unhappy (I, i). It is not difficult to understand why the underground man is sadistic. He has always been tormented by others and has felt himself to be in their power. As an official, he has the petitioners in *his* power and can release some of his suppressed rage by tormenting them. Having been tyrannized as a child, he becomes a tyrant when he has the opportunity to do so. However, his discomfort with this behavior prevents him from wholeheartedly enjoying his vindictiveness. Indeed, he goes on to deny that he was really a spiteful person.

There are a number of reasons why the underground man denies that he was spiteful. He has needs for love, desires for warmth and human closeness, that make him feel that his aggressive behavior does not reflect who he really is; and the inner dictates created by his impulse to move toward people make it impossible for him to admit to himself his anger and cruelty. He must deny these things in order to avoid self-condemnation. At the same time, however, he is mortified by his softness, by the ease with which he can be touched. His aggressive side wants to be unabashedly sadistic and is full of contempt for his sentimentality. Hence, when he is appeased he grinds his teeth at himself and lies awake with shame long after. He is caught in a crossfire of conflicting inner dictates and is bound to hate himself whether he is soft hearted or spiteful. His conclusion that he was "simply scaring sparrows at random and amusing" himself by it (I, i) testifies to his sense of his aggressive self as an empty facade, but it is hardly an explanation of his behavior. It does accord, however, with the dictates of his detachment, which demand that his behavior be undetermined ("random") and that he have no strong feelings (he was simply "amusing" himself). His detachment also requires him to deny that he is embittered, for to be embittered means that other people have been able to injure him, that he has not achieved the indifference to which he aspires. He hates others because they *have* injured him, but if he acknowledged his bitterness, he would have to despise himself for having allowed himself to be hurt.

The violence of the underground man's inner conflicts is evident when he speaks of the "absolutely opposite" elements that have been "swarming" in him all his life and that he will not allow to emerge (I, i). His impulses to move toward people "torment" him because both the aggressive and detached components of his personality make him condemn himself for having such feelings. He will not let these impulses come out because they are profoundly threatening to his other defenses. His aggressive side must suppress trends that would judge it to be evil, and his detached side is deeply afraid of inner forces that would drive him into unbearable intimacy and would expose him to further injury.

Part of the underground man's difficulty, of course, is that his conflicting tendencies are not only very powerful but are all very close to the surface, so that he is driven to "convulsions" and "sickened" by the warfare between them. His detachment, which becomes more and more profound as he grows older, is in part an effort to escape his torment by substituting intellectual awareness for the direct and agonizing experience of his inner contradictions. As is typical of a person who employs this defense, he takes great pride in his intelligence and psychological insight.

Afraid that his auditors will think that he has been expressing remorse and asking forgiveness for something, the underground man proclaims his indifference to what anyone else might think. His aggressive side cannot admit to feelings of repentance; it urges him to get back at his imagined interlocutors, who have been feeling superior, by dismissing the importance of their thoughts. His denial of uncomfortable feelings and his lack of concern about the opinions of others are also generated by his need not to care, not to be vulnerable either to his own softer feelings or to external judgments. They are no more to be taken at face value than his declaration that he is not a spiteful man.

The underground man really is spiteful; he really is remorseful; and he really is indifferent. Like the Russian romantics he describes, he is a "broad" nature, a "many-sided" man (II, i) who is full of contradictory elements. His problem is that because he contains everything, he feels that he is nothing; none of his attributes really define him. "It was not only that I could not become spiteful," he tells us. "I did not know how to become anything: neither spiteful nor kind, neither a rascal nor an honest man, neither a hero nor an insect" (I, i). He cannot become anything because every one of his acts, impulses, and values is subject to almost immediate repudiation by the conflicting components of his personality. It is no wonder that he feels "selfless," without substantial reality. He is in fact a puppet pulled about by his contradictory compulsions who ironically takes his slavery as an evidence of freedom.

CHAPTER 2

ZVERKOV AND LIZA

1. DAY DREAMS, THE VISIT TO SIMONOV, AND THE DINNER FOR ZVERKOV

OUR ANALYSIS OF THE UNDERGROUND MAN'S INNER CONFLICTS CAN shed a good deal of light on the long episode, beginning with the visit to Simonov, that takes up the last half of the novella. As we have seen, the underground man tries to protect himself against the pain of human contact by withdrawing into his private solitude and living in a world of fantasy. He cannot dream for more than three months at a time, however, "without feeling an irresistible desire to plunge into society" (II, ii). Since he has only one "permanent acquaintance," his superior at the office, plunging into society means visiting Anton Antonitch on his at-home day, which is Tuesday. Because it is on a Thursday that he becomes "unable to endure [his] solitude any longer," he goes to see his old classmate Simonov despite his desire to cut himself off from reminders of his miserable life at school. This leads him to invite himself to the dinner for Zverkov, to follow the others to the brothel, and to become involved with Liza. His behavior at every point in this sequence reflects his inner conflicts.

Before he calls on Simonov, the underground man has spent three months "tucked away in [his] corner" dreaming of "the good and the beautiful" (II, ii). We must have a look at his fantasy life if we are to understand his behavior at Simonov's and the events it precipitates.

Once again, Karen Horney's work will be helpful. Horney describes not only the interpersonal strategies of moving toward, against, and away from other people but also intrapsychic strategies that begin with self-idealization. To compensate for feelings of inadequacy and self-hatred, individuals create, with the aid of their imaginations, an "idealized image" of themselves that they endow with "unlimited powers and exalted faculties" (1950, 22). They then embark on a "search for glory," the object of which is to actualize this idealized image.

The process of self-idealization must be understood in relation to the interpersonal strategies of defense, for the idealized image is based on the attributes these strategies celebrate. It reflects not only a person's predominant defense but also the subordinate moves; and since each solution glorifies different behaviors and values, the idealized image has contradictory aspects, all of which press for actualization. Moreover, since people can feel worthwhile only if they *are* their idealized selves, everything that falls short is deemed worthless; and there develops a "despised image" that increases self-contempt. A great many people shuttle, says Horney, between "a feeling of arrogant omnipotence and of being the scum of the earth" (188).

The idealized image generates what Horney calls "the pride system." Individuals take an intense pride in the attributes of their idealized selves; and on the basis of these attributes, they make exaggerated claims on the world. The need to actualize their idealized image leads them to impose stringent demands and taboos on themselves (Horney calls these "tyrannical shoulds"), to compel them to live up to their grandiose conception of themselves. Their inner dictates are determined largely by their predominant interpersonal defense; but because subordinate trends are also represented in their idealized image, they are often caught in a "crossfire of conflicting shoulds." If they obey the demands of one solution, they will be violating the demands of another, so they are bound to hate themselves whatever they do. People often bounce back and forth between various solutions in an effort to appease their contradictory inner dictates. We have already seen this process at work in underground man, and it is dramatized in Dostoevsky's fiction again and again.

* * *

Horney's descriptions of interpersonal defenses help us to understand the underground man's behavior toward other people, and her descriptions of intrapsychic defenses illuminate his inner life and his struggles with himself.

The underground man's fantasies are a major part of his inner life. His dreams serve a number of purposes. As he explains, they are a way of escaping the remorse he feels as a result of his dissipations, they reconcile him to his dreary existence, and they transform him from a chicken-hearted failure into a hero. They allow him "contentedly" to accept the lowest place in reality because he occupies "the foremost" one in his imagination (II, ii). They help him to restore his injured pride, to fulfill his contradictory needs, and to satisfy his craving for glory. Because he has adopted withdrawal as his predominant defense, he can gratify his hungers for love, power, and preeminence only in his fantasies.

Critics often describe the underground man as an egoist who is given to self-aggrandizement. His sense of superiority is in part reality based, for he is better read and more intelligent than the people around him, but his claims for himself are excessive and appear to be an expression of arrogance. They have been explained as a manifestation of narcissism (Guerard 1976), of vanity (Frank 1986), or of archaic grandiose needs (Bouson 1989). I see the underground man's claims as a pride-restoring device, as part of an effort to compensate for the profound sense of unworthiness by which he has always been plagued. When his claims are not honored, his underlying feelings of inadequacy and self-loathing emerge.

The underground man tells us that at school he shut himself away from others "in timid, wounded, and disproportionate pride" (II, iii). His pride is timid because he doesn't really believe in his own value; it is disproportionate because he has idealized himself as a defense against self-hatred; and it is easily wounded because it is fragile and unrealistic. Although his pride compensates for his feelings of unworthiness, it also exposes him to increased self-contempt when others do not honor his claims. At school, he restores his pride in some measure by applying himself to his studies and tyrannizing over his friend. However, as we have seen, his most characteristic defense is withdrawal. This strategy results in further blows to his pride as he falls behind his former schoolmates and is humiliated by his poverty and insignificance.

In his dreams, the underground man maintains his grandiosity and fulfills his conflicting needs by being both full of "loving kindness" and "triumphant over every one" (II, ii). The others are "in dust and ashes" and are "forced spontaneously to recognize [his] superiority."

He is "a poet and a grand gentleman" who falls in love and comes "in for countless millions," which he immediately devotes "to humanity." When he confesses his "shameful deeds," everyone kisses him and weeps, after which he goes "barefoot and hungry preaching new ideas." He then becomes Pope, the Pope having agreed "to retire from Rome to Brazil." His ascension is celebrated by "a ball for the whole of Italy at the Villa Borghese on the shores of Lake Como, Lake Como being for that purpose transferred to the neighborhood of Rome."

In his fantasies, the underground man is a self-sacrificing prophet and benefactor of humanity who is forgiven for his sins and is full of love for his fellows. At the same time, he is a conquering hero, an object of adulation, who is "crowned with laurel" and elevated to a position of great power and eminence (II, ii). The contradictory components of his idealized version of himself are all effortlessly actualized.

There is a good deal of self-mockery in his account of his dreams, whose literariness and absurdity he recognizes. He does not have these dreams *because* of his reading as Joseph Frank contends (1986, 335), but his reading greatly influences their content. His detached side sees through the ridiculousness of his fantasies, which he nonetheless insists "were by no means badly composed" (II, ii). Despite his awareness of what he was doing, his dreams consoled him at the time, and even now he is "to some extent satisfied with them."

As we have seen, a major feature of the underground man's imaginings is the loving kindness he feels "in those 'flights into the good and the beautiful'" (II, ii). This is an expression of his frustrated desire for caring relationships. His "fantastic love" is "never applied to anything human in reality," but it is so abundant that application seems "superfluous." Sometimes, however, his dreams reach "such a point of bliss that it [becomes] essential at once to embrace [his] fellows and all mankind." For this he needs "at least one human being, actually existing," a function that is usually served by Anton Antonitch. During his visits, however, he becomes "stupefied" by the dullness of the company and is "overcome by a sort of paralysis." On returning home, he defers "for a time [his] desire to embrace all mankind."

He has a very different experience when he calls on Simonov. Simonov has two other former schoolfellows with him, Ferfitchkin and Trudolyubov, and the three are planning a dinner for Zverkov, another old schoolmate, now a dashing officer, who is leaving for a distant province. Fresh from his dreams, the underground man craves recognition and longs to give and receive warmth, but "scarcely any notice" is taken of his entrance, and his insecurities are activated: "Evidently they looked upon me as something on the level of a common fly" (II, iii).

After three months of immersing himself in intoxicating fantasies, the underground man is unprepared for the sobering realities he encounters when he steps into the world. Despite all the discouraging signs, he cannot relinquish the hope of having his cravings for fellowship and triumph fulfilled. He invites himself to the dinner for Zverkov, thinking that they will "all be conquered at once" and will look at him "with respect" (II, iii). He soon becomes aware that he is unwelcome, foresees that he will be treated with disdain, and hates himself for his folly. He wishes to withdraw but is "pitch-forked into it" by his compulsive needs.

As the following passage shows, all three of the underground man's defensive moves are powerfully at work in this situation:

> What is more, even in the acutest paroxysm of this cowardly fever, I dreamed of getting the upper hand, of dominating them, carrying them away, making them like me—if only for my "elevation of thought and unmistakable wit." They would abandon Zverkov, he would sit on one side, silent and ashamed, while I should crush him. Then, perhaps, we would be reconciled and drink to our everlasting friendship; but what was most bitter and most humiliating for me was that I knew even then, knew, fully and for certain, that I needed nothing of all this really, that I did not really want to crush, to subdue, to attract them, and that I did not care a straw really for the result, even if I did achieve it. (II, iii)

He wants very much both to crush and to attract them, of course, but he must protect himself against the possibility of failure by feeling indifference. He is humiliated by his full and certain knowledge of his indifference because he sees himself behaving in a way that is quite incompatible with his need not to care. He despises himself because he is not the free and independent being that he wants to be. His tendencies toward detachment are very strong, but at this moment in his life the desires for friendship and mastery are extraordinarily intense and "pitch-fork" him into action. His strongest motive seems to be a desire for a vindictive triumph over Zverkov, toward whom he had felt very competitive in school and who represents the dull, strong-nerved men with whom he is continually comparing himself. He wants acceptance, but he sees it as coming about through the domination and humiliation of his enemies, through a triumph of wit and intelligence. Another force that impels him to go to the dinner is his desire to vindicate himself by carrying out his dreams in reality. In his fantasies he is an exalted being, a saint, a conqueror, a lover of humankind; but in reality he knows that he is only a dreamer and despises himself for it. He is so removed from life that the chance to prove himself rarely occurs. However, once he stumbles into the Zverkov affair, the opportunity is present, and he views it as a challenge. He is caught between his fear that his exalted conception of himself will be shattered by reality and his dread of the self-contempt he will experience if he funks it. When he goes to the dinner, he is in a state of almost hysterical anxiety. He "monstrously" exaggerates the facts because the meaning for him is immense. Now that he is "in for the real thing," his conception of himself is at stake (II, iii).

The dinner turns out disastrously, confirming his worst fears. Instead of vindicating himself, he receives a series of blows that leave him feeling "crushed and humiliated" (II, iv). The others behave as though he "were not in the room." After pacing in front of them for three hours, he cannot stand his exclusion any longer and begs forgiveness for having given offense. Zverkov proclaims, however, that the underground man could "never, under any circumstances," possibly insult *him*. The implication of this statement is that the behavior of so unimportant a person has no significance.

Terribly stung by this, the underground man stands "as though spat upon" (II, iv). He begs Simonov to lend him six roubles so that he can follow the others to the brothel. He resolves to slap Zerkov's face and feels "with horror" that it is going "to happen *now, at once*, and that *no force could stop it*" (II, v; author's emphasis). "Everything is lost," and precipitating a duel is the only way he can make himself felt. By the time he arrives, however, the young men have dispersed and he feels that he has "been saved from death." He may have given the slap, for he desperately needs to restore his pride; but, in any event, the conviction that he would have done so is a great comfort to him. At this point, Liza appears, and his notes are now devoted to his relations with her.

ii. Liza in the Brothel

The underground man's interactions with Liza are brilliantly rendered and require closer scrutiny than they have so far received if we are to appreciate their intricacy. In the lengthy episode that begins in the brothel, his inner conflicts once again come into play. His initial impulse is aggressive. He has been "treated like a rag" and needs to "avenge the insult on some one" in order "to get back [his] own" (II, ix). He masters Liza emotionally by breaking down her reserve and moving her to tears. He later tells her that he was "laughing at her then," that he wanted "power" and "sport." This is the aspect of his relation to Liza that critics have fastened on; but what he says to her in the brothel is motivated also by a longing for human contact, a feeling of identification, and a hunger for self-expression.

The underground man and Liza have much in common. He tells her that he has turned so unfeeling because he grew up without a home, and Liza, it seems, has been sold into prostitution by her father. She too tries to deal with her distress by becoming unfeeling. When the underground man awakens after sex, he sees her "scrutinizing [him] curiously" with eyes that are "coldly detached, sullen, as it were utterly remote" (II, vi). Liza defends herself by regarding him as an object, just as he had regarded her as a means of soothing himself.

Liza's scrutiny weighs on the underground man, inducing him to try to reach out to her. It makes him aware of her as another center of consciousness and leads him to feel the inhumanity of his behavior. During the two hours he has spent with her, he has "not said a single word" (II, vi). The silence gratified him initially because it put Liza in a subordinate position, but now he suddenly realizes "the hideous idea . . . of vice, which, without love, grossly and shamelessly begins with that in which true love finds its consummation." It is not only Liza who is degraded by what has happened between them, but he as well. He has a romantic conception of love and feels sex without mutuality to be hideous. To relieve his oppression, he tries to make conversation, asking Liza questions to which she gives reluctant replies, speaking more and more abruptly and seeming to say, "Let me alone; I feel sick, sad." The underground man feels increasingly "sick and dreary" and later wonders why he did not go away.

So far, the underground man is not speaking to Liza out of a craving for power or sport but from a desire to relieve his discomfort by establishing a more human connection with her. This changes when Liza keeps frustrating his efforts by maintaining her resignation and detachment. He tells her of a scene in the Haymarket that morning in which a coffin containing the body of a prostitute was being brought up out of a basement. To avoid being silent, he comments that it was a nasty day to be buried because it was snowing. However, when Liza abruptly replies that "It makes no difference," he begins "to feel provoked" (II, vi). He then gives Liza a sordid account of the dead woman, much of which he invents, and predicts Liza's rapid descent to the Haymarket and a similar early demise. "Oh, well, then I shall die," Liza replies "quite vindictively," refusing to be moved by his words. When he says he is sorry for her, she replies there is "no need," and he immediately becomes incensed.

The underground man now tries to get Liza to respond to him by attacking prostitution and urging her to change her ways. He says that it was "the exercise of [his] power that attracted [him] most," and although he wants to regain his ascendancy, he has other motives as well. She might still find love, he tells her, and "with love one can live even without happiness," but "here what is there but foulness. Phew!" (II, vi). He begins "to feel [himself] what [he] is saying," for he dreams of love and is sickened by his own "filthy vice" (II, i). He longs "to expound the cherished ideas" he has "brooded over in [his] corner" (II, vi).

The underground man senses the similarities between himself and Liza, and this makes it easier for him both to express his cherished ideas and to "turn [her] young soul" (II, vi). Perhaps he too is "unlucky" like her and "wallow[s] in the mud . . . out of misery." Is the way they came together "loving"? "Is that how one human being should meet another? It's hideous, that's what it is!" "'Yes,' she assent[s] sharply and hurriedly." So she was having the same thoughts as he when she was staring at him before. This is "a point of likeness," he thinks; she "really [does] interest" him. When he speaks of how nice it would be to have a home of her own, to be living in her father's house, she asks, "But what if it's worse than this?" This shocking question suggests horrors in Liza's home life. "I am convinced that some one has wronged you," says the underground man, "and that you are more sinned against than sinning." This is exactly the way he sees himself. When Liza says that some fathers "are glad to sell their daughters, rather than marrying them honourably," the underground man replies, "You must have seen wickedness in your own family, if you talk like that. Truly, you must have been unlucky." The underground man's expressions of empathy are part of his effort to manipulate Liza, but they are also a result of his identification with her and are truly felt. The cherished ideas the underground man expounds to Liza include things he wishes he had had, such as a home in which children are valued, and things he would like to have now. This isolated individual who cannot bear to be with others celebrates the "holy mystery of love" in which there is a "union of souls" and husband and wife have "no secrets between them" (II, vi). The underground man is trying to draw a contrast between a life of marital felicity and the one that Liza is leading, but the contrast applies to himself as well as to her, and he speaks so eloquently because he is giving expression to yearnings of his own. Although he is trying to get at Liza through the pictures he is painting, he "really [is] excited" and speaks "with real feeling," so much so that he "flushe[s] crimson" at the thought that she might laugh at him. Liza says that he speaks "somehow like a book," and this is true, of course, because he has had no first hand experience of the blissful scenes he is depicting and must draw on his reading here as in his other fantasies.

Liza's remark that he speaks like a book offends the underground man and produces another turning point in his attitude toward her. His vanity is wounded, but he is more deeply hurt, I think, by what he takes to be a personal rebuff. He has opened himself to Liza by expressing his cherished ideas, and he hopes for an emotional response. When Liza begins to say something after his long speech, her voice is "not abrupt, harsh, and unyielding as before," but there is "something soft and shamefaced" in it (II, vi). She does not complete her thought, and he asks "with tender curiosity" what she was going to say. He feels "ashamed and guilty" for having manipulated her and has a sympathetic interest in her state of mind. When she says that he talks like a book, there is "a note of irony in her voice" that sends "a pang to [his] heart," and "an evil feeling takes possession" of him. She has pushed him away, and now he is impelled to take a more aggressive approach. Although he later realizes that she was "hiding her feelings under irony," which is the "last refuge of modest people" when "the privacy of their soul is coarsely . . . invaded," he does not see this at the time; and, full of a sense of injury, he determines to break her down.

Instead of painting idyllic pictures of the life for which they both long, he now dwells on the horror of the prostitute's lot, a topic on which he had touched briefly before. Liza's love, a "priceless diamond" that men would have cherished if she were anywhere else, can be "outraged by every drunkard" and is worth nothing here (II, vii). The underground man speaks eloquently of her enslavement and of the fate that awaits her as she ages prematurely, descends to the Haymarket, and dies abandoned by all.

Once again he is drawing on his own preoccupations—not his yearnings this time but his fears. Loss of freedom is one of his greatest anxieties, as we shall see more fully later on, and the end he envisions for Liza is one that he dreads for himself. He tells her that others will have people to visit their graves, "while for you neither tear, nor sigh, nor remembrance; no one in the whole world will ever come to you, your name will vanish from the face of the earth—as though you had never existed, never been born at all!" (II, vii). Given his isolation, this is likely to be his fate as well, and it is no wonder that he works himself "up to such a pitch" that he begins "to have a lump in [his] throat." He senses that he is "turning her soul upside down and rending her heart" and is carried away by the "exercise of [his] skill," but he insists that "it was not merely sport." His motives are mixed, and his identification with Liza is profound.

When Liza weeps and wails in despair, the underground man does not exult in having attained his objective but is "panic-stricken" (II, vii). He is not equipped to deal with either Liza's emotions or the feelings they arouse in him, both of which threaten his detachment. He longs for human closeness, but when Liza moves toward him, he is "in haste to get away—to disappear." Full of remorse, he speaks to her tenderly—"Liza, my dear, I was wrong . . . forgive me, my dear" (author's ellipsis). He is moved by the love letter she produces from a decent young man to show that she too has been "addressed respectfully" and "genuinely loved"; however, he is so eager to leave that, after reading the letter, he departs without a word. As he walks home in the snow, he is "exhausted, shattered," and bewildered.

The underground man's confusion is quite understandable. He had striven to triumph over Liza, but now he is sorry for her and hates himself for having caused her such pain. He wishes to comfort her, but he is terrified of becoming closely involved with another human being and is desperate to get away. He gives her address and tells her to come to him, but an intrusion into the refuge where he "conceal[s] himself from all mankind" (II, viii) is the last thing he wants. Any effort to satisfy one set of needs activates the conflicting components of his personality.

III. LIZA'S VISIT

Once home, the underground man continues to have contradictory thoughts and feelings both before and after Liza appears. Again his oscillations become intelligible in the light of his inner conflicts. When he wakes in the morning, his aggressive and detached tendencies reassert themselves and contend with his feelings of compassion, guilt, and remorse. He is "positively amazed" at his "*sentimentality* with Liza" (author's emphasis), at his "outcries of horror and pity"; and he is disgusted by his "womanish hysteria" the night before (II, viii). He wonders why he had "thrust [his] address upon her" but tells himself that "it doesn't matter" if she comes, that the most important thing is to save his reputation in the eyes of Zverkov and Simonov. He forgets about Liza as he works on this project, but by evening his thoughts once again grow "confused": "Something was not dead . . . in the depths of my heart . . . , and it showed itself in acute depression." He feels "as though some crime were lying on [his] conscience." He dreads Liza's coming not only because she will see how he lives and he will no longer be a hero but also because he will have "to put on that dishonest lying mask again." But how was he dishonest? "I remember there was real feeling in me, too. What I wanted was to excite an honorable feeling in her." There *was* real feeling in him, but his behavior was also dictated by a craving for vindictive triumph disguised as a concern for Liza's welfare, and this weighs on him like a crime. He feels guilty for having reduced her to despair, and as he writes his notes fifteen years later, he is still haunted by the "look of torture" on "her pale, distorted face."

As days go by and Liza does not appear, the underground man's anxiety recedes; and he begins weaving a fantasy in which he will be "the salvation of Liza, simply through her coming to [him] and [his] talking to her" (II, viii). She loves him, she throws herself at his feet; and having transformed her, he takes her to his bosom: "but now you are mine, you are my creation, you are pure, you are good, you are my noble wife." This dream, like others we have seen, satisfies his needs to love and be loved, to be morally noble, and to be worshiped as a savior. His detached side is still operative, however, for he finds his fantasies to be "vulgar" and mocks himself for launching into lofty European "subtleties à la George Sand."

When Liza finally arrives, the reality is quite different from what he had imagined. In his fantasies, she comes into his house "bold and free, / Its rightful mistress there to be" (II, ix); but when she actually appears, he is shrieking at his servant Apollon; and he stands "before her crushed, crestfallen, revoltingly confused." Embarrassed by his poverty, he becomes angry with Liza and knows that he will "make her pay" for his humiliation. At the same time, however, her arrival is momentous because she is someone who might fulfill his need for love. He sends Apollon out for tea, telling him: "This is—everything! . . . you don't know what that woman is!" Then the thought occurs to him that he should "run away" just as he is, in his "dressing-gown, no matter where, and then let happen what would." Impelled to move against, toward, and away from Liza in rapid succession, he has "an hysterical attack," which is his reaction to being torn by inner conflicts. The underground man's behavior seems at first to be dominated by injured pride and a desire to retaliate. He is sure that Liza despises him; and he cannot forgive her for finding him out, for witnessing his tears, for making him loathe himself even more. Such a "horrible spite against her" surges up in his heart that he believes he "could have killed her" (II, ix). He revenges himself by silence, embarrassing her and making it difficult for her to speak. When she haltingly tells him that she wants to leave the brothel, he gives her an account of his behavior there that is partial, distorted, and savagely cruel. He had been humiliated and wanted to salve his feelings by debasing her. He explains that he was laughing at her then, and he is laughing at her now. He had wanted power and sport, to wring out her tears, her humiliation, her hysteria. He had told her lies because he likes to play with words. And much more than this was going on, as we have seen. "Overwhelmed" by the "cynicism" of his speeches, Liza turns "white as a handkerchief," tries to say something, then sinks "on a chair as though she had been felled by an axe."

In addition to rage and humiliation, there is externalized self-hatred behind the underground man's aggression, as he himself understands: "I was angry with myself, but, of course, it was she who would have to pay" (II, ix). Even stronger motives, I believe, are his fear of his softer feelings and his need to protect his detachment. When Liza says that she wants to leave the brothel, his heart "ache[s] with pity" at her "straightforwardness" (II, ix). But "something hideous" at once stifles his "compassion" and provokes him "to greater venom." She has come to him, he tells her, because he "talked sentimental stuff" to her then, and "soft as butter," she is "longing for fine sentiments again." He needs to repudiate his own sentimentality, of which he is ashamed, and to crush Liza's expectations, which deeply frighten him. His object is not simply to avenge his injured pride by hurting Liza but to get rid of her, to drive her away. What he really wants, he tells her, is to be "left in peace." The world can "go to pot" as long as his routine is undisturbed. "What do I care about you," he asks, "and whether you go to ruin there or not?" "Why are you worrying me? Why don't you go?"

The problem is that the underground man really does care. He cannot be cruel to Liza without hating himself. Part of him wants to avenge himself, part of him wants to be left alone, and part of him wants to save Liza and to be saved by her love. Caught in a crossfire of conflicting desires and inner dictates, he is in torment whatever he does. His assaults on Liza are accompanied by even more savage assaults on himself. After he tells her that he would "sell the whole world for a farthing . . . so long as [he] was left in peace," he continues: "Well, anyway, I know that I am a blackguard, a scoundrel, an egoist, a sluggard" (II, ix). Sensing the underground man's torment, Liza throws her arms around him and bursts into tears. He also begins to cry, exclaiming: "They won't let me . . . I can't be good!" Then he falls on the sofa and sobs "for a quarter of an hour in genuine hysterics." He wants to be loving and caring; but his inner compulsions to stifle his softer feelings, to avenge his injured pride, and to keep his distance from other people won't let him be "good."

The underground man is ashamed of his hysteria, which makes him seem "like some silly woman put to shame" (II, ix). Aware that Liza is "now the heroine," while he is "just such a crushed and humiliated creature" as she had been before, he experiences an urge for "mastery and possession" and seeks to restore his pride by having sex with her. After an initial response of "terror" and "amazement" at his advances, Liza "warmly and rapturously" embraces him, only to realize afterward that his "outburst of passion had been simply revenge, and that to [his] earlier, almost causeless hatred was added now a *personal hatred*, born of envy" (II, x; author's emphasis).

As has often been the case, the underground man's defense of his pride results in intensified self-hatred. He feels that Liza now realizes he is "a despicable man" who is "incapable of loving her" (II, x). He envies her because she can love, whereas he cannot. He attacks himself as a "spiteful and stupid" person who even in his "underground dreams" cannot imagine love except as a means of "tyrannizing" over its object. This is not accurate, but it is the expression of his self-lacerating state of mind. The underground man's speeches in the brothel make clear that he has a dream of love as a "holy mystery," based on mutual respect, in which there is a "union of souls" and "happiness in the midst of sorrow" (II, vi). Indeed, at the time of his writing he recognizes that Liza had come "not to hear fine sentiments" but to love him, "because to a woman all . . . salvation from any sort of ruin" is "included in love and can only show itself in that form" (II, x). His inability to respond to Liza means that he is lost, that he has no hope of the "moral renewal" for which he desperately longs.

Instead of availing himself of the opportunity for "reformation" that he feels Liza presents, the underground man is "insufferably oppressed" by her being there: "I wanted her to disappear. I wanted 'peace,' to be left alone in my underground world. Real life oppressed me with its novelty so much that I could hardly breathe" (II, x). Because his primary defense is detachment, he cannot bear to have anyone close to him or to be subject to emotional demands. As Liza is leaving, he puts money into her hands, partly out of spite, to increase her humiliation, and partly to distance himself from her further by denying that what has transpired has any personal significance. Appalled by what he has done, he rushes after Liza "in shame and despair"; but because of his inner conflicts, he calls her name "in a low voice" and returns to his room when he hears the outer door slam. There he finds the five rouble note he had given her lying crumpled on the table; and he runs after her again, only to stop short and return home once more. That evening he is "almost dead with the pain in [his] soul," but he consoles himself with the thought that "exalted suffering" is better than "cheap happiness" and that Liza will be elevated by her resentment of his insult.

The underground man's encounter with Liza has intensified his hopelessness, self-loathing, and withdrawal from "real life." His hopelessness derives in part from his awareness of his inner conflicts, which he sees no way of resolving. He wants to give and receive love, but he knows that his nature will not permit him to do so, and he despises himself for his defectiveness: "Had I not recognized that day, for the hundredth time, what I was worth?" (II, x). He is so full of rage at the injuries he has received and so entrenched in his defenses against further hurt that he cannot allow himself to reciprocate Liza's warmth. His encounter with Liza has lingered painfully in his memory not only because he is so ashamed of the cruelty of his behavior but also because she offered him an opportunity to escape his isolation that he was compelled to reject. His inability to open himself to another human being is the deepest source of his despair.

Chapter 3

The Diarist

1. Introduction

ALL THE EPISODES FROM HIS MIDTWENTIES THE UNDERGROUND MAN recounts in Part II turn out badly, and he is later haunted by his recollection of them. This brings us to the underground man as diarist. One of the reasons he gives for composing his notes is that he hopes to obtain "relief" from his oppressive memories by writing them down (I, xi). Maybe he can "get rid" of them in that way. This effort fails, for at the end he says that his notes have been a form of "corrective punishment" and that he has "felt ashamed" the whole time he has been writing his story. He concludes that he has "spoiled [his] life through morally rotting in [his] corner," through "divorce from real life, and rankling spite in [his] underground world" (II, x). He records his memories in an effort to free himself from psychic discomfort; but when this exacerbates his distress, he decides to stop writing.

Before he does so, however, he makes a characteristic effort to defend his pride and reaffirm his superiority. He castigates not only himself but also his imaginary interlocutors, who he says are just as estranged from themselves and from reality as he. He eases the sting of his self-accusations by generalizing his condition. Out of touch with his own feelings, he often models himself on his reading and envisions others doing the same: "Leave us alone without books and we shall be lost and in confusion. . . . We shall not know . . . what to love and what to hate, what to respect and what to despise" (II, x). He proclaims that "we are all divorced from life, we are all cripples, every one of us, more or less."

The underground man says that he is not "justifying himself" by speaking of "all of us," but he is clearly protecting his pride (II, x). Instead of feeling himself to be worse than others, he sees himself as having only "carried to an extreme" what they "have not dared to carry halfway." They have taken their "cowardice for good sense, and have found comfort in deceiving" themselves, so "perhaps, after all, there is more life" in him than in them. He may be a cripple, but he is better than those he imagines despising him. Here, as elsewhere in his notes, the emergence of self-hatred is accompanied by efforts to cope with it. He sees himself as confronting his own nature more courageously than others and as having greater self-awareness and self-understanding. Unlike them, *he* does not deceive himself.

There is disagreement among critics as to the degree of the underground man's honesty and self-comprehension. According to Mikhail Bakhtin, "there is literally nothing we can say about the hero of 'Notes from Underground' that he does not already know" (1984, 52). James Lethcoe argues, however, that the underground man "is composing his memoirs in a state of self-deception" and that his "testimony cannot be taken at face value" (1966, 9). Because he is "eternally condemned to oscillate between the antithetical poles of his divided soul," he is "completely incapable of attaining his goal of self-honesty" (15). Motivated by a "need to justify himself," he engages in constant "rationalization" (16) and deceives both himself and the reader. Thematic critics tend to regard the underground man as a reliable source of insight into his own condition, whereas those taking a psychological approach question his trustworthiness and self-knowledge.

I side with the psychological critics. According to Bakhtin, among the things the underground man knows "perfectly well" is the "psychopathological delineation of his internal profile" (1984, 52). I disagree. Although the narrator is vividly aware of his inner conflicts and of the oscillations and paralysis they produce, he does not really understand their source or their dynamics. Instead of knowing himself perfectly well, he is often puzzled by his feelings and his behavior. Indeed, one of the things he is trying to do in writing his notes is to fathom the mysteries of his own personality. Why doesn't he "know how to become anything" (I, i)? Why can't he make up his mind whether to be magnanimous or to take revenge? Why is it that the more conscious he is of the good and beautiful, the more deeply he sinks into the "mire" (I, ii)? How is the enjoyment he derives from self-degradation "to be explained?" But "I will get to the bottom of it!"

he proclaims: "That is why I have taken up my pen." He is searching for self-understandings that will relieve his inner torments and enable him to be more at peace with himself.

Complex and sophisticated though they are, the underground man's reflections cannot be regarded as reliable guides to either his own condition or that of his fellow humans. It is evident from the beginning that he is engaged in a series of maneuvers, with both himself and his imagined audience, that are designed to protect his pride. These involve evasion, denial, distortion, exaggeration, rationalization, and externalization. He is sometimes aware of these maneuvers and calls our attention to them, but much of the time he is struggling to maintain a semblance of self-respect and cannot afford to recognize his defensive strategies.

As Lethcoe observes, we must be careful about taking any of the underground man's statements at face value; but in general some parts of his narration seem more trustworthy than others. He is an astute observer of his own subjective states, and he seems most reliable when he is concretely depicting these states and the behaviors to which they give rise. He provides a vivid and self-consistent picture of his inner conflicts and their consequences. He is least to be trusted when he offers interpretations of himself, although even his faulty interpretations contribute to the richness of his self-portrait. There is enough reliable descriptive material to permit us to understand the underground man's character structure; and equipped with this understanding, we can identify his defensive maneuvers and comprehend their function in his psychic economy.

I said in the opening chapter that I would offer an analysis of the underground man that would show his ideas to be the product of his psychology rather than the other way around. Before engaging in such an analysis, I have found it necessary to examine the protagonist's history, personality, and interactions with others. Now I shall explore the ways in which his interpretations of himself and his ideological stance are related to his inner conflicts and his efforts to assuage his distress.

II. Why Can't He Act?

The underground man is sick, knows he is sick, and hates his sickness. Nevertheless, he is trapped by it and must live with it; hence he glorifies it. "People do pride themselves on their diseases," he tells us, "and I do, maybe, more than any one" (I, ii). His withdrawal, his inertia and indecision, and his vacillations and contradictions all become sources of pride, marks of superiority. He is diseased, to be sure, but his disease is that of being "too conscious," too intelligent. Hence it places him far above the stupid normal men of action he both envies and despises. He does nothing because he is so intelligent; and the less he does, the more intelligent he proves himself to be: "perhaps I consider myself an intelligent man because all my life I have been able neither to begin nor to finish anything" (I, v). It is "only the fool who becomes anything"; "an active man is pre-eminently a limited creature" (I, i).

As the underground man sees it, one of the primary differences between the stupid normal man and the man of acute consciousness is the inability of the conscious man to make up his mind to act and particularly to take revenge. When the normal man is possessed "by the feeling of revenge," there is only "that feeling" in his "whole being"; and he "dashes straight for his object," believing in the justice of his cause (I, ii). When the acutely conscious man feels insulted, he is paralyzed. He does not believe in the justice of his cause, but surrounding himself with a "fatal brew" of doubts and questions," he creeps ignominiously into his "mouse hole" to brood on his injury (I, iii). If he revenges himself, it is "piecemeal, in trivial ways, from behind the stove, incognito, without believing" in his "right to vengeance."

He cannot believe in his right to vengeance because he can discover no basic principles on which to judge and act. All science can tell him is that everything is determined and no one is responsible. If he ignores questions of justice and virtue and acts simply out of spite, he finds that he has "not even spite": "In consequence again of those accursed laws of consciousness, anger in me is subject to chemical disintegration" (I, v). If he allows himself to be carried away by his feelings, "without reflection, without a primary cause," he despises himself for his self-deception, and the result is "inertia."

The underground man has given us an accurate picture of his conscious mental processes; but I find it difficult to believe, as many critics seem to do, that he has correctly identified the source of his difficulties. He is incapable of wholehearted feelings of anger, I would say, not because he is acutely aware or philosophically at sea but because, although he is full of wrath, he has powerful taboos against feeling and acting out his rage. His "doubts and questions" derive not so much from hyperconsciousness or intelligence as from his psychological conflicts, which find a sophisticated expression in his relativistic and deterministic attitudes. It is his warring defenses, not the "laws of consciousness," that make his anger subject to disintegration. His vengeful feelings violate the taboos of the self-effacing side of his personality and imperil his detachment by threatening to embroil him in conflict. He handles them on a conscious level by rationalizing them away and on an unconscious level by converting them into self-hatred and self-destructiveness. When he does let out his vengeful feelings, it is "from behind the stove," in a relatively safe though not very satisfying way.

The underground man says that he cannot act because he is forever plagued by doubt, because he can find no foundation on which to build: "I exercise myself in reflection, and consequently with me every primary cause at once draws after itself another still more primary, and so on to infinity. This is just the essence of every sort of consciousness and reflection" (I, v). There is no doubt that his intelligence profoundly affects the his experience; however, the phenomenon the underground man describes has its source not so much in reflection as in inner conflict. Reason alone can never provide the foundation for which he is searching. His intellect is driven by three almost equally powerful defensive strategies, and it oscillates endlessly, settling nowhere. In one of his tirades of self-accusation, he acknowledges that he is "not sure of [his] ground" because his "heart is darkened and corrupt, and you cannot have a full, genuine consciousness without a pure heart" (I, xi). Whatever he means by "a pure heart," it is clear that he knows he is not plagued by doubt only because of his intelligence.

The underground man's inaction is in part a product of his search for glory. By doing nothing, he can preserve the possibility of being a hero. "A man of character, an active man, is pre-eminently a limited creature" (I, i) and limited creatures are "donkeys and mules" who "really are of no consequence" (II, i). He can be a hero in his dreams only because he does not try to do anything in reality. Any real activity is bound to fall short of his goals, to threaten his pride, and to confront him with self-hatred as it has in his devastating experiences with Zverkov and Liza. Hence he gives up active striving, moves away from people, and seeks to actualize his grandiose vision of himself almost wholly in imagination. The needs for love and aggressive triumph he suppresses in daily life have a full flowering in his fantasies.

The underground man is not completely divorced from himself. He concludes, "it is better to do nothing! Better conscious inertia!

And so hurrah for underground!" (I, xi). But he immediately confesses that "it is not underground that is better, but something different, quite different for which I am thirsting, but which I cannot find! Damn underground!" He expresses his longing for a quite different life only once, but it no doubt contributes to his despair and to his efforts at self-honesty. Most of the time he cannot afford to recognize how truly lost he is.

III. "THAT STRANGE ENJOYMENT"

Perhaps the most striking indication of the severity of the underground man's difficulties is the intensity of his self-hatred and self-punishment. From beginning to end, his notes are filled with incidences of extreme self-contempt, self-accusation, self-frustration, self-torture, and self-destructiveness. Alternating with his claim of superiority is a sense of utter insignificance: he describes himself as a fly, a mouse, an eel, an insect. He accuses himself of being morally corrupted, out of touch with life, incapable of love. He calls himself a "blackguard," "the nastiest, stupidest, absurdest, and most envious of all the worms on earth" (II, ix). His liver is diseased, but he won't consult a doctor; Petersburg is too expensive and the climate is bad for him, but he won't leave. He lives in a "horrid" room with a stupid, ill-natured servant who smells bad (I, i). Earlier he had lived for seven years with another servant, Apollon, the "bane of [his] life," whose "very step almost threw [him] into convulsions" and who "despised" him "beyond all measure" (II, viii). At a certain period he repeatedly took strolls along the Nevsky that were not strolls "so much as a series of innumerable miseries" and "humiliations" (II, i). "Why I inflicted this torture upon myself, why I went to the Nevsky, I don't know. I felt simply drawn there at every possible opportunity."

Joseph Frank attributes the underground man's self-loathing to a "dialectic of vanity": his "vanity convinces him of his own superiority and he despises everyone; but since he desires such superiority to be *recognized* by others, he hates the world for its indifference and falls into self-loathing at his own humiliating dependence" (1986, 334; author's emphasis). According to Frank, this dialectic has "an ideological source—not a specific philosophical doctrine . . . , but the general cultural atmosphere of the 1840s, which fostered a forced and artificial Romantic egoism and a sense of superiority to ordinary Russian life that the underground man drank in through every pore" (1986, 334–35).

The protagonist's vanity does generate self-loathing, but Frank takes it as the starting point, whereas I see the underground man's claims for himself as defenses against the self-hatred that originated in his early experiences of rejection and self-betrayal. He exalts himself to compensate for feelings of worthlessness and inadequacy, but his idealized image and the devices he employs to protect it weaken him further and intensify his self-hatred. His dreams of glory offer him moments of "positive intoxication," but when sober he finds these dreams to be "vulgar and contemptible" and despises his ineffectuality (II, ii). His demand for the foremost place forces him to avoid striving for actual achievement, but his withdrawal makes genuine self-esteem impossible. He becomes less and less able to cope with reality even in simple situations, and this intensifies the anxiety from which he is fleeing. As his claims become more grandiose, his vulnerability increases; as his inner dictates become more stringent, his self-hatred intensifies.

The underground man recognizes that his self-idealization and the demands he makes on himself cause him both to despise himself and to feel detested by others: "It is clear to me now that, owing to my unbounded vanity and to the higher standard I set for myself, I often looked at myself with furious discontent, which verged on loathing, and so I inwardly attributed the same feeling to every one" (II, i). His unbounded vanity does not derive from the cultural atmosphere of the 1840s, but from a compensatory process that was set in motion by the deprivation and abuse he experienced in childhood.

The underground man has some understanding of his self-hatred, but there are aspects of it that puzzle him. As we have seen, he does not know why he went to the Nevsky to be tortured, although he is aware that his miseries and humiliations were "just what [he] wanted" (II, ii). He finds an "enjoyment in the very feeling of his own degradation" (I, v) that "sometimes reaches the highest degree of voluptuousness" (I, iv). He is fascinated by "the savour of that strange enjoyment" (I, iii) and has taken up his pen to get to the bottom of it. He finds it "so subtle, so difficult of analysis" (I, iii), however, that humans must reach a higher stage of consciousness before they can "understand all the intricacies of this pleasure" (I, iv). As is the case with other aspects of his behavior, the underground man provides ample material for analysis, and some of his explanations show a great deal of insight; but he is far from knowing himself "perfectly well," as Bakhtin says he does (1984, 52).

The underground man is puzzled by the disparity between his ideals and his actions. He not only fails to live up to his ideals, but he seems compelled to violate them. His spells of dissipation often begin at the very moments when he is "most capable of feeling every refinement of all that is 'good and beautiful,'" and the more conscious he is of the good and beautiful, the more deeply he sinks into his mire (I, ii). At first he struggles against his depravity, then he gnaws at himself for it till "at last the bitterness" turns "into positive real enjoyment." The enjoyment, he explains, is "from the too intense consciousness of one's own degradation; it was from feeling . . . that it was horrible, but that it could not be otherwise; that there was no escape for you, that you could never become a different man."

There are a number of reasons why an intense consciousness of the good and beautiful leads the underground man to embark on a course of dissipation. Part of his idealized version of himself is that he is a high-minded person who is loving and self-sacrificial. His awareness of the good and the beautiful makes him apprehensive, for it presents him with goals that are too lofty to be attained, except in imagination. He protects the virtuous component of his glorified self-image by embracing its opposite and indulging in vice, which puts any attempt at virtue of the question; and if he does not try, he cannot fail. At the same time, his plunging into vice is a form of self-punishment. He cannot be aware of his ideals without also being aware that he is not living up to them, and this generates self-hatred and a need for relief through self-flagellation. He confirms his sense of worthlessness by his vile behavior and takes moral satisfaction in his self-disgust.

Another motive for the underground man's dissipation is his need to rebel against his inner dictates. Being predominantly detached, he cannot stand any form of coercion, and nothing is more coercive than his tyrannical shoulds. As Karen Horney remarks, there may be "a constant shuttling between an 'I should' and 'no, I won't,'" in which the contradictory attitudes toward the shoulds are mistaken for "freedom" (1950, 78).

The underground man's pleasure in his self-degradation is, as he says, quite subtle and intricate. For one thing, he is seeking to escape pain through pain. A "masochistic way of lulling psychic pains," observes Horney, "is to intensify them and wholly surrender to them" (1939, 272). "Wallowing in humiliation" can narcotize the "pain of self-contempt" and turn it "into a gratifying experience." Having to realize his shortcomings is unbearable for the underground man; when he exaggerates his pain and loses himself "in a general feeling of misery or unworthiness, the aggravating experience loses some of its reality, the sting of the special pain is lulled" (Horney 1936, 265). Through an orgy of self-degradation, he converts the agony of self-reproach into the pleasure of self-pity.

The underground man enjoys wallowing not only in feelings of degradation but also in feelings that he can never change. He seeks in this way to protect himself against future blows to his pride and the pain of future defeat. He recognizes that his strange pleasure is, in part, the enjoyment of despair: "in despair there are the most intense enjoyments, especially when one is aware of the hopelessness of one's position" (I, ii). He feels hopeless about resolving his problems and hopeless about living up to his contradictory inner dictates—he cannot be at once good, aggressively triumphant, and indifferent. To escape the pain of his futile struggles and endless self-reproaches, he longs to have his pride crushed, to feel that he is foredoomed, that he might as well sink "in silent impotence . . . into luxurious inertia" (I, iii). His debauchery is a way of crushing his own pride, of proving to himself that he is irremediably lost.

With at least part of his being, the underground man longs to be crushed, to be swallowed up, to have his identity obliterated and his impotence confirmed. This is why he wants to be thrown out of the tavern window and can imagine being glad of a slap in the face: "why then the consciousness of being rubbed into pulp would positively overwhelm one" (I, ii). He wants to escape from his inner torments by having his struggles and agonies subsumed into some larger, implacable phenomenon. This is why he likes to see himself as a helpless victim of the laws of nature. Part of the enjoyment he ascribes to toothache comes from "the aimlessness of your pain, which is so humiliating to your consciousness" (I, iv).

Just as the underground man derives an enjoyment from being in "complete slavery" to his aching teeth (I, iv), so he also takes a certain satisfaction in recognizing his slavery to his compulsions and his inner paralysis, which he sees as a product of "the normal fundamental laws of over-acute consciousness" and "the inertia that [is] the direct result of those laws" (I, ii). He feels that even if he wanted to change, he could not, "because perhaps in reality there [is] nothing . . . to change into." By seeing himself as a victim of the laws of nature, he tries to disclaim responsibility for his weaknesses and to defend himself against his self-hatred and guilt: "a decent man is bound to be a coward and a slave. It is the law of nature for all decent people all over the earth" (II, i). This defense does not work, however; and he turns the fact that he continues to feel guilt into one more reason for feeling trapped, abused, and full of self-pity.

The underground man feels that there is no rational solution to the problem of responsibility, and he sees himself as a victim of existential uncertainty: "it is simply a mess, no knowing what and no knowing who, but in spite of all these uncertainties and jugglings, still there is an ache in you, and the more you do not know, the worse the ache" (I, iii). It is quite natural for him to see his uncertainties as a product of the human condition, but it should be clear by now that they are the result of his inner conflicts. His ache can never be stilled because his personality can never be integrated. His feelings of enslavement and his feelings of responsibility can never be reconciled because they serve contradictory needs.

IV. THE MOST ADVANTAGEOUS ADVANTAGE

The underground man is so famous for his defense of free will and his defiance of necessity that it is somewhat surprising to realize that he also sees himself as a helpless victim of nature's laws and has a number of motives for doing so. His motives for denying necessity are equally strong, if not stronger, and they are evident in the philosophic passages that have attracted so much attention.

Replying to the rationalistic and utilitarian thinkers of his day, the underground man attacks the philosophy of enlightened self-interest. He cannot accept the idea that man "only does nasty things because he does not know his own interest" and that if he were enlightened, "he would see his own advantage in the good and nothing else" and would begin doing good "through necessity" (I, vii). The rationalists have an extremely narrow conception of human nature. They do not realize that man's "capacity for reasoning" is but one-twentieth of his "capacity for life" (I, viii), and that although part of his nature craves well-being, he is sometimes "passionately in love" with suffering, chaos, and destruction, finding it "pleasant . . . to smash things" (I, ix). It follows, therefore, that destructiveness is not simply the product of ignorance but derives in part from nonrational forces in human nature that can never be eradicated by "common sense and science" (I, vii). Since man is governed only in small part by reason, a rational demonstration of his true normal interests will never compel him to will only the good.

Moreover, the rationalists have left out of their calculations man's "most advantageous advantage," which is not "honour, peace, prosperity," or any of the goals dictated by reason, but the exercise of his caprice, the expression of his "own sweet foolish will" (I, vii). "One's own free unfettered choice, one's own caprice—however wild it may be," is the "most advantageous advantage," against which "all systems and theories are continually being shattered to atoms." What man wants "is simply *independent* choice, whatever that independence may cost and wherever it may lead" (I, viii; author's emphasis). Man's craving for independent choice is another source of destructive behavior, for he may consciously desire "what is injurious to himself" so as "to have the right to desire . . . even what is very stupid and not to be bound by any obligation to desire only what is sensible." Such behavior is not really stupid; "it preserves for us what is most precious and most important—that is, our personality, our individuality."

The rationalists dream of a scientific utopia in which all human behavior will be subsumed under the laws of nature and our rational self-interest will be thoroughly calculated. Man will be taught that "he never has really had any caprice or will of his own" and that everything he does "is done of itself, by the laws of nature" (I, vii). Human nature will be "completely re-educated," and man will be "compelled not to want to set his will against his normal interests" (I, vii). As the underground man sees it, humans would never consent to this state of affairs, even if it were attainable, because the price of happiness would be freedom, the most advantageous advantage. They would "kick over the whole show and scatter rationalism to the winds" simply so they could "live once more at [their] own sweet foolish will." It is precisely their "fantastic dreams" and "vulgar folly" they "will desire to retain," to prove to themselves that they are not completely controlled by the laws of nature. Even if it were proved to man "by natural science and mathematics" that he really was "nothing but a piano key," he would not become reasonable but would "contrive destruction and chaos" and "sufferings of all sorts, only to gain his point! . . . for the whole work of man really seems to consist in nothing but proving to himself every minute that he is a man and not a piano key!" (I, viii).

The strongest part of the underground man's argument is his insistence on the influence of nonrational forces on human behavior. His own experience is proof that knowing the good by no means compels one to do it because consciousness of the good and the beautiful produces depravity in him. It is no wonder he sees "theories for explaining to mankind their real normal interest, in order that . . . they may at once become good and noble" as "mere logical exercises" (I, vii). His inner conflicts, the disparity between his ideals and his behavior, and his experience of powerful self-destructive impulses give the underground man a penetrating insight into the inadequacy of rationalist psychology, which simply leaves out of account the existence of irrational forces.

The fact that the underground man makes valid objections to the rationalist psychology does not necessarily mean that his own version of human nature is balanced or accurate. As we might expect, he sees his own traits as characteristic of the species and his own highest value as "the most precious thing for mankind" (I, viii). He does this not only because he is given to generalizing from his experience but also because he needs to believe that in reality everyone is like him. He is very much "worried" by the feeling that there is "no one like" him, that he is "unlike everyone else" (II, ii). One reason he reacts so strongly to the rationalist psychology is that it threatens to intensify his feeling of isolation and reinforce his sense of himself as an anomaly. It is important for him to affirm that it is not simply he who loves suffering, chaos, and destruction but that all men do.

The underground man is threatened not only by the utilitarian philosophers' belief in rationality but also by their contention that human behavior is lawful and can therefore be predicted, explained, and controlled. His arguments on this subject have a vehemence that indicates a high level of anxiety. His attack on the utilitarians is but a single episode in his lifelong battle against necessity. "The laws of nature," he tells us, "have continually all my life offended me more than anything" (I, v). He has "always been afraid of . . . mathematical certainty," and he is "afraid of it now" (I, ix). To him, "mathematical certainty" is "something insufferable": "Twice two makes four seems to me simply a piece of insolence. Twice two makes four is a pert coxcomb who stands with arms akimbo barring your path and spitting. I admit that twice two makes four is an excellent thing, but if we are to give everything its due, twice two makes five is sometimes a very charming thing too."

Why does the underground man so dislike the laws of nature and the fact that twice two makes four? Horney observes that "pride in . . . the supremacy of the mind . . . is a regular occurrence in all neurosis" (1950, 91–92). The laws of nature and of arithmetic limit the power of mind to determine reality. They insufferably frustrate our claims, insolently deny our personal grandeur, and force us to recognize that our idealized image of ourselves is an imaginary construction. Many people, writes Horney, "have an intense . . . aversion to the realization that they [are] subject to *any* necessity. The mere words 'rules,' 'necessities,' or 'restrictions' may make them shudder" (1950, 45; author's emphasis). Because "in their private world everything is possible—to them," the "recognition of any necessity applying to themselves" would "pull them down from their lofty world into actuality, where they would be subject to the same natural laws as anybody else." Horney might have been writing about the underground man. In order to sustain his grandiose version of himself, he must ignore or deny the actual conditions of life.

The underground man's intense aversion to the laws of nature and arithmetic is also a product of his detachment. People in whom detachment is predominant loathe all forms of control or restraint and have a compulsive need for freedom and independence. This need manifests itself "in a hypersensitivity to everything in any way resembling coercion, influence, obligation, and so on. The degree of sensitivity is a good gauge of the intensity of the detachment. What is felt as constraint varies with the individual" (Horney 1945, 77). The underground man's hatred of the laws of nature and fear of mathematical certainty are, in effect, phobic reactions. He is unusually disturbed by twice two makes four.

He is also unusually disturbed by the possibility that human behavior may someday be explicable, that "a formula" will be discovered "for all our desires and caprices" (I, viii). If this happens, he contends, "then, most likely, man will at once cease to feel desire, indeed, he will be certain to. For who would want to choose by rule? Besides, he will at once be transformed into an organ stop or something of the sort." Here, as elsewhere, the underground man confuses descriptive with prescriptive law, but his confusion could never be cleared up by a logical explanation. Because of his hypersensitivity to constraint, he *feels* descriptive laws to be prescriptive. If he must feel and choose by rule, then the only way he can maintain his freedom is to feel nothing and choose nothing. One of the reasons why the doctrine of enlightened self-interest is so abhorrent to him is that, as he perceives it, it contains an element of compulsion: man will be "compelled" by reason "not to want to set his will against his normal interests" (I, vii). If reason compels him to do good, he will, of course, rebel and choose chaos and destruction. If need be, he will "purposely go mad in order to get rid of reason and gain his point" (I, viii).

The underground man's affirmation of freedom as the most advantageous advantage is, like his hypersensitivity to constraint, symptomatic of his detachment. Any appeal to freedom tends to be stirring, but as Horney points out, "the fallacy here" is that the detached person looks on it "as an end in itself and ignores the fact that its value depends ultimately upon what he does with it. His independence . . . has a negative orientation; it is aimed at *not* being influenced, coerced, tied, obligated" (1945, 77; author's emphasis). The underground man does not wish to be free so that he can fulfill his human potentialities. For him freedom is the goal of life, and he is ready to embrace suffering, chaos, and destruction in order to obtain it.

One reason why the underground man wants freedom so much is that he possesses so little of it. His behavior is involuntary; he is aware of the inevitability of his reactions and feels them to be expressions of natural law. His hatred of the laws of nature is in part a hatred of his own compulsions, which he longs to escape. There are times when he mistakes his contradictory attitudes toward his inner dictates for freedom, but his vacillations and rebellions are generated by his inner conflicts. Although he glorifies his self-destructiveness as an evidence of free will and the futility of reason, he is nowhere more driven than in this behavior. He prizes caprice because "it preserves for us what is most precious . . . our individuality" (I, viii), but he is incapable of spontaneity and feels manipulated by forces beyond his control. That is why, to him, "the whole work of man seems to consist in nothing but proving to himself that he is a man and not a piano key!" People who are truly in possession of themselves do not feel a need to fight every minute against the threat of obliteration. It is the underground man's compulsiveness and not the laws of nature, the certitude of mathematics, or the philosophy of the rationalists that threatens to transform him "from a human being into an organ-stop."

It is my contention that, whatever Dostoevsky's thematic or parodistic intentions may have been, the philosophic arguments that take up sections vii–ix of Part I are quite consistent with the underground man's character structure, and they are both better understood and more permanently interesting as manifestations of his personality than as expressions of Dostoevsky's ideology. It is possible to see them as Dostoevsky's reply to utilitarian ethics and rationalist psychology, as a clue to Dostoevsky's conception of human nature and human values, or as an early expression of some of the central motifs of existentialism. Whatever their historical, biographical, or philosophical import, however, they are first and foremost an integral part of

Dostoevsky's remarkably complex and subtle portrait of the underground man. As such they have an enduring aesthetic and mimetic truth that makes them fascinating independently of their ideological content. As Albert Guerard says, Chernyshevsky "is left very far behind in this great masterpiece of psychological literature" (1976, 171).

PART II

CRIME AND PUNISHMENT

CHAPTER 4

RHETORIC IN *CRIME AND PUNISHMENT*

I. INTRODUCTION

CRIME AND PUNISHMENT IS ANOTHER GREAT MASTERPIECE OF psychological literature. Like "Notes from Underground," it has been approached from both thematic and psychological perspectives, with thematic approaches dominating. In "Notes from Underground," the first person narration makes it difficult to determine where the author stands; the work's thematic import can be established only by placing it in its historical context and appreciating its parodistic and satiric characteristics. If we attend to the work by itself, it seems above all a brilliant psychological portrait in which the underground man's philosophic concerns are expressions of his personality and inner conflicts. The situation is different with *Crime and Punishment*. Raskolnikov's ideas are also psychologically motivated, but the implied author's attitudes are much more in evidence, and Raskolnikov exists within formal and thematic structures in terms of which we are invited to view his behavior.

Crime and Punishment is, among other things, a novel of education. Raskolnikov's fall is presented as fortunate: he errs, suffers as a result of his errors, and is transformed as a result of his suffering. Education plots can have either comic or tragic outcomes. In *Crime and Punishment*, Raskolnikov is almost undone by his mistakes, but he learns his lessons in time to profit from them, unlike the protagonists of tragic education plots, such as King Lear or Julien Sorel (see Paris 1974, 1991a). The nature of Raskolnikov's errors and the significance of his transformation are defined for the reader by an authorial rhetoric to which we must pay attention if we are to comprehend how Dostoevsky wants us to perceive his hero.

While a thematic approach is highly appropriate, it cannot by itself enable us to grasp what is going on in the novel. It is important to look at Raskolnikov much as we looked at the underground man, as an imagined human being who can be understood in terms of his history and personality. Looking at him in this way will help us to recover Dostoevsky's psychological intuitions and to appreciate his mimetic achievement. It will also make us aware of certain tensions within the novel. Critics who focus on theme tend to ignore the mimetic portrait of Raskolnikov, while those who employ a psychological approach respond to the richness of the characterization but do not pay much attention to the protagonist's illustrative functions. I shall be concerned with both aspects of the novel and shall explore the ways in which the rhetoric obscures the mimesis and the psychological portrait of Raskolnikov is at odds with the rhetoric.

II. My Approach versus Bakhtin's

Perhaps I can clarify my view of Dostoevsky's art by relating it again to that of Mikhail Bakhtin. In celebrating Dostoevsky as the creator of the polyphonic novel, Bakhtin opposes thematic readings in which the characters have a fixed ideological significance and are subject to the author's "finalizing artistic vision" (1984, 5). Instead, he sees the characters as part of "a great dialogue" in which "the author acts as organizer and participant . . . without retaining for himself the final word" (72). The characters are "not voiceless slaves" but "free people, capable of standing *alongside* their creator, capable of not agreeing with him and even of rebelling against him" (6; author's emphasis). What unfolds in Dostoevsky's works "is not a multitude of characters and fates in a single objective world illuminated by a single authorial consciousness" but "a plurality of independent and unmerged voices and consciousnesses, a genuine polyphony of fully valid voices" (6).

According to Bakhtin, these "equally valid consciousnesses" (1984, 7), each with its own field of vision, "combine in a higher unity" (16). Their autonomy does not disrupt the novels in which they exist, for their "independence and freedom" are "precisely what is incorporated into the author's design" (13), which is to create a polyphonic novel. Seemingly "heterogeneous and incompatible" materials are unified by "this compositional principle" (17).

Bakhtin complains that previous critics have read Dostoevsky incorrectly because they have failed to see his polyphonic design, but subsequent critics have continued to see Dostoevsky's characters from what they take to be the author's perspective. Whereas Bakhtin contends that the characters have equally valid voices and are engaged in open-ended dialogue, almost everyone else feels that the voices of such characters as Sonya, Alyosha, and Father Zossima prevail over those of Raskolnikov or Ivan. Joseph Frank says that Razumikhin "often speaks directly for the author" (1995, 63), and other characters have also been identified with the author's perspective. In *Dostoevsky the Thinker*, James P. Scanlan contends that we can treat the fiction "as providing elaboration of [Dostoevsky's] views, and sometimes even argumentative support for them, rather than as an opaque polyphonic world in which no views are privileged" (2002, 4). Harold Bloom, who is less sympathetic than Scanlan to Dostoevsky's ideas, complains of Dostoevsky's "tendentiousness": "He is a partisan, whose fierce perspective is always explicit in what he writes. His design upon us is to raise us, like Lazarus, from our own nihilism or skepticism, and then convert us to orthodoxy" (2004a, 4). This is Sonya's design on Raskolnikov, of course.

Bakhtin acknowledges that there are monological elements in all of Dostoevsky's novels, but he downplays their importance, contending that they do not "determine the nature of the whole" (1984, 68). He says that there is "a unique conflict" in Dostoevsky "between the internal open-endedness of the characters and dialogue, and the *external* (in most cases compositional and thematic) *completedness* of every individual novel. We cannot go deeply into this difficult problem here. We will say only that almost all of Dostoevsky's novels have a *conventionally literary, conventionally monologic* ending," with *Crime and Punishment* being "especially characteristic in this respect" (39–40; author's emphasis). Although the title of Bakhtin's book is *Problems of Dostoevsky's Poetics*, his study is almost entirely celebratory of Dostoevsky. In the passage I have quoted, he identifies a major problem in Dostoevsky's art, but he says that he cannot go into it. Because the conflict of which Bakhtin speaks is central to my approach, I shall address it more fully than he has done.

Let us begin with the "open-endedness of the characters." According to Bakhtin, Dostoevsky's characters are not puppets but are capable of standing alongside the author and even of rebelling against him. This is an important observation, but I do not believe it applies to all of Dostoevsky's characters as Bakhtin suggests. As numerous critics have pointed out, there are different kinds of characterization. In *The Nature of Narrative*, for example, Robert Scholes and Robert Kellogg distinguish among aesthetic, illustrative, and mimetic characters. Aesthetic characters are stock types who may be understood primarily in terms of their formal and dramatic functions. Illustrative characters are "concepts in anthropoid shape or fragments of the human psyche parading as whole human beings" (1966, 88). We try to understand "the principle they illustrate through their actions in a narrative framework."

A great many works—such as allegories, comedies, satires, and philosophic tales—contain only aesthetic and illustrative characters, but in realistic fiction such as Dostoevsky's, there is a strong "psychological impulse" that leads to the creation of "highly individualized figures who resist abstraction and generalization" (101). When we encounter fully drawn mimetic characters, "we are justified in asking questions about [their] motivations based on our knowledge of the ways in which real people are motivated" (87). Mimetic characters usually serve aesthetic and illustrative purposes; but numerous details have been called forth by the author's imaginative construction of their inner lives, relationships, and predicaments. Bakhtin's observations about the independence of Dostoevsky's characters apply to his major creations but not to minor characters who have mainly aesthetic or illustrative functions or some combination of both.

Dostoevsky is not alone in creating great mimetic characters, and Bakhtin is not alone in declaring their independence. There is much testimony from writers and critics about the tendency of such characters, once created, to escape from their author's designs. John Galsworthy observes that the "enduring characters in literature have kicked free of . . . their creators" (1931, 27), and W. J. Harvey says that the novelist "must accept his characters as asserting their human individuality and uniqueness in the face of all ideology (including his own limited point of view)" (1965, 25). Georg Lukács maintains that a "ruthlessness toward their own subjective world-picture is the hallmark of all great realists" (1964, 11). Characters are not subordinated to the author's *Weltanschauung* but "live an independent life of their own." Their development is "dictated by the inner dialectic of their social and individual existence." Iris Murdoch praises the best realistic novelists for making their fiction "a house fit for free characters to live in" (1959, 271). Their works display a "real apprehension" of other people "as having a right to exist and to have a separate mode of being which is important and interesting to themselves" (257). Their characters "are free, independent of their author, and not merely puppets in the exteriorization of some closely locked psychological conflict of his own." "When a character is born," says the Father in Luigi Pirandello's *Six Characters in Search of an Author*, "he immediately assumes so much independence, even from his own author," that he sometimes "acquires a meaning which the author never dreamed of giving him" (1995, 56).

Bakhtin is right about the conflict in Dostoevsky's novels between what he calls the "open-endedness" of the characters and the formal and thematic components of the works. This conflict is not "unique" to Dostoevsky, however. It is common in realistic fiction and has been brilliantly described by E. M. Forster in *Aspects of the Novel*. The novelist, says Forster, has "a very mixed lot of ingredients to handle" (1927, 64). He or she is telling a story ("life in time") that has a meaning ("life by values"). The story is "about human beings," and the "characters arrive when evoked," but they are "full of the spirit of mutiny." (Forster is speaking here of "round"—or mimetic—as opposed to "flat" characters.) Having parallels "with people like ourselves, [these characters] try to live their own lives and are consequently often engaged in treason against the main scheme of the book. They 'run away,' they 'get out of hand': they are creations inside a creation" who are "often inharmonious" toward the larger whole of which they are a part. If "they are given complete freedom they kick the book to pieces, and if they are kept too sternly in check, they revenge themselves by dying, and destroy it by intestinal decay."

Forster has described the dilemma of realistic writers, the best of whom are faithful to their psychological intuitions even when this leads to the creation of characters who escape their functional roles. He recognizes, as Bakhtin does not, that such characters give rise to unresolved conflicts, that there is no higher harmony into which they are subsumed. They are "creations inside a creation" who can be understood independently of the author and who, when so understood, often subvert the author's designs.

In my view, what Bakhtin sees as the dialogical character of Dostoevsky's novels is a product of tensions between authorial rhetoric and mimetic characterization. As Forster's observations suggest, such tensions are almost bound to arise with the creation of imagined human beings. I have explored such tensions in many psychologically realistic works, from *Antigone* to *Herzog* (see Paris 1974, 1978a, 1986, 1991a, 1991b, 1997, 2003, 2005), and have found in general that the greater the characterization, the greater the subversive effect. The tensions can be either exacerbated or diminished, however, by the author's choice of narrative technique. Emily Brontë's *Wuthering Heights*, with its nesting of multiple narrators, comes closest to achieving the kind of polyphony Bakhtin claims for Dostoevsky (Paris 1997); and once Marlow becomes narrator and begins taking opinions on Jim's case, Joseph Conrad's *Lord Jim* is the kind of dialogical novel that Bakhtin describes (Paris 2005). The tensions between rhetoric and mimesis are minimal in "Notes from Underground," where the author disappears into the first person narration; but they are marked in *Crime and Punishment* and *The Brothers Karamazov*, where Dostoevsky's thematic stance is difficult to ignore. Indeed, the tensions are particularly intense in Dostoevsky because he is at once a great psychological and a great ideological novelist. His ideology is in danger of obscuring his psychological intuitions; and his characters, when independently understood, are often engaged in treason against the main scheme of the book.

III. DOSTOEVSKY'S RHETORICAL TECHNIQUES

I have said that Dostoevsky's thematic stance is difficult to ignore, but how exactly is it established? Much thematic criticism places *Crime and Punishment* in the context of Dostoevsky's other writings, both fiction and nonfiction, of the cultural climate of his time, and of controversies about social, ethical, and theological doctrines. Such work is admirable and considerably enriches our sense of the novel's ideological sophistication. I shall focus on the novel's rhetoric: the internal strategies Dostoevsky employs to influence readers' moral and intellectual responses to characters, their sympathy and antipathy, their emotional closeness or distance (see Booth 1961).

One rhetorical device commonly employed in nineteenth-century fiction is authorial commentary. Bakhtin describes Dostoevsky's narration in the later works as "dry, informative, documentary discourse" that "is, as it were, voiceless" because "the author does not insert . . . any judgment . . . of his own" (1984, 251). This description fits *Crime and Punishment* rather well, better than it does *The Brothers Karamazov*. Indeed, Dostoevsky seems to be characterizing his own technique in his account of the letters Sonya writes to Dunya and Razumikhin from Siberia. At first the letters seem "somewhat dry and unsatisfactory," but it turns out that "they could not have been better written." They

> were full of the most prosaic actuality, the simplest and clearest description of every circumstance of Raskolnikov's life as a convict.... Instead of attempts to explain his psychological condition and his inner life generally, there were only facts, his own words, that is, and detailed reports of his health, of what he expressed a wish for at their interviews, the questions he asked her or the commissions he entrusted to her. All this she communicated with extraordinary minuteness. In the end, the picture of their unhappy brother stood out in relief, exactly and clearly drawn in his own words; there could be nothing misleading about it, because it consisted wholly of factual reports. (Epilogue, i)

The omniscient narrator provides minute accounts of Raskolnikov's inner life, to which Sonya does not have access; but these accounts have the character of factual reports and rarely contain judgments or attempts at explanation.

There are occasional authorial intrusions, to be sure. The narrator tells us, for instance, that behavior like Raskolnikov's "is found among monomaniacs" (II, i), and that, being young, Raskolnikov has "an abstract and consequently cruel mind" (IV, iv). When Raskolnikov is in a state of terror after his unpremeditated murder of Lizaveta, the narrator observes that if he could have seen "all the difficulty of his position and how desperate, hideous, and absurd it was," he probably would have "abandoned everything and given himself up, not out of fear for himself so much as from horror and repulsion for what he had done" (I, vii). This is more than a dry, factual report. The most notable intrusions are in the Epilogue, where the narrator describes the change in Raskolnikov as a "perfect resurrection into a new life" and predicts a "gradual regeneration" that will lead to knowledge of "a hitherto undreamed-of reality" (ii).

Although they are significant, authorial intrusions are very few and they are hardly sufficient to account for our sense that we know how Dostoevsky wants us to understand and feel about Raskolnikov. There are, of course, many devices other than direct commentary that an author can employ to shape our response to a character. In *Crime and Punishment* we are given deep inside views of Raskolnikov that make us sympathetic toward him despite the fact that he is a murderer. We enter into his terror, his fear, his self-loathing, his wrenching inner conflicts. Although he commits a horrible crime,

Raskolnikov is not the villain of the piece but the protagonist. Dostoevsky's rhetoric induces us to see him as good at heart and to hope for his redemption.

Perhaps the major rhetorical device in the novel is Dostoevsky's use of other characters as foils to Raskolnikov and as commentators on him. This has been frequently noted, but there is more to be said about it. The characters so employed include those who reflect the side of Raskolnikov that leads to crime—Lebezyatnikov, Luzhin, and Svidrigaylov—and those who believe in his potential for good—his mother and sister, Razumikhin, Porfiry, and Sonya. These characters are also presented rhetorically, the first group in a negative and the second in a positive light. Through the use of other characters, Dostoevsky surrounds Raskolnikov with explicit and implicit commentary while remaining "as it were, voiceless." Because the positively presented characters tend to say similar things, they serve as a kind of chorus that seems designed to influence how we perceive Raskolnikov and judge him.

Before the murder, Dostoevsky shows his hero alternating between planning the bloody deed and recoiling in horror from the very thought of it. He prays to be released from his evil temptation: "Lord! . . . show me the way, that I may renounce this accursed . . . fantasy of mine!" (I, v). It is his mother who first provides a formulation of Raskolnikov's inner conflicts: "Do you pray to God, Rodya, as you used to do, and do you believe in the mercy of our Creator and Redeemer? I am afraid, in my heart, that you too may have been affected by the fashionable modern unbelief. If that is so, I will pray for you" (I, iii). We are to see Raskolnikov as torn between the secular thought sweeping the educated classes and the Christian beliefs he imbibed in childhood.

IV. FASHIONABLE MODERN UNBELIEF

The modern unbelief that leads Raskolnikov to crime is associated with utilitarianism, again by means of indirect rhetoric. After he first visits Alyona, the thought of the murder begins taking shape in his mind, and it is then reinforced when he overhears a conversation between a student and an officer in which the student says that he "could kill that damned old woman and rob her without a single twinge of conscience" (I, vi). His justification is "simple arithmetic." The old woman is a louse, and thousands can be "saved from corruption and decay" by her money: "What is the life of that stupid, spiteful, consumptive old woman weighed against the common good?" The officer agrees that Alyona does not "deserve to live" but says, "there you are, that's nature." "Don't you see," replies the student, "nature must be guided and corrected, or else we should all be swamped with prejudices. Otherwise there could never be one great man." The student acknowledges the importance of conscience and duty, but how are they to be defined? Presumably in a way that would be compatible with murder. He says, however, that he would not kill Alyona himself, suggesting that in his case nature is stronger than arithmetic.

This conversation introduces some of the novel's main thematic motifs without the use of authorial commentary. Overhearing it influences Raskolnikov profoundly because *"exactly the same ideas"* had "been born in his own brain" during his visit to Alyona (I, vi; author's emphasis). He too believes that if we are to achieve greatness, we must not allow ourselves to be swamped with prejudices and that the beneficial results of the crime "will wipe out one little, insignificant transgression." Unlike the student, Raskolnikov acts on his ideas and finds that he cannot live with what he has done. The novel returns again and again to the opposition between abstract logic that may seem "as straightforward as arithmetic" (I, v) and the whole of human nature, which rejects the conclusions of the utilitarian calculus.

Utilitarianism is presented in a most unsavory light not only through its effect on Raskolnikov but also through the other characters who are associated with it. The chief of these is Lebezyatnikov, whom we see initially through the eyes of Marmeladov. During his conversation with Raskolnikov in the tavern, Marmeladov speaks of his hopelessness about obtaining a loan from Lebezyatnikov. Why "should he give it to me," he asks, "when he knows that I shall not repay it? Out of compassion? But recently Mr. Lebezyatnikov, who is a follower of the latest ideas, was explaining that in this age the sentiment of compassion is actually prohibited by science, and that that is how they order things in England, where they have political economy" (I, ii). According to Marmeladov, Lebezyatnikov has given Katerina Ivanovna "a terrible beating" and has forced Sonya to move away from her family and to carry a prostitute's yellow card. Although Lebezyatnikov later denies these allegations, which seem to be exaggerated, their introduction early in the novel shapes our attitude toward this representative of fashionable modern unbelief.

The narrator is more intrusive in the presentation of Lebezyatnikov than he is with any other character, treating him in an overtly satirical manner:

> Andrey Semënovich really was rather stupid. He had joined the forces of progress and "our younger generation" out of conviction. He was one of that countless and multifarious legion of nondescripts, putrescent abortions, and uninformed obstinate fools who instantly and infallibly attach themselves to the most fashionable current idea, with the immediate effect of vulgarizing it and of turning into a ridiculous caricature any cause they serve, however sincerely. (V, i)

Fashionable modern thought seems absurd, indeed, as espoused by Lebezyatnikov. He advocates harsh attacks on the existing social order and wishes that his mother and father were still alive so that he could "sting them with [his] protests." He believes that things will be better when people are organized into communes, for "environment is everything, and the man is nothing." He says that Sonya has a right to use her "stock" as she does, that he looks "upon her action as a spirited concrete protest against the organization of society," and that he "deeply respect[s] her for it." When he marries, he will urge his wife to take lovers as a sign of his respect for her personal freedom. And, most famously, he says that cleaning cesspits may "be worth more than the activities of some Raphael or Pushkin, because it is more useful!" He proclaims that the only word he understands is "*useful!*"

Although this is admittedly a "ridiculous caricature" of modern thought, it is not counterbalanced by a more equitable presentation. As Dostoevsky portrays them, utilitarian and socialist ideas are either ludicrous or dangerous. They have led to the increase of crime in modern society and to mental disorders. Zosimov observes that people are "frequently more or less deranged" (III, iii), a peasant woman says that "folks is all queer nowadays" (II, vi), and Svidrigaylov calls Petersburg "a town of half-crazy people" (VI, iii). The most sophisticated exponent of contemporary ideas is Raskolnikov, and in him they lead to murder and psychological disintegration. No one can live with such beliefs. The student has no intention of acting on his simple arithmetic, and Lebezyatnikov finds himself behaving in accordance with traditional notions of honor when he denounces Luzhin as a "scoundrel" for falsely accusing Sonya of stealing money (V, iii). The characters espousing fashionable modern unbelief are hardly presented as having equally valid voices engaged in open-ended dialogue but are subsumed by the author's rhetoric into a finalizing artistic vision.

Another character who spouts utilitarian ideas is Dunya's fiancé, Peter Petrovich Luzhin, one of the most unappealing figures in the novel. He has no genuine belief in modern thought but wishes to "ingratiate himself with 'our younger generation'" in order to avoid being denounced by "progressives," whose possible power he fears (V, i). He therefore lodges with Lebezyatnikov, who had once been his ward, and adopts his ideas.

The rhetorical treatment of Luzhin is heavy-handed and leaves no doubt as to where the implied author stands. He is introduced as "a gentleman no longer young, starchy and pompous, with a wary and irritable face," who looks around Raskolnikov's little room "with offensively-unconcealed astonishment" (II, v). Assuming that Raskolnikov and his young friends are progressives, he praises the "new, beneficial ideas" that have been "disseminated, in place of the old fantastic and romantic ones." We have "irrevocably severed ourselves from the past," he proclaims, and made "progress . . . in the name of science and economic truth." He then attacks the old injunction to love thy neighbor, explaining that to do so will impoverish everyone. Science says "love yourself first of all, for everything in the world is based on personal interest. If you love yourself alone, you will conduct your affairs properly" and thus will serve the common good. He is interrupted by Razumikhin, who complains that he is "sick of this kind of self-congratulatory babbling, this ceaseless inexhaustible flow of platitudes, these monotonous repetitions . . . of the same old commonplaces." Here, as elsewhere, Dostoevsky's viewpoint is expressed by a character. Although the narrator is only reporting what Razumikhin said, there can be no doubt as to whose side he is on.

When the conversation turns to the murder of the old moneylender, Luzhin laments the increase of crime in contemporary life, "even in the higher social circles" (II, v). He alludes to robbery, arson, murder, and counterfeiting; and he reasons that the man who killed Alyona "must be a person of some social standing." "How are we to explain this depravity," he asks, "among the civilized elements of our society?" Razumikhin points out that the Reader in Universal History who was the leader of a band of counterfeiters explained that everyone is getting rich by one means or another and that they wanted to get rich too and to do it "at other people's expense, as quickly as possible, and without labour." When Luzhin wants to know what has happened to "morals" and "principles," Raskolnikov asks what he is "making so much fuss about," since things have "worked out in accordance with [his] own theory" about self-interest, which means "that you can cut people's throats" (II, v). Luzhin says this is nonsense, showing that even he cannot stomach the implications of the ideas he is expounding. However, Raskolnikov has already carried them to their "logical conclusion."

Fashionable modern unbelief is also represented by the sinister Svidrigaylov, whom Luzhin describes as "the most depraved, the most completely abandoned to vice" (IV, ii). Dunya accuses him of having poisoned his wife, Marfa Petrovna; he seems to have been responsible for the death of Philip, his serf; and he abused a young girl who then committed suicide. After Marfa Petrovna's death, he comes to St. Petersburg for "a spell of debauchery" (VI, iii). He is a sexual predator, attracted to young girls, who sees no reason why he should "put any restraint on [him]self." He seems to have no qualms about ruining other people's lives in order to satisfy his desires and to escape from his boredom. He feels that he and Raskolnikov have much in common, and Raskolnikov is drawn to him as someone who appears to have transcended the traditional morality and who may show him how to do so as well. Although Svidrigaylov does not preach "progressive" ideas like Lebezyatnikov and Luzhin, he clearly subscribes to them. Having overheard Raskolnikov's confession to Sonya, Svidrigaylov tells Dunya that it was her brother who murdered Alyona and explains his rationale. Raskolnikov's utilitarian calculus is "the same sort of thing," he says, "which makes me . . . consider that a single piece of wrongdoing is allowable, if the chief aim is good" (VI, v). He understands that Raskolnikov is suffering from the fact that although he believes that great men can overstep the law "without pausing to reflect," he is not capable of doing so himself. This means that "he is not a man of genius," "and that, for a young man with a due share of self-esteem, is humiliating, especially in our day." This is one of many instances in which other characters provide precise analyses of Raskolnikov's thoughts and feelings with their social implications, making it unnecessary for the narrator to do so. Svidrigaylov comprehends Raskolnikov so well because he is a kindred spirit, in some respects at least.

Appalled by Svidrigaylov's account of her brother, Dunya asks, "And the pangs of conscience? So you would deny him any moral feeling? Is he really like that?" (VI, v). "In our educated Russian society," Svidrigaylov explains, "there are no sacred traditions," so people make up their own value systems. He himself "make[s] it a rule to condemn absolutely nobody." Svidrigaylov is describing the state of moral anarchy that has resulted from modern unbelief. Svidrigaylov says that he does not condemn anybody, but he is haunted by his own transgressions. He sees ghosts, has terrible dreams, and is full of self-loathing. His hope of salvation lies in Dunya, much as Raskolnikov's lies in Sonya. "Whatever you believe in," he tells her, "I will believe in too" (VI, v). Sonya stands by Raskolnikov, and he eventually adopts her beliefs; but Dunya tells Svidrigaylov that she can never love him, and he leaves her with a "weak, pitiful, mournful smile of despair." He kills himself with the pistol that had misfired when Dunya had tried to shoot him in self-defense.

V. THE RIGHT-MINDED CHARACTERS

There is a dialogue in *Crime and Punishment*, and in Raskolnikov himself, between modern secular thought and traditional Christian beliefs, but the voices are far from being given equal weight. Characters who represent the Christian perspective are presented much more favorably than the unbelievers, and the Christian side of Raskolnikov is ultimately triumphant. The implied author rarely enters into the dialogue directly, but he does not have to do so. Raskolnikov's mother and sister, who are part of his religious background, are deeply disturbed by his apostasy. When Raskolnikov denies that killing Alyona was a crime, Dunya cries out "in despair" that he "really did shed blood" and insists that what he is saying is "quite wrong" (VI, vii). There are a number of right-minded characters who wish Raskolnikov well, believe in his potential for good, and make observations and judgments that seem authoritative. The most important of these are Razumikhin, Porfiry, and Sonya. The conscientious side of Raskolnikov contributes to the rhetorical effect, for he repeatedly condemns the transgressive side of his personality both before and after the murder. He prays to be delivered from temptation, and he later agrees with Sonya that because he has "strayed away from God," "God has stricken [him], and given [him] over to the devil" (V, iv). "I know myself," he tells her, "that it was the devil dragging me along."

* * *

Razumikhin serves as a foil to Raskolnikov as well as a commentator on him. Whereas Lebezyatnikov and Luzhin are satirized, Razumikhin is described in glowing terms. Razumikhin is "so goodhearted as to seem almost simple," but his simplicity conceals "both depth and considerable merit" (I, iv). The "best of his fellow students" understand this and love him. He is a gentle giant: "hot-headed, frank, single-minded, honest, as strong as a hero of legend" (III, i). He is "remarkable . . . in that failure never disconcert[s] him and adverse circumstances" seem "powerless to subdue him" (I, iv). He is very poor, having no resources other than his earnings, but he knows "a thousand and one ways" of making money. Although he has been obliged to leave the university for lack of funds, he regards this as temporary and is "straining every nerve to improve his circumstances in order to continue his studies." Raskolnikov has also left the university, but instead of trying to earn money to return, he has given up tutoring and has been holed up in his room dreaming of making his fortune by murdering the old moneylender. He explains to Nastasya that "teaching children is very badly paid" and that there is not much one can do "with a few copecks" (I, iii). "I suppose you want a fortune straight off?" she asks; he firmly replies, "Yes, I do." He is like the Reader in Universal History who has become a counterfeiter in order to get rich quickly and easily at other people's expense.

Although sometimes naive, as when he is slow to recognize Raskolnikov's guilt, Razumikhin can be extraordinarily perceptive, as his name suggests. (The root of his name is "razum," meaning reason or good sense.) He explains that the workman Nikolay cannot have killed Alyona because he engages in horseplay just after the murder occurs, and if he had committed the act, that would have been a "psychological impossibility" (II, iv). He then correctly reconstructs the murderer's movements following the crime without knowing, of course, that Raskolnikov was the perpetrator. He tells Pulkheria and Dunya that Raskolnikov is "moody, melancholy, proud, and haughty" (III, ii). He "is kind and generous" but "doesn't like to display his feelings, and would rather seem heartless than talk about them." Sometimes, however, he is "inhumanly cold and unfeeling. Really, it is as if he had two separate personalities, each dominating him alternately." This is a brilliant description of Raskolnikov. Razumikhin's depiction of Porfiry is also quite astute: "He likes to mislead people, or rather to baffle them," so that, like moths, they will fly "into the candle" of themselves (III, iv). The narrator can remain "as it were, voiceless" when there are characters who provide such observations.

Razumikhin's beliefs and judgments seem reliable. It is he who most directly articulates the novel's response to utilitarian and socialist ideas.

The socialists contend that "if society is properly organized, all crimes will instantly disappear, since there will be nothing to protest against, and everybody will immediately become law-abiding" (III, v). What this leaves out, says Razumikhin, is "nature": "In their philosophy, it is not humanity, following the path of historical, *living*, development to the end, that will finally evolve into the perfect society, but, on the contrary, a social system, devised by some mathematician's brain, will instantly reorganize humanity, make it righteous and innocent in a flash, with greater speed than any living process, and without the aid of living historical development!" (author's emphasis). The living soul, however, "wants life" and "will not submit to mechanism." "The course of nature" cannot be diverted "by logic alone! Logic can anticipate three possibilities, but there are millions of them!"

Razumikhin sounds here like the underground man, but he is a much more appealing spokesman for these ideas since he is portrayed so positively by the narrator and is held in such high esteem by other characters. Dunya, for example, says, "It was God Himself who sent that man to us" (III, i). The ideas do not emanate from Razumikhin's personality as they do with the underground man, and this is one of the things that makes him seem a mouthpiece for the author. He is not portrayed in psychological depth and is more an aesthetic and illustrative than a mimetic character.

Dostoevsky uses Razumikhin to guide our judgments. He denounces Luzhin's philosophy of self-interest and objects to his treatment of Dunya and Pulkheria. He believes that by pursuing error we can arrive "at the truth," if this is part of a living process (Raskolnikov is a case in point); but Luzhin is merely parroting other people's ideas and is "not on the right path" (III, i). When Raskolnikov discusses his extraordinary man theory with Porfiry, Razumikhin asks, "Are you serious, Rodya?" (III, v). What is "really *original*" in Raskolnikov's article, he is "sorry to say," is the upholding of "bloodshed *as a matter of conscience*" (author's emphasis). This "*moral* permission to shed blood" is "more terrible than official, legal, licence to do so" (author's emphasis). Razumikhin's negative response to Raskolnikov's ideas cannot help but influence the reader, given the favorable light in which he is presented.

The favorable treatment of Razumikhin also influences our response to Raskolnikov in a positive way because Razumikhin remains loyal to his friend even though he is critical of his radical ideas. Razumikhin's support of his friend, like that of his mother and sister, contributes to our sense that, despite his horrible crime, Raskolnikov is being presented as an object of sympathetic concern.

* * *

Another character who understands Raskolnikov well, judges him firmly, and remains sympathetic toward him is Porfiry Petrovich. Like Razumikhin, Porfiry is an illustrative character who functions as a guide to how the author wants us to perceive and feel about his hero. "This is an obscure and fantastic case," he observes to Raskolnikov, "a contemporary case, something that could only happen in our day, when the heart of man has grown troubled. . . . There are bookish dreams here, and a heart troubled by theories" (VI, ii). Raskolnikov's heart is troubled by modern unbelief, and his case is to be seen as symptomatic of the age.

Porfiry speaks of the "one-sided development" of "contemporary intellectuals" and says that, "like all young people," Raskolnikov "esteem[s] the human intellect above all things" (IV, v). "Reality and nature . . . are very important," however, "and sometimes upset the most penetrating calculations," as when the murderer "fall[s] in a faint, and that at the most interesting and shocking point!" It is Raskolnikov's fainting in the police station when the murders are being discussed that first arouses Porfiry's suspicions. "The criminal's own nature" has come "to the rescue of the poor investigator." Reality and nature versus intellect and calculation is a recurring motif in *Crime and Punishment*, as we have seen—one developed by characters who have been endowed with authority.

Porfiry's authority derives in part from his amazing insights into Raskolnikov, insights we know to be accurate because we have been given so much information about the protagonist's inner life. Porfiry has the advantage of having read the article in which Raskolnikov divides humans into ordinary and extraordinary people, with extraordinary people having the right to permit their conscience to overstep "certain obstacles" if their ideas, which may be beneficial for mankind, "require it for their fulfillment" (III, v). But how, asks Porfiry, "do you distinguish these extraordinary people from the ordinary?" Might there not be a mix-up in which "somebody from one category imagined that he belonged to the other and began 'to remove all obstacles'"? This is precisely what Raskolnikov fears has happened in his own case, since he has gone to pieces after committing the crime, whereas, according to his theory, extraordinary people can step over obstacles without feeling guilt or losing their composure. He later acknowledges to himself that Porfiry has "seen right through him" (VI, ii).

Porfiry perceives that there is a conflict in Raskolnikov, not only between his conception of how he should be feeling and behaving if he were an extraordinary man and his actual responses to having murdered, but also between the Christian side of his nature and that which is under the influence of modern thought. According to Raskolnikov, ordinary people "preserve the world and increase and multiply," whereas extraordinary people "move the world and guide it to its goal" (III, v). Both have an equal right to exist, and there will be perpetual conflict between them "until we have built the New Jerusalem, of course!" This is the New Jerusalem of the Saint-Simonians, which is to be a socialist paradise on earth. "You do believe in the New Jerusalem, then?" Porfiry asks, and Raskolnikov replies that he does:

"A-and you believe in God? Forgive me for being so inquisitive."
"Yes, I do," repeated Raskolnikov, raising his eyes to Porfiry.
"A-a-and do you believe in the raising of Lazarus?"
"Y-yes. Why are you asking all this?"
"You believe in it literally?"
"Yes."

Porfiry understands that Raskolnikov is entertaining incompatible beliefs and that the religious side of his nature is still alive despite his pernicious philosophy. His objective becomes not simply to bring Raskolnikov to justice but to help him achieve redemption.

Porfiry is not only Raskolnikov's adversary, then, but also his ally. He tells Raskolnikov, "I sincerely like you and wish you well" (IV, v) and says that he "felt attached" to him as soon as they met (VI, ii). Because he is "a man with a heart and conscience," he does not arrest Raskolnikov when he becomes convinced of his guilt but gives him the opportunity to confess and accept his suffering. He is not just toying with Raskolnikov but is acting out of a concern for his spiritual well-being. His attitude toward Raskolnikov seems be that which the author is trying to instill in the reader. He tells Raskolnikov that although his theory is "mean and base," he is not a mean and base person. Indeed, he looks on him as an "honorable man . . . with elements of greatness" in him, whose crime "resulted from the clouding of [his] faculties."

Porfiry gives explicit expression to some of the central motifs of the novel, such as the paradox of the fortunate fall, the importance of suffering, and the primacy of life over theory. "*Perhaps it is through this,*" he tells Raskolnikov, "*that God seeks to bring you to himself*" (VI, ii; emphasis added). By violating his conscience, Raskolnikov has activated it, making him more aware than he had been before of the divine voice within him. Porfiry says that "suffering is a good thing" and feels that Raskolnikov will benefit from his ordeal. This turns out to be true as Raskolnikov is reborn in Siberia. Porfiry advises Raskolnikov not to "philosophize too subtly": "plunge straight into life, without deliberation; don't be uneasy—it will carry you direct to the shore and set you on your feet." He does not know to what shore Raskolnikov will be carried, but he proclaims it "the sacred truth" that "life will sustain" him and that he will "regain [his] self-esteem." This proclamation foreshadows the ending of the novel and is validated by it. In light of the conclusion, Porfiry's parting words to Raskolnikov seem prescient: "Pleasant thoughts and happy new beginnings!"

* * *

It is Sonya, of course, who is most instrumental in Raskolnikov's ultimate transformation, and it seems we are meant to identify most with her view of Raskolnikov. Sonya is presented from the beginning with a powerfully favorable rhetoric in Dostoevsky's usual way in this novel: by means of another character. She is introduced by Marmeladov, who tells Raskolnikov about her in their conversation in the tavern. She has been driven into prostitution by Katerina Ivanovna, who has sold her, in effect, for thirty silver roubles, thus associating her immediately with Christ. She does not reproach Katerina nor her father when, after the binge that has ruined his family, he asks her "for money to get something for [his] thick head" (I, i). As she gives him her last thirty copecks, she says nothing but only looks at him "in silence . . . A look like that does not belong to this world, but there . . . where they grieve over mankind, they weep for them, but they do not reproach them, they do not reproach!" (author's ellipses).

Sonya is presented as an all-loving, all-forgiving, angelic creature despite her fallen state. On the Day of Judgment, Christ, who alone is "the judge," will pity and forgive "the daughter who gave herself for a harsh and consumptive stepmother and the little children of another" and who "showed compassion to that filthy drunkard, her earthly father" (I, i). According to Marmeladov, Christ will forgive sinners like Sonya and himself because of their humility, because they have not "deemed [themselves] worthy." Marmeladov's words are given additional authority when he dies in a state of grace, receiving absolution, in his daughter's arms, asking her forgiveness (II, vi). This death scene has an aura of holiness, in contrast to that of the proud Katerina Ivanovna, who says she has "no sins" and does not want a priest (V, v). The favorable presentation of Sonya is continued by means of Raskolnikov. He treats Sonya with respect when she calls on him, seats her beside his mother and sister, and kisses her foot when he goes to visit her, prostrating himself, he tells her, "before all human suffering" (IV, iv). He can see that her shame has "touched her only mechanically; no trace of real corruption had yet crept into her heart." This is no doubt how the reader is meant to perceive Sonya.

Sonya is the chief exponent of the religious perspective to which Raskolnikov is ultimately converted. Dostoevsky gives that perspective authority by first challenging it and then constructing an action that validates it. He sets up a contest between Sonya's Christian faith and Raskolnikov's modern unbelief in which Sonya is triumphant. When he first goes to see Sonya, Raskolnikov asks what will happen to the children should she become ill while Katerina is alive and then after Katerina's death. As he pictures various disasters, including Polenka's becoming a prostitute, Sonya keeps insisting that "God will not allow it" (IV, iv). "He lets it happen to others," Raskolnikov observes. "No, no! God will protect her!" Sonya repeats, "beside herself." "Perhaps God does not exist," Raskolnikov replies, "with malicious enjoyment." "What should I do without God?" asks Sonya. She prays to him a great deal, and in return, "He does everything." Raskolnikov decides that this is Sonya's "solution," that her "mind is deranged," that she "expects a miracle to happen." "In two or three weeks' time they will be welcoming her into the asylum." He is afraid that Sonya's "madness" is "catching" and that he will become a "religious maniac" himself.

While the skeptical side of Raskolnikov scoffs at Sonya's beliefs, the religious side of him is drawn to them. He sees the New Testament that was given to Sonya by Lizaveta and asks her to read him the story of Lazarus, in whose resurrection he has told Porfiry he believes. Sonya reads the story as a confession of her own faith. As she approaches "the moment of the greatest, the unheard-of miracle," Sonya's voice rings "like a bell with the power of triumph and joy" (IV, iv). The "blind, unbelieving Jews . . . fall to the ground as if struck by lightning, sobbing and believing." Sonya hopes that Raskolnikov will also be converted by the raising of Lazarus: "'And *he, he* who is also blind and unbelieving, he also will . . . believe. Yes, yes! Here and now!' she dreamed, and trembled with joyful expectancy" (author's emphasis).

Sonya expects a miracle to happen in order to rescue the children; she also expects a miracle in Raskolnikov's life that will be comparable to the raising of Lazarus. Both miracles come to pass, confirming Sonya's faith. The children are saved from the streets and Sonya from a life of prostitution by the intervention of Svidrigaylov (which many critics feel to be contrived), who functions as a *deus ex machina*, providing the necessary funds. Raskolnikov is not instantly converted by Sonya's reading of the story of Lazarus, but what she envisions eventually comes to pass. At the end of the novel, Raskolnikov suddenly seems "to be seized and cast at her feet," after which he clasps her knees and weeps (Epilogue, ii). The narrator says that this is the beginning of "a perfect resurrection into a new life." Like Lazarus, Raskolnikov has been "raised . . . from the dead." Life has "taken the place of logic and something quite different must be worked out in his mind." He takes the New Testament from under his pillow, the one Lizaveta had given to Sonya and for which he himself had asked in the midst of his skepticism; and he wonders if Sonya's beliefs could become his "beliefs now? Her feelings, her aspirations, at least."

Between the reading of the story of Lazarus and Raskolnikov's rebirth, Sonya plays an important role in his life and makes comments so similar to those of Razumikhin and Porfiry that, as I have said, the three characters seem to constitute a chorus. After Raskolnikov confesses to the murders, she asks, "And how could you, you, the man you are . . . bring yourself to do this?" (V, iv; author's ellipsis). This reinforces Dostoevsky's presentation of Raskolnikov as an essentially good man gone astray and is, perhaps, the central question of the novel. Sonya responds to Raskolnikov's utilitarian arguments by insisting that who lives and dies is not for mortals to decide and by rejecting the idea that "a human being" is "a louse." Like Porfiry, she tells Raskolnikov to "accept suffering and achieve atonement through it." She instructs him to stand at the cross-roads, "bow down and kiss the earth you have desecrated," and "say aloud to all the world: 'I have done murder.' Then God will send you life again." Raskolnikov wavers a number of times before he does this; but prodded by Sonya's persistence, he accepts the cross she gives him and enacts her scenario. Even after his confession, he suffers inner conflicts; but Sonya stands by him, and her faith is rewarded.

VI. Dostoevsky's Perspective

I have tried to show that Dostoevsky's thematic stance is difficult to ignore in *Crime and Punishment*, despite Bakhtin's claim that "the author does not insert . . . any judgment of his own" (1984, 251). There is little direct authorial commentary, but there is nonetheless a powerful rhetoric at work in the novel. Fashionable modern unbelief is presented quite negatively through both its effect on Raskolnikov and the satiric treatment of the other characters who embrace it, while traditional Christian values are espoused by characters who are favorably treated, and these values are validated by the action of the novel as a whole. Raskolnikov's movement from skepticism to belief is strongly endorsed by Dostoevsky. The author is "as it were, voiceless" in that he rarely intrudes his own analyses and judgments, but there is a chorus of pronouncements from characters who are rhetorically endowed with authority; and these pronouncements are very astute, very similar to each other, and very much in harmony with the narrator's comments. There can be little doubt that they express Dostoevsky's point of view.

From Dostoevsky's perspective, Raskolnikov is the product of both a religious upbringing and an atheistic culture. His crime and the theories by which he justifies it are symptomatic of the diseased state of modern life in which selfishness and rationality have come to dominate man's spiritual nature. *Crime and Punishment* dramatizes the consequences of modern secular thought. Unbelief leads to nihilism, to crime, and to various forms of self-destruction. The novel also dramatizes the persistence of spirit—of God's power and man's unconscious faith—in the midst of atheism. For those who are not too far alienated from the religious side of their natures, crime may lead to spiritual rebirth. The violation of its dictates awakens the conscience and generates inner conflicts that can only be resolved by turning toward God.

In Raskolnikov, Dostoevsky is presenting a man in whom the spiritual and earthly selves dominate by turns. He is both a believer and an atheist, a lover of mankind and an inhuman murderer, an offspring of the Christian centuries and a product of his time. He is at once a representative of the new thought, which seeks to replace heaven with the New Jerusalem and God with the superman, and a repository of religious beliefs imbibed in childhood that torment him for his sinful thoughts and deeds. The new man triumphs when he commits the murders, but his crimes bring down on him the severe reproaches of his spiritual self, whose dictates they violate. After prolonged and terrible conflict, his spiritual nature gains the upper hand, and he embarks, at the end, on the path of regeneration. Raskolnikov's conversion should come as no surprise. While murdering Alyona is still only a thought, he struggles to reject it; and almost as soon as the crime is committed, he has impulses toward confession. His oscillations and inconsistencies throughout the novel can be seen as manifestations of the conflict between his two selves. His earthly, rational, selfish side consistently triumphs; but supported by the right-minded characters, his spiritual nature becomes stronger as the novel progresses until at last the balance of power shifts. Although he has made a decisive change of course, his conflicts are not over: "the new life . . . must be dearly bought, and paid for with great and heroic struggles yet to come" (Epilogue, ii). That, says the narrator, "might be the subject of a new tale."

CHAPTER 5

HISTORY AND INNER CONFLICTS

I. INTRODUCTION

PULKHERIA ALEXANDROVNA IS AFRAID THAT HER SON HAS BEEN corrupted by the fashionable modern unbelief, and Dostoevsky wants us to see that as Raskolnikov's problem. Porfiry diagnoses him as a contemporary intellectual with a one-sided development who has been led astray by abstract reasoning. Believing that he can govern his life by logic alone, he justifies his crime in utilitarian terms, as a matter of simple arithmetic. From a thematic point of view, Raskolnikov illustrates how modern unbelief leads to crime. He gets into trouble because he has left the religious environment of his native village and has come to St. Petersburg, a hotbed of atheistic humanism.

But why is Raskolnikov so receptive to modern ideas, and why do they lead to such an extreme result in him? Dostoevsky does not raise such questions because they would not serve his ideological purpose; but as a great psychological novelist he provides so much information about Raskolnikov's character, motives, and background that I cannot help asking them. If we confine ourselves to thematic analysis, as most critics have done, we shall miss much of the greatness of *Crime and Punishment*; for it is the mimetic portrait of Raskolnikov, not his illustrative significance, that has made the novel so fascinating to readers of different times, cultures, and beliefs. One need not share Dostoevsky's ideology to find it a marvelous work of art. Looking at Raskolnikov as an imagined human being will help us to recover Dostoevsky's psychological intuitions and to apprehend the tensions—or, as Bakhtin would say, the dialogue—between mimesis and rhetoric.

In this chapter, I shall examine Raskolnikov's relations with his family and the inner conflicts to which they give rise; in the next, I shall consider the ways in which his inner conflicts are manifested in his relations with Sonya and Svidrigaylov and are resolved by his transformation at the end.

II. RASKOLNIKOV AND HIS FAMILY

Just after his plan has begun to take shape in his mind, Raskolnikov overhears the conversation between the student and the officer in which the student says that he could kill the old moneylender "without a single twinge of conscience" and presents a utilitarian rationale for such an action (I, vi). What most impresses Raskolnikov is the student's statement that unless we get rid of our prejudices, there can "never be one great man"; for this addresses one of Raskolnikov's deepest emotional needs. He does not aspire to be a great man because he has fallen prey to modern unbelief, but he is attracted to the new ideas in part because he feels they will allow him to fulfill his ambitions. Dostoevsky suggests that these ideas are responsible for the increase of crime and derangement in contemporary society, but in the case of his protagonist he shows them leading to crime when combined with his individual psychology. Atheistic humanism seems to provide Raskolnikov with a way out of a psychological impasse, enabling him to dismiss the conscientious scruples that block his path to greatness and at the same time to satisfy his moral needs by seeing himself as a benefactor of mankind. According to the ethical calculus articulated by the student, he will be doing far more good than harm by killing the noxious old woman.

Why is Raskolnikov driven to be a great man? The chief reason, I think, is the tremendous pressure he is under to satisfy the needs of his family. A great deal of attention has been given to Raskolnikov's relationships with other characters in the novel, some of whom serve as foils to him or as purer embodiments of aspects of his own personality. From a psychological point of view, his most important relationship is with his mother, but only a few critics have focused on it (see Snodgrass 1960; Laing 1961; Wasiolek 1974; Kiremidjian 1975, 1976; Breger 1989).

Early in the novel, Raskolnikov receives a long letter from his mother that tortures him. As he finishes reading it, his face is "pale and convulsively distorted and a bitter angry smile play[s] over his lips" (I, iii). Before receiving the letter, he had been in terrible conflict about his plan to murder Alyona Ivanovna. He had carried out the rehearsal but then had felt "infinite loathing" toward the "vile, filthy, horrible" act he had been contemplating (I, i). Convinced that he could never do it, he suddenly had a social impulse that took him to the tavern where he became involved with Marmeladov. Raskolnikov vacillates both before and after receiving his mother's letter, but her letter pushes him in the direction of carrying out his plan, and it is possible that without it he would not have committed the crime.

In the third sentence of the letter, Pulkheria Alexandrovna writes, "You know how much I love you; you are all we have, Dunya and I, you are everything to us, our only hope and trust." She repeats these sentiments near the end, adding, "If only you are happy, we shall be happy too" (I, iii). Is it Raskolnikov's happiness that his mother and sister desire? I think not, unless it takes the form of his becoming a great man. When his mother writes that he is their only hope and trust, she means that, as the male in the family, he is the only one who can achieve glory in which she and Dunya can vicariously participate.

Raskolnikov's career is so important to his mother and sister that they are ready to sacrifice themselves to facilitate it. Pulkheria sends money, borrowed on her meager pension, and ruins her eyes with knitting to make a few extra roubles. In order to help her brother, Dunya takes her salary in advance from Svidrigaylov, forcing her to remain in his household after he begins to harass her. The self-sacrificial disposition of both women is well known. Raskolnikov's landlady feels that there is hope of collecting the money he owes "because there is a mama who will come to Rodenka's rescue with her pension of a hundred and twenty-five roubles, if it means going without enough to eat herself, and a sister who would sell herself into slavery for him" (II, iii). Dunya is indeed prepared to sell herself into slavery by marrying Luzhin in order to advance her brother's career. When Luzhin complains that she is not treating his interests as more important than those of her brother, Dunya heatedly replies: "I put your interests alongside of everything that has until now been precious in my life, that has until now formed the *whole* of my life, and you are offended because I set *too little* value on you?" (IV, ii; author's emphasis). Rodya has been everything precious, the whole of her life. What a terrible burden for him!

Raskolnikov is supposed to feel gratitude for the sacrifices of his mother and sister and to repay them by making them proud. In her letter, Pulkheria assures him that she and Dunya are fine, that their sacrifices are nothing, and at the same time lets him know how much she has suffered, how Dunya has been humiliated at the Svidrigaylov's, and how odious Luzhin is. He should love Dunya as she loves him: "her love for you is boundless; she loves you more than herself. She is an angel" (I, iii). Raskolnikov feels that the only way he can reciprocate is by having a glorious career. He is convinced that Dunya has agreed to marry Luzhin because in this way "his happiness may be secured, he may be kept at the University, made a partner in the office, his future provided for; perhaps later on he may be rich, respected, honoured, he may even die famous!" (I, iv). There is a great deal of bitterness here.

There is ample evidence that Raskolnikov has understood his sister correctly, that she was prepared to make an "infamous" marriage for the sake of his future glory. After Svidrigaylov tells her that her brother is a murderer and explains Raskolnikov's theory of the extraordinary man, he recognizes that Dunya's distress is not entirely on moral grounds and says, "Calm yourself. He may yet be a great man" (VI, iv). In parting from his sister, Raskolnikov also tries to reassure her: "Don't cry for me: I shall try to be honourable and manly all my life, although I am a murderer. Perhaps one day you will hear me spoken of. I shall not disgrace you, you will see; I may yet prove. . . . " As his speech trails off, a "strange expression [comes] into Dunya's eyes at the promise of his last words" (VI, vii).

Pulkheria Alexandrovna is even more obsessed than her daughter with visions of Raskolnikov's greatness. This is most evident near the end of the novel in a series of important passages that critics have largely ignored. Despite being distraught by Raskolnikov's state and full of foreboding that "some great misfortune" is in store for him, Pulkheria is tremendously excited by his article and tries to convince herself that he has been so distracted and neglectful because he has been busy with new ideas. Although there is a lot in his article that she does not understand, she has read it three times and tells him that "however foolish" she may be, she "can tell that in a very short time [he] will be one of the first, if not the very first, among our men of learning. And people dared to think [he was] mad!" She laughs and continues, "You don't know, but they really did think that. Wretched crawling worms, how can they understand what true intellect is?" (VI, vii). She had been grieved by his living conditions, but she sees that she "was just being foolish again, because [he] could get anything [he] wanted tomorrow, with [his] brains and talents."

I think we are looking here into Raskolnikov's unconscious, into the attitudes he absorbed from his mother in childhood that have governed him as an adult and that he has elaborately rationalized in his theory of the extraordinary man. His mother's statement corresponds exactly to Raskolnikov's view of himself at the beginning of the novel and helps to explain much of his behavior.

Although Pulkheria understands "that something terrible [is] happening to her son," she cannot relinquish her concern about his career. She asks if he is going far away:

"A very long way."
"What is there there? Some work, a career for you?"
"What God sends . . . only pray for me . . ."
Raskolnikov went to the door, but she caught at him and looked into his eyes with an expression of despair. Her face was disfigured with fear.
"That's enough, mama," said Raskolnikov, bitterly regretting that he had ever thought of coming. (VI, vii)

Raskolnikov is bitter because he understands that at least part of his mother's despair derives from the collapse of her dream of glory. Unlike Sonya and Dunya, she is not a source of spiritual support who can help him accept what God sends.

Pulkheria is so excited about Raskolnikov's article because it seems to promise the fulfillment of her dream. She tells him that his father had "twice sent something to a magazine—first a poem (I have the manuscript still, I will show it to you some time), and then a whole novel (I copied it out for him, at my own request), and how we both prayed that they would be accepted—but they weren't!" (VI, vii). With her husband's failure to redeem their impoverished existence through a glamorous achievement, Pulkheria turned to her son, investing him with all her hope and trust. Now he too has disappointed her, and she soon becomes deranged.

I am not suggesting that her derangement results only from the frustration of her ambition or that she has no other concern for her son, but she remains obsessed with his career. After she falls ill, Dunya and Razumikhin "[agree] on the answers they [will] give to her questions about Raskolnikov, and even [work] out together a complete story of his having gone away to a distant place on the Russian frontier on a private mission which would bring him in the end both money and fame" (Epilogue, i). They know what she needs to hear.

Pulkheria does not ask questions, however, but produces her own account of Rodya's departure (that he is hiding from powerful enemies) and assures Razumikhin that her son will "in time be a great political figure, as was proved by his article and his literary brilliance." She reads his article incessantly, sometimes aloud, all but sleeps with it, and talks about it to strangers. Pulkheria falls into long spells "of dismal brooding silence and speechless tears," from which she often rouses herself "almost hysterically" and begins to talk "of her son, of her hopes, of the future . . . " (Epilogue, i). Trying "to give her a moment of pleasure," Razumikhin tells her about a student and his infirm father whom Rodya had helped while he was at the university and about how he "had suffered from burns in saving the lives of two little children a year ago." This brings Pulkheria's "already disordered mind to a pitch of feverish exaltation," and "in public vehicles or in shops, wherever she [can] find a hearer, she [leads] the conversation round to her son, his article, his helping of the student, his being injured in a fire, and so on." Finally, she falls ill, becomes delirious, develops a burning fever, and dies. In her delirium she reveals "that she suspected far more of her son's terrible fate that they had supposed." It is the frustration of her hopes that kills her, I think, more than the suffering of her son. She cannot go on living after her dream of glory has collapsed.

* * *

When we appreciate the all-consuming character of Pulkheria's need for her son to become a great man, we can begin to understand her effect on him and the sources of his ambivalence. He reacts to her letter at the beginning of the novel with "a bitter angry smile" because it puts him in an unbearable position. He is supposed to be the source of protection and glory for his family, but instead he is impotent and they are sacrificing themselves for him. Their sacrifices make him feel like more of a failure and put him under even greater pressure to fulfill their lofty dreams. He shares his mother's attitude that he *ought* to be able to fulfill these dreams easily by virtue of his superiority to the crawling worms around him. He has dropped out of school in part because completing his education would only have led to a mediocre career, one that would have enabled him neither to protect them nor to satisfy their craving for glory. Instead he has begun to brood about committing a crime that would permit him to achieve these objectives.

But he has powerful taboos against committing the crime and hates himself for even considering it. His mother's letter makes him feel that he *must* go ahead, and he is full of rage with her as a consequence. When he remembers her injunction to love Dunya, who loves him more than herself, and her statement that he is their only hope, "resentment well[s] up in him, more and more bitter, and if he had chanced to meet Mr. Luzhin at that moment, he would have felt like murdering him" (I, iv). This seems to be a displacement of his rage toward his mother and sister onto Luzhin.

There are many evidences of Raskolnikov's rage toward his family. In order to ensure that her precious son will "be rich, respected, honoured," and "may even die famous," Pulkheria Alexandrovna is ready to sell her daughter into a loveless marriage and carry her "conscience . . . to Rag Fair" (I, iv). Raskolnikov feels that "Sonechka's fate is no whit worse" than Dunya's would be if she married Luzhin; indeed, Dunya's may be "even worse, fouler, more despicable" because with Sonya "it is a question simply of dying of hunger." He envisions his sister's "laments," "curses," and "tears" after such a marriage and his mother's suffering "when everything is clearly revealed." "And what of me?" he asks, "How indeed have they been thinking of me?" Under the guise of unselfish love, they subject him to unbearable guilt by proposing to destroy themselves ostensibly for his sake but really to further their own ambitions. He inwardly exclaims, "Oh, ignoble natures! Their love is like hate. O how I hate them all!" (III, iii).

Some critics have suggested that Raskolnikov's murder of Alyona is a form of matricide (see Snodgrass 1060; Wasiolek 1974; Kiremidjian 1975, 1976; Breger 1989), and I think it quite possible that he displaces his rage toward his mother onto Alyona, just as he displaces it onto Luzhin. As a loving son, he usually represses his resentment toward his mother and is mystified when it erupts; but he immediately feels "an irresistible dislike" of the moneylender, who arouses no filial taboos (I, vi). In killing her, he may be symbolically killing Pulkheria. During a spell of near-delirium when he is in the grip of self-hatred and despair, he thinks to himself that "nothing, nothing will make [him] forgive that old witch!" He is, in effect, blaming the murder on Alyona. This is followed immediately by thoughts of his mother and sister: "how I loved them! What makes me hate them now? Yes, I hate them, hate them physically; I cannot bear them near me." The connection, I believe, is that he blames them for his crime, just as he blames Alyona, whom he hates so much that he thinks he "should kill her again if she came back to life!" (III, vi). He later tells Sonya, "I killed myself, not that old creature! There and then I murdered myself at one blow" (V, iv). He hates his mother and Alyona because both, in somewhat different ways, have led him to destroy himself.

In murdering Alyona, he is not only symbolically killing his mother but is showing her what she has done to him and is punishing her for it. By murdering Alyona, he kills himself (or at least his "future") and thereby kills Pulkheria as well. Though only forty-three, she dies not long after. Raskolnikov's crime is an act that he does *for* his mother, *at* his mother, and *to* his mother. He knew in advance that he could not carry it off and what the consequences would be both for himself and Pulkheria. He had almost killed his mother once before when he became engaged to his landlady's plain, sickly daughter. "Would you not think," Pulkheria complains to Razumikhin, "that my tears, my entreaties, my illness, my possible death from grief . . . would have stopped him? No, he would have trampled coolly over every obstacle. But surely, surely he loves us?" (III, ii). He does love her, but he hates her as well and has a need to torment her, as this episode shows. She presents herself as an easy victim, much as Alyona had done, by her readiness to die of grief. It is difficult to say what might have happened if his fiancé had not passed away. Pulkheria would have been crushed had her son made a marriage so out of keeping with her conception of his worth.

* * *

Not only Raskolnikov's murder of Alyona but also the conflicting side of his personality is influenced by his relationship with his mother and the values and example of his family. Pulkheria's letter reinforces his ambition by reminding him that he is their only hope and trust, but it also urges him to pray to God, to "believe in the mercy of our Creator and Redeemer." Afraid that he "may have been affected by the fashionable modern unbelief," his mother reminds him of his religious upbringing: "Remember, my dear, how, when you were a child and your father was still alive, you lisped your prayers at my knee, and remember how happy we all were then!" (I, iii). She wants her son to be a great man but also a good Christian.

Raskolnikov's childhood was steeped in religious feeling. Once or twice a year his pious family visited the cemetery where his grandmother was buried, paying for a requiem in the old stone church: "He loved this church with its ancient icons, most of them without frames, and the old priest with his trembling head" (I, v). The cemetery also contained the grave of a younger brother who had died in infancy. Raskolnikov could not remember his brother, but "every time they visited the cemetery he devoutly and reverently crossed himself before the little grave and bowed down and kissed it." He was a sensitive boy who disliked the village tavern, pressing closer to his father when they passed it, and who felt so sorry for horses when he saw them being beaten that his mother took him away from the window.

Raskolnikov grew up in an atmosphere in which generosity and self-sacrifice were glorified. Indeed, in Dunya and his mother he has examples of women who are heedless of their own well-being and seem only to live for other people. Dunya even tries to save Svidrigaylov, who astutely tells Raskolnikov that "she is the kind of person who hungers and thirsts to be tortured for somebody, and if she does not achieve her martyrdom she is quite capable of jumping out of a window" (VI, iv). Raskolnikov admires Dunya, though he hates being the object of her sacrifice; and he is drawn to martyrs like Sonya who turn the other cheek and seem to love others more than themselves. He is a very compassionate person who is compulsively generous and is given to taking burdens on himself. He is attracted to his fiancé not only because it torments his mother but also because she is ill and unattractive: "If she had been lame as well, or hump-backed, I might very likely have loved her even more" (III, iii). Like his mother and sister, he glorifies sacrifice and derives a masochistic satisfaction from suffering for others.

Pulkheria is extremely proud of this side of her son, which she has done much to cultivate. In her deranged state, she brags not only about his article but also about his having helped a fellow student and his father while he himself was in poverty and having saved two children from a fire, burning his hands in the process. She wants him to be a great man, to be sure, but also a very good one. When he apologizes for having given twenty-five roubles for Marmeladov's funeral, she says, "Don't go on Rodya. I am sure that everything you do is right!" When he says that he "may be no good" but that Dunya ought not to marry Luzhin, she becomes extremely distressed: "And why will you persist in saying you are no good? That I cannot bear" (III, iii).

There is a conflict in Pulkheria between the need for a loving, dutiful son and one with impressive achievements. When Rodion does not come to see her, she rationalizes his neglect: "You may have God knows what plans . . . in your mind, or all sorts of ideas may have sprung up in you; am I to be always jogging your elbow to ask you what you are thinking about?" (VI, vii). She tells her son that he "mustn't spoil" her, that she'll know he loves her even if he can't visit: "I shall read your writings, I shall hear about you from everybody, and from time to time you will come to see me—what could be better?" She then bursts into tears.

Raskolnikov knows how important it is for his mother that he be both great and good, and he strives desperately to reconcile these imperatives, which he has incorporated into the demands he makes on himself. It seems that if he is good he cannot be great and that if he is to be great he cannot be good. No course of action is satisfactory. If he follows his mother's injunction to remember his religious upbringing not only will he fail to achieve greatness but also he will be unable to lift himself out of poverty in time to save her and his sister from sacrificing themselves. He feels that he must commit the crime in order to do his duty toward his mother and prevent Dunya's immoral marriage. If he commits the crime, however, he will be a sinner in the eyes of his family and will be separated from them by guilt. His mother would be destroyed should she learn of what he had done. He would be violating his own humane and conscientious feelings, moreover, and would loathe himself intensely. He will be damned if he commits the murder and damned if he does not.

III. Inner Conflicts

Like the underground man, Raskolnikov emerges from his formative years full of psychological conflicts that lead to internal vacillations and inconsistent behavior. The underground man tries to cope with his inner divisions by distancing himself from other people and from his own feelings. Raskolnikov tries to cope by finding a way to harmonize his contradictory needs and by suppressing the parts of himself that stand in the way of his grandiose aspirations. We see him torn by opposing forces throughout the novel until his conflicts are resolved by his conversion at the end.

We are introduced to Raskolnikov as he sets out for a rehearsal of the murder. For the past month, he has been lying in a corner thinking about the crime that is to make his fortune but not really believing that he is "capable of *that*" (I, i; author's emphasis). Perhaps he is only "amusing himself with fancies, . . . only playing a game." He gradually grows accustomed to "regarding the 'ugly' dream as a real project"; however, as he rehearses his plan, he still does not trust himself to carry it out, and he reproaches himself for his weakness and lack of resolution. After his visit to Alyona, he is overwhelmed with confusion. He regards his design as repulsive and asks how such a horrible idea could enter his mind: "The feeling of infinite loathing that had begun to burden and torment him while he was on his way to the old woman's had now reached such a pitch that he did not know what to do with himself in his anguish." After he stops in a public house and has something to eat and drink, he begins to feel better, leading him to conclude that his panic was simply the result of physical weakness: "'One glass of beer and a rusk and my mind grows keen, my thoughts clear, my resolution firm. Bah, how paltry it all is!' But in spite of the scorn with which he spat out these words, his outlook had grown cheerful, as if he had been suddenly freed from a terrible burden, and he cast friendly glances at the other people in the room."

The most puzzling part of this sequence is Raskolnikov's turnabout when he begins to feel better after eating and drinking. He experiences a renewed resolution, but at the same time he feels freed from a terrible burden and casts friendly glances toward other people. Why does the revival of his resolution to commit murder lead to social impulses and a sense of liberation? He himself "dimly perceive[s] . . . that there [is] something morbid in his sudden recovery of spirits" (I, i).

As in my analysis of the underground man, I find Karen Horney's concept of a crossfire of conflicting inner dictates, or "shoulds," to be helpful in comprehending the protagonist's oscillations. One set of shoulds drives Raskolnikov toward committing the murder, while an opposite set strongly rejects such an action. When one set is dominant, it violates the other, thus activating it and generating self-condemnation. In order to alleviate his discomfort, Raskolnikov swings to the opposite pole, leading to renewed self-hatred and a compensatory move in the other direction. This back-and-forth pattern is repeated throughout the novel with numerous variations. After the murder the main question becomes whether or not to confess. Raskolnikov's oscillations sometimes occur at a conscious level, but sometimes there is an unconscious reaction against the impulses and inner dictates that have become dominant.

In the sequence of psychological states described in the opening chapter, Raskolnikov alternates between entertaining his project and retreating from it. When he entertains it, he feels it to be horrible; when he retreats, he reproaches himself for weakness and irresolution. When he begins to feel better after taking refreshment, he is relieved that the matter seems paltry because now he does not have to condemn himself for being a weakling. At the same time, however, in one of the variations on the pattern I have described, his new sense of resolution allows a suppressed part of himself to emerge. When he began to brood on his horrible plan, he withdrew "from all human contacts, like a tortoise retreating into its shell" (I, iii) in order to avoid distractions; but now confident that he can carry it out, he is drawn to other people and becomes involved with Marmeladov. Momentarily at peace with the conflicting components of his personality, he feels freed from the terrible burden of his inner turmoil. He senses that there is something amiss in his recovery of spirits because it is based on feeling more certain about committing a terrible deed.

Raskolnikov's inner conflicts are reactivated by the letter he receives from his mother, which affects him profoundly, as we have seen. In his agitated state, he goes for a walk, during which he broods on the need "to act, to act at once and with speed" (I, iv). For the past month, and even on the previous day, he could view his homicidal project as "no more than a bad dream"; now it takes on a new reality.

While Raskolnikov is trying to steel himself to act, he becomes very protective toward a drunken young girl, who seems already to have been victimized, being stalked by a Svidrigaylov-like dandy. He attacks the dandy and enlists the aid of a policeman, giving him money to take the girl safely home. This behavior violates the inner dictates that are driving him to be ruthlessly aggressive, and he cries after the policeman to stop: "What is it to you? Drop it! Let him amuse himself! . . . What business is it of yours?" (I, iv). When the policeman does not halt, Raskolnikov cynically envisions him accepting money from the dandy as well and asks why he took it on himself to interfere: "Let them eat one another alive—what is to me?" A world view in which one looks out for other people alternates in Raskolnikov's mind with one in which life is a jungle and all look out for themselves. He castigates himself for his charitable impulses, as he had done earlier when he left money at Marmeladov's; but then he feels compassion again for the poor girl and others like her, whom he sees as doomed to prostitution, disease, and premature death.

Raskolnikov's inner conflicts continue as he realizes that he has been walking toward Razumikhin's flat. Going to Razumikhin means giving up his murderous plan and looking for legitimate ways to earn money. Part of him is drawn to that path, but he rejects it because it does not provide a way out of his difficulties. He will go to Razumikhin, he decides, "the day after, when *that* is over and done with and everything is different" (I, v; author's emphasis). This leads him to recoil from the idea that he might really commit the murder, and he cannot bear the idea of returning to his "dreadful little" room where "the thought of *it* had been maturing in his mind" (author's emphasis). He walks unconsciously into the country, away from the cramped and evil atmosphere of the city. He stops at an eating house, has vodka and a pasty, and becomes sleepy on his way home. Lying down for a nap, he has a terrible dream that indicates how alien the contemplated murder is to the deepest components of his personality.

The dream takes Raskolnikov back to his innocent childhood and to the pious and compassionate part of himself. He is seven years old, and he and his father are passing a tavern that frightens him on their way to the cemetery in which his grandmother and infant brother are buried. In his dream, he and his father witness a drunken peasant named Mikolka savagely beating an old mare, trying to get her to pull an overloaded cart. As the horse is struck on the nose and across the eyes, the seven-year-old Rodion weeps and tries to get adults to intervene. When the mare is beaten to death with a crowbar, "the poor little boy [is] quite beside himself." He runs to the horse, kisses its eyes and blood-spattered muzzle, and then furiously attacks Mikolka, whom one of the bystanders describes as "more like a brute beast than a proper Christian." "'Papa, why did they . . . kill . . . the poor horse?' the boy [sobs], catching his breath. The words [force] themselves out of his choking throat in a scream" (I, v).

This extremely vivid and powerful dream expresses Raskolnikov's horror at what he is planning to do and his rage at himself for his intended unchristian behavior. When he awakens, he asks if it is really possible that he will "take an axe and strike [the old woman] on the head, smash open her skull . . . that [his] feet will slip in warm, sticky blood" (I, v). He feels that he can never perform such a vile and disgusting deed and that he should stop tormenting himself with the thought of it. Once it becomes clear that he will "never summon up enough resolution to do it," he feels that he has "thrown off the terrible burden that had weighed him down for so long" and his "heart [is] light and tranquil."

Having decided that he must act, and act quickly, Raskolnikov finds himself walking in the direction of Razumikhin's lodgings, away from his horrible plan. When he reaffirms his intention to act and decides that he will visit Razumikhin after he commits the crime, he finds himself walking into the country and having his horrible dream. The pattern seems to be that his conscious intentions activate the conflicting side of his personality, which then asserts itself involuntarily.

After his dream, Raskolnikov believes more strongly than ever that he can never commit the murder, but on his way home he passes through the Haymarket and learns that Lizaveta, Alyona's half-sister, will not be at home at seven o'clock the next day. Once he has this information, he does not "reason about anything" but feels "that his mind and will [are] no longer free, and that everything [is] settled, quite finally" (I, v). The forces driving him to do the murder are still very powerful, and learning about this favorable opportunity leads him to change directions again. His sense that "fate [has] laid an ambush for him" enables him to experience his internal compulsions as coming from outside and to disown responsibility for what he is about to do. It provides a defense against his horror and the part of himself that has been revolting against his plan.

IV. AN EXTRAORDINARY MAN

Raskolnikov's inner conflicts are very intense. On one side are temperamental factors: he is compassionate by nature, shrinks from cruelty, and feels pity for those being victimized. These combine with the dictates he has internalized from his Christian upbringing and the example of his family, with its piety, devotion, and self-sacrifice. On the other side are the pressures he is under to rescue his mother and sister, to become a great man for them, and to satisfy his own craving for glory. Given the strength of his aversion to committing the murder, as revealed in his dream, it is no wonder he feels he can never do it. After he confesses to Sonya, she asks, "And how could you, you, the man you are . . . bring yourself to this?" (V, iv). How, indeed? Not only must the forces driving him to the crime have been immensely powerful, but he must have found ways of overcoming his conflicts, temporarily at least. One of these was to externalize his compulsions, to feel that he was being guided by fate. Others include trying to reconcile his inner contradictions with the aid of modern thought and to transcend them by developing an idealized image of himself as an extraordinary man. Once formed, his idealized image creates within him a powerful need to transgress.

As we have seen, Dostoevsky's rhetoric makes fashionable modern unbelief the villain of the piece. It is presented as leading Raskolnikov astray, and he must repudiate it in order to be redeemed. Most critics have followed the rhetoric. Joseph Frank, for instance, sees Raskolnikov as an innocent young man from the provinces who is corrupted by the radical ideas he encounters in St. Petersburg. In *Crime and Punishment*, says Frank, Dostoevsky wants to "pillory" utilitarian morality "as so blurring the line between good and evil, that it could mislead an idealistic and highly compassionate young man, revolted by suffering and injustice, into the commission of a brutal murder" (1986, 69). As usual, Frank gives cultural influences priority rather than examining the role the protagonist's psychology plays in his receptiveness to them.

Modern thought *is* an important factor in Raskolnikov's commission of the murder, but it is not the source of his motivation, which has much more to do with his family. The utilitarian morality does not make Raskolnikov need to save his mother from poverty, to prevent Dunya's marriage to Luzhin, or to be a great man. Rather, it gives him a means of reconciling the plan designed to achieve these objectives with his desire to be a good person. That is why overhearing the student rationalizing Alyona's murder has such a profound effect: "Kill her, take her money, on condition that you dedicate yourself with its help to the service of humanity and the common good: don't you think that thousands of good deeds will wipe out that one little, insignificant transgression?" (I, vi).

After his visit to Alyona, Raskolnikov had begun to have such ideas, and hearing the student articulate them sanctions them, as it were. The student has no powerful motives for killing Alyona and says, "this is not a question of me at all"; however, Raskolnikov does have such motives, and he welcomes the justification the student's words provide.

Raskolnikov later acknowledges to himself that for a month before the murder he had "been importuning all-gracious Providence . . . , calling on it to witness that it was not for [his] own selfish desires and purposes that [he] proposed to act (so [he] said), but for a noble and worthy end" (III, vi). He says that, in the execution of his design, he had tried to secure "the utmost justice accurately calculated by weight and measure: from all the lice on earth, I picked out absolutely the most useless, and when I had killed her, I intended to take from her exactly as much as I needed for my first step," leaving the rest to go "to the monastery for the repose of her soul." This strange amalgam suggests the ways in which Raskolnikov employs utilitarian ethics to harmonize the murder with his religious disposition. He will be serving humanity by killing Alyona and will respect her wishes to have prayers said for her after her death.

Raskolnikov's most radical defense against his inner conflicts is his theory of the extraordinary man. Spurred by his mother's needs for glory, her view of him as an exalted being to whom success ought to come easily, and his own sense of superiority, he develops an idealized image of himself as a person who is above the conventional morality. The particular form his idealized image takes is profoundly influenced by cultural forces, especially atheistic thought and the example of Napoleon.

As Raskolnikov sees it, the death of God means, for those who fully perceive its implications, that historical reality is absurd and there are no absolute values. The liberated man steps into the place of the deity and makes his own laws. Human history shows that great men have somehow realized this and have trampled on the pieties of their own time. From the point of view of their societies, they committed horrible crimes, but later generations have come to celebrate them as heroes. Both history and ideology confirm that might makes right.

Raskolnikov develops a theory that there are two kinds of people: ordinary and extraordinary. Ordinary folk are "staid and conservative," like living in obedience, and exist simply to reproduce their kind (III, v). Extraordinary people have the gift of saying something new. "All law-breakers and transgressors," they have a right to "wade through blood" if that is necessary to the fulfillment of their idea. Being sensitive (like Raskolnikov), they may feel pangs of sympathy for the suffering they cause, but their conscience will be untroubled. This theory gives Raskolnikov permission to do what he feels is necessary to fulfill his ambitions without condemning himself. Although killing Alyona will be an offense in the eyes of society, to an enlightened mind it will not be a crime.

In the article in which he expounds his ideas, Raskolnikov argues that the great man's transgressions are to be justified by his contributions to humanity. His real hero, however, is the man who can dispense with such rationalizations, who can seize "this nonsensical world ... by the tail and fling it to the devil" (V, iv). He takes as his highest authority Napoleon, the man who, in his view, has come closest to doing this. He wants to be able to kill as Napoleon killed, without conscientious scruples and for his own glory. As he explains to

Sonya, "I murdered for myself, for myself alone, and whether I became a benefactor to anybody else . . . *should* have been a matter of complete indifference to me at that moment!"(emphasis added).

Once formed, Raskolnikov's idealized image of himself develops a dynamic of its own and governs much of his behavior. In order to feel that he is an extraordinary man, he must assert claims that are appropriate to his grandiose status. That is one reason why he is so outraged by all the humiliations of his lot, why he "turn[s] nasty" and will not work (V, iv). His life goal is to actualize his exalted conception of himself, and to do this he must commit what society calls a crime without feeling guilt. Raskolnikov has multiple motivations, as we have seen; but this is perhaps the most powerful force driving him to kill Alyona, the one that finally overcomes his horror at the act. If he cannot carry out his plan, his search for glory will be hopeless, and he will despise himself as an ordinary man. Only extraordinary men are "people properly speaking"; ordinary men are simply reproductive "material" out of whom a genius may eventually emerge (III, v).

It is the threat of the self-hatred he will feel should his resolution fail that makes it impossible for Raskolnikov to give up his murderous plan, despite his foreknowledge, like that of Macbeth, that he will hate himself more if he carries it out (see Paris 1991a). In a conversation with Dunya, he describes his dilemma: "you come to certain limit and if you do not overstep it, you will be unhappy, but if you do overstep it, perhaps you will be even more unhappy" (III, iii).

v. After the Murder

In his article, Raskolnikov discusses "the psychological condition of the criminal throughout the commission of the crime" (III, v), theorizing that the ordinary man will experience a collapse of will, whereas the extraordinary man will not. He decides that he would "not be subject to any such morbid subversion, that his judgement and will would remain steadfast throughout the fulfillment of his plans, for the simple reason that what he contemplated was 'no crime'" (I, vi). When the hour for action arrives, however, everything goes awry, and he makes a series of blunders. He becomes inefficient, feels "horror and repulsion" at what he has done, and is repeatedly tormented by the idea that he is losing his mind.

Dostoevsky provides a vivid account of Raskolnikov's collapse. He suffers greatly from anxiety and a sense of moral isolation, of "eternal loneliness and estrangement" (II, i). He faints when he hears the murders being discussed at the police office, thus drawing attention to himself. He becomes absentminded and forgetful, does not even look to see what he has stolen, and is ready to dispose of it by throwing it in the river. He contemplates suicide and decides that water will not do when he sees a woman fail in her attempt to drown herself. After he hides the loot, he falls ill and becomes delirious, almost always Dostoevsky's sign of raging inner conflicts. When he recovers, he wants it all to be over because he cannot "*live like this*" (II, vi; author's emphasis), and he repeatedly has impulses to confess. Indeed, he does confess to Zametov indirectly; and then he returns to the scene of the crime, behaving suspiciously and asking about a pool of blood. He has made up his mind to go to the police when Marmeladov's accident intervenes, followed by the arrival of his mother and his sister.

Raskolnikov goes to pieces partly because he has violated the Christian, conscientious, humane side of himself and is being tormented by expectations of punishment and unbearable self-reproach. That side of him seems predominant in his dealings with the Marmeladovs, which are marked by compulsive generosity and a resurgence of pious feelings. After Marmeladov's accident, Raskolnikov says he will pay for the doctor, comforts Katerina Ivanovna, and gives her the twenty-five roubles he has left from the money sent by his mother. His kindness allays his self-hatred and gives him a feeling of renewed life, like "that of a man condemned to death and unexpectedly reprieved" (II, vii). This leads to a touching scene between him and Polenka, Katerina's eldest child. He asks her if she loves Sonya and if she will love him. She responds by winding her arms around his neck and protruding her lips for a kiss. He then inquires if she knows how to pray and asks her to pray for him. She says she will pray for him all her life and hugs him tightly again.

Earlier we saw that when Raskolnikov feels a renewed sense of resolution after taking refreshment in a public house, a suppressed part of himself emerges, he casts friendly glances at other people, and he becomes involved with Marmeladov. Now something similar occurs, but in reverse. After his kindness to the Marmeladovs and his scene with Polenka, he does a turnabout: "Away with illusions, away with imaginary terrors, away with spectres! Life is! Was I not living just now? My life did not die with the old woman!" (II, vii). "Now comes the reign of reason and light and . . . and freedom and power . . . now we shall see! Now we shall measure our strength!" (author's ellipses).

As his "pride and self-confidence [grow] with every minute," he is puzzled as to "what had so transformed him." The alteration in Raskolnikov is not easy to understand, but I think that Dostoevsky's psychological intuitions are quite brilliant here. Having violated his imperatives to behave as a Christian, Raskolnikov has been living in terror and feeling his life to be over. Satisfying those imperatives diminishes their force and allows the opposite imperatives, from which he has been retreating, to reassert themselves. He now feels his terror to have been the result of beliefs that, from a rational perspective, are nothing but illusions. He will set them aside, stop being afraid of specters, and pursue his original goals of freedom and power. Instead of cowering in his corner, waiting to be apprehended and wanting to confess, he will exercise his strength. Maybe he can still be an extraordinary man. He remembers that he asked for "thy servant Rodion" to be remembered in Polenka's prayers: "'well, that's just in case!' he added, and laughed at his own childish quibbling. He was in excellent spirits" (II, vii).

Raskolnikov is in excellent spirits because he has momentarily satisfied the conflicting demands that have been tearing him apart. His scenes with the Marmeladovs and Polenka have enabled him to feel like a good person, and the subsequent resurgence of his scorn for conventional beliefs allows him to hope that he can still be an extraordinary man. He has achieved an unstable equilibrium that does not last very long, for soon he will be hating himself once more for what he has done and then hating himself for hating himself.

Raskolnikov's psychological torment after the murder derives as much from having failed to live up to his image of himself as an extraordinary man as from having committed such a terrible act. The murder was to be the test of his claims to be above the conventional morality, and he has failed the test. He has brought himself to do the deed, but his subsequent reactions have been those of an ordinary person. His will and judgment fail in the way he had predicted for such beings, he cannot bear his anxiety and guilt, and at times he seems to be seeking punishment. In discussing his article, Porfiry raises the possibility of a mix-up in which "somebody from one category imagined that he belonged to the other and began 'to remove all obstacles'" (III, v). Raskolnikov acknowledges that this "very frequently happens" but observes that there is nothing to worry about because people who make such a mistake never go far: "there is no need even for anyone to carry out the punishment: they will do it themselves, because they are very well conducted." They even "impose on themselves various public penances," with a "beautifully edifying result." Later, on his way to turning himself in, Raskolnikov will kneel in the middle of the square, bow to the ground, and kiss "its filth with pleasure and joy" (V, viii).

We can see how much Raskolnikov hates himself for his failure to obey the imperatives of his grandiose self when he returns home after his conversation with Porfiry and is accosted by a stranger who calls him a murderer. He is conscious with repulsion of how weak he has become as a result of the accusation, and he berates himself: "'How, knowing myself, foreknowing myself, dared I take the axe and stain my hands with blood? It was my duty to know beforehand . . . Ah! But really I did indeed know beforehand! . . . ' he whispered despairingly" (III, vi). The chief source of his despair is his realization that he is not, and never can be, an extraordinary man. Raskolnikov compares himself with Napoleon, "the *real* ruler, to whom everything is permitted" (author's emphasis), who is "plainly not made of flesh, but of bronze" (III, vi). Napoleon "destroys Toulon, butchers in Paris, *forgets* an army in Egypt, *expends* half a million men in a Moscow campaign" (author's emphasis), and then is commemorated by statues when he is dead. He, by comparison, has murdered a "withered old woman" and crawled under her bed looking for loot. And he has not even done that properly. He was trying to kill a principle by overstepping "all restrictions as quickly as possible": "but as for surmounting the barriers, I did not do that; I remained on this side." He feels himself to be "a louse, nothing more." He mocks himself for having called on Providence to witness that he was not going to murder for his own selfish ends and for having devoted so much attention to "securing the utmost justice" in the execution of the crime. These are signs of his ordinariness, of his inability to transcend the attitudes of his culture. The prophet Mahomet could mow "down the innocent and the guilty, without deigning to justify himself," but Raskolnikov can't even kill a worthless old woman without going to pieces: "Obey, trembling creature, and—*do not will*, because that is not your affair!" (author's emphasis).

Raskolnikov's inner conflicts continue unremittingly until his conversion in Siberia. He cannot live with what he has done, and he cannot live with the fact that he cannot live with it. He alternates between feeling like a sinner for having committed the murder and feeling like a louse for feeling like a sinner. When he moves in the direction of confession, he recoils and feels that he can still put up a fight. Confessing will quiet the clamor of one set of inner dictates, but it will violate the other, and he will still hate himself, though for different reasons. His problem seems insoluble, and most critics feel that the resolution at the end is contrived. I shall argue in the next chapter that Raskolnikov's conversion makes good psychological sense and gives him a way of harmonizing his contradictory needs. I am less enthusiastic than is Dostoevsky, however, about the solution at which his protagonist arrives.

CHAPTER 6

SONYA, SVIDRIGAYLOV, AND RASKOLNIKOV'S CONVERSION

1. INTRODUCTION

RASKOLNIKOV'S INNER CONFLICTS ARE RENDERED SOMEWHAT DIFFERENTLY in the second half of the novel than in the first. We are still given inside views of his psyche, but his mind is befogged much of the time, and there are aspects of his psychology that Dostoevsky portrays more explicitly in other characters, especially Sonya and Svidrigaylov, than in Raskolnikov himself. When Raskolnikov is drawn to or recoils from these characters, he is reacting to external embodiments of his own tendencies; and we are given deeper insight into both the tendencies themselves and his conflicting attitudes toward them. His behavior toward these characters reveals the action of unconscious forces that only gradually make their way into his awareness.

It has often been observed that Sonya and Svidrigaylov function as Raskolnikov's "doubles," but to appreciate just what aspects of his psyche they mirror and to which they appeal, we shall have to pay more attention to them as mimetic characters than has usually been done. Their illustrative functions are important and have been much discussed, but they are also imagined human beings who employ defensive strategies to which Raskolnikov is drawn. Each seems to offer him a way of coping with his problems, and a central question in the second half of the novel is whether he will take up one of their solutions. He oscillates from one stance to another, sometimes quite rapidly; however, he ultimately adopts Sonya's values and beliefs, making hers the predominant voice in the novel.

Raskolnikov's conversion at the end has struck most critics as psychologically unconvincing and artistically contrived. I agree with David Matual, however, that Raskolnikov "is psychologically capable of the metamorphosis" he is presented as undergoing and that there are numerous elements in the body of the novel that "prepare the reader for the concluding scene" (in Bloom 2004b, 113). I have discussed many of these elements in Chapter 4. Matual does a good job with imagery and theme, but neither he nor other critics give much attention to Raskolnikov's psychology after he confesses to the police. I believe that Raskolnikov's conversion is entirely credible in motivational terms, especially when we understand the significance of the dream by which it is preceded. I feel that the epilogue is much more successful than has generally been thought. At the same time, I share some of the discomfort readers have expressed because I too find the happy ending to be discordant with the grimness of the rest of the book.

II. Raskolnikov and Sonya

Like his deceased fiancé, Sonya is one of the sufferers, one of the "poor, meek, gentle creatures" (III, vi), for whom Raskolnikov feels great compassion and to whom he is attracted. Part of her appeal may be that she would upset his mother, as his landlady's daughter had done. Indeed, as soon as Pulkheria meets Sonya she is concerned about her son's interest in her (III, iv). More important, however, is the fact that Sonya represents to Raskolnikov a source of acceptance and a model for obtaining forgiveness for his crime. He first comes to know of her through Marmeladov's account of her as the saintly daughter who does not reproach her drunken father but who displays a Christ-like compassion for human weakness and whose own transgressions will be pardoned because of her humility.

After the murders, Raskolnikov is tormented by "a dreary feeling of eternal loneliness and estrangement" (II, i); he feels cut off "from everybody and everything, as if by a knife" (II, ii). His recurrent impulses to confess are motivated in part by his need to reestablish a connection with his fellow humans. When Pulkheria and Dunya arrive, he assures his mother that there will "be plenty of time for [them] to talk to [their] heart's content"; but then he turns pale as he realizes not only that he can no longer "talk himself out, but that now he could never talk *at all*, to anybody" (III, iii; author's emphasis). His sense of alienation in the presence of his family is so painful that he breaks off relations with them as soon as their security has been assured by Dunya's inheritance from Marfa Petrovna and Luzhin has been dismissed. He says he may come to them later, but he asks them to give him up if they love him and puts them in the care of Razumikhin. In his mind he has "made a complete break" with his family and has no plans to see them again (IV, iv). He says that whatever happens to him, he wants "to be alone" (IV, iii). He cannot bear isolation, however, and on leaving his mother and sister, he goes directly to Sonya.

He tells Sonya he has deserted his family and that now he has only her. He has come to her because they "are both alike accursed" (IV, iv). She too has "stepped over the barrier" by destroying a life, her own. "If you remain *alone*," he tells her, "you will go out of your senses, like me. . . . so we must go together by the same path!" (author's emphasis). Raskolnikov's feeling that they are both guilty of similar transgressions makes it possible for him to turn to Sonya as a kindred spirit, a source of human community and of possible answers as to how he can live with his crime. He is hoping to find a way to hold onto his sanity through her.

How, he wonders, is Sonya able to live with what *she* has done? It seems to him that there are only three paths open to her: "to throw herself into the canal, to end in a madhouse," or "to abandon herself to debauchery that will numb her mind and turn her heart to stone" (IV, iv). She has evidently considered suicide, as he also has done, and has rejected that idea. Her solution, he concludes, is to expect a miracle. He sees this as "religious mania," a form of "madness" he is afraid of catching himself, and he thinks that "in two or three weeks' time" they will both be welcomed "into the asylum." Raskolnikov will regard Sonya's solution much more positively by the end of the novel.

Sonya's solution is glorified by the rhetoric, as we have seen, and she is usually regarded as a figure who is there to serve Dostoevsky's purposes. Thematic critics emphasize her embodiment of "all the Christian virtues" (Terras 1998, 53), especially humility and selfless love, while a psychoanalytic critic like Louis Breger focuses on her role in facilitating Raskolnikov's reclamation. Breger observes that her "saintliness makes her quite unreal as a character and has posed a problem for critics. Dostoevsky was clearly capable of creating characters of full-bodied reality," but Sonya is "one-sided to the point of artificiality" (1989, 49). She never displays anger and responds to all provocations with "resignation, sympathy for the other, and understanding." Dostoevsky has made her this way, says Breger, "because this is precisely what Raskolnikov needs." She is the "perfect therapist" whose all-accepting attitude enables Raskolnikov to overcome the split between love and murderous rage in his feelings toward women.

Sonya has many functions, to be sure, but she is also an imagined human being whose behavior makes sense in motivational terms. Victor Terras feels that she is "almost a credible character" (1998, 72) despite her lack of "psychological complexity" (62). She does not have the complexity of a Raskolnikov, but I think her behavior is entirely credible when we understand her defenses, which are grounded in her personality and experience. It is their rigidity that makes her so one-sided as to appear artificial. Approaching Sonya as a mimetic character will help us to appreciate the subtlety of Dostoevsky's portrait and to recover his psychological insights. It will free us from seeing Sonya only from the author's perspective and permit us to appraise her solution for ourselves.

With Marmeladov as her father, Sonya grows up in a turbulent environment and has no one to rely on for protection. She receives little nurturing, anticipates maltreatment, and lives in constant fear of imminent calamity. Profoundly insecure, she has always been "very shy" and dreads "seeing new faces and making new acquaintances" (V, i). Her chief method of dealing with her anxiety is most clearly revealed when it begins to break down, after Luzhin accuses her of theft:

> Sonya, with her meek nature, had always been conscious that she was more vulnerable than other people, and could be insulted with impunity. She had, nevertheless, until this moment thought that she could somehow manage to avoid disaster—by caution, meekness, submissiveness to anybody and everybody. Her disillusionment was too grievous. She was, of course, capable of bearing everything, even this, with patience and almost without murmuring. But at first she found this burden too heavy. (V, iii)

Aware "of her helplessness in the face of insult and injury," she becomes hysterical and runs from the room.

Sonya has made a bargain with fate in which if she submits to everything *without murmuring*, she will be spared the worst disasters (for a discussion of bargains with fate, see Paris 1991a). As a result she has powerful taboos against complaining about injustice or feeling abused. Her hysteria in this scene results in part from her sense that her bargain is not working and in part from her fear that she will violate its demands by being angry at the unfairness of Luzhin's accusations. We can see the importance to her of not feeling resentment when she gives her father her last thirty copecks so that he can continue drinking. It is impossible to know if Sonya is at some level aware that, as Marmeladov observes, "it hurts more, when there are no reproaches" (I, ii), but even if she is not, her behavior has other rewards. She is regarded by many as a saint, and according to her father, because of her sense of unworthiness she will be forgiven her sins.

Sonya's fear of her own anger becomes evident when she is questioned by Raskolnikov:

> "I suppose Katerina Ivanovna used to beat you . . . when you lived at your father's?"
> "Oh, no. Why do you say that? No!" Sonya looked at him almost with terror. (IV, iv)

The blame implied in Raskolnikov's query frightens Sonya because it arouses her deeply buried resentment and thus threatens her bargain. Katerina did beat her, of course, but Sonya says, "What of it?" Katerina is ill and unhappy and becomes exasperated because "she believes there ought to be justice in everything," a claim the self-abasing Sonya does not dare to make. Katerina has not only beaten her but also has sent her out to sell her virginity for thirty silver roubles, forcing her into a life of prostitution. Given her extreme shyness and her religious values, she is "monstrously . . . tormented" by her position, but Sonya "loves" Katerina, pities her misery, and defends her passionately to Raskolnikov: "But how clever she used to be . . . how generous . . . how good! You know nothing, nothing at all" (author's ellipses). Instead of blaming Katerina for what she had done to her, Sonya accuses herself of cruelty: "And how often I have driven her to tears, how often!" She reproaches herself for not having given Katerina some collars for which she had asked, a refusal that not only upset Katerina but also violated Sonya's need to be entirely unselfish. She is haunted by the fact that she was capable of wanting something for herself and of hurting Katerina by asking what use the collars would be to her. Even a small act of aggression generates a great deal of self-hatred in Sonya.

Sonya's bargain is not essentially with human beings but with God. If she is meek and humble, if she gives up everything for others and asks nothing for herself, then God will listen to her prayers. When Raskolnikov confronts her with the terrible plight of the younger children should Katerina die or she become ill, Sonya cannot face this problem or think about it in realistic terms. Her response is that God will not let such things happen. She *does* expect a miracle. The fact that God has let horrible things happen to *her* is something Sonya cannot afford to register. She gets around the problem through her "infinite self-humiliation" (VI, i), by not feeling that she has any rights and by patiently accepting her suffering.

The reward for her self-effacement is great. When Raskolnikov asks what God does for her, Sonya replies that "He does everything" (IV, iv). "That is the solution!" Raskolnikov decides. Through her faith in the miraculous power of God, Sonya is able to live under conditions that might otherwise drive her to madness or suicide: "He understood that those feelings in fact constituted her real long-standing *secret*, cherished perhaps since her girlhood, in the midst of her family, with an unhappy father, a step-mother crazed by grief, and hungry children, in an atmosphere of hideous shrieks and reproaches." Through her submission to the unintelligible dictates of an all-powerful deity, Sonya gains a feeling of enormous potency. The master of the universe does everything for her.

Sonya's confidence that Katerina's children will be saved from penury and Polenka from prostitution turns out to be well founded. It is Dostoevsky, of course, who answers her prayers. The threat to the children is removed by a gift of money from Svidrigaylov, thus validating Sonya's bargain. Sonya is rewarded not only with economic security for herself and the children (Svidrigaylov also gives money to her) but with glory as well. Like Christ, she too performs the miracle of raising a man from the dead.

In the early stages of their relationship, Sonya sees mainly the kind and generous side of Raskolnikov's personality. She is drawn to him as a strong, protective man who is socially and intellectually above her and through whom she can gratify her needs for devotion, submission, and a vicarious sense of superiority. When she begins to learn his true state, she immediately casts herself in the role of his savior. Through her love, fidelity, and piety, she will bring about his redemption.

Raskolnikov comes to Sonya because with part of himself he wants to relinquish his pride and to be reborn as a Christian. In his quest for renewal, which is largely unconscious, he asks her to read the story of Lazarus. The power of God is most vividly manifested in this story: when Lazarus is raised from the dead, the laws of this world are set to nought. As Sonya approaches the climax of the story, her voice is "filled with immense triumph" (IV, iv). Her dream is that, like the "blind, unbelieving Jews," Raskolnikov will be converted. She wants to repeat the miracle, to raise Raskolnikov from the dead as Christ raised Lazarus. The conversion does not occur immediately as she hopes it will; but her dream comes true at the end, when Raskolnikov is "cast at her feet" (Epilogue, ii).

Sonya is frightened at his placing himself beneath her, but when she understands that the moment of resurrection has come, "infinite happiness [shines] in her eyes." She cannot experience conscious triumph on her own behalf, and she immediately places herself in the subordinate role; however, the effect of the whole scene is to glorify Sonya's solution and to celebrate the miraculous power of submissive faith and love.

Whether or not we find Sonya to be credible depends on our sense of how human beings behave. Her self-sacrifice and apparent lack of resentment are extreme, to be sure, but I have encountered numerous characters like her in literature, including Chaucer's Griselda (Paris 1997), Antonio in *The Merchant of Venice* (Paris 1989), Helena in *A Midsummer Night's Dream*, (Paris 1991a), the poet in Shakespeare's sonnets (Paris 1991a), Fanny Price in *Mansfield Park* (Paris 1978), and Dobbin and Amelia in *Vanity Fair* (Paris 1974). In discussing these characters, and many more like them, I have drawn on Karen Horney's accounts of the compliant solution in *Our Inner Conflicts* (1945) and the self-effacing solution in *Neurosis and Human Growth* (1950). My understanding of Sonya has also been influenced by these accounts. Great literary artists intuitively grasped and mimetically portrayed the defensive strategies of people like Sonya long before psychologists described them in conceptual terms.

Sonya is not an unusual figure in nineteenth-century fiction, which is full of terrible childhoods, some much more vividly depicted than hers. Often the rhetoric of a novel asks us to see the resulting adults as wonderful persons, while the mimesis shows that they have been hurt by their early experience and are troubled human beings. The rhetoric obscures the mimetic portraits, and the action may be contrived to make the protagonists' solutions work or at least to save them from some of the consequences of their psychological problems (see my discussions of Charlotte Brontë's *Jane Eyre* in Paris 1997 and of George Eliot's *Middlemarch* in Paris 2003). This usually happens when the defenses a character adopts are favored by the author. I believe that such is the case with Sonya, a crushed human being whose magic bargain corresponds to the teachings of the version of Christianity the rhetoric is designed to promote. There is a similar glorification of a self-effacing solution in the presentation of Alyosha in *The Brothers Karamazov*. In his mimetic portrayal of such characters, Dostoevsky has made a contribution to our understanding of the psychology of religion, despite his proselytizing intent. There is no similar glorification of characters like the underground man and Ivan Karamazov, who also have wretched childhoods but whose resultant defenses do not meet with the author's approval. Whereas nineteenth-century novels often propose that suffering makes one a better person, the underground man and Ivan are presented as having been seriously damaged by the early frustration of their emotional needs. Although the rhetoric would have us believe otherwise, Sonya has been badly damaged also.

* * *

Raskolnikov's movements toward and away from Sonya are a direct reflection of his inner turmoil and of the relative strength of his conflicting tendencies at any given time. He has very mixed feelings about his attraction to her, and until the very end, every movement toward her brings on an almost immediate recoil in the opposite direction.

After Sonya reads the story of Lazarus at his request, Raskolnikov is not converted to her perspective but warns her that she will go mad unless she joins him on his path: "You must judge things seriously and directly at last, and not weep like a child and cry that God won't allow it" (IV, iv). He again paints a picture of what is likely to happen to Polenka and the other children should Sonya become ill after Katerina dies. "But what must we do? What must we do?" Sonya responds, "crying hysterically and wringing her hands." She cares desperately about the children for whom she has been sacrificing herself.

Raskolnikov replies, they must "demolish what must be demolished, once and for all, . . . and take the suffering on [themselves]!"

(IV, iv). This is another of Raskolnikov's turnabouts as his expansive attitudes come to the fore and he begins to sound like the Grand Inquisitor, assuming the burden of dreadful freedom that comes with the death of God. What they must do is destroy the traditional order, with its dependence on a nonexistent deity, and take power by stepping over the barriers posed by Christian morality. Raskolnikov is once again aspiring to become an extraordinary man. After he departs, the bewildered Sonya sees that "he must be dreadfully unhappy" and takes comfort in his having said "that he could not live without her."

Before he leaves, Raskolnikov tells Sonya that if he comes to see her the next day, he will tell her who killed Lizaveta. He says that he chose her "to tell this thing to" when Marmeladov talked to him about his daughter, while Lizaveta was still alive (IV, iv). He seems to have anticipated his inability to bear his moral isolation and to have felt that he could tell Sonya about his crime because of her attitude toward her father. After another interview with Porfiry and the calamitous funeral dinner, he returns to Sonya and confesses.

The bond between Raskolnikov and Sonya is firmly established in this scene. She has run home after Luzhin's accusation; and when Raskolnikov appears, she immediately says, "What would have become of me without you?" (V, iv). Lebezyatnikov's intervention on her behalf had been more crucial than Raskolnikov's support, but she casts Raskolnikov in the role of her savior. Raskolnikov feels as dependent on Sonya as she does on him. He cannot carry his burden alone and has come to ask her not to leave him. Sonya says she will never forsake him but will follow him wherever he goes. Raskolnikov sees Sonya as his only hope, and she sees him as her sole source of love and protection. Each fulfills the other's desperate needs.

As the scene between them unfolds, Raskolnikov swings back and forth between accepting Sonya's perspective and clinging to his conception of himself as an extraordinary man. He asks Sonya not to forsake him; but when she says she will follow him to prison, he feels "a sudden shock," smiles at her almost mockingly, and replies that perhaps he doesn't "mean to go to prison yet" (V, iv). In "his changed tone," Sonya hears "the voice of the murderer" and asks how a man like him could have committed such a deed. As he explains his behavior, he alternately condemns and justifies his actions.

His primary motive was that he "wanted to make [himself] a Napoleon," and he behaved as he felt his "authority" would have done. He acknowledges that "killing the old woman . . . was wrong" but then argues that he "only killed a louse" (V, iv). Sonya protests against calling a human being a louse, and Raskolnikov expresses agreement with her sentiments. But he then expounds the "gloomy creed" that led him to the murder and in which, with part of himself at least, he still believes. The "man of strong and powerful mind" is "master" of the stupid masses, who regard the person who "tramples on the greatest number of things [as] their law-giver." He wanted to have the courage to fling this "nonsensical world" to the devil and take power for himself.

The horrified Sonya proclaims that Raskolnikov has "strayed away from God," who has given him over to the devil, and he immediately accedes: "I know myself that it was the devil dragging me along" (V, iv). The fact that he had been in conflict about his right to transgress indicates that he did not have such a right, and his coming to Sonya means that he is "just as much a louse as everybody else." He cannot bear being in this position, however, and he hates himself for having come to her.

In despair, Raskolnikov asks Sonya what he should do; but when she tells him to seek atonement through confession and the acceptance of suffering, he rejects her advice. Those in power "destroy millions of people themselves, and count it as a virtue," so why should he submit himself to them? They would laugh at him as "a fool and a coward" (V, iv), something his pride could not bear. Sonya says that if he does not confess, he will be cut off from his fellows and will cease "to be a human being." "How can you live then?" she asks. Despite her "desperate supplication" that he not destroy himself, Raskolnikov cannot give up the possibility that perhaps he is "*still* a man and not a louse" (author's emphasis), that perhaps he "can still put up a fight!"

Raskolnikov's second visit to Sonya is in some ways a success. He cannot bear his moral isolation and is seeking relief. When his mother and sister arrived, he felt that he could never speak freely again with anyone, but he is able to talk himself out with Sonya. The visit is like a therapy session in that Raskolnikov is able to explore his motives and to arrive at a clearer understanding of himself. He realizes that he could have remained at the university if he had not "turned nasty" and that he did not commit murder because of poverty or to benefit mankind or for the sake of his mother and sister but because he wanted to prove to himself that he was an extraordinary man. "It is a long time," he says, "since I have told or known the truth" (V, iv). Speaking with someone who responds to his revelations by empathizing with his unhappiness enables him to get in touch with some truths about himself.

Joseph Frank argues that *Crime and Punishment* is "focused on the solution of an enigma: the mystery of Raskolnikov's motivation" and that he finally discovers "that he killed, not for the altruistic-humanistic motives he believes he was acting upon, but solely because of a purely selfish need to test his own strength" (1995, 102). The mystery is solved during his second visit to Sonya, but this does not bring him any closer to the resolution of his conflicts. Instead, it exacerbates them and intensifies his torments. He had come to Sonya because he felt she was "his only way out," but he has rejected her path, and now feels burdened by her love and is "conscious that his unhappiness [is] immeasurably greater than before"(V, iv). He hates himself not only for his crime and his inability to commit it without feeling guilt but also for the pain he is causing Sonya by burdening her with his confession and refusing to accept his punishment. He feels great tenderness toward her and almost takes the cross she offers because he "does not want to distress her." He cannot embrace her solution, however, until he can find a way to do so without despising himself.

III. Raskolnikov and Svidrigaylov

After Raskolnikov, the character in *Crime and Punishment* who has received the most attention from critics is Svidrigaylov. One volume of Harold Bloom's series on major literary characters includes essays on Svidrigaylov as well as on Raskolnikov. Two of Bloom's contributors quote Philip Rahv's observation that Svidrigaylov "is so fascinating a character in his own right . . . that at times he threatens to run away with the story" (Bloom 2004a, 81, 119). Indeed, Middleton Murray had argued in1916 that Svidrigaylov is the "most striking figure in *Crime and Punishment*" (Bloom 2004a, 81). Bloom himself sees Svidrigaylov as a character who "runs away from Dostoevsky's ferocious ideology, and indeed runs out of the book" (6). For Bloom he is a creation inside a creation, a character who develops a life of his own and escapes the main scheme of the work. He is a round character who displays, in W. J. Harvey's words, "a surplus margin of gratuitous life" (1965, 188). Caught up in imagining a human being, Dostoevsky supplies many more details about Svidrigaylov than are required by his formal and thematic functions, thus making him an object of interest in his own right.

My purpose here is not to explore the full richness and complexity of Dostoevsky's psychological portrait or even all the ways in which Svidrigaylov serves as Raskolnikov's double, such as his embodiment of Raskolnikov's repressed sexuality (see Wasiolek 1974 and Curtis 1991). Rather, I shall focus on those aspects of Svidrigaylov's personality that are important for our understanding of Raskolnikov's search for a way of managing his inner conflicts.

Raskolnikov confesses to Sonya because he feels that she is "his only hope, his only way out"; but when she tells him that he must accept his suffering and go to prison, he begins to feel that he has misjudged himself and that he can "still put up a fight" for his grandiose conception of himself (V, iv). His movement toward Sonya makes him feel like a "louse," and he finds himself "immeasurably" more unhappy than before. To escape his misery, he withdraws into a state of blunted consciousness that enables him "to avoid a full and clear understanding of his position" (VI, i). The most important aspect of this stage of his development is his preoccupation with Svidrigaylov. After he parts from Sonya, he finds himself "hurrying to see Svidrigaylov" without knowing exactly what he "hope[s] for from him" (VI, iii). Svidrigaylov seems to offer Raskolnikov another means of coping with his problems, one that might provide "some way of escape." Svidrigaylov is a man who has attempted to immobilize his inner conflicts and assuage his sense of guilt by employing the defense of detachment. This appeals to Raskolnikov because he has strong tendencies toward detachment himself. Indeed, he is often extremely withdrawn, and he has many characteristics in common with the underground man and Ivan Karamazov, who are predominantly detached people. What distinguishes him from them, and from Svidrigaylov, is his need to act, to be a great man not just in imagination but in reality. Like them, he is a worshiper of freedom, but it is not his primary value. "Freedom and power," he exclaims to Sonya, "but above all power! Power over all trembling creatures, over the whole ant heap! . . . That is the goal!" (IV, iv).

Svidrigaylov initially seems to Raskolnikov to be one of the men of bronze he so admires. He has repudiated traditional values and appears to have been able to transgress without feeling guilt. Subscribing to no moral code, he makes "it a rule to condemn absolutely nobody" (VI, v). This includes himself, of course, and is a defense against self-hatred. He tells Raskolnikov that he is "not particularly interested in anyone's opinion of him" (IV, i), an indifference Raskolnikov envies and wishes he could emulate.

What Raskolnikov does not see at first is that Svidrigaylov is plagued by inner conflicts that are similar to his own, though configured somewhat differently, and that his detachment is both highly problematic and far from complete. Svidrigaylov says that he does not want to get "involved" in other people's affairs (VI, vi), but he does get involved, and he feels a "heavy anger" at himself for his efforts to help the little girl in his last dream. He insists on his freedom, as in his marital arrangement with Marfa Petrovna, and avoids committing himself to any set of responsibilities or line of work. As a result of his disengagement, he is "bored to death" (IV, i): "if only I were something—a landowner, say, or a father, or an officer in the Lancers, a photographer, a journalist . . . but I'm nothing. I have no specialty" (VI, iii). He engages in a variety of aggressive acts without experiencing hostile feelings: "I never greatly hated anybody, I never even felt particularly revengeful. . . . I didn't like quarreling either, and never got heated" (VI, vi). He himself recognizes that these are "bad signs" and says "there is something wrong with me, although I honestly don't know what" (IV, i). He is suffering from profound self-alienation.

As a result of his lack of real connection either with himself or with the world, Svidrigaylov's life is empty and he is emotionally dead. His sadistic behavior and his sexual perversions are, in part at least, efforts to bring excitement into his life and to generate some kind of feeling, some sense of being alive. "Debauchery," he tells Raskolnikov, is "in its way . . . an occupation. . . . If it were not for it, one might have to shoot oneself without more ado" (VI, iii).

In addition to suffering from the despair that accompanies the sterility of his existence, Svidrigaylov experiences considerable self-hatred, despite his scorn for the values of his society. He has nightmares; he is visited by the ghosts of Marfa Petrovna and his servant Philip, in both of whose deaths he is implicated; he is haunted by the suicide of the young girl he has sexually abused; and he feels that "one little room . . . black with soot, with spiders in every corner" is the kind of eternity he deserves (IV, i). He sees no reason to "put any restraint" on himself (VI, iii), but like Raskolnikov he cannot commit crimes with impunity and is tormented by guilt. He too has a kind and generous side that leads to compensatory acts of beneficence; he too longs for renewal; and he too turns to a woman for salvation.

There are several things going on in Svidrigaylov's relation with Dunya. Her regal air makes her a desirable conquest, and her inaccessibility elevates her all the more and drives him into a frenzy of passion. Svidrigaylov pursues her partly out of a desire for mastery (the achievement of which would no doubt kill his ardor) and partly out of a desire to be submissive: "Let me kiss the hem of your dress, let me! . . . Say to me, 'Do this!' and I will do it. I will do anything. I will do the impossible. Whatever you believe in, I will believe in too. I will do anything, anything" (VI, v). He sees Dunya as a "godlike" being who has the power to reform him. His desire to submerge himself in Dunya, to get a new self from her, is stronger even than his desire for sexual triumph. He finally gets her in his power; but when she tells him that she can never love him, he cannot go on living. She was his last hope: "she might . . . have re-moulded me somehow" (VI, vi). Dunya's rejection is at once a crushing blow to his pride and a sign that he will never be able to escape his self-hatred. He can find peace now only in death.

Svidrigaylov fascinates Raskolnikov because he is a man who is reputed to have committed horrible crimes, ranging from the abuse of young girls to murder, and who does not seem to be troubled by what he has done. Raskolnikov's virtuous side recoils from Svidrigaylov's vileness (Raskolnikov is unusually moralistic in his presence), and he fears for Dunya's safety; but Svidrigaylov seems at first to have solved the problem with which Raskolnikov is grappling himself, and he has a desperate hope that Svidrigaylov can show him a way out of his conflicts. When Raskolnikov hears that Svidrigaylov has committed suicide, that his solution has failed, this means that Sonya's is the only path open to him, and he confesses to the police.

IV. RASKOLNIKOV'S CONVERSION

Although many critics stop their analysis of Raskolnikov at this point, his confession to the police is not the culmination of his development. The confession shows the force of Sonya's influence, but it does not mark Raskolnikov's final acceptance of her beliefs. His inner conflicts persist, and he must find a way to resolve them before his conversion can take place.

Immediately after he confesses to Sonya, Raskolnikov feels that he may have misjudged himself, that perhaps he is "still a man and not a louse" (V, iv). He admits that "killing the old woman . . . was wrong," but in a later conversation with Dunya he denies, in "a sudden access of rage," that he is guilty of a crime (VI, vii). He is not a criminal, but a stupid blunderer: "I understand less than ever why what I did was a crime! Never have I been stronger, never have I held my convictions more firmly, than now!" With the collapse of his ambitions, Raskolnikov holds onto his pride by refusing to acknowledge his guilt and admitting only to incompetence.

After he goes to prison, Raskolnikov clings even more tenaciously to his defiant attitudes. His chief fear beforehand is that he will be crushed by suffering and will give up his pride, that he will "whine and whimper before people, branding [him]self a criminal" (VI, vii). Once he admits his deed, thus satisfying one set of needs, it is of the greatest importance to him not to feel remorse, thus satisfying another. He theories look as reasonable to him as ever; he has only carried to its logical conclusion the line of action that lesser "prophets of denial" cannot bring themselves to complete (Epilogue, ii). He admits to having performed "an illegal action," but his "conscience is easy" because he does not feel guilty of a crime.

Raskolnikov's only regret is that he has not succeeded. The first steps of his heroes "were successfully carried out, and therefore *they were right*, while [his] failed" (Epilogue, ii; author's emphasis). In the terms of his philosophy that might makes right, events have proved him wrong; however, as long as he feels no remorse he can hold onto his image of himself as an extraordinary man, and this is what is essential to the defense of his pride. His renewed feelings of grandiosity lead him to deny even that he is a blunderer. He stops raging at himself and finds it "completely impossible to think [his actions] as stupid and monstrous as they had seemed to him before." He sees himself now as a victim of "blind fate."

The trouble with this defense is that it is poorly adapted to his situation, and Raskolnikov begins to suffer in a new way. "How happy he would have been," observes the narrator, "if he could have put the blame on himself! Then he could have borne anything, even shame and infamy" (Epilogue, ii). He would have felt that his punishment was deserved and could have accepted his lot. As it is, he is outraged at being the victim of an irrational destiny. He is being compelled to submit to forces he had aspired to master and for which he has no respect. He is "ashamed ... because he, Raskolnikov, [has] perished so blindly and hopelessly, with such dumb stupidity, by some decree of blind fate." He falls ill, the narrator tells us, from "the wound to his pride." His illness, which is preceded by a period of defensive withdrawal from others, is in part a response to his psychological impasse: he can neither give up his pride nor find a way to maintain it. His life in prison is a constant humiliation.

The side of Raskolnikov that is drawn to Sonya's solution has not disappeared, but his punishment has diminished its strength, and it has receded into the background. He feels "in his heart," however, "that there [is] something profoundly false in himself and his beliefs" (Epilogue, ii). Raskolnikov sees this as the bondage of social conditioning, which he cannot shake off, and he despises himself for "his weakness and worthlessness." The narrator sees it as "the herald of a coming crisis in his life, of his coming resurrection, of a future new outlook on life."

Whatever we may think of the solution Raskolnikov embraces at the end, Dostoevsky is correct in perceiving that it is the only one that will work for him at this time. At some level Raskolnikov also perceives this, and in the dream he has when he is ill, he finds a way of reconciling Sonya's beliefs with his need to be a great man. This dream is crucial to an understanding of Raskolnikov's transformation, but it has not received the attention it deserves. As many critics have observed, it shows Raskolnikov the catastrophic consequences of modern secular thought, but this does not account for its power to resolve his inner conflicts.

Raskolnikov dreams "that the whole world [is] condemned to fall victim to a terrible, unknown pestilence"—the pestilence of unbelief (Epilogue, ii). People who are infected become "like men possessed and out of their minds," but they feel themselves to be "wise" and "unshakable in the truth": "Never had they considered their judgements, their scientific deductions, or their moral convictions and creeds more infallible." The result is chaos of every sort: "none could understand any other; each thought he was the sole repository of truth. . . . they did not know what was evil and what good." No common enterprise is possible; "the most ordinary callings [are] abandoned"; and the end result is universal war, fire, famine, and finally cannibalism. This dream embodies Dostoevsky's vision of the disaster toward which the world is heading if the forces of atheism are not checked. In terms of Raskolnikov's psychology, it is his Christian side's vision of where his radical philosophy is taking the world. He is seeing himself as one of those "men possessed" who has the illusion of infallibility. The clear message of the dream is that he has chosen the wrong path, that men must submit to religious authority if they are to be saved. The dream lingers "painfully" in his memory and pushes him toward a renunciation of his skeptical attitudes.

This aspect of the dream has been frequently discussed, but its most important function has not been properly appreciated. The dream is so significant in Raskolnikov's development because it offers him a way out of his impasse by showing him how he can embrace Sonya's solution without relinquishing his search for glory. In the dream "only a few [can] save themselves, a chosen handful of the pure, who were destined to found a new race of men and a new life, and to renew and cleanse the earth" (Epilogue, ii). This is a revised version of Raskolnikov's earlier fantasies. The world is still divided into an elite group of extraordinary men and the mass of mankind who are destined to perish meaninglessly. In this version, however, the extraordinary men are not the great criminal conquerors but those who have kept alive spiritual truth. The ordinary men are the freethinkers, the original minds who "put forward [their] own ideas." As long as Raskolnikov aspires to be a Napoleonic figure, he is doomed to unbearable frustration and self-hatred. There seems to be no way in which he can reconcile his need to be great and his need to be good. The dream shows him that he can be great not by repudiating traditional values but by preserving them in a world that is in danger of being destroyed by unbelief. He can become one of the chosen few who are destined to cleanse the earth.

Sonya has accompanied Raskolnikov to Siberia, but as long as he clings to his pride in himself as a prophet of denial, she is a threat to him, and he treats her with coldness. He has suppressed his awareness of his conflicts, but they war within him nonetheless and precipitate the psychological crisis from which he falls ill. After he recovers he does not consciously understand the meaning of his dream, but the forces within him that generated it seize him and cast him at Sonya's feet. The moment of transformation has arrived. That night Raskolnikov takes a New Testament from under his pillow—"it was [Sonya's], the very one from which she had read to him the raising of Lazarus"—and an idea flashes through his mind: "Could not her beliefs become my beliefs now? Her feelings, her aspirations at least . . . " (Epilogue, ii). In the hurry of bringing his novel to a close, Dostoevsky does not spell out the details of his protagonist's new life, but his dream clearly suggests that he will become one of the chosen few by promulgating Sonya's beliefs.

Understanding Raskolnikov's dream enables us to see that Dostoevsky does *not* sacrifice plausible characterization to the need for formal and thematic closure. The change Raskolnikov undergoes is well motivated and in keeping with his psychology. Indeed, Dostoevsky's mimetic portrait of Raskolnikov is so detailed and so independent of his ideology that readers can form their own interpretations and judgments. Dostoevsky sees Raskolnikov as moving in the direction of spiritual health, toward a "perfect resurrection" (Epilogue, ii). Some critics agree, while others have difficulty seeing Raskolnikov as adopting a Sonya-like humility. I see him as moving away from a failed defensive strategy to one that is better adapted to his situation. He has worked his way out of his impasse, he has found a way to go on living, and his new solution is more humane than the old one; however, he is still engaged in a search for glory, and his new model, Sonya, is hardly an exemplar of psychological well-being.

The change in Raskolnikov is entirely believable, but we need not subscribe to Dostoevsky's celebration of it. Biographical evidence suggests that Raskolnikov's story embodies a version of Dostoevsky's own development and that his conversion has parallels with the author's experience in Siberia. Dostoevsky has a powerful vested interest in seeing Raskolnikov's change as spiritual growth. His need to glorify the solution at which Raskolnikov arrives is such that he is unable to recognize its limitations, although he presents a faithful picture of its destructive effects in characters like Marmeladov and Sonya, whose mimetic portraits I feel are at odds with the rhetoric.

v. The Happy Ending of *Crime and Punishment*

The majority of critics have been uncomfortable with the conclusion of *Crime and Punishment*. I think this is partly because, having failed to see the solution at which Raskolnikov arrives in his dream, they find his conversion too sudden and too radical to be convincing. Bloom argues, for instance, that "Raskolnikov never does repent and change, unless we believe the epilogue, in which Dostoevsky himself scarcely believed.... Konstantin Mochulsky is surely right to emphasize that Raskolnikov never comes to believe in redemption, never rejects his theory of strength and power" (2004b, 2). I think that the ending completes aesthetic and thematic patterns established earlier in the novel, that Raskolnikov unconsciously refashions his image of himself as an extraordinary man, and that this leads to his movement toward Sonya and her solution.

Yet I too feel discomfort with the conclusion of the novel. What disturbs me, and accounts for some of the dissatisfaction of others as well, is that the ending is so happy as to be out of keeping with the gritty realism of most of the book. Bloom observes that until the epilogue "no other narrative fiction drives itself onwards with the remorseless strength of *Crime and Punishment*, truly a shot out of hell and into hell again. To have written a naturalistic novel that reads like a continuous nightmare is Dostoevsky's unique achievement" (2004b, 2). But at the end, the nightmare turns into a wish-fulfillment dream.

In reaching for greatness, Raskolnikov commits a crime that threatens to destroy him, along with his victims, and that results in the early death of his mother. Instead of destroying him, however, his crime ultimately leads to a vision of his becoming even greater than he had imagined himself to be in his Napoleonic fantasies. The sinner may become a savior of the world, one of the handful of men destined to keep truth alive and purify the earth.

Leaving aside its consequences for Alyona, Lizaveta, and Pulkheria Alexandrovna (none of whom is deeply mourned), Raskolnikov's fall has been fortunate indeed. He does not become humble in the manner of Sonya—that *would* be unconvincing. Rather, he will pursue a grand destiny by espousing Sonya's beliefs, by opposing atheistic humanism, and by preaching Christian doctrine—like a Zossima or perhaps a Dostoevsky. He is only at the beginning of his new path, and there are "struggles yet to come," but they will be "great and heroic" (Epilogue, ii). The novel holds out the prospect that the craving for glory by which Raskolnikov and his family have been obsessed will be fulfilled, that had she lived his mother would have been proud.

Things turn out quite well for other characters also. Dunya puts herself in jeopardy to further her brother's career, but she is saved from Svidrigaylov and Luzhin, finds love with Razumikhin, and is made financially secure by Marfa Petrovna's bequest. The goodhearted Razumikhin marries the woman he adores and is lifted out of poverty by her inheritance. Katerina Ivanovna's children are rescued by Svidrigaylov, an intervention with which even critics sympathetic to Dostoevsky's perspective are uncomfortable. Svidrigaylov has inner conflicts, to be sure, but his kind and generous side is not fully enough developed to make his beneficence seem an inevitable expression of his character. He appears to me, and to others, to be fulfilling the author's needs more than his own. Through him, and through Marfa Petrovna, the economic problems that had loomed so large in the novel are simply made to disappear.

Among those who are saved by the shower of money is Sonya. Like Dunya, she has been driven into behavior harmful to herself by a combination of financial pressures and a compulsively self-sacrificial nature. Svidrigaylov's largesse enables her to give up prostitution and accompany Raskolnikov to Siberia. Her life had seemed irrevocably spoiled, but she wins the love of the potentially great man who understands that she is pure at heart. She saves Raskolnikov from his moral and emotional isolation, and he saves her from the apparent hopelessness of her social position. They both have been "raised . . . from the dead" (Epilogue, ii).

Sonya is so exultant at the end not only because she knows that Raskolnikov will love her forever after she had despaired of ever being cherished but also because she too has a dream of glory that is coming true. The transformation she had hoped for as she read the story of Lazarus finally occurs when, after his illness, Raskolnikov casts himself at her feet. Her belief in the power of her prayers and of her magic bargain is justified by the escape of Katerina's children and the resurrection of Raskolnikov. She retains the humility on which her potency depends by submerging herself in Raskolnikov and living "only in his life" (Epilogue, ii).

In *Crime and Punishment*, we find two of the major patterns of Western fiction, those of education and of vindication (see Paris 1997). Raskolnikov's story has an education plot based on the pattern of the fortunate fall. The plot is comic rather than tragic in this novel in that Raskolnikov will be able to profit from the wisdom he has gained. He will go on to have a much better life than he would have had if he had never sinned. Sonya's story has a vindication pattern, based on the Cinderella archetype, in which a virtuous but persecuted heroine finally achieves the recognition and status she deserves (other examples are Jane Austen's *Mansfield Park* and Charlotte Brontë's *Jane Eyre*; see Paris 1978, 1997). Like most protagonists of vindication plots, Sonya has early defenders (Marmeladov, Katerina, and Raskolnikov), but initially she is stigmatized as a fallen woman and is surrounded by detractors. As the story progresses, the detractors fall away, and she becomes an object almost of veneration to the people in her life. She is highly prized by Raskolnikov and will share his future glory. What has been a very dark novel has an ending like that of a fairy tale.

Part III

The Brothers Karamazov

CHAPTER 7

THEMATIC ANALYSIS OF *THE BROTHERS KARAMAZOV*

I. INTRODUCTION

IN MY OPINION, DOSTOEVSKY IS THE WORLD'S GREATEST NOVELIST and *The Brothers Karamazov* is his greatest novel. The novel rivals Dante's *The Divine Comedy* and Milton's *Paradise Lost* in the loftiness of its ideological aspirations, and its intricate formal patterns are endlessly rewarding to contemplate. It contains, moreover, a brilliant array of mimetic portraits that embody Dostoevsky's profoundest psychological intuitions. Ivan is one of the greatest character creations in literature; and he and Alyosha (along with Father Zossima) generate the dialectic that is at the thematic heart of the novel.

The illustrative significance of these characters has been much discussed, but they are also imagined human beings whose beliefs are expressions of their personality and experience. Before I approach them from this perspective, I should like to consider their roles in the larger creation of which they are a part. This will make it easier to perceive the relationship in the novel between rhetoric and mimesis.

An examination of the novel's thematic structure must inevitably deal with familiar topics, but I shall keep it as brief as I can and shall offer some new observations. The analyses of characters in subsequent chapters will offer a fresh perspective on *The Brothers Karamazov* and will focus on aspects of the novel that have been largely ignored.

Before embarking on a thematic analysis, I must say another word about Mikhail Bakhtin. Despite his contention that the characters in the novel "are all equally privileged participants in the great dialogue" (1984, 92), I find *The Brothers Karamazov* to be as heavily rhetorical as *Crime and Punishment*. Bakhtin argues that "upon entering his polyphonic novel," the ideas of Dostoevsky the journalist and thinker "are liberated from their monologic isolation" and "become thoroughly dialogized." As a consequence, it is "absolutely impermissible to ascribe to these ideas the finalizing function of authorial ideas in a monologic novel." It is true that Dostoevsky's religious positions are challenged in the novel by Ivan's perspective and are not presented as they are in his journalism; but I do not believe that the "partiality . . . for specific ideas and images" which "is sometimes sensed" in Dostoevsky's novels "is evident only in superficial aspects" of the works, such as the "conventionally monologic epilogue to *Crime and Punishment*." I have tried to show that there is a powerful rhetoric at work from the beginning of *Crime and Punishment* that shapes our attitude toward the characters and their beliefs.

The same thing is true in *The Brothers Karamazov* (see Belknap 1978). Indeed, the novel is prefaced with an epigraph that makes the pattern of the fortunate fall, which emerges only gradually in *Crime and Punishment*, quite explicit from the beginning: "Verily, verily, I say unto you, except a corn of wheat fall into the ground and die, it abideth alone: but if it die, it bringeth forth much fruit" (John 12:24). This pattern becomes a recurring motif. Immediately after the epigraph comes "From the Author," in which the narrator identifies Alyosha as the hero of the story. Acknowledging that his protagonist is "odd, even eccentric," he argues that "sometimes such a person . . . carries within himself the very heart of the universal" from which "the rest of the men of his epoch" have been torn away. The reader is left in little doubt from the outset as to where the implied author stands. Indeed, the rhetoric of *The Brothers Karamazov* is often more explicit than that of *Crime and Punishment*.

Bakhtin himself recognizes, as do the vast majority of critics, that the voices of Zossima and Ivan are not equally privileged but that Zossima's is dominant. He tries to reconcile this awareness with his insistence on the polyphonic quality of the novel by means of an argument that has received little attention. Dostoevsky creates a world "of yoked-together . . . human orientations" (Bakhtin 1984, 97). Among these, he "seeks the higher and most authoritative orientation, and he perceives it not as his own true thought, but as another authentic human being and his discourse." Zossima's discourse is in his own voice rather than in the author's, to be sure, but it is validated by a variety of rhetorical devices that give it the author's endorsement. Bakhtin continues: "The image of the ideal human being or the image of Christ represents for [Dostoevsky] the resolution of ideological quests. This image or this highest voice must crown the world of voices, must organize and subdue it." Bakhtin usually contends that in real life there is no authoritative orientation and that the faithful reflection of this aspect of the human condition is what makes Dostoevsky's polyphonic fiction so truthful and profound. In this passage, however, he recognizes that there is indeed a dominant perspective in *The Brothers Karamazov*, one that subdues the other voices and organizes the competing orientations.

Thematically, *The Brothers Karamazov* is Dostoevsky's attempt to justify the ways of God to man. His technique is to pose through Ivan the most devastating form of modern unbelief and then to answer Ivan's challenge through Zossima's words and Ivan's own experiences, along with those of other characters. Dostoevsky was proud not only of his response to Ivan (about which he had much anxiety while composing) but also of the negations expressed through his character, which he felt were far more powerful than those of the atheists who looked down on him as an unsophisticated advocate of obsolete ideas.

II. Ivan's Challenge

Ivan poses the problem of evil in a way that makes it impossible to maintain a rational belief in the existence of a just and omnipotent deity. Adults have sinned and therefore may have deserved the suffering that befalls them; but children are "innocent," yet "they, too, suffer horribly on earth" (V, iv). Try as they might, rational people can find no justification for the abominations inflicted on these pitiful victims. Religion tells us that they are being punished for the sins of their fathers, who have eaten the apple, "but that reasoning," says Ivan, "is of the other world and is incomprehensible for the heart of man here on earth. The innocent must not suffer for another's sins, and especially such innocents!" Because of the senselessness of children's suffering, Ivan concludes that historical reality is absurd.

So far, Ivan's position presents Dostoevsky with no great difficulty. Like many religious thinkers of his time (and our own), Dostoevsky begins with the assumption that reality cannot be understood in rational terms and that attempts to do so lead only to despair. There *is* a moral order in the universe, but it is not one that is commensurate with our human understanding or that corresponds to our human conceptions of justice. God is not an anthropomorphic but a transcendent being. He is good and just but not necessarily in the human sense of these terms. If we would be at peace with life and gain some intimation of its meaning, we cannot judge God by our values. We must accept his will without understanding it; we must trust in his benevolence; and we must have faith that if we are humble and loving, the divine mystery will be revealed to us—in glimpses while we are on earth and fully thereafter. We believe in God because life must have meaning, but from the human point of view it does not.

Ivan's most powerful negation is his acceptance of the possibility of a transcendent moral order and his rejection of that order *even if it exists*. He does not actually believe that such an order exists, but he knows that he cannot disprove it and that the affirmation of such an order is the most incontrovertible response to the problem of evil. So, for the sake of argument, he accepts God: "and what's more I accept His wisdom, His purpose—which are utterly beyond our ken; I believe in the underlying order and the meaning of life; I believe in the eternal harmony in which they say we shall one day be blended" (V, iii). However, he does not accept God's world.

At the heart of Ivan's position is his refusal, as Albert Camus would put it, to commit philosophical suicide, to give up his human point of view. He accepts the believer's most powerful argument. Let us say that there is a God, that there is a meaning to life, that there is a divine plan that will reconcile us to the seeming absurdity of human existence. I cannot understand this God, however, or this meaning, or this plan with my limited, earthly, Euclidian mind, which is the only knowing faculty I have. You say that I shall understand these things in the hereafter, at the world's finale, and perhaps I shall. But I am alive now, with my human faculties, and a need to make sense of reality, a craving for justice and order. A meaning that will be intelligible to me on the last day will comfort me then, but it is of no help to me in this life. A meaning that is unintelligible to me as a human being is no meaning to me at all; it does not satisfy my needs and is simply irrelevant.

I have invoked Camus because his position and Ivan's are very similar. A passage in Camus' *The Myth of Sisyphus* may help us to understand the thinking of Dostoevsky's character:

> What I know, what is certain, what I cannot deny, what I cannot reject—this is what counts. . . . I don't know whether this world has a meaning that transcends it. But I know that I do not know that meaning

and that it is impossible for me just now to know it. What can a meaning outside my condition mean to me? I can understand only in human terms. What I touch, what resists me—that is what I understand. And these two certainties—my appetite for the absolute and for unity and the impossibility of reducing this world to a rational and reasonable principle—I also know that I cannot reconcile them. What other truth can I admit without lying, without bringing in a hope I lack and which means nothing within the limits of my condition? (1960, 38)

The plight Camus describes is exactly that of Ivan. Humans have an appetite for clarity, for order, for justice; but this appetite cannot be satisfied within the limits of the human condition.

Like Camus, Ivan refuses to go beyond what he knows.

"We know what we know!"
"What do you know?" [asks Alyosha]
"I understand nothing.... I don't want to understand anything now. I want to stick to the fact. I made up my mind long ago not to understand. If I try to understand anything, I shall be false to the fact and I have determined to stick to the fact.... I am a bug, and I recognise in all humility that I cannot understand why the world is arranged as it is.... With my pitiful, earthly, Euclidian understanding, all I know is that there is suffering and that there are none guilty; that cause follows effect, simply and directly ... but that's only Euclidian nonsense, I know that, and I can't consent to live by it!... I must have justice, or I will destroy myself. And not justice in some remote infinite time and space, but here on earth, and that I could see myself. (V, iv)

Our Euclidian minds can explain suffering in terms of cause and effect, but this cannot satisfy our demand for a moral explanation that will enable us to accept suffering as just and hence to be reconciled to our condition.

Ivan refuses to accept God's world not only because its order is incomprehensible from a human point of view but also because its order is unjust in any intelligible sense of that term and hence is unacceptable on moral grounds. Ivan arraigns God in the name of human values. At the end of time, "everything that lives and has lived" may cry aloud: "Thou art just, O Lord, for thy ways are revealed" (V, iv). However, if this is so, this final harmony requires the suffering of innocent children, and it is "beyond all comprehension why they should suffer and why they should pay for the harmony." To accept the suffering of the innocent in the name of this harmony is to betray our human values, to worship as good that which from our point of view is unmitigated evil. Ivan proclaims, therefore, that he does not want transcendent harmony: "From love for humanity I don't want it. . . . I would rather remain with my unavenged suffering and unsatisfied indignation, *even if I were wrong*" (author's emphasis).

Ivan makes human beings the measure of God, and from the human point of view, God is morally defective. In order to preserve his human sense of dignity, integrity, and justice, Ivan returns to God "the ticket" (V, vi). If a transcendent harmony exists and he rises again to see it, he too "may cry aloud with the rest, looking at the mother embracing her child's torturer, 'Thou art just, O Lord!'"; however, he doesn't "want to cry aloud then" (V, iv). While he is on earth, therefore, he makes "haste to take [his] own measures" by renouncing "the higher harmony altogether. It's not worth the tears of that one tortured child who beat itself on the breast with its little fist and prayed in its stinking outhouse, with its unexpiated tears to 'dear, kind God!'"

Ivan's highest values are justice and happiness, both of which are denied by God's universe. The miseries of the human condition need no elaboration. To the argument that humans will be happy in the hereafter, Ivan replies much as he did to the argument that God's justice will be revealed at the world's end. The happiness promised by such an argument is not commensurate with human notions of happiness because it is based on the suffering of the innocent and is therefore ignoble. Ivan gets Alyosha to agree that if he had the power to create "a fabric of human destiny with the object of making men happy in the end" with the condition that "it was essential and inevitable to torture to death only one tiny creature," he would not consent to do so (V, iv). Ivan's conclusion is that "too high a price is asked for harmony."

Ivan is aware, of course, that human unhappiness can be justified in the name of freedom. God could have created people so that they would be automatically good. If he had done so, they would have been spared the self-hatred generated by their own sins and the suffering caused by the sins of others. The price of their happiness would have been freedom, however. Instead of being autonomous agents with the capacity to determine their own destiny, humans would be like the beasts of the fields whose ignorance of good and evil leaves them devoid of spiritual dignity. Ivan's response to this position is that freedom is simply not worth the sacrifice of human happiness: "Why should [we] know that diabolical good and evil when it costs so much? Why, the whole world of knowledge is not worth that child's prayer to 'dear, kind God'!" (V, iv).

* * *

Ivan's protest against the elevation of freedom over happiness is elaborated in "The Grand Inquisitor," which is an attack not so much on God as on the Christian religion. Being a determinist, Ivan does not believe that humans have unconditioned free will. They are the products of heredity and environment, and their behavior is a manifestation of the laws of their nature. That is why "'there are none guilty'" (V, iv). Since there is no God and consequently no absolutes, people create their own values and are free in a moral sense. "Nothing is more seductive for man," says the Grand Inquisitor, "than his freedom of conscience, but nothing is a greater cause of suffering" (V, v). Since most people are weak, vicious, ignoble creatures who are incapable of living either with themselves or with others in a state of freedom, what they need is an unquestioned principle of authority to which to submit. They need to be controlled, disciplined, and enslaved for their own happiness, otherwise they will suffer unbearable moral anxiety and will move inexorably toward a state of anarchy and mutual destruction.

A religion designed to promote human happiness would relieve humans of their "fearful burden" of freedom (V, v). It would supply their material necessities and exercise absolute temporal power. Under the banner of miracle, mystery, and authority, it would dispel all doubts and would tell them exactly what to believe and what to do. If he had accepted the devil's wise advice, Christ could have provided such a religion; instead he chose "all that is exceptional, vague, and enigmatic," thereby burdening "the spiritual kingdom of mankind with its sufferings forever." By choosing what "was utterly beyond the strength of men," Christ acted "as though [he did] not love them at all," even though he came to give his life for them.

Out of love for humanity, the Grand Inquisitor and those who are like him will correct Christ's work. Taking upon themselves the dreadful burden of freedom, they will assume absolute authority, both spiritual and temporal, and will "plan the universal happiness of man"

(V, v). True martyrs, they will suffer the spiritual torments of consciousness so that others can have "the quiet humble happiness" commensurate with their nature.

Like the philosophical sections of *Notes from Underground*, "The Grand Inquisitor" is often anthologized and is discussed independently of its context. It must be considered in relation to the novel as whole, however, if it is to be properly understood. When we examine it in its context, we see that it serves three distinct functions. It is part of Ivan's assault on religion, particularly on the defense of Christianity in the name of human freedom, and it is also part of Dostoevsky's refutation of Ivan's blasphemies. Dostoevsky wants the reader to see the denial of freedom and dignity that results from Ivan's position and to recoil from it. In addition, it is an expression of Ivan's personality. It is a fantasy that reveals Ivan's dreams of glory and longings for power and superiority. I shall examine the second function of "the Grand Inquisitor" in the next section, where I take up Dostoevsky's response to Ivan's arraignment of God. I shall discuss its third function when I analyze Ivan in motivational terms.

III. CONTRADICTION IN IVAN'S POSITION

Before we consider Dostoevsky's response to Ivan, there is a contradiction in Ivan's position that must be examined. As we have seen, although Ivan accepts the possibility of a transcendent God for the sake of argument and in order to show its irrelevance, his real conclusion from the absence of an intelligible moral order in the universe is that there probably is no God and that there are, therefore, no moral laws outside of humans to which they must conform. This leads to his famous proclamation that "all is lawful." From Dostoevsky's point of view, this is an inevitable consequence of Ivan's rejection of God, for Dostoevsky regards God as the source of all values and nihilism as the logical consequence of unbelief. The conclusion that all is lawful is not required, however, by Ivan's arraignment of God; it is, in fact, in conflict with it.

Ivan's protest against the order of the universe is made in the name of human values such as justice and happiness. Since the world order cannot be explained in such a way as to satisfy our legitimate cravings for fairness and fulfillment, Ivan concludes that if God exists, he must be a transcendent being whose consciousness is not commensurate with our own and whose values are beyond our understanding. Nevertheless, Ivan judges this God by human standards and finds his ways repugnant. To accept the will of such of God is to betray humankind. Ivan would rather not go to heaven if the price of admission is the acceptance of a "harmony" that is evil from the human point of view.

Ivan's position is similar to that of John Stuart Mill in *An Examination of Sir William Hamilton's Philosophy*. "If in ascribing goodness to God I do not mean what I mean by goodness," says Mill, then "what reason have I for venerating it"? (1961, 437). "To say that God's goodness may be different in kind from man's goodness, what is it but saying, with a slight change of phraseology, that God may possibly not be good?" Mill continues: "Whatever power such a being may have, he shall not compel me to worship him. I will call no being good, who is not what I mean when I apply that epithet to my fellow-creatures; and if such a being can sentence me to hell for not so calling him, to hell I will go" (1961, 438).

Having rejected God's nature, and for all practical purposes his existence, in the name of human values, Ivan then deduces from the absence of an intelligible God the absence of all values. The values in the name of which he has rejected God have not disappeared, however, except in Ivan's thinking. They are generated by human nature, and they still exist as criteria of human as well as of divine conduct. According to Miüsov, Ivan contends not only that without immortality everything is lawful but also "that for every individual . . . who does not believe in God . . . , the moral law of nature must immediately be changed into the exact contrary of the former religious law, and that egoism, even to crime, must become, not only lawful but even recognized as the inevitable, the most rational, even honourable outcome of his position" (II, vi). From a philosophic point of view, this makes no sense. If God is to be judged in terms of our notions of justice and our cravings for happiness, why are egoism and crime, which bring misery and injustice to others, lawful for human beings?

How are we to account for Ivan's illogicality? One possibility is that Dostoevsky is manipulating his characterization of Ivan for thematic purposes in order to illustrate his own beliefs. Dostoevsky contends that a justification of criminality is the inevitable outcome of unbelief; perhaps he makes Ivan believe this not because it is something that a person like Ivan would believe but because he wants to demonstrate the horrible consequences of atheistic humanism. Another possibility is that Ivan's contradictions are a product not of his rational intelligence, which seems much too acute to make such mistakes, but of his psychological problems. In this view, which I embrace, Ivan's philosophy as a whole, including his contradictions, is a reflection of his defensive strategies and of the conflicts between them. I shall develop this point when I turn from thematic to motivational analysis.

IV. Responses to Ivan

Dostoevsky responds to Ivan's rejection of God or of God's world in a variety of ways. He affirms the existence of a mystic sense that puts us in touch with transcendent realities; he demonstrates the spiritual value of suffering; he celebrates freedom as a higher good than happiness; he protests that we, not God, are responsible for human sinfulness and misery; and he shows the consequences of unbelief through Ivan's deterioration.

"To Chestov," says Camus, "reason is useless but there is something beyond reason. To an absurd mind reason is useless and there is nothing beyond reason" (1960, 27). Ivan's is the absurdist position, while Dostoevsky's is that of Chestov. "If God exists," argues Ivan, "and if He really did create the world, then, as we all know, He created it according to the geometry of Euclid and the human mind with the conception of only three dimensions in space" (V, iii). Since we have only earthly Euclidian minds, it is "utterly inappropriate" for us to speculate on such questions as the existence of God or the transcendental meaning of life.

From Dostoevsky's point of view, Ivan's problem is that he has metaphysical needs that are generated by his spiritual nature, but he insists on trying to satisfy those needs in a purely empirical way. He rejects God's world because it does not make sense, whereas it is only by first accepting God's world that its meaning can be apprehended. "If you love everything," explains Zossima, "you will perceive the divine mystery in things. Once you perceive it, you will begin to comprehend it better every day" (VI, iii). The meaning we perceive will not be a rational one, nor will we perceive it with our rational faculties. To compensate for the limitations of our Euclidian minds, we have been given "a precious mystic sense of our living bond with the other world, with the higher heavenly world, and the roots of our thoughts and feelings are not here but in other worlds. That is why the philosophers say that we cannot apprehend the reality of things on earth."

Dostoevsky explained to his publisher that he wanted to depict in Book V ("Pro and Contra") "the most extreme blasphemy and the seeds of destructive ideas in our time among our youth, which have torn themselves away from reality" (Wasiolek 1967, 3). The reality from which they have torn themselves is "the higher heavenly world" of which Zossima speaks, and the most destructive of their ideas is that man's earthly Euclidian mind is his only source of knowledge. In *The Idiot*, Aglaya distinguishes between Myshkin's "surface mind," which is "a little affected," and his "real mind," which is "far better" than those of all of his detractors "put together." "Because really," she concludes, "there are *two* minds—the kind that matters, and the kind that doesn't matter" (III, viii). By trying to live exclusively from their surface, rational minds, the empiricists deny their deeper, spiritual minds. When we do this, says Zossima, the "heavenly growth" within us "die[s] away" (VI, iii). The results are alienation and despair and every form of moral perversion and social chaos.

Part of Dostoevsky's reply to Ivan is his dramatization of the destructive consequences of Ivan's philosophy. Dostoevsky feels that it is only a belief in God that checks our potentially monstrous egoism. Having deposed God, Ivan wishes to become God himself. Ivan is not driven, like Raskolnikov, to overstep the barriers of the old morality in order to prove to himself that he is the man-god. He has a different psychology. Nevertheless, his philosophy that all things are lawful leads to the murder of his father, and he discovers, like Raskolnikov, that he cannot live with his transgression. Dostoevsky dramatizes not only the consequences of unbelief but also the persistence of God's spirit even in those who have denied his reality, as Ivan's conscience forces him to feel and to act in ways that contradict his rational beliefs. Instead of being able "lightheartedly [to] overstep all the barriers of the old morality" (XI, ix), the thought of parricide is so horrible to him that he tries desperately to escape an awareness of his own responsibility. Ivan's conflicts are so severe that his personality begins to split apart, and he is overcome by illness after he testifies at Dmitri's trial.

Ivan's rejection of God has resulted in crime and madness, but his feelings of guilt bring on a spiritual crisis that may lead to his regeneration. The best clue that we have to the outcome is in Alyosha's observations to himself immediately before the trial: "'God will conquer!' he thought. 'He will either rise up in the light of truth, or . . . he'll perish in hate'" (XI, x). Dostoevsky shows us through Ivan's story that man cannot live in rebellion. Either he submits and is saved or he perishes.

v. Seeds That Bear Much Fruit

It is not only Alyosha's hope that God will conquer but also the design of the novel as a whole that leads us to believe that Ivan will "rise up in the light of truth." The novel's aesthetic and thematic structures are both dominated by the pattern introduced in the epigraph: "verily, verily, I say unto you, except a corn of wheat fall into the ground and die, it abideth alone: but if it die, it bringeth forth much fruit" (John 12:24). This is the pattern of the fortunate fall, and its repetition is one of the major devices by which Dostoevsky justifies the ways of God to man. It appears in a variety of ways in the stories of Zossima, Markel, Mihail, Dmitri, Grushenka, Alyosha, and Ilusha. Part of the pattern is present in Ivan's story, and it would have been completed, we may presume, had Dostoevsky lived to write his sequel to *The Brothers Karamazov*. Sin and suffering are not the absurdities Ivan makes them out to be; they are, rather, seeds that bear much fruit. They are part of a divine plan in which good comes out of evil and triumphs in the end.

People are led by their animal passions, their pride of intellect, and the corruptions of the world to ignore the promptings of their spiritual nature and plunge into sin. If they have not become too far alienated from their spiritual selves, however, their sins may be the instruments of their salvation. The commission of a particularly heinous act may awaken their conscience and fill them with moral revulsion at their own iniquity.

This is what happens to Mihail, Zossima's mysterious visitor, who murders the woman he loves in order to prevent her from marrying another man. At first he is untroubled by pangs of conscience, but eventually he begins to brood on his crime and comes to realize that it is only by confessing that he can "heal his soul and . . . be at peace for ever" (VI, ii). Worldly fears prevent him from acting on this realization until he is inspired by the example of Zossima, who apologizes publicly to his adversary in a duel. After Mihail confesses, he finds heaven within and is saved from the worldly consequences of his act by God's providence, which leads everyone except Zossima to think him insane.

Zossima's story has a similar pattern. At the time of his conversion he is an army officer who, under the influence of his companions, has become "a cruel, absurd, almost savage creature" (VI, ii). He looks on the common soldiers "as cattle," and devotes himself to "drunkenness, debauchery, and devilry." He is on the verge of attempting to murder a fellow human in a duel when his brutal assault on his orderly

Anfansy awakens his conscience, and he undergoes a spiritual transformation. He too is thought crazy when he acts in a righteous way, but his fellow officers forgive him for violating their code of honor when they learn that he plans to become a monk. The sins of Mihail and of Zossima cause suffering to the innocent, but they also bear spiritual fruit, both to the perpetrators and to the others who benefit from their regeneration. Indeed, Zossima becomes one of the few righteous men on whose teachings the future salvation of the world depends.

The cases of Markel, Dmitri, and Grushenka are somewhat different. These people are all leading unrighteous lives at the time of their conversion, but it is not their own sins so much as a blow of fate that awakens their spirituality. When he is seventeen, Zossima's brother Markel makes friends with a political exile who has been banished from Moscow for freethinking, and under his influence, he rejects religion as "silly twaddle" (VI, i). He soon falls ill with consumption, however, and as he lies dying, "a marvelous change passe[s] over him, his spirit seems[s] transformed." He dies full of spiritual wisdom and at peace with life.

Dmitri's reformation begins when he is unjustly accused of the murder of his father. Exhausted by the ordeal of interrogation, he falls asleep, dreams of the babe, and awakens into a new spiritual state: "I've sworn to amend, and every day I've done the same filthy things. I understand now that such men as I need a blow, a blow of destiny to catch them with a noose, and bind them by a force from without'" (IX, ix). Because he is guilty of having wanted his father's death, even though he did not kill him, Dmitri accepts his suffering and hopes to be purified by it. Ivan dreams of becoming the "new man" who steps into the place of God and becomes his own lawgiver. There is in Dostoevsky's scheme of things a "new man" who is born within us when we acknowledge our sinfulness, submit to fate, and heed the voice of the Deity. After two months in prison, Dmitri tells Alyosha, "Brother.... a new man has risen up in me. He was hidden in me, but would never have come to the surface, if it hadn't been for this blow from heaven" (XI, iv).

Dmitri's arrest has a similar effect on Grushenka. She sees her wickedness in tormenting both Fyodor and Dmitri and wishes to share Dmitri's suffering. She falls into one of those illnesses that, in Dostoevsky's works, are at once the sign of intense spiritual conflict and the harbinger of renewal. After five weeks of suffering, during one of which she is unconscious, she emerges "very much changed" (XI, i).

Instead of avariciously pursuing wealth, she is now charitable. She opens her home to Maximov and is compassionate even toward the Poles, whose daily requests for money she never refuses. Her spiritual self is now dominant, but like Dmitri, she is not entirely free of her old personality. There is "scarcely a trace of her former frivolity," but her eyes gleam "with the old vindictive fire" when she is disturbed by her jealousy of Katerina Ivanovna.

The stories of Markel and Dmitri could be seen from Ivan's point of view as examples of absurd suffering: Markel dies prematurely and Dmitri is punished for a crime he did not commit. From Dostoevsky's perspective, these blows of fate are the means by which God manifests his power. They shake men out of their sinful ways and make them aware of spiritual realities. The "victims" themselves embrace their suffering as a source of spiritual rebirth.

The fate of Ilusha is more difficult to justify. We are dealing here not with a sinful man but with an innocent child who is neither being punished for his sins nor reformed by his ordeal. Ilusha seems to be one of those examples of suffering children on which Ivan bases his indictment of God. It is through Ilusha's story, of course, that Dostoevsky responds to Ivan's charges by showing once again, in this most difficult of cases, the spiritual meaning of suffering.

Dostoevsky develops the seed imagery contained in the epigraph in a number of ways. Sin and suffering bring forth spiritual fruit both in those who sin and suffer and in the people around them who are influenced by their example. The memory of his brother Markel is a seed that lies dormant in Zossima while he is being corrupted by the influence of worldly companions but that flowers at the moment of his conversion, when he recalls everything Markel had said. Zossima's example, in turn, is a source of inspiration to Mihail, leading him to make his confession. Dmitri's fate arouses in Kolya a longing for self-sacrifice: "So he will perish an innocent victim! . . . though he is ruined he is happy! . . . Oh, if I, too, could sacrifice myself some day for truth! . . . I should like to die for all humanity" (Epilogue, iii). Such spiritual influences are especially potent when we receive them as children, for as Alyosha explains, "there is nothing higher and stronger and more wholesome and good for life in the future than some good memory, especially a memory of childhood." Ilusha's suffering bears spiritual fruit by providing such a memory to the boys to whom Alyosha is directing these remarks at the end.

When we first encounter Ilusha, Dmitri has humiliated his father; and he is in conflict with his schoolfellows, whose teasing about the incident he cannot tolerate. When he falls ill, however, the children draw around him; and with the help of Alyosha, they become bound both to him and to each other by their loving concern. After the funeral they gather at Ilusha's stone, and Alyosha formulates the meaning that the death of their friend will have for them. They may "grow wicked later on" and "be unable to refrain from a bad action," but their memory of how their love of Illusha united them in a "kind, good feeling" will remain with them and may keep them "from great evil" someday (Epilogue, ii).

Ilusha will live on not only in their memories but also in the afterlife. "Karamazov," cries Kolya, "can it be true what's taught us in religion, that we shall all rise again from the dead and shall live and see each other again, all, Ilusha too?" (Epilogue, iii). "Certainly," Alyosha replies, "we shall all rise again, certainly we shall see each other and shall tell each other with joy and gladness all that has happened!" Death is the seed out of which immortality grows. The novel ends with this triumphant reply to Ivan's indictment of God.

VI. WE ARE RESPONSIBLE FOR ALL

"With my pitiful, earthly, Euclidian understanding, all I know," says Ivan, "is that there is suffering and that there are none guilty" (V, iv). It is Dostoevsky's belief that "every one is really responsible to all men for all men and for everything" (VI, i). This is a spiritual truth that cannot be explained logically but that is grasped intuitively by those who are in touch with their higher selves. Alyosha acts on it without thinking, and Markel, Mihail, Zossima, and Dmitri all come to proclaim it as a result of their conversions.

Dmitri's dream of the babe poses the same questions that lead Ivan to reject God: "Why is the babe poor? Why is the steppe barren? . . . Why are they so dark from black misery? Why don't they feed the babe?" (IX, viii). The suffering of the innocent so heartrendingly symbolized by the weeping of the babe does not move Dmitri to indignation with God but to "a passion of pity" and a desire to "do something for them all," so that "no one should shed tears again from that moment."

Dmitri awakes from this dream "with a new light, as of joy, in his face" and proceeds to accuse himself and to embrace his suffering: "Gentlemen, we're all cruel, we're all monsters, we all make men weep, and mothers, and babes at the breast, but of all, let it be settled here, now, of all I am the lowest reptile!" (IX, ix). It is Dmitri, in fact, who has made Ilusha weep and who bears a heavy responsibility for his death, for Ilusha becomes ill after being hit in the chest by a stone thrown by one of his schoolmates with whom he is fighting as a result of Dmitri's insult to his father. In prison, confronted with the prospect of going to Siberia for a crime he did not commit, Dmitri realizes the full implication of his dream: "It's for the babe I'm going. Because we are all responsible for all. For all the 'babes,' for there are big children as well as little children. All are 'babes.' I go for all, because some one must go for all. . . . I accept it" (XI, iv). This is why Kolya says that though Dmitri is ruined, he is happy.

There is, proclaims Zossima, "only one means of salvation" (VI, iii): to hold ourselves "responsible . . . for all human sins. . . . For . . . every one of us is undoubtedly responsible for all men and everything on earth, not merely through the general sinfulness of creation, but each one personally for all mankind and every individual man" (II, i). This truth cannot be explained rationally, but "as soon as [we] sincerely make [ourselves] responsible for everything and all men, [we shall] see at once that it is really so, and that [we] are to blame for every one and for all things" (VI, iii). Once we see this, our hearts will grow "soft with infinite, universal, inexhaustible love" (II, i). If we deny our own responsibility, we "will end by sharing the pride of Satan and murmuring against God" (VI, iii). This is what happens to Ivan.

Confronted with the reality of evil, then, we must choose between blaming God or blaming ourselves. If we blame God, life will be absurd and we'll be filled with hatred and despair. Blaming ourselves, we'll love God and our fellows and will be filled with spiritual joy. We will seek to relieve human suffering and "will have the power to win over the whole world by love and to wash away the sins of the world with [our] tears" (IV, i).

Because humans are the source of evil, they have the power to eradicate it. This cannot be achieved by the socialistic schemes of the environmental determinists, which are misguided attempts to master fate. It can be accomplished only by the spiritual regeneration of humanity, by the emergence of humility and love as its primary values. It is Alyosha's, Zossima's, and Dostoevsky's dream that such a regeneration is possible. Atheistic humanism will lead human beings to such chaos and despair that they will turn once again to the "purity of God's truth," which has been preserved from olden times by the humble Russian monks (VI, iii). Not only individuals but also humankind as a whole will follow the pattern of sin, suffering, and regeneration. When they are reborn, people will embrace spiritual truths that have been there all along, awaiting "the day and the hour, the month and the year."

VII. FREEDOM VERSUS HAPPINESS

Zossima's vision of humankind's ultimate destiny is Dostoevsky's alternative to the vision of Ivan as embodied in "The Grand Inquisitor." In Ivan's view, the only hope for happiness lies in the establishment of a totalitarian regime that embraces the functions of both church and state, whereas for Dostoevsky, harmony and joy are to be attained through the spiritual regeneration of individuals who freely embrace God's truth. Human happiness is not entirely dependent, however, on the realization of Zossima's dream. Those who in the present state of the world are faithful to spiritual values may be scoffed at by their unregenerate brethren from whose sins they will suffer; but they possess a paradise within that leads them to feel that life is joyful and that they are "in heaven now" (VI, i).

Dostoevsky feels, moreover, that it is better for people to be free and miserable than happy on Ivan's terms. Dostoevsky and Ivan have the same understanding of Christianity. For both it is a religion that compels neither belief nor obedience but that requires a leap of faith and a voluntary submission to the will of God. Ivan feels that Christianity is wrong to give humans a freedom they are not fit to bear and that will doom them to the miseries of doubt and disorder. He rejects the argument that it is better for God to have made people free than to have made them ignorant of good and evil like the beasts of the field. Ivan protests that this freedom costs too much. For Dostoevsky, human freedom and dignity are well worth the price of happiness. He tries to show us through Ivan's very words how right Christ was to have rejected the various means of compelling obedience and belief and how demeaning it is to be deprived of freedom.

Instead of seeing human beings as possessed of a spiritual faculty that rises above their earthly natures and gives them the ability to make unconditioned choices according to eternal principles, Ivan sees his fellows as "feeble, unruly, incomplete, empirical creatures created in jest" (V, v) who must be disciplined like little children if they are to be made happy. "This question," Dostoevsky wrote to his editor, "is posed in the section: 'Do you, future saviors of mankind, feel contempt or respect for mankind?'" (Wasiolek 1967, 4).

CHAPTER 8

IVAN: CHARACTER STRUCTURE AND BELIEFS

1. INTRODUCTION

THERE HAVE BEEN MANY BRILLIANT DISCUSSIONS OF IVAN KARAMAZOV'S thematic significance, but little attention has been paid to the richness of Dostoevsky's mimetic portrait of this character. There is a great deal of psychological detail that looms very large when we approach Ivan as an imagined human being and try to understand his motivations. All of the brothers, including Smerdyakov, have terrible childhoods that lead them to feel unsafe, unloved, and unvalued in a chaotic and threatening world; and they develop defensive strategies to cope with their injuries, resentments, and anxieties. Their strategies vary because of differences in their situations and temperaments, but all are profoundly affected by their father's mistreatment of them. Three of the brothers are full of murderous rage, while Alyosha develops a radical defense against feeling hurt and angry that is similar to that of Sonya Marmeladov.

While all of the brothers are splendidly portrayed, Ivan and Alyosha are the most complex, and I shall concentrate on them. They are interesting to consider together because their psychological differences give rise to such contrasting responses. In this chapter, I shall discuss Ivan's defenses and inner conflicts and the ways in which they influence his thoughts and relationships. In the next two chapters, I shall examine how the breakdown of his defense system leads to his involvement in the murder of his father and his psychological collapse. The concluding chapters will focus on Alyosha and his relationship with Father Zossima.

II. Detachment

We do not know much about Ivan's childhood, but what we do know is highly significant. Upon his mother's death when he is seven, he and Alyosha are "completely forgotten and abandoned by their father"(I, iii), as their half-brother Dmitri had been. While their mother was alive, she was abused by their father; after her death, they are looked after by Grigory for three months. Then they are found, "unwashed and dirty," by the general's widow who had raised their mother and are taken away. When she dies soon after, leaving the boys 1,000 roubles each, they are cared for by her principal heir, Yefim Petrovitch Plenov, a benevolent man who educates them at his own expense. He is particularly fond of Alyosha, who lives as one of his family for a long time, but he is also kind to Ivan.

Ivan early displays "a brilliant and unusual aptitude for learning" (I, iii), and Yefim Petrovitch sends him to a gymnasium at the age of thirteen, arranging for him to board with "a celebrated teacher." Yefim is "captivated by the idea that the boy's genius should be trained by a teacher of genius." Neither Yefim nor the teacher is alive when Ivan enters the university, and Ivan has not yet received his inheritance, so he is short of money for the first two years and is forced to support himself. He does so by giving lessons and writing for newspapers. He has been a student of natural science, but it is not clear what career he is pursuing when he comes to visit his father, partly at Dmitri's request, at the age of twenty-four.

Whereas Alyosha is at ease about being supported by Yefim Petrovitch, Ivan is "bitterly conscious" from childhood "of living at the expense of his benefactor" (I, iv). When he is ten years old, he realizes that they are "living not in their own home but on other people's charity, and that their father [is] a man of whom it [is] disgraceful to speak" (I, iii). Feeling humiliated by his dependent position and his father's evil reputation, he seeks to restore his pride by his academic achievements. When he enters the university and is in need of money, he does "not even attempt to communicate with his father, perhaps from pride, from contempt for him, or perhaps from his cool common sense, which told him that from such a father he would get no real assistance." He has felt from an early age that there is no one out there to love, value, and protect him, that he cannot depend on anyone and needs to be self-sufficient. As a boy he is "morose and reserved, though far from timid"; as an adult he is isolated and detached. Despite his appearance of self-possession, he is a troubled, unhappy person who is "often . . . depressed" (V, vi).

The action of the novel is set in motion by the coming together of the Karamazov brothers at their birthplace. It seems strange to the townspeople that a young man as learned, proud, and cautious as Ivan "should suddenly visit such an infamous house and a father who had ignored him all his life" (I, iii). Ivan has been living with his father for two months, however, and they are "on the best possible terms." Ivan hates and loathes his father, but he has distanced himself from his feelings and seems able to have a cordial relationship with him. During the painful scene in Father Zossima's cell, Alyosha is on the verge of tears. He had rested his hopes on Ivan, "who alone had such influence on his father" that he could have checked his unruly behavior, but his brother sits "quite unmoved, with downcast eyes, apparently waiting with interest to see how it would end, as though he had nothing to do with it" (II, ii). After the scene, Miüsov is outraged by Ivan's indifference to what has occurred, while he himself is humiliated by Fyodor's buffoonery, though he is only a distant connection. He looks at Ivan "with hatred" because he is going to the Father Superior's dinner "as though nothing had happened" (II, vi). Ivan refuses to take responsibility for anyone else and insists that he is not his brother's keeper.

Ivan attracts wide notice by his article on the position of the ecclesiastical courts, a strange topic for an atheist. His argument that "the Church ought to include the whole State" (II, v) is conducted in such a way that the article is applauded by churchmen and secularists alike. When the article becomes known in the local monastery, the monks are "completely bewildered by it" (I, iii). "Some sagacious persons opined," says the narrator, "that the article was nothing but an impudent satirical burlesque." No doubt they are correct. Ivan's playing with ideas he doesn't take seriously and the elusiveness of his position are manifestations of his detachment.

Even when he is expressing ideas that he does take seriously, Ivan treats them lightly. He tells Alyosha that after Christ kissed the Grand Inquisitor, the old man adhered to his position. "'And you with him, you too?' cried Alyosha, mournfully" (V, v). Ivan laughs at this: "Why, it's all nonsense, Alyosha. It's only a senseless poem of a senseless student. . . . Why do you take it so seriously? Surely you don't suppose I am going straight off to the Jesuits, to join the men who are correcting His work? *Good Lord, it's no business of mine*" (emphasis added). Ivan has no intention of becoming involved in human affairs and trying to carry out his ideas in real life. He lives inside of his head and experiences his triumphs there. Indeed, Ivan seems to have little connection with his fellow human beings. Alyosha yearns for a response from him, but Ivan remains aloof: "There has been a continual look of expectation in your eyes, and I can't endure that. That's how it is that I've kept away from you" (V, iii). Ivan doesn't expect anything from anyone, and he doesn't want anyone to expect anything from him. He finally tells Alyosha that he wants to be friends with him, "for I have no friends and want to try it"; but he waits until the day before his departure to approach his brother. "I want to get to know you once for all," he tells Alyosha, "and I want you to know me. And then to say good-bye. I believe it's always best to get to know people just before leaving them." Ivan can get close to another person only if it is to be a fleeting experience. Even when he is trying to connect with Alyosha, he cannot help being condescending, calling him a "little fellow" and a "little man." Moreover, their conversation in the tavern consists mostly of an attack on Alyosha's beliefs, as Ivan rejects God's universe and narrates his prose poem on the Grand Inquisitor.

Ivan is unhappy with the outcome of their meeting. As they are about to part, he expresses his frustration: "I thought that going away from here I have you at least . . . but now I see that there is no place for me even in your heart, my dear hermit. The formula, 'all is lawful,' I won't renounce—will you renounce me for that?" (V, vi). Alyosha responds by kissing Ivan on the lips as Christ had kissed the Grand Inquisitor. As a result of this gesture, the brothers part friends, but Alyosha runs to the monastery to be saved from Ivan by Father Zossima, and Ivan is angry with himself. He is vexed "at having failed to express himself, especially with such a being as Alyosha, on whom his heart had certainly been reckoning." He has expressed himself brilliantly, of course; but he has frightened Alyosha rather than gotten close to his brother, as at least part of him had wanted to do. Ivan is also vexed at having violated his taboo against opening himself to other people. Hitherto he has "been silent with the whole world and not deigned to speak," but now he has let someone else see his thoughts. He has been seduced by his needs for intimacy and self-expression, which he has always tried to suppress. Because he has not been as self-contained and reserved as he would like to be, he has exposed himself to disappointment. After he parts from Alyosha, he sadly reflects that he will "again be as solitary as ever."

Ivan's sense of isolation is intensified by the fact that he has just terminated his relationship with Katerina Ivanovna. Ivan has a craving for love that gets the better of him at times, and he has come to town partly out of a desire to be near Katerina. He is in love with Katerina and he feels that she loves him; but he realizes that she has a compulsive need to restore her injured pride by behaving nobly toward Dmitri however badly he treats her, and he concludes that she will devote her life to this project. Indeed, he may have been drawn to Katerina by the fact that she was committed to another man. He could have the experience of loving and being loved without the danger of becoming permanently involved in an intimate relationship.

Ivan's break with Katerina contributes to his sense of loneliness, but it also satisfies the need for freedom that is so important to the detached side of his personality. When Alyosha finds him dining alone in the tavern, Ivan says that he was thinking of ordering champagne "to celebrate [his] first hour of freedom. Tfoo! It's been going on nearly six months, and all at once, I've thrown it off" (V, iii). He had roared with laughter after he left Katerina that morning, and Alyosha observes that he seems "very merry about it now." "But how could I tell," says Ivan, "that I didn't care for her a bit! Ha-ha! It appears after all I didn't." He is enormously relieved that he is not in the grip of a powerful emotion over which he has no control, that he is not deeply distressed after all by his parting from Katerina. He had been afraid of being trapped in a hopeless situation and "could never have guessed how easy it would be to put an end to it." Ivan says it may take Katerina fifteen or twenty years to find out that she loves him rather than Dmitri but that it is "better so," for he "can simply go away for good." Katerina's obsession with Dmitri makes it much easier for Ivan to extricate himself from an uncomfortable intimacy. He invites Alyosha to join him in drinking to his freedom: "Ah, if only you knew how glad I am!"

III. ANGER AND AGGRESSION

During Ivan's final interview with Smerdyakov, the valet astutely observes, "you mind most of all about living in undisturbed comfort, without having to depend on anyone—that's what you're most about" (X, vii). Ivan's detachment may be what he is most about, but there are other sides of his personality that are in conflict with his primary defense and that must be reconciled with it.

There is a great deal of anger and aggression in Ivan that he must find a way to satisfy while maintaining a safe distance from his emotions and refraining from acting them out. He is full of rage and contempt toward his father and longs to avenge his injuries, but he represses these feelings during the first two months of his visit. The emergence of his fury under the influence of Dmitri and Smerdyakov destroys his precarious equilibrium and precipitates his psychological crisis. I shall examine these developments in the next chapter. Before his bitterness and wrath begin to affect his actions, they manifest themselves in his mental life: in his wish for his father's death, his preoccupation with the injustices done to children, his arraignment of God, and his fascination with human cruelty.

Ivan manages the conflict between his aggressive impulses and his need to remain detached by experiencing vicarious gratification when others do what he would like to do himself. He says that he'll always defend his father but reserves the right to wish for his death. Rakitin perceptively observes to Alyosha, "some murderous conflict may well come to pass from all this, and that's what your brother Ivan is waiting for. It would suit him down to the ground" (II, vii). During Ivan's second visit to Smerdyakov, shortly before Dmitri's trial, the valet says, "As for the murder, you couldn't have done that and didn't want to, but as for wanting someone else to do it, that was just what you did want" (XI, vii). Smerdyakov is correct on all points. Ivan did not want to commit the murder himself and could not have done it because that would have violated his need to remain uninvolved, but he did want someone else to kill his father.

Ivan's rage with his father also takes the form of collecting stories about the sufferings of children. If children "suffer horribly on earth," it must be "for their father's sins," but "the innocent must not suffer for another's sins, and especially such innocents" (V, iv). Ivan feels that as a child he had to suffer for his father's sins, and he is outraged at the injustice. Adults have "eaten the apple" and are "disgusting and unworthy of love," so their suffering is less unfair; but up to the age of seven children are innocent and deserving of affection. They are different from grown-up people, "as it were, of a different species." We should note that it was during his first seven years, while his mother was still alive, that Ivan was exposed to his father's vile behavior; after that he was abandoned and never given a thought. Ivan identifies with the victims in the stories he has collected about cruelty to children and is indignant with God, if he exists, on their behalf. God should have been a benevolent father but instead has created an absurd and hideous universe. Ivan cannot forgive his sufferings as a child, and he does not want to be reconciled with those responsible. He strengthens his indictment of the powers that be by invoking extreme cases of inhumanity. The severity of the suffering of the children in his stories and his murderous feelings toward his father suggest the magnitude of his feelings of injury. Although his mistreatment appears to have been mild compared with the horrors he describes, he *feels* terribly abused. His stories are a kind of objective correlative of his sense of how badly he has been victimized. If there is a transcendent moral order that he will understand some day and that will reconcile him to the torture of innocents, he wants no part of it but would rather hold onto his indignation and sense of injustice. He has other motives for returning the ticket, as we shall see, but the intensity of his bitterness is an important one.

Ivan seems to identify not only with the children who suffer horribly on earth but also with their tormentors. He tells Alyosha that he is "awfully fond of children" (V, iv), and it is clear that he feels genuine outrage on their behalf; but he observes that "cruel people, the violent, the rapacious, the Karamazov's are sometimes very fond of children." Ivan is a Karamazov, of course. He also says that the "historical pastime" of people of his nationality "is the direct satisfaction of inflicting pain." The lines in Nekrassov "describing how a peasant lashes a horse on the eyes" are "peculiarly Russian," he proclaims.

As Ivan recites his tales of horror to Alyosha, he makes no effort to separate himself from the tormentors. The "love of torturing children is a peculiar characteristic of many people," he explains (V, iv). "To all other types of humanity these torturers behave mildly and benevolently, like cultivated and humane Europeans, but they are very fond of tormenting children." It is just the defenselessness of children "that tempts the tormentor, just the angelic confidence of the child who has no refuge and no appeal, that sets his vile blood on fire. In every man, of course, a demon lies hidden—the demon of rage, the demon of lustful heat at the screams of the tortured victim, the demon of lawlessness let off the chain." If this demon lies hidden in every man, it also lies hidden in Ivan. Indeed, Ivan seems to be defending himself against self-hatred by ascribing his own sadistic tendencies to everyone. Ivan seems to be both condemning the behavior he is describing and confessing his own propensity toward it. He understands that children are the targets of cruelty because they are helpless. People who are full of rage at their own mistreatment in childhood can satisfy the impulse to do unto others what has been done to them, especially in relation to the small and the weak, now that they are adults. It is a psychological commonplace in our time, though it was not in Dostoevsky's, that those who were abused in childhood often become abusers themselves.

I am not suggesting, of course, that Ivan abuses children. He is too aloof from human relationships and too immobilized to do that. He satisfies the sadistic side of his personality in a characteristically detached way, by collecting stories about horrible cruelties inflicted on children and vicariously enjoying the screams of the victims. He is a voyeur who likes to see other people acting out the desires he has suppressed in himself. This does not negate the fact that he also feels great pity for the children and indignation with their tormentors. He is full of contradictions.

The most striking evidence of Ivan's sadistic tendencies is his response late in the novel to Lise's enjoyment of the story of a four-year-old child being crucified. She tells Alyosha that she has read about the trial of a Jew who cut off the child's fingers, nailed him to a wall, and looked on in admiration while the moaning child took four hours to die (XI, iii). Lise says, "That's nice!" She is full of sorrow and pity for the child and also of delight. After she reads the story, she shakes "with sobs all night. I kept fancying how the little thing cried and moaned (a child of four understands, you know)." She likes to imagine, however, that it was she who crucified the boy: "He would hang there moaning and I would sit opposite him eating pineapple compote. I am awfully fond of pineapple compote." All the time she was sobbing, she tells Alyosha, "the thought of pineapple compote haunted me." In the morning, she writes to Ivan, asking him to visit: "He came and I suddenly told him all about the child and the pineapple compote. *All* about it, *all*, and said that it was nice. He laughed and said it really was nice." Lise is afraid that now Ivan despises her, but Alyosha assures her that he does not: "No, for perhaps he believes in the pineapple compote himself." "Yes, he does believe in it," says Lise, "with flashing eyes."

IV. SEARCH FOR GLORY

Collecting stories about the horrible suffering of children has many functions for Ivan. It feeds his self-pity, expresses his rage toward father figures, and confirms his sense of the vileness of human nature and the unfairness of life. It provides a vicarious satisfaction of his sadistic impulses, a way of enjoying the exercise of power and the infliction of pain that is compatible with his primary defense of detachment.

It serves other of Ivan's needs as well. Ivan cannot bear the idea of being coerced, and his indignation on behalf of tortured children justifies his returning the ticket should God exist and ultimately prove to be just in a way that transcends our human understanding. His rejection of God's universe enables him to preserve his freedom and independence. It is also a means of affirming his moral values. Like many who have been badly treated in childhood, Ivan has a highly developed sense of unfairness, of how different things are from the way they ought to be. He refuses to give up his conception of justice and condemns the order of things for failing to correspond to it, holding his values to be superior to those of the Creator, if he exists. Moreover, since there is no justice perhaps there is no God; and if God does not exist, Ivan can occupy the foremost place himself. Ivan's rejection of God as either immoral or nonexistent because of the suffering of children is an essential component of his search for glory.

Having been abandoned by his father, Ivan tries to protect himself against further injury by restricting his wishes and looking for little from other people. At the same time, however, he has "great hopes, and great—too great—expectations from life" (V, vi). Because he is so detached, his aspirations remain nebulous: he "could not have given any definite account of his hopes, his expectations, or even his desires." He emerges from childhood with the shaky sense of worth that is inevitable in a child who has been neglected, abandoned, and forgotten. His brilliant aptitude for learning is recognized and encouraged, however, and this enables him to develop a compensatory sense of himself as a superior person. His intellectual abilities give him a basis for great hopes and expectations, but his need to keep a safe distance from life makes it difficult for him to envision how his yearning for preeminence can be satisfied. He does not aspire to be another Napoleon, like Raskolnikov. Rather, his search for glory takes place in the realm of the mind, through an arraignment or denial of God and fantasies of mastery and power, like his poem on the Grand Inquisitor.

Ivan accepts the idea that God exists and is just in a way that transcends our understanding only for the sake of argument, to make an ethical objection to his ways. The existence of such a God would not reconcile him to innocent suffering, which would still be unacceptable in human terms. Ivan sees himself as a morally superior being whose values are better than God's. He is even ready to sacrifice his salvation in order to preserve his conception of justice and his protest on behalf of humanity.

But Ivan doesn't really believe that God exists. The incompatibility of the order of things with his sense of justice leads him to conclude that in this absurd universe there is neither a deity nor an afterlife. He then makes the move that I have already shown to be illogical: he proclaims that if there is no God "everything [is] lawful, even cannibalism" (II, vi). First he argues that there is no God because the order of things is unfair; then he concludes that everything is permitted because there is no God. Is there is no basis for objecting to the suffering of innocent children unless there is a God? What has happened to the values in the name of which Ivan has arraigned or denied God to begin with, to the conception of justice he returns his ticket in order to preserve? What is going on here?

A partial explanation is provided, I believe, by Ivan's search for glory. If God exists, Ivan sees himself as morally superior to the deity. But if God does not exist, his glory is greater still. His thinking is most fully revealed late in the novel by the devil that appears to him in hallucinations and in a dream. Whatever we make of his devil from a psychiatric perspective, it is clear that he lets us know what was going on in Ivan's mind before his psychological breakdown. Once we "destroy the idea of God in man," says this side of Ivan, the old morality "will fall of itself . . . and everything will begin anew" (XI, ix). Because of the "inveterate stupidity" of human beings, "this cannot come about for at least a thousand years," but "every one who recognises the truth even now may legitimately order his life as he pleases, on the new principles. In that sense, 'all things are lawful' for him." Even if the new period never comes about, "the new man may well become the man-god, even if he is the only one in the whole world, and promoted to his new position, he may lightheartedly overstep all the barriers of the old morality of the old slave-man, if necessary. There is no law for God. Where God stands, the place is holy. Where I stand will be the foremost place."

By saying that everything is permitted if there is no God, Ivan lays claim to a God-like position for himself. Everything is permitted in the sense that there are no absolutes to which he must submit. It is he who will determine what is lawful. Like Raskolnikov, he distinguishes between ordinary people, who are stupidly submissive, and clever people like himself, who understand their true position. Unlike Raskolnikov, however, Ivan does not seek to convince himself of his superior status by overstepping the old morality. His search for glory does not take place in the world but only in his mind, in a way that is consistent with his detachment.

By saying that everything is permitted, Ivan is not necessarily abandoning his moral values. Indeed, he has visions of a humanistic utopia. When it finally comes to pass that everyone has denied God, people

> will unite to take from life all it can give, but only for joy and happiness in the present world. Man will be lifted up with a spirit of divine Titanic pride and the man-god will appear. From hour to hour extending his conquest of nature infinitely by his will and his science, man will feel such lofty joy from hour to hour in doing it that it will make up for all his old dreams of the joys of heaven. Every one will know that he is mortal and will accept death proudly and serenely like a god. His pride will teach him that it's useless for him to repine at life's being a moment, and he will love his brother without need of reward. Love will be sufficient only for a moment of life, but the very consciousness of its momentariness will intensify its fire, which now is dissipated in dreams of eternal love beyond the grave. (XI, ix)

Dostoevsky regards this as a foolish and sacrilegious fantasy, and Ivan is embarrassed by these thoughts when they are repeated by his devil, but they reflect major components of his personality. In this vision, the death of God leads not to anarchy, chaos, and cannibalism but to unity and brotherly love. The human community will not be destroyed because people no longer believe in immortality; instead, love will be intensified and earthly joys will be relished all the more. Ivan's craving for glory is fulfilled here in a variety of ways; people like him will enjoy God-like power, display God-like love, and possess a God-like serenity.

This fantasy is compatible with Ivan's protest against the suffering of innocent children, but he does not always find the denial of God to have such benign implications. As we have seen, having rejected God's existence or goodness in the name of the human demand for compassion and justice, he then denies the values that led to that rejection. During the meeting in Father Zossima's cell, Miüsov reports that five days earlier Ivan had declared that "if there had been any love on earth hitherto, it was not owing to a natural law, but simply because men have believed in immortality" (II, vi). Without a belief in immortality and God, nothing "would be immoral." This position is not compatible with either Ivan's moral indignation or his utopian dream.

Even less compatible is Ivan's assertion that for those who do "not believe in God or immortality, the moral law of nature must immediately be changed into the exact opposite of the former religious law" (II, vi). Father Païssy agrees that "there is no virtue if there is no immortality," that crime is "the inevitable and the most rational outcome of his position for every infidel." It makes sense that he should do so in view of his religious beliefs, and it also makes sense for Father Zossima to agree. I fail to see, however, the rational basis for *Ivan's* positing that in the absence of God crime is lawful, inevitable, and honorable. What would the innocent victims, for whom Ivan is an advocate, have to say?

There may be a psychological basis for Ivan's illogical conclusion. We have seen that he at once identifies with suffering children, on whose behalf he is morally indignant, and seems to take a sadistic delight in contemplating their agonies. There is a dark side of Ivan that he describes as demonic. He is a bitter, angry, vindictive man who is full of suppressed violence. He takes a dim view of the human condition and an even dimmer view of human nature. He denies the human capacity for love (although sometimes he affirms it), and he sees everyone as bristling with nastiness the way he is himself. His contention that in the absence of God crime is lawful, inevitable, and honorable may be a way of justifying the side of his nature of which he is most ashamed, of defending himself against self-hatred by claiming that his darker impulses are natural and universal. His inconsistencies and self-contradictions are manifestations of his psychological conflicts, and his lapses in logic may also be products of his inner divisions.

Or, they may be a mark of manipulation, the result of Dostoevsky's attributing to Ivan beliefs that show the evils of atheism because that is what he wants Ivan to illustrate. For the most part Ivan seems a brilliant mimetic creation, but I cannot help wondering if sometimes Dostoevsky's ideological agenda intrudes upon his psychological portrait.

V. THE GRAND INQUISITOR

As I observed in the last chapter, "The Grand Inquisitor" serves three distinct functions in *The Brothers Karamazov*. It is part of Ivan's assault on religion, part of Dostoevsky's refutation of Ivan's blasphemies, and part of Dostoevsky's psychological portrait of Ivan's character. I have discussed the first two functions; it is time to consider the third.

Ivan has composed "The Grand Inquisitor" in his mind, but he has never written it down or shared it with anyone until his conversation with Alyosha on the day before his departure. Its recitation is evoked by the dynamic of the conversation and of the interaction between the brothers.

Ivan has very mixed feelings toward Alyosha. When he expresses a love of life in spite of logic, Alyosha says that he is half-way to salvation, for it is only by loving life that we can understand its meaning. You are "trying to save me," replies Ivan, "but perhaps I am not lost!" (V, iii). Later, however, after he has proclaimed that he cannot accept God's world, Ivan says that he has "led the conversation to [his] despair," perhaps because he wants "to be healed" by Alyosha. Ivan feels superior to Alyosha, treats him with condescension, and attacks his beliefs; but at the same time, he wants Alyosha's friendship and hopes that his brother can somehow alleviate his despair. He has powerful moral, intellectual, and psychological reasons for denying God's existence or his justice if he exists, but he is distressed by the sense of the absurdity of life he experiences as a result. "I must have justice," he tells Alyosha, "or I will destroy myself" (V, iv). Ivan envies Alyosha's faith, which would satisfy his need for meaning and his appetite for clarity if only he could share it.

This is not, however, his dominant response to his brother. When he says that he has led the conversation to his despair, Alyosha asks him to explain why he doesn't "accept the world" (V, iii). "Dear little brother," Ivan replies, "I don't want to corrupt you or to turn you from your stronghold, perhaps I want to be healed by you." Part of him wants to be healed, but he is on the attack throughout the conversation and clearly wants to turn Alyosha from his stronghold, to undermine his beliefs.

One of Ivan's motives seems to be competition with Father Zossima. He gets Alyosha to agree that the general who set his hounds on the child deserves to be shot and is delighted by his brother's "pale, twisted smile" when he reluctantly gives his assent: "You're a pretty monk! So there's a little devil sitting in your heart, Alyosha Karamazov!" (V, iv). When Alyosha protests that "what [he] said was absurd," Ivan is more delighted still. He proclaims that "the world stands on absurdities" and that he is determined not to cancel them out by going beyond the facts. "'Why are you trying me?' Alyosha crie[s], with sudden distress. 'Will you say what you mean at last?'" "You are dear to me," Ivan replies, "I don't want to let you go, and I won't give you up to your Zossima."

Another reason why Ivan wants to break down Alyosha's beliefs is that he finds them threatening: they endanger his search for glory by dismissing the importance of reason, in which he has invested his pride, and by consigning human beings to a subordinate position. Alyosha's version of human nature is contrary to Ivan's and makes him feel like a monster because of his own aggressive tendencies. He is full of hostility and rage and has sadistic and retaliatory impulses. He wants his suffering to be avenged, and he desires the death of his father. He needs to feel that all humans are like this and that they are incapable of Christ-like forgiveness.

At the same time, Ivan is genuinely compassionate, is horrified by human cruelty, and recoils from the thought of parricide. There is a conflict in him, as there is in Raskolnikov, between the side of him that holds everything to be lawful and the kind, caring, conscientious part of his nature. His utopian vision testifies to his wish to believe in a natural human capacity for brotherhood and love. To Ivan, Alyosha represents a suppressed side of himself, one that makes him uncomfortable with his vindictive and cynical attitudes and that will trouble him profoundly after his father's murder. He denigrates Alyosha and his beliefs in order to reduce his inner conflicts and alleviate his self-condemnation. His effort to sway Alyosha is motivated in part by a need to reinforce his own convictions.

Ivan's recitation of "The Grand Inquisitor" follows on his stories of the horrible sufferings of children, such as those of the boy who is torn apart by the general's hounds and the five-year-old girl who is punished for soiling her bed by having her face smeared and mouth filled with excrement and being shut up in a freezing privy all night. Ivan cannot imagine a just order in which such suffering can be atoned for and the torturers forgiven. "From love for humanity," he does not want a higher harmony in which he will be forced to relinquish his indignation, and he returns his entrance ticket while he is still alive. "Is there in the whole world," he asks Alyosha, "a being who would have the right to forgive and could forgive?" Alyosha replies that Christ is such a being, and Ivan offers his prose poem on the Grand Inquisitor as a response.

* * *

Although "The Grand Inquisitor" is presented as a rejoinder to Alyosha's invocation of Christ, Ivan had composed it in his mind earlier, and it reflects his ongoing preoccupations and inner conflicts. It is above all, I think, a fantasy of being an extraordinary man, of occupying the foremost place. It is part of Ivan's search for glory.

At the end of the poem, Alyosha exclaims, "Your inquisitor does not believe in God, that's his secret!" (V, v). Ivan immediately agrees: "It's perfectly true that that's the whole secret, but isn't that suffering, at least for a man like that, who has wasted his whole life in the desert and yet could not shake off his incurable love of humanity? In his old age he reached the clear conviction that nothing but the advice of the great dread spirit could build up any tolerable sort of life for the feeble, unruly, 'incomplete empirical creatures created in jest.'" The inquisitor was once a believer who had "eaten roots in the desert and made frenzied efforts to subdue his flesh to make himself free and perfect." He came to realize, however, that most people cannot live up to the Christian ideal, and out of love for humanity, "he turned back and joined the clever people," the atheists. As an unbeliever, the inquisitor joins those who have corrected Christ's work by devising a religion that is adapted to human nature and the human condition. His religion conceals the absence of God and an afterlife from its followers, deceiving them on their journey to death so that "the poor blind creatures may at least on the way think themselves happy."

Throughout his speech, the Grand Inquisitor describes the mass of human beings in strongly negative terms. They are vicious, worthless, rebellious, sinful, ignoble, impotent, base, childlike, vile, and weak. The inquisitor's main criticism of Christ is that he thought "too highly of men" and showed them "too much respect" (V, v). He would have loved humans more had he asked less of them.

The greatest burden Christ placed on human beings was freedom of faith and of choice. "Thou didst desire man's free love, that he should follow Thee freely, enticed and taken captive by Thee. In place of the rigid ancient law, man must hereafter with a free heart decide for himself what is good and what is evil, having only Thy image before him as his guide" (V, v). But freedom is unbearable to humans, however much they may prize it. They prefer "peace, and even death, to freedom of choice in the knowledge of good and evil." Christ, however, made their freedom greater than ever.

The Grand Inquisitor's objective is to facilitate the happiness of human beings by ridding them of this dreadful burden while persuading them that they are perfectly free. In order to achieve this, he will give the feeble, unruly creatures what they need by following the path rejected by Christ when Satan offered it. Christ refused to turn stones into bread; but give humans bread and they will be "like a flock of sheep, grateful and obedient" (V, v). They cannot have both freedom and enough to eat, "for never, never will they be able to share between them." Humans need more than bread, of course; they also need an indisputable object of worship and someone to keep their conscience. The religion over which the inquisitor presides has provided these things by founding itself on miracle, mystery, and authority, something Christ had declined to do. Once more subjects of an authoritarian, rule-bound religion like that of the Old Testament, "men rejoiced that they were again led like sheep, and that the terrible gift that had brought them such suffering was, at last, lifted from their hearts." In addition to bread and an object of worship and obedience, humans also crave universal unity; here too Satan showed the way by displaying to Christ "all the kingdoms of the earth." The inquisitor and his predecessors have taken "Rome and the sword of Caesar, and proclaimed [themselves] sole rulers of the earth." Their power is being challenged, but when they ultimately triumph, they will "plan the universal happiness of man."

It is not difficult to see how Ivan's poem is "in praise of Jesus, not in blame of Him," as Alyosha says (V, v). Deprived of freedom, human beings lose their dignity, and the happiness they gain in exchange is that of "pitiful children." "The Grand Inquisitor" is clearly part of Dostoevsky's response to Ivan. My question here is, What functions does it serve for Ivan? Does it make sense as an expression of his psychology?

I think we can see "The Grand Inquisitor" as part of Ivan's search for glory, which is carried out in his mind. The fantasy expresses his sense of the superiority of clever atheists like the inquisitor and himself to the docile, pathetic believers who constitute the mass of mankind. The clever people know there is no God and no immortality, and they can live with these truths, whereas most people cannot do without the deceptions of religion. They regard other humans with enormous condescension, and the people they despise "will marvel at [them] and look on [them] as gods, because [they] are ready to endure the freedom which they have found so dreadful" (V, v). They are heroic figures who take on themselves the awesome task of creating values and making choices in a universe that is devoid of meaning. As

Victor Terras observes, there is "a basic emotive undercurrent" present in "The Grand Inquisitor": "the weak, lowly wretched masses of humanity and the wise and mighty few. A steady stream of abuse is heaped upon the former, a steady flow of self-congratulatory adulation descends on the latter. The former are ultimately reduced to so much 'cattle' and 'geese,' while the latter become gods'" (1998, 124).

"The Grand Inquisitor" is a fantasy of power as well as of superiority. The clever people are masters of the multitude. When Christ reappears in Seville, the townsfolk recognize him and are drawn to him with love; however, the inquisitor orders the guards to arrest him: "And such is his power, so completely are the people cowed into submission and trembling obedience" that they readily allow Christ to be taken away (V, v); then they bow "down to the earth, like one man, before the old inquisitor." The inquisitor has power not only over the people but also over their deity, thus enhancing his status as a god-like being. He threatens to burn Christ at the stake the next day and tells him that "the very people who have today kissed Thy feet, tomorrow at the faintest sign from me will rush to heap up the embers of Thy fire."

The inquisitor envisions having complete control of his subjects, both physical and mental. He tells Christ that having learned "the value of complete submission," the people "will crawl fawning to our feet" (V, v). When they realize that they cannot have both freedom and bread, they will give up their freedom and say, "Make us your slaves, but feed us." They "will be awe-struck before us, and will be proud at our being so powerful and clever, that we have been able to subdue such a turbulent flock of thousands of millions." They will regard their rulers as saviors, have no secrets from them, and look to them for permission to sin.

"The Grand Inquisitor" reflects Ivan's sadistic tendencies in its references to the burning of heretics, but it expresses even more the side of him that professes love for mankind. Christ wants human beings to be free, but freedom is incompatible with happiness, and the inquisitor wants them to be happy. If they are to be happy, they must relinquish their freedom to the inquisitor; like Hamlet, he explains that he must be cruel only to be kind. He sees those who are like himself as enlightened despots who suffer for the sake of their subjects: "For only we, who guard the mystery, shall be unhappy. There will be thousands of millions of happy babes, and a hundred thousand sufferers who have taken upon themselves the curse of the knowledge of good and evil" (V, v). With a contemptuous benevolence, he will provide his pitiful dependents with the absolutes they crave.

The inquisitor criticizes Christ for having come "to the elect and for the elect," whereas the inquisitor and his church will save all. He himself had striven to be one of Christ's elect by pursuing moral perfection, but then he awoke and "would not serve madness" (V, v). He "left the proud and went back to the humble, for the happiness of the humble." The inquisitor seems to be deceiving himself here, for he has hardly ceased to be proud.

Like his creator, Ivan, the Grand Inquisitor has conflicting needs. He wants at once to see himself as a benevolent man who is more humane than Christ and to occupy a position of power over the masses that feeds his pride. He is still a member of the elect, but he has redefined the elect not as imitators of Christ but as the clever people who do not believe in God. Although the inquisitor expresses concern for the happiness of the humble, his primary concern seems to be establishing himself as one of the unhappy few. Like Ivan, he says that happiness is a higher value than freedom, but that is a choice he makes for other people rather than for himself. His ability to bear the burden of freedom sets him apart from ordinary folk and is the basis of his claim to dominance. Those whose happiness he serves through his despotic rule are the objects of his scorn.

His fantasy of "The Grand Inquisitor" furnishes Ivan with a number of satisfactions. It feeds his sense of superiority and provides an imagined fulfillment of his cravings for power, glory, and preeminence. In it, clever people like himself are both righteously cruel and grandly benevolent and are objects of worship and awe. In the absence of God, they step into the foremost place themselves, exercise their existential freedom, and become the creators of values and laws. Their freedom is a burden from which they greatly suffer, but their rewards are also great. Instead of the childlike happiness of believers, they enjoy the pleasures of domination and of being venerated as gods.

Ivan's fantasy serves his needs in a way that is consistent with his detachment. It neither activates his conflicts nor involves him with the lives of other people. As we have seen, when Alyosha expresses concern about his adhering to the inquisitor's ideas, Ivan dismisses his recitation as "only a senseless poem" and says that correcting Christ's work is "no business" of his (V, v). He shares his poem with Alyosha as part of his attempt to get closer to his brother and to win him away from Father Zossima. It was bound to have the opposite result, but

Ivan is blind to this reality because he is carried away by his desires and the urge to express his thoughts at last.

The brothers part on friendly terms, but Alyosha flees back to Zossima, and Ivan feels disappointed and depressed. His depression has less to do with Alyosha, however, than with Smerdyakov, who is waiting for him at home. Ivan is about to give his consent to the murder of his father, an act that is incompatible with his values and his detachment and that precipitates his psychological collapse.

CHAPTER 9

IVAN: BEFORE THE MURDER

1. THE EMERGENCE OF IVAN'S INNER CONFLICTS

AS WE HAVE SEEN, IVAN IS FULL OF INNER CONFLICTS THAT HE MANAGES by being detached from other people and from himself. He does not try to fulfill his needs in actuality but contents himself with vicarious satisfactions and mental maneuvers that give safe expression to the warring facets of his personality. His strategy is working fairly well when we first encounter him in the novel, for he gets along with his father despite his resentments and remains undisturbed when others are upset.

Even at the beginning, however, there are signs that Ivan's detachment has been weakening. He visits his father partly at the request of his brother Dmitri, who hopes that Ivan will mediate between their father and himself. Ivan thus exposes himself to the possibility of becoming embroiled in a violent family quarrel. He comes to visit also because Katerina Ivanovna is staying in the town, and he wants to be near her. This entangles him not only with Katerina but also with Dmitri, to whom Katerina is betrothed. By responding to his brother and pursuing Katerina, Ivan is abandoning his strategy of remaining aloof, independent, and uninvolved in human affairs. His need for intimacy and love surfaces in relation not only to Katerina but also to Alyosha, with whom he wishes to be friends.

What most destabilizes Ivan is the emergence of his anger toward his father. First he allows himself to wish for his father's death, and then he succumbs to the temptation to be revenged on the man he hates by colluding with Smerdyakov. He tries to defend himself against his inner conflicts by suppressing his awareness of what he is doing, but his conflicts erupt after he consents to the murder, precipitating a psychological crisis that threatens to destroy him.

* * *

Ivan tells Alyosha that in every man "a demon lies hidden" (V, iv). This is, among other things, a "demon of rage." The primary object of Ivan's rage is his father, whose neglect, abandonment, and humiliation of him in childhood he deeply resents. Ivan does not express his rage toward his father directly, however; he displaces it onto those who torture children in the stories he collects and onto God with whom Ivan is indignant because he permits such things to happen. In Ivan's world, there is no kind, protective father who is loving and just, either in heaven or on earth. From the time he is taken away as a seven-year-old child until his return at the age of twenty-four, Ivan has kept his distance from his father, both physically and emotionally. He expects nothing from his parent, even when he needs money to continue his education, and he seems not to be consciously aware of his anger. This is what allows him to return home and to be on good terms with his father for the first two months of his visit. But the hidden demon of rage is there, and it gradually manifests itself.

The first visible manifestation occurs after the scandalous scenes in Father Zossima's cell and at the Father Superior's dinner. While Alyosha is deeply distressed by his father's behavior and Miüsov is angry and embarrassed, Ivan seems to be cooly looking on from a position of aloof unconcern. As he and his father are leaving the monastery, Maximov runs alongside Fyodor's coach, asking to be taken along. Fyodor tells him to jump in, but Ivan gives Maximov "a violent punch in the breast and [sends] him flying" (II, viii). Fyodor is shocked, asks Ivan what he is about, and wants to know why he is angry: "'You've talked rot enough. You might rest a bit now,' Ivan snap[s] sullenly." When Fyodor insists that he'll take Alyosha away from the monastery, even though Ivan does not approve, Ivan shrugs "his shoulders contemptuously," stares at the road, and is silent the rest of the way home.

At least two critics have commented on Ivan's brutal behavior toward Maximov, a harmless old man who is succored by Grushenka later in the novel. Joseph Frank suggests that Ivan's "action dramatizes all the pent-up hatred for his father that [he] does not allow himself to express directly" (2002, 581), and Victor Terras observes that this "seemingly trivial incident. . . . starts a pattern" (1998, 120)—presumably that of Ivan becoming more aggressive. Frank is right, I believe, that Ivan's attack on Maximov is a displacement of his anger with his father, which he then expresses more directly through his words, his body language, and his silence.

Ivan's rage and contempt have been there all along, but he has tried to preserve his equilibrium by means of his detachment. His feelings are now beginning to emerge as a result of his close proximity to his father and his exposure to the turbulent emotions of his brothers. His father's withholding of money and pursuit of Grushenka outrage Dmitri, and he verbally attacks him and threatens physical violence. Fyodor's ill treatment of Smerdyakov generates a smoldering resentment in the bastard son that resonates with Ivan, establishing an unspoken connection between them. Even Alyosha stirs up Ivan's loathing of his father, despite his own accepting attitude and apparent lack of anger.

There is an important scene in which Fyodor tells Alyosha and Ivan about his ways of dealing with women, including their mother, his second wife. He says that he insulted her only once, when he tried to "knock [the] mysticism out of her" because she turned him out of her room during the feast of Our Lady:

> "Here," said I, "you see your holy image. Here it is. Here I take it down. You believe it's miraculous, but here, I'll spit on it directly and nothing will happen to me for it!" . . . When she saw it, good Lord! I thought she would kill me. But she only jumped up, wrung her hands, then suddenly hid her face in them, began trembling all over and fell on the floor . . . fell all of a heap. (III, viii; author's ellipses)

As Fyodor is speaking, Alyosha behaves as his mother had done. He jumps up from his seat, wrings his hands, hides his face in them, and falls "back in his chair, shaking all over in an hysterical paroxysm of sudden violent, silent weeping." His mother initially reacted with rage at Fyodor's desecration of her cherished icon. Fyodor says he thought she would kill him. Alyosha initial reaction also seems to be anger at his father's mistreatment of the object of his devotion: "He flushed crimson, his eyes glowed, his lips quivered." Neither Alyosha nor his mother can tolerate their own aggressive feelings, and both become hysterical as they stifle their rage, dramatize their distress, and are torn by inner conflicts.

This scene has a powerful effect on Ivan. Fyodor urges him to get water for Alyosha, as he himself used to do for "the crazy woman" (III, viii). "He's upset about his mother, his mother," he explains. "But she was my mother, too, I believe, his mother. Was she not?" says Ivan, "with uncontrolled anger and contempt." The old man shrinks before Ivan's "flashing eyes," much as he might have shrunk when he thought his wife would kill him. His father's account of his cruel treatment of his mother and Alyosha's intense reaction bring Ivan's buried feelings to the surface and make it impossible for him to control his rage any longer.

At this point Dmitri bursts in, looking for Grushenka. Fyodor rushes to Ivan, screaming in terror: "He'll kill me! He'll kill me! Don't let him get at me!" (III, viii). When Dmitri attacks his father, throwing him on the floor and kicking him in the face, Ivan pulls him away with Alyosha's help and cries, "Madman! You've killed him!" (III, ix). However, after Dmitri departs, Ivan seems to regret his intervention:

> "Damn it all, if I hadn't pulled him away perhaps he'd have murdered him. It wouldn't take much to do for æsop, would it?" whispered Ivan to Alyosha.
> "God forbid!" cried Alyosha.
> "Why should He forbid?" Ivan went on in the same whisper, with a malignant grimace. "One reptile will devour the other. And serve them both right, too."
> Alyosha shuddered.
> "Of course I won't let him be murdered as I didn't just now. Stay here Alyosha, I'll go for a turn in the yard. My head's begun to ache."

Ivan assures Alyosha that he won't let his father be murdered but says that he reserves the right to wish for his death.

After the scenes at the monastery, Fyodor and Ivan are no longer on good terms. Fyodor feels that Ivan despises him, and he pleads with his son not to be angry with "a feeble old man": "I know you don't love me, but don't be angry all the same. You've nothing to love me for" (III, viii). His exposure to the emotions of Dmitri and Alyosha release Ivan's own suppressed feelings, leading him to express them more openly and to wish for his father's demise. He justifies that wish by saying that "all men live so and perhaps cannot help living so," but his inner stress is evident when his head begins to ache. Sensing the change in his son, Fyodor tells Alyosha that he is more afraid of Ivan than he is of Dmitri: "You don't suppose he too came to murder me, do you?" (IV, ii). He says that Ivan is a "scoundrel," which is what Ivan later calls himself.

Ivan's exposure to his father's behavior and his brother's emotions makes it impossible for him to continue to repress or displace his hostility, and he begins to wish for revenge. There is a side of him that feels he ought to protect his father, and he has no intention of doing violence on him himself, but he has become vulnerable to the temptation offered by Smerdyakov. When he succumbs to it, he destroys the precarious equilibrium he had achieved.

ii. Ivan and Smerdyakov

As Ivan returns home after his meeting with Alyosha in the tavern, he is overcome by "insufferable depression" (V, vi). He does not know why he is so depressed and wonders if it is because of the imminent renewal of his solitude, his disappointment in the outcome of his effort to win over his brother, or his loathing for his father's house. When he sees Smerdyakov sitting on a bench at the garden gate, he realizes that it is this man by whom he is oppressed, that upon Alyosha's mention of his encounter with Smerdyakov, he had "felt a sudden twinge of gloom and loathing, which had immediately stirred responsive anger in his heart." Ivan's relationship with Smerdyakov, so crucial to the main action of the novel, is portrayed by Dostoevsky with remarkable subtlety. It is marked by compulsive behavior, self-deception, externalization, and inner conflict. It precipitates the murder of Fyodor and Ivan's subsequent psychological crisis.

Ivan is friendly toward Smerdyakov at first, but then he develops an increasingly intense dislike of him. Initially he takes an interest in Smerdyakov, thinks him original, and discusses philosophical questions with him. Smerdyakov looks up to Ivan as his mentor and is deeply impressed by his contention that everything is lawful. Although Ivan regards Smerdyakov as "a lackey and a mean soul" (III, viii), Smerdyakov's high opinion of him feeds his pride. Ivan's aversion develops when Smerdyakov begins "to betray a boundless . . . and a wounded vanity" (V, vi), thus challenging Ivan's condescending attitude. What irritates Ivan most is a "peculiar revolting familiarity" that Smerdyakov displays toward him. Although he is very respectful, Smerdyakov speaks in a tone that suggests that they have "some kind of compact, some secret between them, that had at some time been expressed on both sides, only known to them and beyond the comprehension of those around them." As Smerdyakov shows this familiarity more and more markedly, Ivan's dislike intensifies. "During the last few days," he has noticed in himself a feeling "almost of hatred for the creature"; and as he approaches Smerdyakov sitting at the garden gate, he wonders "with insufferable irritation" if it is possible "that a miserable, contemptible creature like that can worry [him] so much."

To understand what is going on here, we must look for a moment at Smerdyakov. The son of "stinking Lizaveta" and probably of Fyodor, Smerdyakov is raised by Grigory and Marfa. He is an unfriendly, unsociable, taciturn child who looks "at the world mistrustfully" and is "very fond of hanging cats, and burying them with great ceremony" (III, vi). His sadistic impulses are manifested in adulthood when he induces Illusha to give food with pins in it to a stray dog. Smerdyakov is full of rage and a desire to hurt others as he has been hurt. As the bastard child of "a filthy beggar," he occupies a shameful position; and he is told by the disapproving Grigory that he is "not a human being. You grew from the mildew in the bath-house. That's what you are." Smerdyakov can "never forgive" Grigory "those words." After Grigory teaches him to read the Bible, he asks where light came from on the first day if the sun, moon, and stars were created on the fourth. He is slapped by Grigory for asking such a question, withdraws into his corner, and a week later has his first attack of epilepsy. Fyodor takes an interest in him at this point, and because he is so fastidious about food, he decides to make him his cook. He sends him to Moscow for training, and Smerdyakov returns, still unsociable, to serve as cook and valet. He is very talented in the kitchen, is a shrewd theologian, and has a high opinion of himself.

We can get an idea of Smerdyakov's state of mind from his conversation with Marya Kondratyevna, in what seems to be a courting scene. When Marya compliments him on his cleverness, he replies, "I could have done better than that. I could have known more than that, if it had not been for my destiny from my childhood up" (V, ii). Smerdyakov deeply resents the fact that his birth has made it impossible for him to develop his intellect and defend his honor. "I would have shot a man in a duel," he tells Marya, "if he called me names because I am descended from a filthy beggar and have no father. And they used to throw it in my teeth in Moscow. It had reached them from here, thanks to Grigory Vassilyevitch." What he is saying is that he would have challenged those who insulted him had he been in a position to do so. But he is not. He compares himself with Dmitri, probably his half-brother, who is "lower than any lackey in his behaviour, in his mind, and in his poverty. He doesn't know how to do anything, and yet he is respected by every one." Despite Dmitri's inferiority to him in intelligence and talent, people of high birth treat him as an equal. If Dmitri "were to challenge the son of the first count in the country, he'd fight him. Though in what way is he better than I am?"

Smerdyakov is "ready to burst with rage" when either he or his mother is treated in a demeaning manner. He blames the class structure of his society and tells Marya that he "hate[s] all Russia" and wishes that Napoleon had triumphed in 1812, for then "a clever nation would have conquered a very stupid one and. . . . we should have had quite different institutions" (author's ellipsis). Perhaps he is thinking of the ability of talented men of low birth to rise under Napoleon.

Smerdyakov is bitterly unhappy at the injustice of his lot. He tells Marya that Grigory blames him "for rebelling against [his] birth," but he says, "I would have sanctioned their killing me before I was born that I might not have come into the world at all" (V, ii). This is a very strong statement, suggesting the intensity of Smerdyakov's misery and resentment.

When Ivan comes to visit, Smerdyakov admires him and hopes to receive his approval. Both have been mistreated by father figures, do not believe in God, rely on logical thinking, and look down on others because of their sense of intellectual superiority. When Smerdyakov employs casuistical reasoning to argue that a Russian soldier would not jeopardize his salvation if he renounced Christ in order to avoid being martyred by Turks, Fyodor whispers to Ivan, "He's got this all up for your benefit. He wants you to praise him" (III, vii). Fyodor is right, but Ivan regards Smerdyakov as "a stinking lackey" (V, ii), and Smerdyakov is aware of this. Toward the end of the novel, during their third and last interview, Smerdyakov observes to Ivan, "you've always thought no more of me than if I'd been a fly" (XI, viii). When he then produces a brilliant analysis of Ivan's character, Ivan is struck and says, "You are not a fool." "It was your pride made you think I was a fool," Smerdyakov replies.

We can now begin to understand what is going on between Ivan and Smerdyakov. Smerdyakov has a sense of himself as an exceptionally intelligent and gifted person who has been deprived of opportunities and scorned by others because of his birth. He had hoped to receive recognition from Ivan, but Ivan looks down on him. Hence Smerdyakov displays the wounded vanity to which Ivan has such an aversion. As Ivan's detachment breaks down and his rage toward his father emerges, Smerdyakov begins to behave with a "revolting familiarity." He understands that Ivan has no intention of killing his father himself but that he would like to see someone else do it. Ivan has provided a rationale for the act by proclaiming that everything is lawful, and Smerdyakov feels that Ivan wants him to arrange the murder. Therefore Smerdyakov behaves as though there is a secret compact between them. Smerdyakov's motive, like Ivan's, is a desire to avenge the injustices done to his mother and himself. In addition, Smerdyakov wants enough money to leave his past behind and begin a new life by opening a restaurant in Moscow.

As Ivan's murderous feelings grow stronger, Smerdyakov becomes increasingly familiar. He is enjoying the sense that he and Ivan are on the same level as coconspirators. Ivan's and Smerdyakov's homicidal impulses reinforce each other. Smerdyakov's familiarity is so revolting to Ivan not only because it offends his pride but also because it confronts him with a side of himself from which he recoils. His hatred of Smerdyakov is in part an externalization of his self-loathing, of his revulsion at his own bloodthirsty thoughts.

On returning to his father's house after his conversation with Alyosha, Ivan is overcome "by insufferable depression" (V, vi). He feels that his depression has an "external character"; and when he sees Smerdyakov sitting in the gateway, he realizes that it is he who has triggered it. He is so depressed, I believe, because Smerdyakov activates inner conflicts that cannot be resolved and that threaten him with unbearable guilt. Ivan wishes for the death of his father, but he is appalled by the idea of parricide. He *says* that everything is lawful, but this is only a theoretical position and is not how he *feels*. He has strong human-centered values in the name of which he arraigns God, and he cannot commit crimes against others without condemning himself.

As Frank observes, the continuing power of *The Brothers Karamazov* "derives from its superb depiction of the moral-psychological struggle of each of the main characters to heed the voice of his or her own conscience, a struggle that will always remain humanly valid and artistically persuasive whether or not one accepts the theological premises without which, as Dostoevsky believed, moral conscience would simply cease to exist" (2002, 571). I believe that Ivan is struggling with his conscience, however we account for its existence, and that his insufferable depression derives from its imminent violation by his unconscious collusion with Smerdyakov. His struggle at this point in the novel is not to heed the voice of his conscience but somehow to evade it.

Ivan's inner divisions are manifested in the disparity between his feelings and his actions and in his behaving in ways that are the opposite of his conscious intentions and are surprising to himself. Dostoevsky's depiction of the operation of unconscious forces in Ivan is brilliant. Ivan tries "to pass in at the gate without speaking or looking at Smerdyakov" (V, vi), but when Smerdyakov rises from the bench, indicating that he wants to talk, Ivan looks at him and stops. The fact that he stops "instead of passing by, as he meant to the minute before, [drives] him to fury." I think he is furious with himself for his lack of self-mastery. The side of Ivan that wants to collude with Smerdyakov is stronger than the side of him that is full of "anger and repulsion" and that shrinks from their alliance. Shaking, he is about to say, "Get away, miserable idiot. What have I to do with you?" But "to his profound astonishment," he hears himself say, "Is my father still asleep, or has he waked?" He asks the question "softly and meekly, to his own surprise, and once again to his own surprise, [sits] down on the bench." He feels "almost frightened," as well he might. He has striven to remain self-possessed and at a safe distance from life, but now he is compulsively becoming complicit in an act for which he can never forgive himself.

III. TEMPTATION AND FALL

In the conversation that follows, Smerdyakov tries to assure himself that he has Ivan's approval for what he is planning to do and to make Ivan his accomplice. The conversation takes place on several levels. Smerdyakov's facial expressions and manner of speaking suggest that they are two clever people who understand one another in a way that goes beyond the surface meaning of their words. Ivan feels that he ought to show anger, and Smerdyakov seems to be waiting to see if he will, but he does not. When he makes a move to get up from the bench, Smerdyakov lets him know that his father will be murdered if he leaves town. Ivan had planned to go to Moscow the next day, but it is not clear that Smerdyakov is aware of this. In any event, it is important to Smerdyakov that Ivan make a decision to leave *after* he knows what will happen if he does, for then Ivan will be his partner in crime. Smerdyakov presents Fyodor's death as inevitable should Ivan go away, and Ivan gives him the signal he has been seeking by declaring that he will leave for Moscow in the morning.

Ivan's behavior is conflicted throughout the conversation. At the beginning, he realizes "with disgust" that he is "feeling an intense curiosity and would not, on any account, have gone away without satisfying it" (V, vi). He wants to know what Smerdyakov has in mind, but he is disgusted with himself for becoming involved with a man he despises in a project he abhors. As soon as Smerdyakov urges him to go to Tchermashnya, Ivan knows what he is up to, but he cannot allow himself to be aware of his knowledge and behaves as though he does not understand.

Smerdyakov is not taken in by this, but he plays along with Ivan by pretending to be frightened as he spells out a scenario in which his father will be killed. He will have a fit, which he lets Ivan know he is capable of feigning; Grigory and Marfa will be laid up; and Dmitri knows the secret of the knocks that will induce Fyodor to open his door. "What a rigamarole!" exclaims Ivan. "And it all seems to happen at once, as though it were planned" (V, vi). Smerdyakov protests that whatever happens will not be his doing, that everything will depend on Dmitri; however, Ivan understands that his father's murder is indeed being planned. As Smerdyakov explains later, he expected Dmitri "to kill Fyodor Pavlovitch. I thought that was certain, for I had prepared him for it" (XI, viii). Smerdyakov is setting Dmitri up not only to kill his father but also to be deprived of his undeserved position, to be beneath Smerdyakov, where he belongs. Through his Iago-like scheme, Fyodor, Dmitri, and Ivan will all have been brought down.

When Smerdyakov makes it clear that he does not expect Grushenka to come to Fyodor, Ivan asks why Dmitri should kill his father if she is not there. Smerdyakov explains that Dmitri is in need of money and that he would benefit financially from Fyodor's death. If Fyodor marries Grushenka, she will be his heir, and the brothers will not inherit anything. If Fyodor were to die now, however, there would be at least forty thousand roubles for each of the sons. Smerdyakov is not only explaining why Dmitri might kill his father even if Grushenka has not come but also is tempting Ivan to collaborate in order to get his share. Neither Dmitri nor Ivan is likely to kill for money, but Smerdyakov hopes to profit from Fyodor's death. He can take the three thousand roubles that have been set aside for Grushenka because he has lied to Dmitri about their hiding place, and as he tells Ivan later, he expects to be rewarded by him when he receives his inheritance.

I doubt that the money tempts Ivan, but he thinks that Dmitri might be tempted, and the prospect of the murder takes on a new reality for him (V, vi). His reaction reflects his inner conflicts. A shudder passes over his face, and he asks Smerdyakov "why on earth" he has advised him to go to Tchermashnya:

> "What did you mean by that? If I go away, you see what will happen here." Ivan drew his breath with difficulty.
> "Precisely so," said Smerdyakov, softly and reasonably, watching Ivan intently, however.

"You seem to be a perfect idiot," says Ivan, "and what's more . . . an awful scoundrel, too" (author's ellipsis). He rises from the bench and is about to pass through the gate, but "in a sudden paroxysm" he bites his lip, clenches his fists, and is about to fling himself on Smerdyakov. His impulse of violence toward Smerdyakov is in part an externalization of his self-condemnation, but he does not act it out. Instead, he turns "in perplexity" to the gate and tells Smerdyakov angrily that he will be leaving for Moscow in the morning. "That's the best thing you can do," responds the valet, "as though he had expected to hear it": "you can always be telegraphed for from Moscow, if anything should happen here." Ivan does not attack Smerdyakov; his desire to have him carry out his plan is more powerful than his loathing for him and what he means to do.

Having assented to the murder of his father, Ivan breaks into a laugh, but not, we are told, "from lightness of heart": "he could not have explained himself what he was feeling at that instant. He moved and walked as though in a nervous frenzy." Ivan has been tempted at the entrance to the garden, and he has fallen. His craving for revenge has proven to be stronger than either his conscientious scruples or his defensive detachment, and he is in deep psychological trouble from this moment on. Dostoevsky does not explain what is happening in Ivan, but he portrays it mimetically with perfect insight.

* * *

Ivan's nervous frenzy continues after he enters the house. He tries to pass by his father without even looking at him, perhaps, says the narrator, because "the old man was too hateful to him at that moment" (V, vii). His father is so hateful not because of anything new he has done but because Ivan's revulsion and rage have more fully emerged. Ivan sits up very late that night in a state of "intense excitement." After midnight, he has a strong "inclination to go down, open the door, go to the lodge and beat Smerdyakov"; but he could not have said why, exactly, "except perhaps that he loathed the valet as one who had insulted him more gravely than any one in the world." Smerdyakov has insulted him by treating him as a man who is ready to conspire in the murder of his father, and Ivan's sense of the gravity of the insult indicates his horror of the act. He will later feel that Dmitri is a monster because he commits parricide, and he now feels like a monster because by going to Moscow he has agreed to leave his father to be murdered. He cannot afford to confront his own culpability, so he displaces his self-punitive impulses onto Smerdyakov. Although Ivan continues to practice denial, deep down he knows what he has done: "A feeling of hatred was rankling in his heart, as though he meant to avenge himself on some one" (V, vii). He means to avenge himself on his father for all the insults and injuries he has suffered, but he does not allow himself to be fully conscious of who is the object of his revenge.

Ivan's psychological crisis has begun. He feels that he has "lost his bearings," and his mind is in a whirl (V, vii). His head aches, he is giddy, and he is overcome more than once "by a sort of inexplicable humiliating terror" that paralyzes him. He is terrified by the guilt he is about to incur and by the collapse of his lifelong way of coping with external threats and internal difficulties. No longer able to maintain his aloofness, he is now subject to fierce inner conflicts. Not only does he hate his father and Smerdyakov but "he even hate[s] Alyosha," and "at moments he . . . intensely" hates himself. Ivan hates Smerdyakov because he tempts him to give in to his vindictive impulses and commit an act with which he knows he cannot live. He hates Alyosha because Alyosha represents the side of himself that condemns him for succumbing to that temptation. He hates himself because he has violated the inner dictates of his strategy of detachment and has thereby exposed himself to self-reproach, confusion, and anxiety. He hates himself for his murderous aggression against his father, he hates the side of himself that hates his aggression, and he hates himself for losing self-control and being governed by his emotions.

In the course of the evening, Ivan "stealthily" leaves his room, goes out on the staircase, and "listen[s] to Fyodor Pavlovitch stirring down below" (V, vii). He listens for about five minutes "with a strange sort of curiosity, holding his breath while his heart throb[s]." The narrator tells us that "long afterwards" Ivan recalls his behavior "with peculiar repulsion," that he characterizes the action as "infamous" for the rest of his life, and that he thought of it as "the basest" thing he had ever done. This indicates that Ivan will recover from his brain fever and will pass a harsh judgment on himself. Ivan could not have said why he was listening because he cannot acknowledge his motives to himself, but it seems clear that he knows what is going to happen to his father and is savoring the thought. He moves stealthily because he feels like a criminal, and he experiences "no hatred" for Fyodor "at that moment" because his craving for revenge is soon to be satisfied. Listening to his father stirring below gives him a feeling of power and mastery. He is experiencing the voyeur's guilty enjoyment in studying the actions of a condemned man who does not know he is about to be executed or of an insect about to be squashed. He goes out on the staircase twice to relish this sadistic pleasure.

When Ivan leaves for Moscow the next morning, his father asks him to do some business for him in Tchermashnya on the way. Going to Tchermashnya has become code between Smerdyakov and Ivan for Ivan's consenting to Smerdyakov's plan. When Ivan departs, therefore, he says to Smerdyakov, "You see . . . I am going to Tchermashnya" (V, vii). "It's a true saying then," replies Smerdyakov, that "'it's always worth while speaking to a clever man.'" He looks "significantly at Ivan," confirming their understanding. It may seem that Ivan knows perfectly well what he is doing, but "nothing [is] clear in [his] soul," and he seems still to be simultaneously comprehending and obtuse. He suddenly feels very happy as the carriage rolls away, perhaps because he feels momentarily free of his rage; but after a while he begins to wonder why he told Smerdyakov he was going to Tchermashnya and what the valet meant by saying it is always worthwhile speaking to a clever man. The thought seems "suddenly to clutch at his breathing." He decides not to go to Tchermashnya but to go directly to Moscow instead. This shows an inclination to repudiate his assent. If he had truly repudiated it, of course, he would have returned to his father's house.

As the train leaves for Moscow, Ivan looks forward "to a new life, new places, and no looking back," but "instead of delight his soul was filled with such gloom, and his heart ached with such anguish, as he had never known in his life before" (V, vii). He spends the entire night in thought, and when the train approaches Moscow at daybreak, he whispers, "I am a scoundrel" to himself.

CHAPTER 10

IVAN: AFTER THE MURDER

I. INTRODUCTION

AFTER THE MURDER, THERE IS A STEADY INTENSIFICATION OF IVAN'S inner conflicts. He continues to fend off conscious awareness of his role in the murder, but he is haunted by what he has done, and he moves toward a self-recognition that will tear him apart. On his way back from Moscow, he keeps thinking of his last conversation with Smerdyakov, but he makes no mention of it to the authorities, and he acts as though he does not comprehend its significance during his first interview with the valet. His need not to perceive his role in the crime indicates the severity of his self-condemnation. His loathing of Dmitri is in part an affirmation of his moral values and in part an unconscious externalization of the self-hatred he feels for having violated them. Each meeting with Smerdyakov weakens his defenses, heightens his inner turmoil, and brings him closer to unbearable truths. In hallucinations and dreams, he begins to have encounters with a devil who embodies the skeptical ideas that he now feels to be the worst part of himself. He oscillates between denial and self-knowledge, unbelief and stirrings of faith.

Critics have discussed Ivan's behavior after the murder mostly in terms of Dostoevsky's ideology, as an example of "God . . . and His truth . . . gaining mastery over [the] heart" of the atheist (XI, x), and I have considered its thematic importance in Chapter 7. It is also largely intelligible in terms of Dostoevsky's portrait of Ivan as an inwardly motivated imagined human being (I say *largely* intelligible because there are puzzles, as we shall see). A creation inside a creation,

Ivan is a fascinating character, whether we perceive him from the author's perspective or not.

If we are to understand Ivan as a mimetic character, we must comprehend what is going on between him and Smerdyakov in their three meetings after Fyodor's murder. The first two meetings have, as Smerdyakov says, the quality of a farce (XI, viii), with both guilty men evading the truth and presenting themselves as innocent. Ivan is deceiving himself, and Smerdyakov is lying to Ivan. Each finds their encounters extremely unsettling, and the psychological disturbance of each is exacerbated by that of the other. The farce comes to an end in the third interview, when Smerdyakov describes how he killed Fyodor and accuses Ivan of being the real murderer.

Once Ivan learns that Smerdyakov is the murderer and fully recognizes his own contribution, he must decide what to do with his knowledge. He is in terrible turmoil about this, as his nightmare about the devil indicates, and his conflict intensifies after Smerdyakov's suicide makes his testimony of little value to Dmitri. He finally testifies, confessing his complicity, but he has not resolved the internal strife that is responsible for his psychological crisis.

II. THE FIRST MEETING WITH SMERDYAKOV

Ivan visits Smerdyakov on the first day of his return to town, after both Alyosha and Dmitri have said that the valet is the killer. Smerdyakov is in the hospital and is very ill, having had a series of violent seizures. The doctors had feared for his life but now feel confident of his survival. Ivan has been brooding about his conversation with Smerdyakov the night before his departure and has been puzzled and suspicious. He has made enquiries, apparently in Moscow, about whether Smerdyakov could have foretold the exact time of his fit and has been informed that he could not. His suspicions have been heightened by Alyosha and Dmitri, and he asks Smerdyakov's doctors if he could have been shamming a seizure at the time of the catastrophe. They assure him that the seizure was genuine, but we later learn that the first real fit occurred the day after the murder.

The interaction between Ivan and Smerdyakov in their first interview is elusive and complex. I have examined it many times without fully grasping its dynamics, and I have not found any detailed discussions of it in the criticism. In pondering it again, I have come to see that it has a complex pattern of attack, defense, and counterattack.

Smerdyakov is quite weak and has difficulty talking. His left eye is scrunched up, however, and seems to be saying that "it is always worthwhile speaking to a clever man" (XI, vi). He reminds Ivan of the understanding he thought they had established before his departure. Ivan is solicitous at first, asks Smerdyakov if he is strong enough to talk, and says that he won't tire him. He becomes very aggressive, however, when Smerdyakov sighs after Ivan refers to the mess Smerdyakov "[is] in here": "Why do you sigh, you knew of it all along?" When Smerdyakov protests that he could not have predicted what would happen, Ivan exclaims, "Don't prevaricate! You've foretold you'd have a fit on the way down to the cellar, you know. You mentioned the very spot." Warning Smerdyakov not to play with him, he keeps asking how he could have foretold "the day and the hour." He tries to frighten Smerdyakov by threatening to report his ability to sham fits to the authorities, and he asks why Smerdyakov had advised him to go to Tchermashnya.

Smerdyakov offers a variety of explanations, all of them false, and tries to put Ivan on the defensive. He claims that the fit was brought on by his fear of it and that he urged Ivan to go to Tchermashnya out of his wish to spare him the upcoming trouble. If Ivan went to Tchermashnya, moreover, rather than directly to Moscow, that might serve as a deterrent to Dmitri and would make it easier for Ivan to return if he were needed. Actually, however, says Smerdyakov, he hoped that Ivan would see what would happen if he left and would "remain at home to protect [his] father" (XI, vi). "You might have said it more directly, you blockhead!" Ivan retorts. "But I thought at the time that you quite guessed," Smerdyakov parries. "If I'd guessed, I should have stayed," cries Ivan. Ivan concedes that he "ought to have guessed," but then he reminds Smerdyakov that he had praised him for going to Tchermashnya by saying that "it's always worthwhile speaking to a clever man." Smerdyakov protests that Ivan misunderstood him, that when he said those words "it was not by way of praise, but of reproach." "What reproach?" asks Ivan. "Why, that foreseeing such a calamity you deserted your own father, and would not protect us," Smerdyakov replies.

Ivan tries to regain the offensive by saying that if he feared anything then, it was "some wickedness" from Smerdyakov, and he asks Smerdyakov why he had told him that he could fake a seizure (XI, vi). Smerdyakov says that in his simplicity he was boasting and that he has never shammed a seizure in his life. Would he have told Ivan beforehand that he could if he intended to do so as part of a design against Fyodor? Struck by this argument, Ivan backs off. He tells Smerdyakov that he does not suspect him and thanks him for setting his mind at rest. Although Ivan seems to have been convinced of the valet's innocence, as he departs he finds himself saying that he won't mention Smerdyakov's being able to fake a fit, and he advises Smerdyakov to keep quiet about it also. Smerdyakov replies, "I quite understand" (XI, vi). He has been puzzled by Ivan's behavior and has been afraid, as he puts in their final interview, that Ivan knows "everything and [is] trying to 'throw it all on him to his face'" (XI, viii), hence his lies and his counterattack. Ivan's parting words seem to reinstate the understanding Smerdyakov thought they had reached the night before the murder, and he says that if Ivan doesn't speak of his ability to fake a seizure, he will say nothing of their conversation before Ivan's departure. As Ivan walks down the hospital corridor, he suddenly feels that there is "an insulting significance in Smerdyakov's last words," but he dismisses this as "nonsense!" and resists the impulse to turn back (XI, vi). The significance, of course, is that Smerdyakov is reminding Ivan of his complicity, which is something Ivan has not yet admitted to himself.

After his meeting with Smerdyakov, Ivan's "chief feeling [is] one of relief at the fact that it was not Smerdyakov, but Mitya, who had committed the murder" (XI, vi). After his second interview with Smerdyakov, he tells Katerina Ivanovna that if Smerdyakov "is the murderer, and not Dmitri, then, of course, I am the murderer, too" (XI, vii). This idea is not conscious within him during the first interview, but it seems to be dimly present and to account for his relief that Smerdyakov is innocent. I must admit that some aspects of Dostoevsky's portrayal of Ivan puzzle me. In their conversation at the garden gate, Smerdyakov sketches out a scenario in which Dmitri will kill Fyodor if Ivan goes away. Smerdyakov expects Dmitri to commit the murder, and he is seeking Ivan's participation in a plan that will facilitate that outcome. Ivan departs the next morning and Fyodor is slain, presumably by Dmitri. Why, then, is Ivan relieved when he concludes that Dmitri is the murderer? Ivan says he did not believe Dmitri "would steal" but that he "was prepared for any wickedness" from Smerdyakov (XI, vi). However, in the garden gate conversation, he displays alarm at the danger to his father after Smerdyakov explains that Dmitri needs money and will lose his inheritance if Fyodor marries Grushenka. This seems to indicate that Ivan is prepared for wickedness from Dmitri as well.

After his first meeting with Smerdyakov, Ivan learns of the evidence against Dmitri and dismisses all doubts as to his guilt. He cannot think of his brother "without repulsion" (XI, vi). He abandons himself "hopelessly to his mad and consuming passion" for Katerina, suggesting the further breakdown of his detachment and the emergence of his suppressed emotions (his relishing of Lise's fantasy about the pineapple compote also points to this). For the next two weeks, he almost forgets about Smerdyakov's existence, but then he again starts brooding about his behavior before and after the murder. Why had he crept out on the stairs to listen to his father's movements, and why had he recalled that action with such repulsion? Why had he been so depressed on his journey the next day, and why had he called himself a scoundrel on his arrival in Moscow? These "tormenting thoughts" take such complete possession of him that he thinks he'll forget Katerina, by whom he has been obsessed.

It is clear that being convinced that Dmitri is the murderer has not given Ivan peace of mind. When he encounters Alyosha on the street, he asks him if he thought he had wanted Dmitri to kill their father and was "prepared to help bring that about" (XI, vi). "I want the truth," he insists, "the truth!" Ivan is looking for reassurance, but what Alyosha tells him is not what he hopes to hear. Alyosha admits that he had indeed thought these things, and Ivan begins to dislike him and to keep his distance. His most immediate response to Alyosha's words is to go to see Smerdyakov again.

III. THE SECOND INTERVIEW

Ivan's first visit to Smerdyakov ends on a positive note for both men. Ivan is convinced that Dmitri is the murderer, which temporarily relieves his personal uneasiness, and Smerdyakov feels that their original understanding has been tacitly renewed. Smerdyakov has recovered from his illness and looks quite well when Ivan calls on him again, but Ivan has become deeply troubled. Ivan's second visit to Smerdyakov has a quite different conclusion. Both men are so disturbed by the interview that they become physically and psychologically ill.

Ivan goes to see Smerdyakov after his conversation with Alyosha because he is upset by Alyosha's confirmation of his fears about himself, and he hopes to convince himself that he did not participate in the murder of his father. He is angry with Smerdyakov because his offer not to "tell the investigating lawyer all [their] conversation at the gate" (XI, vii) implies that he was, indeed, complicit in the deed, and he needs to reject this unbearable idea. Immediately sensing Ivan's aggressive state of mind, Smerdyakov responds by behaving almost uncivilly. He is upset that Ivan is still playing the innocent, and he scorns his moral timidity. "Were you threatening me?" asks Ivan. "Have I entered into some sort of compact with you?" Ivan *has* entered into a compact, of course. It is terribly important to Smerdyakov that Ivan recognize that compact, and it is equally important to Ivan to deny it.

Full of resentment, Smerdyakov now attacks Ivan directly. What he meant, he says, by offering not to report *all* of their conversation, was that he would conceal that Ivan had desired his father's death and left him to his fate when he knew he would be killed. "Do you suppose I *knew* of the murder!" Ivan protests, bringing down "his fist violently on the table" (XI, vii, author's emphasis). When Smerdyakov says that Ivan wanted his father's death, Ivan strikes him "with all his might," knocking him against the wall. Ivan's reactions are so intense because of his need to deny truths with which he cannot live. By striking out at Smerdyakov, he is protesting his innocence and demonstrating his horror of parricide.

Smerdyakov does not back off, however. He explains that he stopped Ivan at the gate precisely to find out whether he wanted his father to be murdered. If Ivan and Dmitri wanted the same thing, "then the business was as good as settled" (XI, vii). Still in denial, Ivan asks what he could "have done to put such a degrading suspicion into [Smerdyakov's] mean soul." Why should he have wanted his father's death? Smerdyakov's response reflects his own preoccupations and his own version of Ivan, which is modeled on what he is consciously aware of in himself. His explanation is that Ivan wanted his inheritance, which would be greater if Dmitri were the murderer and forfeited his rights. "There's not a doubt," he tells Ivan, "you did reckon on Dmitri Fyodorovitch." He is right about that. When Ivan repeats that if he had reckoned on anyone then, it was Smerdyakov, the valet replies that if Ivan had had a foreboding about him "and yet went away, [Ivan] as good as said to [him], 'You can murder my parent, I won't hinder you!'" Ivan insists that he didn't expect anything to happen, and Smerdyakov insists that he should "have stayed to save [his] parent's life."

This second meeting with Smerdyakov has a devastating effect on Ivan (and on Smerdyakov as well, as we shall see). When Ivan tells

Smerdyakov that he suspects him of the crime and will drag him to justice, Smerdyakov replies that if Ivan accuses him, he will tell everything, for he must defend himself. "Shaking all over with indignation," Ivan stalks out, "a nightmare of ideas and sensations fill[ing] his soul" (XI, vii). He asks himself why he set off for Tchermashnya and remembers "for the hundredth time how, on that last night in his father's house, he had listened on the stairs." He remembers it now "with such anguish that he [stands] still on the spot as though he had been stabbed. 'Yes, I expected it then, that's true! I wanted the murder, I did want the murder! Did I want the murder? Did I want it?" Smerdyakov has shaken his defenses, but Ivan still cannot accept his guilt and is in an agony of doubt.

Ivan goes straight to Katerina and repeats the whole conversation to her. He is "like a madman," and she is alarmed (XI, vii). He says that if Smerdyakov is the murderer, then he shares his guilt because he "put him up to it." But Ivan says, "Whether I did, I don't know yet." Again, I do not understand why Ivan says this, for he still does not think Smerdyakov was the killer, and he himself is just as much at fault if it was Dmitri. Perhaps this is his way of allowing himself to acknowledge his sense of guilt while leaving himself the possibility of eluding it. In any event, his statement has an important function in the plot: it leads Katerina to produce Dmitri's damning letter, which will later seal his fate in court. "Completely reassured" by the letter, Ivan now "wonders how he could have been so horribly distressed at his suspicions and thinks "of Smerdyakov and his gibes with contempt."

Once again, being reassured that Dmitri is the murderer does not soothe Ivan for very long. He makes no further inquiry about Smerdyakov, though he happens to hear that he is sick. However, Ivan begins to have hallucinations of being visited by a devil, and toward the end of the month, he himself begins to feel very ill. He hates Dmitri more and more every day "*because he was the murderer of his father*" (XI, vii, author's emphasis), indicating his horror of the crime and his need to externalize his self-loathing. He plans Dmitri's escape, to which he will contribute thirty thousand roubles, because Smerdyakov has pointed out that he will benefit from his brother's conviction and he needs "to heal that sore place." He begins to ask himself, moreover, if he also wants Dmitri to escape because he is just "as much a murderer at heart." Something deep down is "burning and rankling in his soul."

IV. The Final Visit to Smerdyakov

Ivan's final visit to Smerdyakov is precipitated by an encounter with Katerina and Alyosha on the eve of Dmitri's trial. Alyosha calls on Katerina after having seen Dmitri and finds Ivan on his way out. Katerina summons both men to her and begins to express her doubts about Dmitri's guilt: "But did he do it? Is he the murderer?" she cries, turning to Ivan (XI, v). Alyosha sees that she had asked Ivan that question before he arrived, perhaps "for the hundredth" time, "and that they had ended by quarreling." This is puzzling because Katerina had convinced Ivan that his brother was the murderer by showing him the letter in which Dmitri says he'll kill his father. Now in doubt, she accuses Ivan of having persuaded her of Dmitri's guilt. Ivan is mystified by her behavior (he has not tried to persuade her), and I cannot explain it either. When Katerina says that she has been to see Smerdyakov, Ivan departs abruptly, and Katerina urges Alyosha to run after him, saying that "He's mad!"

Catching up with Ivan, Alyosha insists that Dmitri is not the murderer and assures Ivan that he is not either, despite the fact that he has accused himself many times. Ivan *has* accused himself in his conversations with his devil, and he thinks that Alyosha must have witnessed this in his room. Alyosha tells Ivan that God has put it into his heart to tell him that he is not the murderer, but saying that he cannot endure "messengers from God" (XI, v). Ivan breaks off relations with him. This is also difficult to understand. How does Alyosha know that Ivan has accused himself, and why does he affirm Ivan's innocence? Alyosha is invested with a great deal of authority by the rhetoric of the novel, but I don't think we are supposed to feel that Ivan's self-accusations are unwarranted. One might think, moreover, that Ivan would welcome Alyosha's words, but he tells Alyosha that he doesn't want to see him again. Perhaps he feels threatened by Alyosha's insight and by what he thinks Alyosha's judgment would be if he knew what he had done. Alyosha represents to Ivan the part of himself that is driving him crazy, the conscience he has been trying to escape and by which he stands condemned.

After his conversation with Alyosha, Ivan goes to see Smerdyakov in obedience to "a sudden and peculiar impulse of indignation" (XI, vii). He is indignant with Katerina for accusing him of having persuaded her of Dmitri's guilt and for being uncertain about it now. He connects her uncertainty with her having spoken to Smerdyakov and wonders what the valet could have said. He feels a "violent anger" toward Smerdyakov and thinks he may kill him this time. There is a great deal of rage in Ivan, not only toward Katerina and Smerdyakov, but also toward Dmitri, Alyosha, and himself. His emotions are out of control, and he has a need to discharge his anger by striking out. En route to Smerdyakov's lodging, he encounters a drunken peasant for whom he feels "an intense hatred"—a displacement, no doubt, of his hatred of more significant people in his life (XI, viii). After acting on "an irresistible impulse to knock [the peasant] down," he leaves him to freeze and continues on his way. If the peasant dies, Ivan, who has been horrified of murder, will be responsible for his demise. For the moment, the vindictive side of him has the upper hand.

When Ivan sees Smerdyakov, he is struck by how ill he looks and says that he won't keep him long. He just wants to know if Katerina has visited him. Smerdyakov says that she has, that it is a matter of no importance to Ivan, and that he wants Ivan to let him alone. Ivan persists in his questioning, however, and Smerdyakov stares "at him with a look of frenzied hatred, the same look that he had fixed on him at their last interview, a month before" (XI, viii). Smerdyakov now observes that Ivan is also very ill: his face is sunken and the whites of his eyes have turned yellow. "Are you so worried?" he asks, then "smile[s] contemptuously" and laughs.

Smerdyakov is attributing Ivan's illness to his mental state, and he is right, of course. Their prior meetings have made them both ill, Ivan because they have stirred up his guilt by forcing him to be more aware of his role in the murder and Smerdyakov because they have shaken his faith in Ivan and challenged the beliefs that had sanctioned his killing of Fyodor. When Ivan warns Smerdyakov not to play with him at the beginning of their first interview, Smerdyakov asks, "Why should I play with you, when I put my whole trust in you, as in God Almighty?" (XI, vi). Having adopted Ivan as his authority, Smerdyakov has acted on his pronouncement that everything is permitted because God does not exist. Ivan's evasions and denials, and his anguish at the thought of his complicity, are deeply disturbing to the valet because they indicate that Ivan himself cannot live with the consequences of his philosophy, hence Smerdyakov's "insane hatred" of Ivan and his "incredibly supercilious tone" (XI, viii).

Smerdyakov scorns Ivan for not having the courage of his convictions ("You were bold enough then. You said 'everything is lawful,' and how frightened you are now" [XI, viii]), and he hates him because Ivan's moral squeamishness has undermined his own defense against guilt. Deprived of Ivan's support, Smerdyakov is torn by inner conflicts.

He continues to deny the existence of God and to maintain that everything is lawful, but he starts reading "The Sayings of the Holy Father Isaac the Syrian," and during their last interview, he says that God is there with them in the room. Like Raskolnikov, he murders for money and then loses interest in his loot; like Ivan, he is torn between atheism and belief.

Ivan and Smerdyakov are both suffering terribly from guilt. Ivan is still trying to defend himself by denial, and Smerdyakov now places all the blame on Ivan. Scornful of Ivan's trembling anxiety, Smerdyakov assures him that he will say nothing against him at the trial and tells him to go home: "*you* did not murder him" (XI, viii). Ivan says, "I know it was not I," and Smerdyakov retorts, "Do you?" When Ivan then demands that Smerdyakov tell him everything, Smerdyakov "whisper[s] furiously," "Well, it was you who murdered him," and "I was only your instrument, your faithful servant, and it was following your words I did it."

Smerdyakov now recounts exactly what happened, with the object of proving to Ivan that he is "responsible for it all": "You knew of the murder and charged me to do it, and went away knowing all about it. . . . you are the only real murderer in the whole affair, and I am not the real murderer, though I did kill him" (XI, viii, author's emphasis). "Why, why, am I a murderer? Oh, God!" cries Ivan. It would seem that Ivan can no longer escape a recognition of his guilt, but even now he equivocates: "perhaps I, too, was guilty; perhaps I really had a secret desire for my father's . . . death, but I swear I was not as guilty as you think, and perhaps I didn't urge you on at all. No, no, I didn't urge you on!" (author's ellipsis).

Despite his reservations and denials, Ivan says he will testify at the trial, even giving evidence against himself. They'll go together, and Smerdyakov must confess. Smerdyakov says, "There'll be nothing of the sort" (XI, viii). He predicts that Ivan won't go because he is "very proud," he "like[s] to be respected," and he "won't want to spoil [his] life forever" by taking "such a disgrace" on himself. Ivan reaffirms his determination and says the only reason he hasn't killed Smerdyakov is that he needs him for tomorrow. "Well, kill me. Kill me now," says Smerdyakov: "'You won't dare do that even!' he added, with a bitter smile. 'You won't dare to do anything, you, who used to be so bold!'"

Smerdyakov foils Ivan's plan by committing suicide before the trial begins. He seems to have taken this determination by the end of

Ivan's visit, for he calls "Good-bye!" as Ivan is walking out. Why does Smerdyakov do away with himself? His deterioration and his placing all the blame on Ivan indicate that he is troubled by guilt, and he may be escaping his inner torments. Seriously ill, perhaps dying, he is in despair about himself. He had dreamed of using the three thousand roubles he had stolen to begin a new life either in Moscow or abroad, but he gives the money to Ivan in a gesture of hopelessness about his own future. By killing himself, he also escapes the ordeal of being accused by Ivan and subjected to the investigation that would follow. Even if his guilt could not be proved, he would always be an object of suspicion. Moreover, by killing himself Smerdyakov controls his own fate and removes himself from the power of others.

I think too that Smerdyakov's suicide is an act of aggression against Dmitri and Ivan. The person in the novel who understands Smerdyakov best is the defense attorney, Fetyukovitch. According to him, Smerdyakov is by no means the simple, weak-minded man portrayed by the prosecutor: "I found in him, on the contrary, an extreme mistrustfulness concealed under a mask of naïveté, and an intelligence of considerable range" (XII, xii). He believed himself to be the illegitimate son of Fyodor Pavlovitch, was ashamed of his parentage, and resented his position in relation to his half-brothers: "They had everything, he had nothing. They had all the rights, they had the inheritance, while he was only the cook." As Fetyukovitch says, Smerdyakov was "a distinctly spiteful creature, excessively ambitious, vindictive, and intensely envious." The prosecutor asks why, if his conscience prompted him to kill himself, Smerdyakov did not leave a confession behind. Fetyukovitch replies that "the suicide may not have felt penitence, but only despair. Despair and penitence are two very different things. Despair may be vindictive and irreconcilable, and the suicide, laying his hands on himself, may well have felt redoubled hatred for those whom he had envied all his life." This sounds right to me. By committing suicide before the trial, Smerdyakov makes it impossible for Ivan to salve his conscience by rescuing Dmitri and ensures the conviction of a man whose superior position he has always felt to be undeserved. He kills Fyodor not only for the sake of money but also out of bitter hatred and a desire for revenge. He tells Ivan that "the longing to get it done came over me, till I could scarcely breathe" (XI, viii). He kills himself partly out of vindictiveness also, to inflict suffering on those he has envied all his life.

v. Continued Inner Conflicts

When Ivan parts from Smerdyakov, he feels that "the wavering that had so tortured him of late" has come to an end (XI, viii). He has taken a resolution to testify at the trial, and he is certain this will not change. With "something like joy" in his heart, he saves the peasant he had previously left to freeze, taking him to the police and paying for his medical care. Feeling at peace with himself, he is confident of his sanity, but this state does not last very long. After he decides not to go to the prosecutor at once but to wait until he testifies the next day, "almost all his gladness and self-satisfaction" disappears. This is followed by Ivan's nightmare, in which his conflicts continue to rage, and by his wavering behavior and ultimate collapse at the trial.

Ivan's encounters with his devil are presented as symptoms of an impending attack of brain fever, a term we now use for such viral ailments as meningitis and encephalitis but that in Dostoevsky's day was used much more broadly, often to designate psychosomatic symptoms brought on by moral and emotional crises. When Ivan consults the doctor Katerina has brought from Moscow, he is informed that "hallucinations are quite likely in your condition" (XI, ix). Evidently, he has told the doctor about being visited by the devil. The night before the trial, when the narrator says that he is "on the very eve of an attack of brain fever," Ivan is visited again, this time in a nightmare in which the devil identifies himself as both a hallucination and a figure in a dream. Ivan may be dreaming that he is having a hallucination.

It is difficult to make sense of Ivan's experience in terms of our current medical science, and it may seem that Dostoevsky has abandoned psychological realism and shifted to a different genre in his account of Ivan's nightmare. There are important distinctions between hallucinations and dreams, which Dostoevsky seems to ignore, and Ivan's nightmare is too coherent and full of elaborately articulated ideas to seem like a dream to us. If the nightmare is an artificial device for developing thematic concerns (and it certainly does develop such concerns), is it appropriate to treat it as part of the mimetic depiction of Ivan?

According to Konstantin Mochulsky, Dostoevsky did not regard the nightmare as a device but strove "for absolute precision in his representation of his heroes' psychological states" (1967, 594). In support of this contention, he cites a letter Dostoevsky wrote to Nikolai Liubimov, his editor, on August 10, 1880, regarding Ivan's dream: "I have for a long time consulted the opinion of doctors (and not of only one). They maintain that before a 'cerebral fever' not only are such nightmares possible, but also hallucinations. My hero, of course, does see hallucinations too, but he confuses them with his nightmares." It seems that Ivan's interaction with his devil was meant to be realistic, and I shall treat it as part of Dostoevsky's portrayal of Ivan's state of mind. Despite its problematic nature, it yields important insights into the conflicts that are tormenting Ivan as a result of his father's death and his meetings with Smerdyakov.

After Ivan testifies against himself at the trial, Katerina produces Dmitri's letter and describes Ivan as having "a tender, overtender conscience! He tormented himself with his conscience!" (XII, v). For Dostoevsky, conscience can only have a supernatural origin, but I think that his psychological portrait of Ivan makes sense either with or without that premise. If it did not, *The Brothers Karamazov* would not have such a widespread appeal. We have seen that Ivan has a firm set of values (even though he argues that everything is permitted if there is no God), that he is horrified by parricide, and that he condemns himself so severely for his participation in the crime that he refuses to allow himself to be consciously aware of what he has done. He does indeed have a tender conscience by which he is tormented. Because he sees his atheistic beliefs as having led to the murder and to the terrible guilt he feels as a consequence, he has been moving in the direction of repudiating those beliefs, although he has not given them up.

In his nightmare, Ivan ascribes his atheistic beliefs to the devil, whom he addresses as "the incarnation of myself, but only of one side of me . . . of my thoughts and feelings, but only the nastiest and stupidest of them" (XI, ix). Ivan is ashamed when the devil refers to "The Grand Inquisitor," and he covers his ears and trembles all over when the devil describes the utopia that will arise once the idea of God has been destroyed. He responds to the devil's repetition of his argument that recognizing that all things are lawful will enable him to step into the place of God by flinging a glass at him in imitation of Luther's throwing his inkstand.

While the side of Ivan with which we are most familiar is embodied in his devil, there is also in him a longing for faith that has been growing stronger and that seems in his dream to have gained the upper hand. Indeed, this longing is also present in his devil, who would like to become "incarnate once for all . . . in the form of some merchant's wife weighing eighteen stone, and believing all she believes" (XI, ix). His ideal "is to go to church and offer a candle in simple-hearted faith. . . . Then there would be an end to my sufferings." The devil longs to shout "hosannah" and laments the fact that he has been "predestined 'to deny'" because without negation and suffering life would be "transformed into an endless church service" and "would be holy, but tedious." Through his devil Ivan is responding to his own arraignment of God: "nothing but hosannah is not enough for life, the hosannah must be tried in the crucible of doubt."

The sufferings the devil would like to escape through simple-hearted faith seem to be those of uncertainty, which are similar to Ivan's. When Ivan asks, with "savage intensity," if there is a God or not, the devil replies, "My dear fellow, upon my word I don't know" (XI, ix). His devil shares Ivan's lack of certitude about transcendental matters, and he speaks with great eloquence about the agony of doubt. Ivan admits to wanting to believe that his devil really exists and is not just a hallucination or a dream, for this would constitute "a tiny grain of faith" that could grow into an oak tree. According to his devil, Ivan is secretly longing "to enter the ranks of 'the hermits . . . and the saintly women.'" He wants to "wander into the wilderness to save [his] soul!" But Ivan cannot distinguish between dream, hallucination, and reality, and his devil observes that "hesitation, suspense, conflict between belief and disbelief—is sometimes such torture to a conscientious man, such as you are, that it is better to hang oneself at once."

Why, we might ask, is Ivan, who has denied God's existence and returned the ticket if he does exist, now demonizing this side of himself and moving toward religious faith? In his last interview with Smerdyakov, he says that the devil has helped the valet and that "God sees" (XI, viii). Ivan's movement is in accord with Dostoevsky's belief that by activating the conscience, crime brings the sinner to God, and one cannot help wondering if Ivan is becoming a purely illustrative character who is being manipulated by the author in order to confirm his ideology.

Ivan *is* an illustrative character, of course, and his movement toward faith is part of the pattern of the fortunate fall, of death and rebirth, that is repeated again and again in the novel. At the same time, however, I think that his inner struggles make sense in terms of Dostoevsky's mimetic portrayal of his psychology. Ivan has never been comfortable with his lack of faith. When he says during the unfortunate gathering at the monastery that "there is no virtue if there is no immortality," Father Zossima observes that Ivan is "blessed in believing that, or else most unhappy" (II, vi). Zossima thinks that Ivan probably does not believe in the immortality of the soul, that the question is "still fretting [his] heart," and that he is diverting himself in his "despair" with arguments about God and ecclesiastical courts. It is Ivan's "great grief," says Zossima, that he cannot answer the question about immortality in either the affirmative or the negative: "You know that that is the peculiarity of your heart, and all its suffering is due to it. But thank the Creator who had given you a lofty heart capable of such suffering." Ivan seems to acquiesce in Zossima's view of him: he goes up to him, receives his blessing, kisses his hand, and returns to his place in silence.

Ivan wants to find God but cannot do so because he tries to answer metaphysical questions by rational means, cannot believe in a beneficent father, and wants to occupy the foremost place himself. Father Zossima seems to be right in thinking that Ivan is "most unhappy" in his unbelief. As Mochulsky observes, "Ivan is not a self-satisfied atheist" but a man "who experiences lack of faith as a personal tragedy" (1967, 613). Ivan's Grand Inquisitor is a former holy man who has joined the clever people and who sees himself as heroically enduring the burden of freedom so that ordinary people, like the devil's eighteen-stone woman, can enjoy the bliss of unreflecting faith. In his long conversation with Alyosha in the tavern, Ivan tries both to befriend his brother and to undermine his beliefs, but he has another motive as well. When he tells Alyosha that he cannot accept the world God has created, he says, "I've led the conversation to my despair" (V, iii). Perhaps he does want to be healed by Alyosha. Ivan cannot live with his own philosophy. Causal explanations are no comfort to him: "I must have justice," he says, "or I will destroy myself." He sees himself "living in spite of logic" until he is thirty, then losing his "unseemly thirst for life."

Ivan is in psychological difficulty before he becomes involved in his father's murder. He appears to be an atheist who once had faith (though we do not see this phase of his development), and as Father Zossima perceives, he seems to have a terrible nostalgia for the comforts of religion. He is preoccupied with ultimate issues. He is one of those Russian youths he describes to Alyosha, for whom the eternal "questions of God's existence and of immortality . . . come first and foremost . . . and so they should" (V, iii). Ivan has a craving for justice, for immortality, for an absolute meaning to life, all of which require a God. He experiences instead the sentiment of the absurd, which arises, says Albert Camus, from the human "longing for clarity" confronting the "unreasonable silence" of the universe (1960, 16, 21). As Zossima also perceives, this fills Ivan with despair.

There is, then, a part of Ivan that welcomes the death of God, for reasons I have examined, and a part of him that wants to believe, that longs to be rescued from his hopelessness. Before the murder of his father, the disbelieving side of Ivan is stronger by far; after the murder, a movement toward belief slowly gains strength. As it does, Ivan's inner conflicts intensify, and he experiences more and more the agonies of doubt his devil describes.

Another nonbeliever might have concluded that there are values even without God and have arrived at a naturalistic ethic or a Religion of Humanity as did some of Ivan's (and Dostoevsky's) contemporaries (see Paris 1965). But for Ivan, as for Dostoevsky, guilt and a sense of right and wrong have supernatural origins. If there is no God, there is no virtue; but if there is virtue, God may exist. Ivan is not entirely sure, however, that his sense of right and wrong has a divine source. When Alyosha arrives with the news of Smerdyakov's suicide, Ivan says that the devil has been teasing him: "'Conscience! What is conscience? I make it up for myself. Why am I tormented by it? From habit. From the universal habit of mankind for the seven thousand years. So let us give it up, and we shall be gods.' It was he said that, it was he said that!" (XI, x). Ivan would be "awfully glad to think it was *he* and not I"; and Alyosha cries, "And not you, not you?" Ivan now curses his skeptical thoughts and wishes to disown them, but clearly they plague him still.

* * *

Although a major shift is taking place in Ivan, his conflicts have not been resolved, and his wavering continues both in his conversation with Alyosha and at Dmitri's trial. His conscientious side is dominant through most of his conversation but not at the end. He tells Alyosha that he lied about Lise's having tried to seduce him, he tries to distance himself from the aspect of himself his devil represents, and he tells Alyosha that he loves his face. He intends to confess at the trial that Smerdyakov murdered his father at his instigation. His devil says that Ivan is tortured by the fact that he will be performing "an act of heroic virtue" without believing in virtue, and Ivan says that the devil knows what he is talking about (XI, x). Because he does not believe in virtue and his testimony will do no good after Smerdyakov kills himself, Ivan does not know why he is going to confess. The devil points out that it cannot be "for the sake of principle," since there is no basis for principle in Ivan's philosophy, and proposes that Ivan will "go because [he] won't dare not to go." He won't dare not to go because he is "a coward." Ivan's devil calls him a coward because he cannot live in accordance with his belief that everything is permitted: "It is not for such eagles to soar above the earth." In anguish, Ivan tells Alyosha that "Smerdyakov said the same." Ivan's "pride" has been "suffer[ing] cruelly" for the past month (XI, vii) because of his timidity and guilt. He has not been able to become his own lawgiver and occupy the foremost place. He had meant to soar beyond moral constraints, but instead he has been tormented by self-reproach.

Now filled with self-contempt, Ivan feels that Katerina, Lise, and Alyosha all despise him, and he tells Alyosha that he is "going to hate [him] again!" (XI, x). He had stayed away from Alyosha when he dreaded his judgment but had felt warmly toward him while he was repudiating his devil. Stung by his devil's (that is, his own) judgment of himself as a coward, he scorns himself for his qualms of conscience and withdraws from Alyosha once more. He says that he hates Dmitri and doesn't want to save him: "Let him rot in Siberia! He's begun singing a hymn! Oh, to-morrow I'll go stand before them, and spit in their faces!" Ivan is recoiling against his scruples and his movement toward belief. He is repelled by Dmitri's hymn. Caught in a crossfire of conflicting inner dictates, he condemns himself for his role in his father's murder and condemns himself for condemning himself.

Ivan's wavering continues in court the next day. Instead of standing before them and spitting in their faces, Ivan tells the president that he has "something interesting" to reveal (XII, v). But when asked if he has a "special communication to make," he replies, "No . . . I haven't. I have nothing particular" (author's ellipsis). He asks to be excused because he is feeling ill, starts walking out of the court, and then returns to testify. He produces the three thousand roubles Smerdyakov had given him, declares that the valet had murdered his father, and confesses that he had "incited him to do it." Having satisfied his conscience by admitting his guilt, Ivan moves in a different direction. Attacking his auditors with "furious contempt," he defends himself by externalizing his self-hatred. He universalizes his own behavior by declaring that "all desire the death of their fathers." Those attending the trial pretend to be horrified, but they are really pleased that their own parricidal wishes have been acted out, and they are enjoying the spectacle. Reverting to his earlier vindictive attitudes, Ivan again sees human beings as reptiles devouring each other. As he is escorted from the court clutching his head, he returns to accusing himself. He assures everyone that he is "not mad," that he is "only a murderer." This is the last we see of Ivan.

Unlike Raskolnikov's, Ivan's inner conflicts are not resolved by the end of the novel. There are intimations in his story of the pattern of the fortunate fall, and he does testify on Dmitri's behalf despite his awareness of the futility of his sacrifice. He achieves no peace, however, and is overcome by his illness. There are references to his later life that lead us to believe that Ivan will survive, but we are given no clear indication of what he will be like when he recovers. I find it difficult to imagine a solution that will work for Ivan, and Dostoevsky may have had the same problem.

After he visits Ivan the evening before the trial, Alyosha begins "to understand Ivan's illness": "The anguish of a proud determination. An earnest conscience!' God, in Whom he disbelieved, and His truth were gaining mastery over his heart, which still refused to submit" (XI, x). Ivan is being sickened by the conflict between his proud determination to persevere in his atheistic beliefs and his earnest conscience, which calls those beliefs into question. As Alyosha is about to fall asleep, the thought floats through his mind that Ivan will testify despite the fact that no one will believe his evidence. He smiles softly and thinks, "God will conquer!"

This may seem to be Dostoevsky's way of letting us know the outcome of Ivan's struggle, but he is too great a novelist to fit Ivan so neatly into the work's ideological structure. For one thing, Alyosha is not always right about his brother. He tells Ivan that he has been sent by God to assure him that he is not the murderer, and when Ivan accuses himself at the trial, Alyosha cries, "He is ill. Don't believe him; he has brain fever" (XII, v). He is right about the illness but wrong in dismissing what Ivan has said. Alyosha's prediction that God will conquer is also called into question by Alyosha's own misgivings about the outcome. After he smilingly thinks to himself that God will conquer, Alyosha adds "bitterly": "He will either rise up in the light of truth, or . . . he'll perish in hate, revenging on himself and on every one his having served the cause he does not believe in" (XI, x). Then he prays for Ivan again.

Alyosha seems to understand that Ivan hates himself because his conscience makes him feel guilty but that if he obeys his conscience by testifying, he may hate himself even more. His testimony increases his inner turmoil and brings on the mental collapse he has been trying to avoid. We are left wondering how Ivan can resolve his uncertainties, cope with his guilt, and stop despising himself for failing to become the soaring eagle he has aspired to be.

CHAPTER 11

ALYOSHA: HISTORY, PERSONALITY, AND RELATIONSHIP WITH ZOSSIMA

I. INTRODUCTION

IN "FROM THE AUTHOR," DOSTOEVSKY IDENTIFIES ALYOSHA AS HIS hero, and although the story is as much about the other brothers as it is about Alyosha, Richard Peace is right in arguing that Alyosha is "at the centre of the novel" (1971, 229). As Peace points out, except for the events surrounding the murder of Fyodor, "there is scarcely one important scene" at which Alyosha is not present (221). Ivan, Dmitri, and Fyodor open their hearts and minds to him, he overhears the conversation between Smerdyakov and Marya Kondratyevna, and we see Father Zossima largely through his eyes. The account of Zossima's recollections, conversations, and exhortations in Book VI ("The Russian Monk") is presented as having been compiled by Alyosha. As Peace observes, it is through contact with Alyosha that such characters as Rakitin, Katerina Ivanovna, Grushenka, Lise Hohlakov, Captain Snegiryov, and Kolya Krassotkin "reveal their true natures" (229). It is Alyosha who reconciles Illusha and his classmates and who sounds the novel's final note with his speech at Illusha's stone.

As I observed in Chapter 7, in addition to performing numerous formal functions, Alyosha plays a major role in the novel's thematic structure. As the brother in whom the spiritual self is dominant, he serves as a foil to the sensual Mitya and the rational Ivan and, along with Zossima, constitutes the novel's moral norm. A Christ-like figure, he acts as a conscience to many other characters and is frequently called a "cherub," an "angel," and a "saint." He turns the other cheek; loves, forgives, and suffers for his fellows; takes no thought for worldly matters; and is surrounded by disciples at the end. It is he who saves Kolya from becoming another Ivan. His faith is shaken by Zossima's premature decomposition and then is reestablished on a firmer footing, making him all the more effective as an exponent of the novel's religious themes.

I have included Alyosha in this study of Dostoevsky's greatest characters because he not only has important aesthetic and illustrative functions but also is a splendidly realized imagined human being. *The Brothers Karamazov* is full of richly developed mimetic characters, the greatest of whom is Ivan. For me, Alyosha is the next most fascinating figure.

My view of Alyosha is not widely shared. Most critics would agree with Konstantin Mochulsky that Alyosha is "more palely" drawn than his siblings (1967, 626). According to Eliseo Vivas, none of Dostoevsky's "good or saintly characters . . . is endowed with as dense and authentic a humanity" as his evil ones because "genuine goodness and saintliness are harmonious, unassertive and hence undramatic, dull affairs" (1955, 62). Although Richard Peace makes a strong case for the centrality of Alyosha's position in the novel, he too remarks that the youngest Karamazov "does not compel the imagination to the same extent as his brothers" (1971, 221).

Joseph Frank observes that Alyosha's character and behavior conform "closely to the hagiographical pattern" and that "the narrator makes no attempt to explain [them] psychologically" (2002, 577). He feels that the "forces that move" Alyosha "are left deliberately vague so as to suggest a possible otherworldly inspiration." Valentina Vetlovskaya shows in detail that Alyosha is presented as though he were the subject of a saint's biography, a genre with which Dostoevsky was quite familiar. His sympathy, humility, lack of pride, indifference to material things, naive trustfulness, and nonresentment of insults all correspond to the "usual representation of the hero of the *vita*," as do his gift of making himself loved and his withdrawal from the world (1984, 210). Like that of his namesake—Saint Aleksey, the Man of God—Alyosha's faith is tested by a series of trials.

I think that critics who point to the hagiographical pattern are undoubtedly correct. In "From the Author," Dostoevsky says that despite his oddness and eccentricity, Alyosha "carries within himself the very heart of the universal" from which "the rest of the men of his epoch" have been "temporarily torn" away. Vetlovskaya notes that the heroes of saints' lives are characterized by oddness and eccentricity and seem "strange to ordinary people and ordinary perception" (1984, 208).

But Dostoevsky is not only following the hagiographical pattern; he is also imagining Alyosha as a real person, and he supplies so much concrete detail that his protagonist *does* possess the dense and authentic humanity saintly characters are said to lack. Although Dostoevsky makes no attempt to explain Alyosha's personality and behavior psychologically, his mimetic portrayal of his hero makes it possible for us to do so. I have already suggested that, like Sonya in *Crime and Punishment*, Alyosha copes with a threatening environment by becoming extremely self-effacing, and I think that many of the traits that Frank, Vetlovskaya, and others associate with the hagiographical pattern can also be seen as emanating from his ways of defending himself—as can his beliefs and his relationships, especially his attachment to Father Zossima.

Although I shall argue that Alyosha is a realistically drawn character, I feel that at times there is an aura of unreality about him. This derives, I think, from certain magical elements in his thinking and in that of Father Zossima that are honored by Dostoevsky because they correspond to his own religious beliefs. The world of the novel, of which the author is the creator, is one in which Alyosha's defensive strategies work well, whereas those of most other characters do not. It seems to me that in the case of Alyosha, we have an almost entirely mimetic character in a not-quite-realistic world. It is a realistic world for Dostoevsky, of course, because it reflects his conception of the order of things.

Like Dmitri and Ivan (and Smerdyakov also), Alyosha has a traumatic childhood that forces him to develop coping mechanisms at a very early age. These profoundly affect his character structure and the ways in which he relates to the surrounding environment. When he returns home at the age of nineteen to seek out his mother's grave, he is drawn to the local monastery because the life he finds there reinforces his defenses and serves his psychological needs, including his need for glory. At the monastery, he encounters the famous elder, Zossima, with whom he identifies and to whom he turns over the direction of his life. Zossima's teachings provide a source of authority for what Alyosha is already disposed to believe. A great crisis occurs when Zossima does not receive the posthumous glory Alyosha feels he deserves, and it is resolved when Alyosha's pride is restored.

II. Alyosha and His Mother

Like Ivan, Alyosha was exposed to the atmosphere of debauchery and disorder created by his father and was "forgotten and abandoned" after his mother's death (I, iii); however, his temperament was different from Ivan's, and he developed a different way of coping with a frightening environment. Moreover, his mother was an important formative influence to him, which does not seem to have been the case with his brother.

Alyosha's mother was Sofya Ivanovna, Fyodor Pavlovitch's second wife, a "meek and gentle creature" who married at the age of sixteen to get away from the general's widow in whose house she grew up after she was orphaned as a child (I, iii). "So terrible were her sufferings from the caprice and everlasting nagging" of the old woman that she had once been cut down from a noose from which she was hanging in the attic. Attracted by her innocence and beauty, Fyodor persuaded her to elope, leading her benefactress to disown her. "Making her feel that she had 'wronged' him" because of her lack of a portion, Fyodor "took advantage of her phenomenal meekness and submissiveness to trample on the elementary decencies of marriage" by bringing loose women into the house and engaging in "orgies of debauchery" in her presence. "Kept in terror from her childhood," and now maltreated by her husband, Sofya fell into the "kind of nervous disease which is most frequently found in peasant women who are said to be 'possessed by devils.' At times after terrible fits of hysterics she even lost her reason." Alyosha was born into a household in which his extremely fragile mother was being driven mad by the depravity of his father.

Although he was only four when his mother died, we are told that Alyosha remembered her face and her caresses all his life. She was evidently very attached to her second child, who resembled her much more than her first. Alyosha's most vivid memory is of a summer evening, "the slanting rays of the setting sun," and his mother on her knees before a holy image (I, iv). "Sobbing hysterically with cries and moans," she takes him in her arms, "squeezing him close till it hurt, and praying for him to the Mother of God, holding him out . . . to the image as though to put him under the Mother's protection." Then a nurse rushes in "and snatches him from her in terror," presumably afraid that she will do him harm.

Sofya has turned to religious faith as a refuge from the horrors of her life, and in this scene she is seeking protection for Alyosha from the same source. "Here is safety," she seems to be saying to her son. When Alyosha returns to his birthplace later on, it is to visit his mother's grave, and the narrator says that memories of childhood may have brought him to the monastery in the town: "Perhaps the slanting sunlight and the holy image to which his poor 'crazy' mother had held him up still acted upon his imagination" (I, v). Alyosha may have felt that his pious mother had devoted him to a religious life.

Alyosha's similarity to his mother is made clear in the scene I discussed in connection with Ivan, in which Fyodor describes how he tried to knock the mysticism out of his wife by threatening to defile her holy image. At first he thought she would kill him, but "she only jumped up, wrung her hands, then suddenly hid her face in them, began trembling all over and fell on the floor" (III, viii). As Fyodor speaks, a change comes over Alyosha: he flushes crimson, his eyes glow, and his lips quiver. He jumps up, wrings his hands, hides his face in them, and is overcome by "an hysterical paroxysm of sudden violent, silent weeping." Fyodor is deeply impressed by Alyosha's "extraordinary resemblance to his mother."

Sofya is enraged by Fyodor's threatened desecration of her holy image, and Alyosha is enraged by his father's treatment of his mother, but both are incapable of expressing anger directly, and the suppression of their fury results in paroxysms of hysterical behavior. They manifest their feelings indirectly, in ways that do not threaten others and that evoke concern rather than retaliation. Karen Horney observes that in people who have adopted self-effacement as a defense "vindictive resentment" is characteristically expressed "through suffering" (1950, 232). Through her hysterics and loss of reason, Sofya is showing Fyodor what he has done to her, just as she had shown the widow what she had done through her attempted suicide. Instead of striking out at her tormentors, she inflicts suffering on herself. Neither the widow nor Fyodor are the sort of people who respond to her misery as she hopes, so she does not improve her situation by enacting her distress.

Both Alyosha and his mother have powerful taboos against aggression and are wracked by inner conflict when their anger threatens to erupt. It is clear that Sofya's initial manifestation of resentment, when

Fyodor thinks she will kill him (III, viii), is an extraordinary event, an exception to her "phenomenal meekness and submissiveness" (I, iii). Alyosha's reaction to his father's account of his abuse is also an unusual occurrence, but it points to an underlying rage, perhaps of murderous proportions, that may be responsible for the later negligence that has led some to argue that he is partly responsible for his father's death (see Mochulsky 1967, 598–99; Peace 1971, 250, 259). Like his mother, Alyosha stifles his fury and becomes hysterical instead of lashing out.

III. Alyosha's Defenses

The narrator acknowledges that Alyosha is "very strange" and says that he has been so "from his cradle" (I, iv). Inheriting some temperamental traits from his mother and exposed to the combination of her anxious love, her "nervous disease," and his father's brutality, Alyosha develops powerful defenses at a early age that make him seem odd.

One of these is his response to being injured. As a schoolboy, we are told, "he never resented an insult": "It would happen that an hour after the offence he would address the offender or answer some question with as trustful and candid an expression as though nothing had happened between them. And it was not that he seemed to have forgotten or intentionally forgiven the affront, but simply that he did not regard it as an affront" (I, iv). This suggests a severe repression of retaliatory impulses. Horney observes that a person who has adopted a self-effacing strategy "is terrified lest anybody be hostile toward him, and prefers to give in, to 'understand' and forgive" (1950, 219). This sounds very much like Sonya Marmeladov. Alyosha's defense is more extreme. He does not have to forgive injuries, because he refuses to register them. This prevents the escalation of hostilities and enables him to be on good terms with everyone: his schoolmates are "captivated" by his not being offended (I, iv). It also allows him to remain on good terms with himself, for it is clear that he has powerful taboos against feeling angry or aggrieved. As Horney says, in a person who adopts this kind of strategy, "vindictive drives remain unconscious and can only be expressed indirectly and in a disguised form" (219).

That aggressive impulses are present in Alyosha is most vividly revealed in the dream he shares with Lise. Lise tells him that she sometimes dreams of devils:

> It's night, I am in my room with a candle and suddenly there are devils all over the place, in all the corners, under the table, and they open

the doors, there's a crowd of them behind the doors and they want to come and seize me. And they are just coming, just seizing me. But I suddenly cross myself and they all draw back, though they don't go away altogether, they stand at the doors and in the corners, waiting. And suddenly I have a frightful longing to revile God aloud, and so I begin, and then they come crowding back to me, delighted, and seize me again and I cross myself again and they all draw back. (XI, iii)

"I've had the same dream, too," says Alyosha. As we have seen, when Ivan asks Alyosha what the general who set his hounds on the serf boy deserves, Alyosha replies, "To be shot" (V, iv). Alyosha is deeply disturbed by his vindictive feelings, which he says are "absurd," but they are there, as the dream of the devils indicates. Dmitri and Ivan react to their father's unjust treatment with anger, which extends to God in the case of Ivan. Alyosha's having the same dream as Lise indicates that he too is full of rebellious resentment. His internal demons are kept at bay by his religious faith, which Ivan does not share.

Alyosha's refusal to register insults works well at school: it is difficult to torment someone who does not become angry or feel hurt. His schoolmates mock his "wild fanatical modesty and chastity," and when he puts his fingers in his ears to shut out their vulgar talk, they sometimes "crowd round him, pull his hands away, and shout nastiness into both ears" (I, iv). Alyosha then slips to the floor and tries "to hide himself without uttering one word of abuse, enduring their insults in silence." This spoils their fun, and eventually they leave him alone.

Alyosha deals with a threatening world by being unthreatening himself. He is modest, unassertive, undemanding. He is very bright and does well in school, but he is not competitive and is never first in his class. Because he never tries to show off, he is not afraid of his schoolfellows, whom he has given no reason to resent him. He is "not proud of his fearlessness" (I, iv), however, for that would violate his need to be unassuming, and it might tempt others to challenge him. He seems to be "unaware that he [is] bold and courageous," just as he is unaware of having been insulted. Alyosha is very good at blocking out thoughts and feelings that do not fit his sense of how he ought or needs to be. Being proud of himself would not only arouse rivalrous feelings in the other boys, it would also clash with the humility that makes him feel secure.

Alyosha maintains his nonthreatening posture by not caring "to be a judge of others" (I, iv). He never takes "it upon himself to criticise" and would never "condemn any one for anything." Dmitri and Ivan are full of indignation at having been mistreated, but Alyosha is not; he "accept[s] everything," and no one can "surprise or frighten him even in his earliest youth." Alyosha inures himself to his father's behavior at an early age in order to avoid being overwhelmed by it, as is his mother, so that nothing his father does can take him unawares or fill him with disgust—at least not consciously. When he returns to the "sink of filthy debauchery" that is his father's house, he simply withdraws "in silence when to look on [is] unbearable, but without the slightest sign of contempt." His accepting attitude endears him to his father, who feels that he is "the only creature in the world who has not condemned [him]."

Again, there is a striking lack of affect in Alyosha's response. Because he seems to be impervious to his surroundings, Fyodor regards Alyosha as an "angel" whom nothing can touch, and this also seems to be Dostoevsky's perspective. Alyosha does not become detached in the manner of Ivan, but his deep inner denial and aloofness protect him from unbearable realities and keep him from having reactions that would jeopardize his self-image and sense of security.

Alyosha feels that because no one has reason to be afraid of him, he need not be afraid of other people. His defenses are designed to counteract anxiety, and they seem to be working, for Dostoevsky stresses his lack of fear. He is "fully persuaded that his father might hurt any one else, but would not hurt him" (III, iii). Given his father's fondness for him, this is not an unreasonable conviction, but Alyosha's sense of safety goes much farther: he "was certain that no one in the whole world ever would want to hurt him, and, what is more, he knew that no one could hurt him. This was for him an axiom, assumed once for all without question, and he went his way without hesitation, relying on it." This is a very striking belief. As a matter of fact, both Grushenka and Rakitin want to hurt Alyosha, but he emerges unscathed from their designs, as we shall see in the next chapter.

Alyosha seems from early childhood to have entered into a world of his own, one in which to be amiable, unassertive, and undemanding will ensure the satisfaction of his needs. Within the fortress of his defenses, he has a sense of invulnerability. He is convinced that if he does not threaten anyone, resent anything, feel or express hostility, or make demands for himself, he cannot be injured. He has a magic bargain in which obeying his inner dictates will produce the results he desires.

Having this bargain does not make Alyosha an unrealistic character, for such deals are a common feature of human psychology (see

Horney 1950; Paris 1991a, 1994a). Alyosha's bargain is similar to that of Saul Bellow's Moses Herzog, who clings to a childish credo from Mother Goose:

> I love little pussy, her coat is so warm
> And if I don't hurt her, she'll do me no harm.
> I'll sit by the fire and give her some food,
> And pussy will love me because I am good.

Herzog is in crisis because the world does not honor his bargain: his unloving wife does him harm, and he is betrayed by his best friend (see Paris 1986, 66–78). What creates an aura of unreality around Alyosha is that his bargain is made to work by the author, who is, as it were, the God of this universe. The order of things affirmed by the novel validates Alyosha's claims: no one will harm him because he doesn't hurt anyone. By retreating into a world of his own and behaving according to the laws of that world, Alyosha transforms his environment into a safe and nurturing one. He controls reality by means of his own behavior, which is magically efficacious. That is the object of bargains with fate, but usually they do not succeed.

The traits Alyosha develops make him not only unthreatening but also an object of affection: people love him because he is good. He was loved "wherever he went, and it was so from his earliest childhood" (I, iv). When he enters the household of Yefim Petrovitch Polenov, he gains "the hearts of all the family," so that they look "on him as quite their own child." This does not happen with the "morose and reserved" Ivan (I, iii), though he too is treated kindly by his benefactor.

The narrator says that Alyosha "entered the house at such a tender age that he could not have acted from design nor artfulness in winning affection. So that the gift of making himself loved directly and unconsciously was inherent in him, in his very nature so to speak" (I, iv). There are no doubt temperamental factors involved, but children can begin to develop defensive strategies that are in keeping with their temperament when they are quite young, and this seems to have been the case with Alyosha. He responded to an unstable environment in which he had a devoted mother who could not protect him by being a good boy and making himself easy to get along with. Dmitri responds to his turbulent childhood by acting out aggression, while Ivan withdraws into himself and strives to be independent of an untrustworthy world. The object of Alyosha's solution is getting himself cared for.

Through his trustfulness, docility, and endearing personality, he turns a threatening world into a fostering one.

One of Alyosha "strange" (i.e., saintly) characteristics is his lack of concern for money. We are told that if he suddenly came into a large fortune, he wouldn't "hesitate to give it away for the asking, either for good works or perhaps to a clever rogue" (I, iv). He would have difficulty making discriminations and being self-protective. When he is given pocket-money, for which he never asks, he is "either terribly careless of it so that it [is] gone in a moment, or he [keeps] it for weeks together, not knowing what to do with it." When he decides to return to his native town, the distant relations of Yefim Petrovitch with whom he has gone to live after his benefactor's death provide him liberally with money for his journey; however, he returns half of it, announcing that he plans to go third class. It is important to Alyosha not to be grasping or self-indulgent or to care for material comforts. He has difficulty wanting things for himself or treating himself well. He is more at ease traveling third class because this accords with his modesty and self-minimization.

Alyosha takes no thought for worldly matters such as money because he is confident that he will cared for, and Dostoevsky lets us know that his confidence is well founded. Pyotr Alexandrovitch Miüsov, "a man very sensitive on the score of money," gives the following account of Alyosha:

> Here is perhaps the one man in the world whom you might leave alone without a penny, in the centre of an unknown town of a million inhabitants, and he would not come to harm, he would not die of cold and hunger, for he would be fed and sheltered at once; and if he were not, he would find a shelter for himself, and it would cost him no effort or humiliation. And to shelter him would be no burden, but on the contrary, would probably be looked on as a pleasure. (I, iv)

This can be seen as one of the hagiographical elements in Alyosha's story, but the testimony comes from a Westernized freethinker, so it seems meant to be taken as a sober account of the way things are. Alyosha just assumes that people will provide for him, and they do.

The mimetic portrait of Alyosha shows him as the product of a highly disturbed family who develops radical strategies for warding off anxiety and fulfilling his emotional needs. Although the strategies are extreme, they make sense psychologically and increase our admiration of Dostoevsky's intuitive understanding and mimetic skill. Alyosha's strategies work to perfection in the world of the novel, particularly at the beginning and at the end, much better, I think, than they would in life. Alyosha lives in a world constructed by an author who wants to glorify these strategies and to show them as being in accord with reality and having a transformative power.

Through his defenses, Alyosha finds safety, love, and belonging, despite his initially dim prospects for obtaining these things. His needs for esteem are also gratified. He is lavishly praised by other characters, who open their hearts to him and value his judgment. At times he becomes an object of veneration. When Dmitri confides in him, he says: "You are an angel on earth. You will hear and judge and forgive. And that's what I need, that some one above me should forgive" (III, iii). The rewards are great for Alyosha's self-abnegation and accepting attitude.

IV. Alyosha and Father Zossima

Alyosha does not finish his studies at the gymnasium but says that he is going to see his father about a plan. We hear nothing further about the plan but are told that Alyosha returned to his native town in order to look for his mother's grave, that this was probably not the whole reason for his return, and that he himself "did not understand and could not explain" what had drawn him to a new path (I, iv). Presumably, he is being led into the orbit of Father Zossima by supernatural forces. Soon after he visits his mother's grave, he announces that he wants to enter the local monastery. He has been there for a year before the arrival of his brothers, and he seems "willing to be cloistered there for the rest of his life" (I, iii).

Alyosha is drawn to the monastery because it provides a refuge from the confusions and dangers of the world, thus enabling him to preserve his innocence. He is drawn also because the monastery offers him a path by which he can pursue his search for glory. Once there, he becomes attached to Father Zossima, in whose fame he vicariously participates and who articulates for him, in a more conscious and elaborate way, the inner dictates and beliefs to which he has already been led by his defenses.

The narrator tells us that Alyosha was not "a sickly ecstatic" or "a pale, consumptive dreamer" but was "radiant with health" (I, v). There is nonetheless something of the dreamer and the ecstatic about him. As a child, he talks little, displays "a sort of inner preoccupation," and likes to creep "into a corner to read" (I, iv). At school he is "dreamy," "rather solitary," and somewhat remote from those around him. He enters the monastery, we are told, because he is "simply an early lover of humanity," and the monastic life strikes him "as the ideal escape for his soul struggling from the darkness of worldly wickedness to the light of love" (I, iv). This may be so, but he is also a very ambitious young man engaged in a quest for the absolute. He seeks the truth, wishes "to serve it at once with all the strength of his soul," and is "ready to sacrifice everything, life itself, for it" (I, v). He chooses his path with a "thirst for swift achievement." "It is written: 'Give all thou hast to the poor and follow Me, if thou wouldst be perfect.'" Alyosha wants to be perfect, and the narrator observes that he may have come to the monastery "only to see whether here he could sacrifice all." The problem of how to pursue his search for glory may be what he has been brooding about in his inner preoccupation. Once he becomes a novice, his dreaminess disappears.

Alyosha does not enter the monastery because Father Zossima is there, but once he encounters Zossima, he focuses his life on the elder. Dostoevsky is unsympathetic to a craving for glory when it occurs in unbelievers like Ivan but not when it takes a religious form. As we have seen in the cases of Sonya and Raskolnikov, religion provides a glory system of which Dostoevsky approves. The monastery that receives Alyosha has had three elders who have made it famous. Zossima is now dying, and there is no one to take his place. This is of great concern, the narrator explains, because before the elders the monastery "had not been distinguished by anything in particular"; it "had neither relics or saints, nor wonder-working ikons, nor glorious traditions, nor historical exploits. It had flourished and been glorious all over Russia through its elders, to see and hear whom pilgrims had flocked for thousands of miles from all parts" (I, v).

Mirroring the rhetoric of the novel, most critics contrast Ivan's pride, his desire to stand in the foremost place, with Alyosha's meekness and humility; but both brothers aspire to become extraordinary men, perhaps to compensate for early humiliations. Although we are told that Alyosha became attached to Zossima "with all the warm first love of his ardent heart" (I, iv), his attachment derives mainly from the fact that "his youthful imagination [is] deeply stirred by the power and fame of his elder" (I, v). He fully believes "in the spiritual power of his teacher and rejoice[s] in his fame, in his glory, as though it were his own triumph." Through his identification with Zossima, Alyosha can fulfill his own craving for glory without violating his need to be humble.

Alyosha has a vested interest in Father Zossima's greatness. His heart throbs, and he beams all over when the elder receives the adulation of the pilgrims waiting to see him. He understands why the peasants love Zossima so much: here is someone exalted and holy who is the "custodian of God's truth" (I, v). Alyosha is not troubled by Zossima's "standing as a solitary example before him": "No matter. . . . He carries in his heart the secret of renewal for all." In Zossima lies the "power which will, at last, establish truth on earth" and bring about "the true Kingdom of Christ." Here are power and glory indeed. The fact that Zossima stands alone increases his stature in Alyosha's eyes and intensifies his pride in him. Alyosha is extremely uncomfortable at Zossima's having been asked to mediate the dispute between Dmitri and his father because he "tremble[s] for his glory, and dread[s] any affront to him" (II, ii). When Fyodor treats Zossima with disrespect, Alyosha is "on the verge of tears."

There is a widespread conviction that Zossima's death will be followed by "miracles" and that his relics will bring "great glory to the monastery" (I, v). The anticipation of "extraordinary glory" is "stronger in Alyosha" than in anyone else, and a "deep flame of inner ecstasy" burns "more and more strongly in his heart." He may not be sickly, but he is an ecstatic. It is no wonder that Zossima's premature decomposition precipitates a psychological crisis of great severity.

v. Zossima's Teachings

Alyosha finds in Father Zossima the truth for which he has been thirsting. Through obedience to the elder, he can achieve the perfection he craves and the comfort of submitting to absolute authority, like the subjects of the Grand Inquisitor. His inner dictates are made explicit in Zossima's teachings and are reinforced by his example. Zossima says, "Be not angry if you are wronged" (II, iii); we have seen how Alyosha suppresses his rage at his father's treatment of his mother and weeps hysterically instead. Zossima tells him to love everyone, including sinners, and he does. He not only stifles his anger with his father and refuses to judge him, as Zossima has taught, but he displays "a perfectly natural unaffected devotion to the old man who deserved it so little" (III, i). I do not trust Dostoevsky's narrator here; I think that Alyosha is alienated from his deepest feelings about his father because they clash with his inner dictates and his quest for moral perfection. Unaffected devotion would hardly be natural in his case, but it is what he thinks he ought to feel toward a parent and what the narrator claims that he does. Other major precepts set forth in Zossima's teachings are to be happy, to be selfless, to work unceasingly for the welfare of others, to be humble, and to hold oneself responsible for all the evil in the world.

According to Zossima the order of things is such that obedience to these dictates will bring one power and glory, joy and ecstasy. Usually the problem with magic bargains is that the external world has not signed on to them (see Paris 1991a), but Zossima teaches that it has, and the universe of the novel is one in which bargains like Zossima's and Alyosha's work. If they live up to their inner dictates, their claims are bound to be honored—eventually, if not right away. While satirizing the dreams of unbelievers, the rhetoric of the novel supports Alyosha's and Zossima's faith that some day *their* dreams will come true.

Maintaining humility is essential to Zossima's method of controlling reality, but both he and Alyosha see themselves as extraordinary people and must struggle constantly against experiencing their sense of superiority. In his dying speech to his fellow monks, Zossima insists that those who have "shut [themselves] within these walls . . . are no holier" than those on the outside (IV, i). In fact by coming there they have confessed that they are "worse than others, than all men on earth." He then contradicts himself by observing that "monks are not a special sort of men, but only what all men ought to be." Having said this, he quickly adds, "Be not proud."

In his discourse on "The Russian monk and his possible significance," Zossima envisions the salvation of Russia, and indeed of the world, coming from "these meek monks who yearn for solitude" (VI, iii). It is they who have preserved "the purity of God's truth," and "when the time comes they will show it to the tottering creeds of the world. That is a great thought. That star will rise out of the East." Again, having expressed such thoughts, Zossima is concerned about pride because he is afraid of losing the magic power he attributes to humility. He preaches that "humble love" can "subdue the whole world," that "loving humility is marvelously strong, the strongest of all things." "God will save His people," Zossima proclaims, "for Russia is great in her humility." Zossima is engaged in a search for glory by means of a humility for which he makes extravagant claims and of which he is afraid of being proud.

Zossima really is proud, of course, and so is Alyosha, who makes no claims for himself but participates in Zossima's grandeur. Both have a condescending attitude toward the mass of mankind that they take great pains to deny. When Alyosha explains to Lise that Captain Snegiryov will accept money from Katerina Ivanovna should it be offered again because his initial refusal has satisfied his sense of honor, Lise asks if they are not "showing contempt" for the "poor man—in analyzing his soul like this, as it were, from above" (V, i). "How can it be contempt," says Alyosha, "when we are all just the same, no better. If we are better, we should have been just the same in his place." This is a wonderful reply, which I have quoted elsewhere with approval (Paris 1974), but it makes Alyosha uncomfortable because it seems to be saying that they *are* better than Captain Snegiryov, and this he must deny: "I don't know about you, Lise, but I consider that I have a sordid soul in many ways, and his soul is not sordid; on the contrary, full of fine feeling." Alyosha needs to feel inferior to Snegiryov, just as Zossima must insist that monks are worse than all men on earth.

Alyosha goes on to say, however, that Father Zossima once told him "to care for most people exactly as one would for children, and for some of them as one would for the sick in hospitals" (V, i). This is very benevolent, but it is also patronizing. (Didn't the Grand Inquisitor also regard most people as children, to be looked after by those in the know?) "Ah, Alexey Fyodorovitch, dear, let us care for people as we would for the sick," Lise enthusiastically replies, but Alyosha becomes very tentative. "Let us, Lise; I am ready. Though I am not altogether ready in myself. I am sometimes very impatient and at other times I don't see things. It's different with you." "Ah, I don't believe it!" says Lise. I don't believe it either. Having cast himself as healthier or more grown up than most people, Alyosha must now retreat by saying he is unready, unperceptive, and impatient and by placing the immature and unstable Lise above himself. "Be not proud," Father Zossima has taught, and Alyosha tries to obey.

Zossima's central teaching is "that every one of us is undoubtedly responsible for all men and everything on earth, not merely through the general sinfulness of creation, but each one personally for all mankind and every individual man" (IV, i). "This knowledge," he proclaims, "is the crown of life for the monk and for every man." It is the knowledge at which those in Zossima's stories of conversion arrive. This knowledge is so important because through it we maintain our humility, guard against judging others, and avoid rebelling against God. We cannot judge a criminal until we recognize that we are "just such a criminal as the man standing before [us], and that [we] perhaps [are] more than all men to blame for that crime." If people are "spiteful and callous" and will not hear us, we must "fall down before them and beg their forgiveness, for in truth [we] are to blame for their not wanting to hear [us]." If evil doing moves us "to indignation" and a desire to punish the perpetrator, we must seek suffering for ourselves as though we ourselves were "guilty of that wrong." And we *are* guilty, for we "might have been a light to the evil-doers" and we "were not a light to them."

Zossima seems to be aware that his teaching is difficult to grasp, but he insists that "as soon as you sincerely make yourself responsible for everything and for all men, you will see at once that it is really so" (VI, iii). Once we commit ourselves to that belief, our experience will confirm it, just as accepting God's world to begin with will enable us to sense its meaning. The evidence for our faith comes only after we have made the leap. I must confess that I have not made the leap. Zossima seems to me to be advocating irrational guilt and self-reproach.

The belief that "we are to blame for every one and for all things" is so important that Zossima identifies it as the only "means of salvation" (VI, iii). If we do not subscribe to it, we will throw our "own indolence and impotence on others" and will "end by sharing the pride of Satan and murmuring against God." Taking responsibility for all the ills of the world is, in effect, a solution to the problem of evil. It is not the Creator but each of us individually who is to blame for the suffering and injustice that plague human existence and of which Ivan Karamazov complains. God is OK, but we are not. It is no wonder that after Alyosha has been shaken by Ivan's rebellion, he runs back to the monastery to be saved by Father Zossima—Zossima has the answer to Ivan's arraignment of God.

I find it striking that even as he is discoursing on the importance of blaming ourselves for everything, Zossima's vision of glory surfaces once more. Evildoers might have been saved by our light had it been shining, but perhaps it was shining and they nonetheless were not saved. We must not for that reason doubt "the power of heavenly light. Believe that if they were not saved, they will be saved hereafter. And if they are not saved hereafter, then their sons will be saved, for your light will not die even when you are dead" (VI, iii). As long as we abide by Zossima's precepts, we cannot fail: "The righteous man departs, but his light remains. Men are always saved after the death of the deliverer. Men reject their prophets and slay them, but they love their martyrs and honour those whom they have slain." If they are not appreciated now, the righteous will receive due recognition in time. They have an immediate reward, moreover, in "the spiritual joy which is only vouchsafed to the righteous man." Presumably the righteous man is one who recognizes that he is lower than all others and is responsible for all the sin and suffering on earth. This recognition makes him a prophet, possibly a martyr, one of the spiritually elite. In Zossima's way of thinking, the more one lowers oneself, the higher one ascends.

Father Zossima's teachings come to us through Alyosha's transcription. Alyosha accepts them completely and tries to live by them.

CHAPTER 12

ALYOSHA: TRIALS AND RESOLUTIONS

I. ALYOSHA IN THE WORLD

AS WE HAVE SEEN, IN FATHER ZOSSIMA'S TEACHINGS ALYOSHA FINDS A sophisticated articulation of the view of human nature, human values, and the human condition that he had already adopted in a less conscious way as part of his strategy of defense. His inner dictates are henceforth formulated in Zossima's terms, and he is at peace when he is what Zossima wants him to be and distressed when he is not. His belief system is called into question by the elder's premature decomposition, but ultimately Zossima's glory and Alyosha's solution are reaffirmed.

The narrator tells us that Alyosha was "very thoughtful, and apparently very serene" when he returned to his birthplace (I, v). The wording suggests that Alyosha may not have been as serene as he appeared to be. He enters the monastery because it offers "an ideal means of escape for his soul from the darkness of worldly wickedness to the light of love" (I, iv). The worldly wickedness from which he is escaping may be that which he has been witnessing in his father's house. He refrains from passing judgment, but the sexual orgies in which his father engages are disturbing to him, and he withdraws from the spectacle. They may remind him of his father's maltreatment of his mother, and they may arouse his own erotic desires. He says again and again that he is a Karamazov and hence a sensual being; at the same time, he displays a "wild fanatical modesty and chastity." He is deeply afraid of his sexual urges and sees becoming a monk as a means of avoiding temptation.

Becoming a monk is also a means of escaping the complications of life in the world. When Madame Hohlakov observes that Father Zossima looks "so gay and happy," the elder replies that she could never say anything that would please him so much: "For men are made for happiness, and any one who is completely happy has a right to say to himself, 'I am doing God's will on earth.' All the righteous, all the saints, all the holy martyrs were happy'" (II, iv). In the world of the monastery, Zossima is an object of veneration and is entirely at peace with himself. His happiness shows his acceptance of God's will and is a sign of divine beneficence. God wants us to be happy. Alyosha would like to be gay and happy also, but whereas Zossima is the Christian in the monastery, Alyosha is to be the Christian in the world. He is told he must leave the monastery after Zossima's death and that he must "seek happiness" in sorrow (II, vii).

Because of the turmoil in his family, Alyosha becomes involved in worldly trials while Zossima is still alive. Indeed, as we have seen, the turmoil even enters the monastery when Fyodor and Dmitri arrive for mediation. Alyosha's involvement with his family exposes him to experiences that disturb his serenity. During one of his returns to the monastery in the midst of his efforts to help his brothers, Alyosha asks: "Why, why had he gone forth? Why had [the elder] sent him into the world? Here was peace. Here was holiness. But there was confusion, there was darkness in which one lost one's way and went astray at once" (III, xi). In their conversation in the tavern, Alyosha tells Ivan that he feels "somehow depressed" (V, iii). "Yes," Ivan observes, "you've been depressed a long time, I've noticed it."

It is hard to say exactly when Alyosha's depression begins, but he has a series of unsettling experiences that are undoubtedly responsible for it. Critics have referred to these experiences only in very general ways—saints are subject to trials and tribulations. I must recapitulate what happens to Alyosha in some detail if we are to understand his state of mind.

Alyosha becomes disturbed when he is summoned by Katerina Ivanovna, of whom he is afraid. We are told that it is "not her beauty" that makes him apprehensive but something he cannot define (III, iii). It may be her pride and imperiousness, his sense that she will create difficulties despite the nobility of her aims. He crosses himself as he turns uneasily in the direction of her house, and "a shiver" runs "down his back" as he draws near.

Before he reaches Katerina, however, he encounters Dmitri, who seizes the occasion to unburden himself. Alyosha is weighed down by Dmitri's confessions, but he also feels that perhaps "his work lay here" (III, iii). Richard Peace points out that Alyosha's name means "helper." This is fitting for someone who takes it as his mission to come to the aid of troubled souls. Dmitri's problems turn out to be more than Alyosha can handle, however, and he is left with a feeling of failure.

Dmitri's account of his inner conflicts stirs up Alyosha's anxieties about himself. Dmitri begins his "confession" with Friedrich Schiller's "Hymn to Joy," one verse of which says that insects have been given "sensual lust," while angels have "visions of God's throne" (III, iii). All the Karamzovs "are such insects," he tells Alyosha, "and, angel as you are, that insect lives in you, too, and will stir up a tempest in your blood." Human nature is "too broad," Dmitri complains: "God and the devil are fighting there and the battlefield is the heart of man." Alyosha does not feel exempt from this conflict.

Dmitri goes on to recount his love of vice and the ways in which he has taken advantage of innocent girls. As he speaks, Alyosha blushes and his eyes flash. Fearing he might be misunderstood, Alyosha explains that he did not blush at what Dmitri has said or done but because he is the same:

"You? Come, that's going a little too far!"
"No, it's not too far," said Alyosha warmly (obviously the idea was not a new one). "The ladder's the same. I'm at the bottom step, and you're above, somewhere about the thirteenth. That's how I see it. But it's all the same. Absolutely the same in kind. Anyone on the bottom step is bound to go up to the top one."
"Then one ought not to step on at all."
"Any one who can help it had better not."
"But can you?"
"I think not." (III, iv)

Dmitri then tells Alyosha that Grushenka has said she'll "devour [him] one day."

Clearly, this conversation exacerbates Alyosha's fear of women, of Grushenka, and of his own sexuality. He seems to have a sense of being doomed to fulfill the fate from which he has been fleeing, to become like Dmitri and his father. This is a terrifying prospect given his need for holiness and moral perfection.

Alyosha's anxieties had already manifested themselves in a similar conversation with Rakitin. After Rakitin says that Dmitri cannot tear himself away from Grushenka, Alyosha suddenly jerks out, "I understand that" (II, vii). So you've already thought about sensuality, observes Rakitin: "Oh, you virgin soul! You're a quiet one, Alyosha, you're a saint, I know, but the devil only knows what you've thought about, and what you know already! You are pure, but you've been down into the depths. . . . You're a Karamazov yourself; you're a thorough Karamazov. . . . You're a sensualist from your father, a crazy saint from your mother." When Alyosha begins to tremble, Rakitin is convinced of the truth of what he has said. Then he too brings up the subject of Grushenka: "Do you know, Grushenka has been begging me to bring you along. 'I'll pull off his cassock,' she says."

It is evident that Alyosha has erotic impulses, as would be normal for a healthy young man of twenty, and that he's afraid he won't be able to resist them as he must if he is to retain his purity. Just having such impulses makes him feel depraved. Of all women he fears Grushenka most, perhaps because he finds her quite attractive. He may understand Dmitri's inability to tear himself away because he is similarly obsessed.

Alyosha's encounter with Dmitri ends on a very disturbing note. Dmitri wants him to ask his father for three thousand roubles so that he can repay Katerina the money he owes her and to go to Katerina with or without the money to tell her that Dmitri "sends his compliments"—that is, bids her farewell (III, v). Dmitri says that if Grushenka comes to his father while he is lying in wait, he will kill the old man. Dmitri has given Alyosha very disagreeable tasks and has made him fear for his father's life.

Alyosha's visit with his father is more disturbing still. First there is a conversation in which Ivan denies the existence of God and then Ivan openly shows his anger with his father. Fyodor is afraid of Ivan and asks Alyosha not to love him. This puts Alyosha in an impossible position because he is supposed to love everyone. There follows the scene in which Fyodor describes how he tried to knock the mysticism out of Sofya Ivanovna, and both Alyosha and Ivan are convulsed with rage. Next, thinking Grushenka is in the house, Dmitri rushes in and attacks his father. Ivan restrains him and says that he won't let Fyodor be murdered, but Fyodor says that he's more afraid of Ivan than he is of Dmitri, and Ivan tells Alyosha that he reserves the right to wish for his father's death.

When Alyosha leaves his father's house, he is "even more exhausted and dejected in spirit than when he had entered it" (III, x). His mind seems "shattered and unhinged" and he feels "something bordering upon despair [translators agree on this word], which he had never known till then." The narrator explains that he is haunted by "the fatal insoluble question" of how things will end between his father, Dmitri, and Grushenka. His father has refused to give Dmitri the money he is demanding, and Alyosha fears that his brother, "feeling himself dishonoured and losing his last hope, might sink to any depth." The whole affair involves more people "than Alyosha could have supposed before," and there is "something positively mysterious in it."

The narrator seems to be explaining Alyosha's despair as a result of his concern for his family and his fear that something terrible is going to happen, and this is no doubt part of it. Despair is mainly about oneself, however, and I think that, overwhelmed by the complexity of his family's problems, Alyosha feels hopeless about being able to rescue his loved ones as he is supposed to do. He is in despair because he does not see how he can live up to Father Zossima's expectations and his demands on himself.

Alyosha now goes to see Katerina in hopes of finding "guidance from her" (III, x). Katerina tells him that Grushenka is there, that her Polish officer has sent for her, and that she has promised to break with Dmitri. When Grushenka enters the room, "a violent revulsion passe[s] over Alyosha": "He fixed his eyes on her and could not take them off. Here she was, that awful woman." In the course of their conversation, Alyosha becomes "flushed, and faint," and "imperceptible shivers [keep] running down him." Grushenka tells Katerina that she hasn't really promised anything and refuses to kiss her hand after having already received a kiss from Katerina. Katerina becomes enraged and Alyosha has to keep her from rushing at Grushenka. He urges Grushenka to go away at once, and Grushenka asks "Alyosha, darling" to see her home, saying that he'll "be glad of it afterwards." The terrified Alyosha turns away, "wringing his hands," and after parting from his hostess, he walks "out into the street, reeling" and feeling as though "he could have wept."

As Alyosha hurries back to the monastery, he encounters Dmitri, who has been waiting for him, and he begins to cry—"he had been on the verge of tears for a long time, and now something seemed to snap in his soul" (III, xi). Alyosha reproaches his brother for playing a prank on him ("Your money or your life!") after having "almost killed" his father, and Dmitri confides his suicidal thoughts. When he tells Dmitri about the scene at Katerina's, he is disturbed that his brother "appear[s] pleased" at Katerina's "humiliation."

Entering the monastery, Alyosha wonders why Father Zossima had sent him into the world, where there is darkness and confusion and "in which one lost one's way and went astray at once" (III, xi). Alyosha has had a series of traumatic experiences as he has encountered the passions of other people and the tangled web of life, and he longs for the holiness and peace of the monastery. He has also encountered components of his own nature, particularly his sexuality, that arouse his anxiety. It is striking, I think, that when Alyosha returns to the monastery, his focus is not on his family's woes but on himself. He has been overwhelmed by the emotions and the problems to which he has been exposed, and he has been unable to perform his mission or even to maintain his composure. He feels that he has been a failure and has lost his way. It is not surprising that he is depressed.

II. COMFORTS AND COMPLICATIONS

Alyosha is temporarily soothed by the note from Lise that a servant has handed him. Upon opening it in the monastery, he finds it to be a declaration of love, a proposal that they get married when she comes of age. It also contains an expression of anxiety about her reputation. Alyosha reads the note twice "in amazement" and then laughs "a soft, sweet laugh" (III, xi). He crosses himself as he lies down, and his "agitation" passes: "God have mercy upon all of them, have all these unhappy and turbulent souls in Thy keeping, and set them on the right path." He crosses himself again and falls "into peaceful sleep."

There are several things going on here. By placing the unhappy and turbulent souls in God's keeping, Alyosha frees himself of the responsibility of solving their problems. God is love and will "send joy to all." This thought quiets Alyosha's concern. Praying for others relieves his feeling of impotence, and submitting himself to a higher power restores his sense of virtue. He no longer feels embroiled in the messiness of life but seems to be looking at troubled people from a position that is above them. He is full of serene benevolence, much like Father Zossima.

Most important perhaps is the fact that Lise's proposal of marriage sets his mind at ease about his erotic desires. When he later discusses the letter with Lise, he assures her that he did not laugh at her: "As soon as I read it, I thought that all that would come to pass, for as soon as Father Zossima dies, I am to leave the monastery. Then I shall go back and finish my studies, and when you reach the legal age we will be married. I shall love you. Though I haven't had time to think about it, I believe I couldn't find a better wife than you, and Father Zossima tells me I must marry" (IV, iv). Marrying Lise will enable him to obey Father Zossima's commands and to take care of his sexual needs in a way that is free of the Karamazovs' gross sensuality. Lise later asks why Alyosha should "choose a little idiot, an invalid like [her]" (V, i), but she is an ideal mate for him. Lise does not sexually bewitch him as Grushenka seems to do, and he will be doing a good deed by marrying her. In response to Lise's question, Alyosha explains: "*He* told me to marry, too. Whom could I marry better than you—and who would have me except you?" (author's emphasis). Lise's feeling that she is not worthy of Alyosha makes him uncomfortable. He reestablishes his humility by saying that it is she who will be doing him a favor because no one else would have him.

Alyosha's serenity does not last very long, however, and when he meets Ivan in the tavern, he still describes himself as depressed. In the interim he has visited his father and given him what turns out to be a farewell kiss, Illusha has bitten him, and he has seen Katerina and Ivan at Madame Hohlakov's. He is again caught up in the darkness and confusion of life in the world. Not only is there a rivalry between his brother and father over Grushenka but also there are additional "grounds for hatred and hostility in their family" (IV, v), for Ivan seems to be in love with Katerina, who is Dmitri's fiancé: "And with which of them was Alyosha to sympathise? And what was he to wish for each of them? He loved them both, but what could he desire for each in the midst of these conflicting interests? He might go quite astray in this maze" (IV, v). This is precisely the kind of situation with which Alyosha cannot cope. We are told that "if he loved any one, he set to work at once to help him," but how can he help both of his brothers when he cannot "know for certain what [is] best for each?" And what is best for one may not be good for the other.

Alyosha quickly feels that he *has* gone astray again. Katerina says she's not sure she loves Dmitri anymore but that she'll never abandon him, even if he marries Grushenka. Ivan approves of her decision, but Katerina wants Alyosha's approval also, and Alyosha doesn't know what to say. When Ivan announces that he is leaving for Moscow the next day, Katerina professes to be glad, and Alyosha accuses her of acting, saying that someone must tell the truth. He tells her she is "torturing

Ivan" because she loves him and because she loves Dmitri "with an unreal love," "through 'self-laceration'" (IV, v). The enraged Katerina calls him "a little religious idiot." Ivan assures Alyosha that Katerina has never cared for him, analyzes Katerina's "heroic fidelity" to Dmitri as an expression of her pride, announces that he will never come back, and leaves without saying goodbye.

Alyosha is distraught. He cries "desperately" after Ivan to return and feels responsible for the rupture. He longs "to beg [Katerina's] pardon, to blame himself, to say something," but Katerina leaves the room before he has a chance to speak (IV, v). "It was all my fault. I am horribly to blame," he tells Lise, "hiding his face in his hands in an agony of remorse for his indiscretion." Lise says that he "behaved like an angel," and what he said was on the mark, but Alyosha feels that he has gone terribly astray: "He had rushed in like a fool, and meddled in what? In a love-affair. 'But what do I know about it? What can I tell about such things?' he repeated to himself for the hundredth time, flushing crimson" (IV, vi). He is grieved by the thought that he has "caused more unhappiness" when "Father Zossima sent [him] to reconcile and bring them together." He has failed, to be sure, but at a hopeless task.

Once again Alyosha finds a source of consolation. Katerina has asked him to give two hundred roubles to Illusha's father, Captain Snegiryov, the man Dmitri has insulted. Thinking about this is "a relief," and Alyosha resolves not to brood about "the 'mischief' he [has] done, and not to torture himself with remorse, but to do what he [has] to do, let come what would. At that thought he [is] completely comforted" (IV, vi). Here is a new mission for Alyosha, one he thinks he can accomplish. After an initial misstep, he does indeed succeed. His relationship with the Snegiryov family becomes extremely important as the novel proceeds.

Alyosha is still depressed, however, when he sees Lise the next day. She asks him why he has "been so sad lately. . . . I know you have a lot of anxiety and trouble, but I see you have some special grief besides, some secret one, perhaps?" (V, i). Alyosha acknowledges that he has a secret grief but says that he'll tell Lise about it later—"afterwards. . . . Now you wouldn't understand it perhaps—and perhaps I couldn't explain it." Lise knows that his father and brothers are worrying him, and Alyosha speaks of how they are "destroying themselves" and "others with them" as well:

> "It's 'the primitive force of the Karamazovs,' as Father Païssy said the other day, a crude, unbridled, earthly force. Does the spirit of God

move above that force? Even that I don't know. I only know that I, too, am a Karamazov . . . Me a monk, a monk! Am I a monk Lise? You said just now that I was."
"Yes, I did."
"And perhaps I don't even believe in God."
"You don't believe? What is the matter?" said Lise quietly and gently. But Alyosha did not answer. There was something too mysterious, too subjective in these last words of his, perhaps obscure to himself, but yet torturing him.
"And now on top of it all, my friend, the best man in the world is going, is leaving the earth! If you knew, Lise, how bound up in soul I am with him! And then I shall be left alone. . . . " (author's ellipses)

We have here most of the things that are oppressing Alyosha—a litany of his woes. His secret grief is probably the imminent death of Father Zossima, something he plans to tell Lise about "afterwards" but cannot help mentioning now. The only thing of importance that he omits is his feeling of personal failure at being unable to solve everyone's problems, his sense that he has been blundering and making things worse.

The most surprising thing Alyosha says is that he may not even believe in God. What can be the source of such doubt? Perhaps it is his sense, after encountering yet more complications, that the prayer that had given him peaceful sleep is not going to be answered. He has asked God to have mercy on "all these unhappy and turbulent souls" and to "set them on the right path. All ways are Thine. Save them according to Thy wisdom. Thou art love. Thou wilt send joy to all!" (III, xi). Since then he has instinctively given his father a goodbye kiss, he has been bitten by Illusha and learned of Dmitri's role in the Snegiryov family's sorrows, and he has been denounced as a religious idiot by Katerina. He now wonders if "the spirit of God moves above" the "crude, unbridled, earthly force" of the Karamazovs (V, i). It seems impossible that the people about whom he is so concerned will be shown the right path and find joy.

Thus Alyosha is already in a precarious state when he has his conversation in the tavern with Ivan. He has been wanting to get close to Ivan, but when Ivan takes a step toward him after defending his father from Dmitri's attack, Alyosha is "frightened" (III, x). Ivan is a formidably intelligent atheist, and Alyosha might be afraid that his faith will be challenged. It is challenged indeed by Ivan's arraignment of God. Alyosha suffers as Ivan depicts the agonies of innocent children, and when Ivan asks if he would consent to be the architect of an order in which the final happiness of humankind had to be founded on even a single baby's being tortured to death, Alyosha softly replies, "No, I wouldn't consent" (V, iv). Yet Ivan is clearly saying that such an order—indeed, one far worse—is what God has apparently created. Alyosha has almost totally suppressed his resentment and his retaliatory impulses, but they emerge in a disturbing way when he agrees that the general who set his dogs on the peasant boy deserves to be shot. Alyosha makes valiant efforts to hold his own against Ivan's attacks on God and religion, and he scores some points, but after they part, he races to the monastery: "Here is the hermitage. Yes, yes, that is he, Pater Seraphicus, he will save me—from him and for ever!" But this is the last day of Father Zossima's life, and Alyosha's distress is greatly intensified by what happens after the elder's death.

III. Rebellion: The Death of Zossima

As we have seen, Alyosha, along with many others, "anticipated miracles and great glory to the monastery" from Father Zossima's remains (I, v). There had been saints in the monastery in the past "whose relics, according to tradition, showed no signs of corruption" (VII, i). But instead of showing no signs of corruption, Zossima's body begins to give off an odor of decomposition not long after his death. Those who had been jealous of the elder are "extremely delighted," and as they denounce Zossima's teachings and accuse him of pride and self-indulgence, "a kind of frenzy seem[s] to take possession of them." Shocked by this turn of events, Alyosha undergoes a painful crisis that ultimately strengthens him, we are told, "for the rest of his life."

The narrator assures us that Alyosha's faith is "holy and steadfast," but it clearly seems to waver when he sees the man he has venerated being "put to shame" (VII, ii). He does not need miracles, says the narrator, "but only 'the higher justice'" that has been "outraged by the blow that had so suddenly and cruelly wounded his heart." However, the justice he is looking for takes "the shape of miracles to be wrought immediately by the ashes of his adored teacher." Alyosha's sense of injustice derives from the fact that his claims on Zossima's behalf are not being honored. This deprives him of his participation in the splendor of the elder and calls his whole solution into question. He believes that Zossima should have been "exalted above every one in the whole world," but "instead of receiving the glory that was his due," he is "suddenly degraded and dishonoured." Alyosha cannot bear without "mortification" and "resentment" that "the holiest of men should have been exposed to the jeering and spiteful mockery of the frivolous crowd so inferior to him." He has been deprived of the superior position from which he can look down on ordinary mortals with magnanimous benevolence. Why "this humiliation," why "this 'sign from heaven,'" why this absence of Providence at such a "crucial moment"? The narrator attributes Alyosha's response to his great love for Zossima, but the mimesis shows that much more is going on.

Alyosha's response is partly attributable to his conversation with Ivan, which now haunts his mind. His fundamental faith has not been shaken, we are told, but "the evil impression left by this conversation" is "forcing its way to the surface of his consciousness," and he is "suddenly murmuring against" his God (VII, ii). "I am not rebelling against my God," he tells Rakitin, "I simply 'don't accept His world.'"

Alyosha certainly seems to be rebelling, however, to be engaging in what Rakitin calls "a regular mutiny, with barricades!" (VII, ii). He leaves the hermitage without asking for permission or a blessing, and his resentment surfaces in the form of irritability. "Your face is quite changed," Rakitin observes. "There's none of your famous mildness to be seen in it. Are you angry with some one?" Alyosha has always suppressed his anger, but now he "can shout at people like other mortals." "That's quite a come-down from the angels," says Rakitin. Alyosha is angry with Providence, of course, much like Ivan. Rakitin seizes on the opportunity Alyosha presents to tempt him to be unruly. He offers him some sausage, which Alyosha accepts, and invites him to his place for a drink. "Give me some vodka too," says the novice.

It then occurs to Rakitin that this is the right moment to take Alyosha to Grushenka, and Alyosha immediately agrees to go. Rakitin has a "revengeful desire to see 'the downfall of the righteous'" (VII, ii), and he also wants the money Grushenka has promised if he brings Alyosha to her. "So the critical moment has come," he thinks "with spiteful glee." If we have understood the intensity of Alyosha's fear of sex and hence of Grushenka's charms, we can appreciate the significance of his visit to her house. He is rebelling against his inner dictates and allowing his natural appetites to emerge. What is the point of denying himself, of remaining pure, when Providence has allowed the holiest of men to be mocked and scorned? He might as well accept the fact that he's a Karamazov after all.

Alyosha also rebels against his sense of duty, his mission to help others with their troubles. As he was dying, Father Zossima had urged Alyosha to "leave everything and make haste" to find Dmitri: "Perhaps you may still have time to prevent something terrible" (VI, i). Prior to receiving this injunction, Alyosha had been searching for his brother despite his eagerness to be with his ailing mentor: "Even if my benefactor must die without me, anyway I won't have to reproach myself all my life with the thought that I might have saved something and did not.... If I do as I intend, I shall be following his great precept" (V, ii). After Zossima's death, however, he entirely forgets Dmitri and Captain Snegiryov, both of whom he had been concerned about the night before. He is not yet rejecting his duty—not consciously, at least—but he is failing to remember it in his anguish at Zossima's "disgrace." The image of Dmitri does rise before his mind as he goes to Grushenka; but he dismisses it, even though "it remind[s] him of something that must not be put off for a moment, some duty, some terrible obligation." We are told that he remembers this "a long while afterwards." It is Alyosha's neglect of his "terrible obligation" that has led some critics to see him as sharing responsibility with his brothers for his father's death. If he had prevented Dmitri from going to Fyodor that night, Smerdyakov would not have done the murder, for the valet later tells Ivan that nothing would have happened if Dmitri hadn't come.

IV. Raised from the Depths

Grushenka has been wanting to seduce Alyosha because she thinks that he despises her, which makes her feel ashamed (VI, iii). Like Rakitin, she wants to pull down the saint. Alyosha, as we have seen, is ready to be pulled down. Their encounter turns out quite differently than anyone had thought it would, however. It is uplifting to Alyosha and Grushenka and profoundly disappointing to Rakitin.

Rakitin has brought Alyosha at an unpropitious moment for Grushenka, and she is initially displeased. She has heard from the Polish officer who was her first seducer and is preparing to fly to him. On reflection she decides that it may be better that Alyosha "has come now" and not before (VI, iii). Struck by the "kind expression in her face," Alyosha is surprised to find her "altogether different from what he had expected."

Asking why he is "so depressed," Grushenka tries to cheer her "pious boy" by sitting on his knee:

> Alyosha did not speak. He sat afraid to move, he heard her words, "If you tell me, I'll get off," but he did not answer. But there was nothing in his heart such as Rakitin, for instance, watching him malignantly

from his corner, might have expected or fancied. The great grief in his heart swallowed up every sensation that might have been aroused, and, if only he could have thought clearly at that moment, he would have realised that he had now the strongest armour to protect him from every lust and temptation. (VI, iii)

This is crucial moment for Alyosha. Grushenka is sitting on his knee, and he is not becoming sexually aroused. He doesn't realize that grief has deadened his response and may wonder if perhaps he is a saint after all. In any event, his fear of women, and of Grushenka in particular, disappears, at least for the moment: "This woman, this 'dreadful' woman, had no terror for him now, none of that terror that had stirred in his soul at any passing thought of woman." He has "dreaded [Grushenka] above all women," but he is able to regard her now with "a feeling of the . . . purest interest."

This is the first in a series of pride-restoring experiences that contribute to the resolution of Alyosha's crisis. Instead of having to hate himself for being a bestial Karamazov, he regards Grushenka with pure concern as he is supposed to do. And she says that she loves him "with all [her] soul," in a "quite different" way from that in which she loves her officer (VI, iii). She has long regarded Alyosha as her conscience and has been afraid that he "must despise a nasty thing" like her. She has mistaken his fear and shyness in her presence for contempt. The fact that Grushenka has looked up to him and says she loves him in a nonerotic manner is an antidote to Alyosha's impulse to express his rage and despair by plunging into sin.

Grushenka's response when she learns that Father Zossima has died is extremely important to Alyosha: "'Good God, I did not know!' She crossed herself devoutly. 'Goodness, what have I been doing, sitting on his knee like that at such a moment!' She started up as though in dismay, instantly slipped off his knee and sat down on the sofa" (VI, iii). Her respect for Zossima and pity for Alyosha are restorative. His mutiny over, Alyosha firmly tells Rakitin not to taunt him "with having rebelled against God." He had come to see Grushenka because he was drawn to evil, but he has found "a loving heart," "a treasure," "a true sister" here instead: "Agrafena Alexandrovna, I am speaking of you. You've raised my soul from the depths." "'She has saved you, it seems,' laugh[s] Rakitin spitefully. 'And she meant to get you in her clutches, do you realise that?'" Grushenka says that Alyosha's praise makes her ashamed because she is "bad and not good." She did want to corrupt him, but "now it's all different." Their emotional intensity annoys Rakitin, who feels as though he's "in a madhouse" and is afraid they'll soon "begin to cry." Grushenka says that she *will* begin to cry: "He called me his sister and I shall never forget that."

The visit ends with Grushenka and Alyosha having saved each other, much to Rakitin's discomfiture. Grushenka continues her self-accusation, comparing herself to the wicked woman in her story of the onion and telling Alyosha not to praise her. Alyosha continues to celebrate her, however, saying that "she is more loving" than he because she is ready to forgive her seducer "after five years in torment" (VI, iii). Irritated by her attachment to Alyosha and the frustration of his plans, Rakitin asks Grushenka what Alyosha has said that is "so special." She cannot say exactly, but whatever it was went "straight to [her] heart": "He is the first, the only one who has pitied me." She falls on her knees before Alyosha and asks, "Why did you not come before, you angel? . . . I've been waiting all my life for someone like you. I knew that some like you would come and forgive me. I believed that, nasty as I am, some one would really love me, not only with a shameful love!"

Alyosha is now successfully fulfilling the role of rescuer that he has been assigned. Grushenka looks up to him, calls him an angel, and regards him as her conscience. She feels loved and forgiven by him, and she venerates him in return, much as Zossima is venerated by those who seek him out. Under his influence, Grushenka tries to make peace with Rakitin and sends her greetings to Dmitri, asking Dmitri not to remember evil against her despite the fact that she has "brought him misery" (VI, iii). Her encounter with Alyosha prepares her to accept her culpability when Dmitri is arrested in Mokroe. "Well, so you've saved the sinner?" Rakitin spitefully remarks. "Have you turned the Magdalene into the true path? Driven out the seven devils, eh? So you see the miracles you were looking out for just now have come to pass!" Embittered by this unexpected outcome, Rakitin damns Alyosha as they part, saying he doesn't want to know him from now on. Symbolically this signifies the departure of the dark side of Alyosha, which had briefly gained the upper hand. As a result of his visit with Grushenka, his soul has been raised from the depths.

v. One of the Elect

When Alyosha returns to the monastery, his search for glory is back on course. He regards Zossima's coffin as a holy shrine and is no longer troubled by the odor of corruption. He kneels to pray, but "worn out with exhaustion," he begins to doze as Father Païssy is reading about the marriage in Cana of Galilee (VI, iv). The gospel account of the miraculous transformation of water into wine is in the background as Alyosha dreams that he is at the wedding. Father Zossima is also there, having been "called and bidden," and he summons Alyosha to join them. Referring to Grushenka's story of the wicked woman who has a chance of redemption because of her one good deed, Zossima says that he is there because he has given "an onion to a beggar" (thus preserving his humility) and that Alyosha too has "known how to give a famished woman an onion today." "Begin your work, dear one, begin it, gentle one!" Zossima enjoins him. Alyosha has already begun it with Grushenka, of course. He is afraid to look at the radiant Christ, but Zossima urges him to have no fear: "He is terrible in his greatness, awful in his sublimity, but infinitely merciful."

With a glow in his heart and "tears of rapture" in his eyes, Alyosha utters a cry and awakens. The message of his dream is that Zossima is at the side of Christ and that he too has been deemed worthy to be a member of that exalted company. His sense of himself as an exceptional person has been restored by a dream, much as Raskolnikov's pride is restored by his dream at the end of *Crime and Punishment*.

His soul "overflowing with rapture," Alyosha goes out into the beauty of the night and gazes at the heavens. Suddenly he throws himself down on the earth: "He did not know why he embraced it. He could not have told why he longed so irresistibly to kiss it, to kiss it all. But he kissed it weeping, sobbing and watering it with his tears, and vowed passionately to love it, to love it for ever and ever. 'Water the earth with the tears of your joy and love those tears,' echoed in his soul" (VI, iv). The narrator says that Alyosha does not know why he embraces the earth, but the words that echo in his mind provide an explanation. They are part of Alyosha's account of Father Zossima's teachings: "Love to throw yourself on the earth and kiss it. Kiss the earth and love it with an unceasing, consuming love. Love all men, love everything. Seek that rapture and ecstasy. Water the earth with the tears of your joy and love those tears. Don't be ashamed of that ecstasy, prize it, for it is a gift of God and a great one; *it is not given to many but only to the elect*" (VI, iii; emphasis added).

Alyosha is following the scenario laid out by his mentor, as he will for the rest of the novel and perhaps for the rest of his life: "It was as though some idea had seized the sovereignty of his mind—and it was for all his life and for ever and ever. He had fallen on the earth as a weak boy, but he rose up a resolute champion, and he knew it and felt it suddenly at the very moment of his ecstasy" (VI, iv). By experiencing the rapture Zossima has described, Alyosha assures himself that he is one of the elect and confirms the glory bestowed on him in his dream. Within three days Alyosha leaves the monastery "in accordance with the words of his elder, who had bidden him 'sojourn in the world'" (VI, iv). When he goes back into the world, he encounters unhappy and turbulent souls once again, but this time he is able to pursue his work successfully, without being overwhelmed. The tragedy he was trying to forestall has already occurred, so he is no longer faced with the impossible task of preventing it. He serves as a source of support to Lise and Grushenka, Dmitri and Ivan. He succors Illusha and his family, reconciling Illusha and his classmates in the process. He saves Kolya from becoming another Ivan. And he becomes the spiritual mentor to a group of young disciples who shout "Hurrah for Karamazov" at the end. He is doing Zossima's bidding, fulfilling his mission, becoming what he is supposed to be. His solution is now working to perfection, thanks to favorable arrangements of the plot.

VI. Conclusion

I find Alyosha to be a truly fascinating imagined human being until he leaves the monastery following Zossima's death. After that he becomes mostly an illustrative character, an example of the Christian in the world. He serves Dostoevsky's thematic purposes, but mimetically he is less interesting than he had been before. The main signs of his earlier struggles are when he assures Ivan that he is not the murderer (X, v), says "don't believe him" when Ivan accuses himself at the trial (XI, v), and readily participates in the plans for Dmitri's escape (Epilogue, i). He may have forgotten about his duty to seek out Dmitri during his period of rebellion because part of him was enraged with his father and would not mind seeing him dead, and he may be so defensive of his brothers after the murder because he does not want to face his own failure to fulfill his "terrible obligation."

Like *Crime and Punishment*, *The Brothers Karamazov* is a grim novel with a very happy ending. Ivan's crisis is unresolved, but the humbled Dmitri and Grushenka will have a new life together in America. Ivan is profoundly uncomfortable about his grandiose aspirations in his colloquy with the devil, but Alyosha's and Zossima's dream of glory is celebrated by the rhetoric, their condescension is obscured, and their sense of election is confirmed. Thematically, Ivan and Alyosha are opposites. When we approach them as mimetic characters, however, we can see that they have much in common and that their similarities have a subversive effect on the main scheme of the book. Alyosha occupies the moral high ground throughout, but Ivan seems to have the more sensitive conscience. He is tormented by his sense of guilt, while Alyosha successfully represses his.

References

Bakhtin, Mikhail. [1963] 1984. *Problems of Dostoevsky's Poetics*. Ed. and trans. Caryl Emerson. Minneapolis: University of Minnesota Press.
Belknap, Robert. 1978. "The Rhetoric of an Ideological Novel. *Literature and Society in Imperial Russia, 1800–1914*. Ed. William Mills Todd III. Stanford University Press. In Bloom 1988, 125–53.
Bloom, Harold, ed. 1988. *Fyodor Dostoevsky*. Philadelphia: Chelsea House
———, ed. 2004a. *Raskolnikov and Svidrigailov*. Philadelphia: Chelsea House.
———, ed. 2004b. *Fyodor Dostoevsky's Crime and Punishment*. Philadelphia: Chelsea House.
Booth, Wayne. 1961. *The Rhetoric of Fiction*. Chicago: University of Chicago Press.
Bouson, J. Brooks. 1989. *The Empathic Reader: A Study of the Narcissistic Character and the Drama of the Self*. Amherst: University of Massachusetts Press.
Breger, Louis. 1989. *Dostoevsky: The Author as Psychoanalyst*. New York: NYU Press.
Camus, Albert. 1960. *The Myth of Sisyphus*. Trans. Justin O'Brien. New York: Vintage Books.
Curtis, Laura. 1991. "Raskolnikov's Sexuality." *Literature and Psychology* 37: 88–106.
Dostoevsky, Fyodor. 1865. *Crime and Punishment*. Trans. Jessie Coulson. Norton Critical Edition. Ed. George Gibian. New York: W. W. Norton, 1964.
Forster, E. M. 1927. *Aspects of the Novel*. London: Edward Arnold.
Frank, Joseph. 1961. "Nihilism and *Notes from Underground*." *Sewanee Review* 69: 1–33.
———. 1986. *Dostoevsky; The Stir of Liberation, 1860–1865*. Princeton, NJ: Princeton University Press.
———. 1995. *Dostoevsky: The Miraculous Years, 1865–1871*. Princeton, NJ: Princeton University Press.
———. 2002. *Dostoevsky: The Mantle of the Prophet, 1871–1881*. Princeton, NJ: Princeton University Press.

Galsworthy, John. 1931. *The Creation of Character in Literature*. Oxford: Clarendon Press.
Goodheart, Eugene. 1968. *The Cult of the Ego: The Self in Modern Literature*. Chicago and London: University of Chicago Press.
Guerard, Albert J. 1976. *The Triumph of the Novel: Dickens, Dostoevsky, Faulkner*. New York: Oxford University Press.
Harvey, W. J. 1965. *Character and the Novel*. Ithaca, NY: Cornell University Press.
Horney, Karen. 1936. *The Neurotic Personality of Our Time*. New York: W. W. Norton.
———. 1939. *New Ways in Psychoanalysis*. New York: W. W. Norton.
———. 1945. *Our Inner Conflicts*. New York: W. W. Norton.
———. 1950. *Neurosis and Human Growth: The Struggle toward Self-Realization*. New York: W. W. Norton.
Kiremidjian, David. 1975. "Dostoevsky and the Problem of Matricide." *Journal of Orgonomy* 9: 69–81.
———. 1976. "*Crime and Punishment*: Matricide and the Woman Question." *American Imago* 33: 403–33.
Laing, R. D. [1961] 1971. *Self and Others*. Baltimore: Penguin Books.
Lethcoe, James. 1966. "Self-Deception in Dostoevskij's *Notes from the Underground*." *Slavic and East European Journal* 10: 9–21.
Lukács, Georg. 1964. *Studies in European Realism*. New York: Grosset & Dunlap.
Matlaw, Ralph E. 1958. "Structure and Integration in *Notes from the Underground*." *PMLA* 73: 101–9.
Matual, David. 1992. "In Defense of the Epilogue of *Crime and Punishment*." *Studies in the Novel* 24: 26–34. In Bloom 2004b, 105–14.
Mill, John Stuart. 1961. *The Philosophy of John Stuart Mill*. Ed. Marshall Cohen. New York: Random House.
Mochulsky, Konstantin. 1967. *Dostoevsky: His Life and Work*. Trans. Michael A. Minihan. Princeton, NJ: Princeton University Press.
Murdoch, Iris. 1959. "The Sublime and the Beautiful Revisited." *Yale Review* 49: 247–71.
Paris, Bernard J. 1965. *Experiments in Life: George Eliot's Quest for Values*. Detroit: Wayne State University Press.
———. 1973. "*Notes from Underground*: A Horneyan Analysis." *PMLA* 88: 511–22.
———. 1974. *A Psychological Approach to Fiction: Studies in Thackeray, Stendhal, George Eliot, Dostoevsky, and Conrad*. Bloomington: Indiana University Press.
———. 1978a. *Character and Conflict in Jane Austen's Novels: A Psychological Approach*. Detroit: Wayne State University Press.
———. 1978b. "The Two Selves of Rodion Raskolnikov." *Gradiva* 1: 316–28.
———, ed. 1986. *Third Force Psychology and the Study of Literature*. Rutherford, NJ: Fairleigh Dickinson University Press.
———. 1989. "The Not So Noble Antonio: A Horneyan Analysis of

Shakespeare's Merchant of Venice." *The American Journal of Psychoanalysis* 49: 189–200.

———. 1991a. *Bargains with Fate: Psychological Conflicts and Crises in Shakespeare and His Plays.* New York: Plenum.

———. 1991b. *Character as a Subversive Force in Shakespeare: The History and the Roman Plays.* Rutherford, NJ: Fairleigh Dickinson University Press.

———. 1991c. "A Horneyan Approach to Literature." *The American Journal of Psychoanalysis* 51: 324–32.

———. 1994a. *Karen Horney: A Psychoanalyst's Search for Self-Understanding.* New Haven, CT: Yale University Press.

———. 1994b. "Pulkheria Alexandrovna and Raskolnikov, My Mother and Me." In *Self-Analysis in Literary Study.* Ed. Daniel Rancour-Laferriere. New York: NYU Press.

———. 1997. *Imagined Human Beings: A Psychological Approach to Character and Conflict in Literature.* New York: NYU Press.

———. 2003. *Rereading George Eliot: Changing Responses to Her Experiments in Life.* Albany: State University of New York Press.

———. 2005. *Conrad's Charlie Marlow: A New Approach to "Heart of Darkness" and Lord Jim.* New York: Palgrave Macmillan.

Peace, Richard. 1971. *Dostoevsky: An Examination of the Major Novels.* Cambridge: Cambridge University Press.

Pirandello, Luigi. [1922] 1995. *Six Characters in Search of an Author and Other Plays.* Trans. M. Musa. London: Penguin Books.

Rimmon-Kenan, Shlomith. 1996. *Narrative Fiction: Contemporary Poetics.* New York and London: Routledge.

Scanlan, James P. 2002. *Dostoevsky the Thinker.* Ithaca, NY: Cornell University Press.

Scholes, Robert, and Robert Kellogg. 1966. *The Nature of Narrative.* New York: Oxford University Press.

Simmons, Ernest J. 1940. *Dostoevsky: the Making of a Novelist.* New York: Random House.

Spilka, Mark. 1966. "Playing Crazy in the Underground." *Minnesota Review* 6: 233–43.

Terras, Victor. 1998. *Reading Dostoevsky.* Madison: University of Wisconsin Press.

Vetlovskaya, Valentina. 1984. "Alyosha Karamazov and the Hagiographic Hero." In *Dostoevsky: New Perspectives,* ed. Robert Louis Jackson, 206–26. Englewood Cliffs, NJ: Prentice Hall.

Vivas, Eliseo. 1955. "The Two Dimensions of Reality in *The Brother's Karamazov.*" In *Creation and Discovery,* 47–70. New York: Noonday Press.

Wasiolek, Edward, ed. 1967. *The Brothers Karamazov and the Critics.* Belmont, CA: Wadsworth Publishing Company.

———. 1974. "Raskolnikov's Motives: Love and Murder." *American Imago* 31: 252–69.

INDEX

Abbreviations: "Notes" for "Notes from Underground," *CP* for *Crime and Punishment*, *BK* for *The Brothers Karamazov*

Aglaya Ivanovna (*The Idiot*), 127
Alyona (moneylender in *CP*), 58–59, 60, 63, 72, 79–80, 113
Alyosha Karamazov, 53, 102, 117, 118, 122, 131, 137, 139, 142, 170
  aggressive impulses in, 194–95
  anger, taboo against, 193–94, 216, 217
  bargain of, 196–97, 202
  and Captain Snigiryov, 203, 214
  childhood of, 135, 136, 191–93
  and children, 130–31, 189, 222
  depression of, 208–18 *passim*
  and Dmitri, 189, 209–10, 211–12, 217–18, 222
  Dmitri, comparison with, 195–96, 197
  election, sense of, 221–22
  and father, 157, 189, 193–94, 196, 201, 207, 210, 222
  formal functions of, 189–90
  and Grushenka, 209–10, 211, 217–20, 221, 222
  hagiographical pattern of story of, 190–91
  and Ilusha, 189, 199, 222
  as illustrative character, 189–90, 222
  as imagined human being, 190–91
  inner conflicts of, 194–95, 209–10
  and Ivan, 138, 147–53 *passim*, 173, 176, 186–87, 189, 213–14, 215–16, 217, 222
  Ivan, comparison with, 195–96, 197, 200, 222–23
  on Ivan, 127, 176, 186, 210
  and Katerina Ivanovna, 208, 211, 213–14
  and Kolya, 222
  and Lise, 194–95, 203, 212–13, 214, 222
  and mother, 157, 191–94, 210
  pride restoring experiences of, 219–22
  psychological crisis of, 192, 201, 216–18
  and Rakitin, 210, 217–20
  Raskolnikov, comparison with, 221
  rebellion of, 216–18
  religious doubt of, 215
  search for glory of, 191, 199–201, 207, 216, 220–22
  self-effacing defenses of, 191, 193–99

INDEX

sexual urges, fear of, 207, 209–10, 211–13, 217, 219
Sonya Marmeladov, comparison with, 191, 194
unreality, aura of, 191, 197
worldly trials of, 208–16 *passim*
and Zossima, 138, 189–90, 191, 199–205 *passim*, 207–8, 211, 212, 216–17, 220–22
Amelia Sedley (*Vanity Fair*), 101
Antigone, 56
Anton Antonitch ("Notes"), 17
Antonio (*Merchant of Venice*), 101
Apollon ("Notes"), 28, 38
Aspects of the Novel (E. M. Forster), 55
Austen, Jane, 114

Bakhtin, Mikhail, xii, 71, 74
on *The Brothers Karamazov*, 117–19
on dialogical novel, 52–53, 56
disagreements with, xiv–xv, 5–6, 52–56, 117–19
on Dostoevsky as polyphonic novelist, 52–53, 55
on the underground man, 34, 39
Belknap, Robert, 118
Bellow, Saul, 197
Bloom, Harold, 53, 105, 112, 113
Booth, Wayne C., 56
Bouson, Brooks, 6, 19
Breger, Louis, 74, 79, 97–98
Brontë, Charlotte, 102, 114
Brontë, Emily, 56
Brothers Karamazov, The, 56, 102, 117–223
atheistic humanism, consequences of in, 132
Crime and Punishment, comparison with, 222–23
Dostoevsky's response to Ivan in, 126–27

fortunate fall, pattern of in, 118, 128–32
freedom vs. happiness in, 133, 149–52
mystic sense in, 126–27
puzzling aspects of, 172, 175, 176
seed imagery in, 128–31 *passim*
suffering, spiritual meaning of in, 130–31
thematic analysis of, 117–33
unreliable narrator in, 201

Camus, Albert, 120–21, 126, 184
characterization
Bakhtin on, xiv, 53–54
Dostoevsky's skill in, xi–xvi
mimetic, 54–56
round, xi, 55
Shakespeare's, xi
synchronic approach to, xiii
taxonomy of, 54
Chaucer, Geoffrey, 101
Chernyshevsky, Nikolai, 4, 47
Chestov, Leon, 126
Cinderella archetype, 114
Conrad, Joseph, 56
Crime and Punishment, 51–114
authorial commentary in, 56–57, 60, 71–72, 110
The Brothers Karamazov, comparison with, 222–23
Christian beliefs in, 58, 63–72
Dostoevsky's perspective in, 71–72
education, as novel of, 51, 114
epilogue of, 96–112
foils, use of in, 58–72 *passim*
happy ending of, 112–14
ideology and psychology, relation of in, 56, 87
life vs. logic in, 65, 66, 67–86, 70
modern unbelief in, 58–63, 71, 87

"Notes from Underground," comparison with, 51
rhetoric in, 56–72, 87
rhetoric vs. mimesis in, 52, 56, 73–74, 113
right-minded characters in, 63–70
secular thought (utilitarianism, socialism), satiric treatment of in, 58–62, 64–65, 71
suffering, value of in, 67–68, 70
thematic analysis of, 51–72
vindication pattern in, 114
Curtis, Laura, 106

Divine Comedy, The, 117
Dmitri Karamazov, 164, 170, 222
and Alyosha, 199, 209, 211–12
Alyosha, comparison with, 197
childhood of, 135, 136, 197
dream of babe, 131–32
and father, 158, 195, 210
and Ilusha, 131–32
inner conflicts of, 209
and Katerina Ivanovna, 175
reformation of, 129
Dobbin, William (*Vanity Fair*), 101
Dostoevsky
Alyosha Karamazov's defensive strategies, validation of, 196, 197, 198–99, 202
characterization, skill in, xi–xvi
and editor (*BK*), 126–27, 133
experience in Siberia and Raskolnikov's, 112
on freedom vs. happiness, 133
Ivan, responses to in *BK*, 126–27
negations, proud of, 119
perspective of in *CP*, 71–72
as philosophical novelist, xi–xii
as realistic novelist, xii
religious glory systems, approval of, 200
rhetorical techniques of in *CP*, 56–70
spiritual regeneration, dream of, 132
tendentiousness of, 53
tensions between rhetoric and mimesis in, 52, 56, 73–74, 113
Dostoevsky the Thinker (Scanlan), 53
Dunya (Raskolnikov's sister), 58, 62, 63, 65, 75–76, 77, 81, 97, 108, 113, 114

Examination of Sir William Hamilton's Philosophy, The (J. S. Mill), 125
existentialism, 46

Fanny Price (*Mansfield Park*), 101
Forster, E. M. (Edward Morgan), xi, 55
fortunate fall, pattern of in *BK*, 128–31
in Dmitri's story, 129, 130
in Grushenka's story, 129–30
in Ivan's story, 182
in Markel's story, 129, 130
in Mihail's story, 128–29
in Zossima's story, 128–29
Frank, Joseph, 13, 19, 20
on *BK*, 156–57, 162 190, 191
on *CP*, 87, 105
emphasis on intellectual climate, xii
on "Notes," 3–5, 6–7, 38
Fyodor Karamazov, 136, 137
and Alyosha, 196
and Ivan, 156–59, 210
and Sofya Ivanovna (second wife), 157, 192–94

Galsworthy, John, 54
George Eliot, 102
"Grand Inquisitor, The," 146–53 passim
and Alyosha, 147–53 *passim*

Christ in, 149, 150, 151, 152
freedom vs. happiness in, 151–52
functions of, 124, 146–47
Ivan's psychology, as expression of, 149–53
power, as fantasy of, 151
sadistic elements in, 151
search for glory in, 150–51
Grand Inquisitor (character)
arguments of, 123–24, 149–52
conflicting needs of, 152
former holy man, 183
Zossima, comparison with, 203
Grigory (*BK*), 136, 160, 161
Griselda (Chaucer, "Clerk's Tale"), 101
Grushenka, 164
and Aloysha, 196, 211, 218–20
and Dmitri, 220, 222
and Katerina Ivanovna, 211
transformation of, 129–30, 219–20
Guerard, Albert, 3, 6, 19, 47

Hamlet, 151
Harvey, W. J., xiii, 54, 105
Helena (A Midsummer Night's Dream), 101
Herzog (Saul Bellow), 56, 197
Horney, Karen, 83, 193
on hypersensitivity to coercion, 44–46
on interpersonal strategies of defense, 9–10
on intrapsychic strategies of defense, 17–18
on masochism, 40–41
on pride in supremacy of the mind, 44–45
on self-effacing solution, 101, 194, 197
"Hymn to Joy" (Schiller), 209

Idiot, The, 127

Illusha (*BK*), 130–31, 160
Ivan Karamazov, 53, 102, 117, 131, 132, 197, 200
and Alyosha, 122, 137–38, 139, 147–53, 155, 157–58, 166, 173, 176, 177, 183, 185–86, 215–16
Alyosha, comparison with, 197, 222–23
anger and aggression of, 140–42, 156
brain fever of, 180
Camus, comparison with, 120–21
childhood of, 135–36, 143
children, on suffering of, 119, 121–22, 140, 148
confession of, 184–85
contradictions in position of, 125–26, 144–46
detachment of, 136–39, 143, 152, 155
Dostoevsky's response to rejection of God of, 126–27
and his devil, 144, 169, 175, 180–82, 184–85
and Dmitri, 155, 158, 169, 172, 174, 175, 177, 185, 210
at Dmitri's trial, 181, 184–87
faith, longing for, 181–84
and father, 136–37, 140, 155–59, 165–67, 195, 210
freedom, need for, 136, 143
on freedom vs. happiness, 122–24, 133
God, arraignment of, 121–22, 124, 141, 144
guilt feelings of, 177–78, 181, 184
and "The Grand Inquisitor," 137, 146–53 *passim*, 181
inner conflicts of, 127, 139–40, 146, 148, 155, 162–63, 164–66, 169–70, 181–82, 184–87

justice, challenge to belief in God's, 119–24
and Katerina Ivanovna, 139–40, 155, 173, 175, 176, 181, 185, 213–14
and Lise, 142, 173, 184, 185
and mother, 157–58, 210
nightmare of, 180–82
psychological crisis of, 166, 170
puzzling aspects of portrayal of, 172, 175
Raskolnikov, comparison with, 127, 145, 148, 186
sadistic tendencies of, 141–43, 146, 167
search for glory of, 124, 143–46, 149–52
self-hatred of, 166–67, 169, 175, 185–87
self-hatred, defenses against, 146, 148, 162, 166, 185
and Smerdyakov, 159–66 *passim*, 169–79 *passim*
Smerdyakov on, 139–40, 153
tender conscience of, 181, 223
utopian vision of, 145, 148, 181
values of, 181
victimization, sense of, 140–41
Zossima, comparison with, 147–48, 152

Jane Eyre, 102, 114
Julian Sorel (The Red and the Black), 51

Katerina Ivanovna (CP, Marmeladov's wife), 68, 69, 90, 99, 114
Katerina Ivanovna (*BK*), 139, 175, 176, 181, 211, 213–14
Kellogg, Robert, 54
King Lear, 51
Kiremidjian, David, 74, 79

Kolya Krassotkin (*BK*), 130, 131, 132, 222

Laing, R. D., 74
Lebezyatnikov (CP), 58, 59–60, 61, 62, 63, 103
Lethcoe, James, 5, 34, 35
Liza ("Notes")
  in brothel, 23–26
  detachment of, 23–24
  home life of, 24
  and underground man, 23–31
  visit of, 27–31
Lizaveta (*CP*, Alyona's sister), 57, 69, 113
Lise Hohlakov (*BK*)
  and Alyosha, 203, 212–13
  dream of, 194–95
  and story of crucified boy, 142
Lord Jim (Conrad), 56
Lukács, Georg, 54
Luzhin (*CP*), 58, 60, 61–62, 63, 65, 75, 79, 97, 103, 113

Markel (BK, Zossima's brother), 129, 131
Marmeladov (*CP*), 59, 68–69, 75, 90, 103, 112, 114
Matlaw, Ralph, 5
Macbeth, 89
Mansfield Park (Jane Austen), 101, 114
Marfa Petrovna (*CP*, Svidrigaylov's wife), 97, 107, 113
Matual, David, 96
Maximov (*BK*), 156
Merchant of Venice, The, 101
Middlemarch (George Eliot), 102
Midsummer Night's Dream, A, 101
Mihail (*BK*, mysterious visitor), 130–31
Mill, John Stuart, 125
Miüsov (*BK*), 137, 156, 198
Mochulsky, Konstantin, 112, 180, 183, 190, 194

Murdoch, Iris, 54–55
Murray, John Middleton, 105
Myshkin, Prince (*The Idiot*), 127
Myth of Sisyphus, The (Camus), 120–21

Napoleon, 88–89, 92, 103, 161
Nature of Narrative, The (Scholes and Kellogg), 54
Neurosis and Human Growth (Horney), 101
"Notes from Underground," 3–47
   comparison with *CP*, 51, 56
   parodistic characteristic of, 3–4
   relation of ideology and psychology in, 4–5, 46–47
   satire in, 4
   thematic components of, 3–5, 46

Our Inner Conflicts (Horney), 101

Päissy, Father (*BK*), 146
Paradise Lost, 117
Peace, Richard, 189, 190, 194, 209
Pirandello, Luigi, 55
Porphiry Petrovich (*CP*), 58, 63, 64, 66–68, 70, 91, 102
Problems of Dostoevsky's Poetics (Bakhtin), 53
psychoanalytic criticism, xii–xiii
Pulkheria Alexandrovna (Raskolnikov's mother), 58, 63, 65, 73, 113
   dream of glory of, 76–78
   letter to Raskolnikov of, 74–76
   and Raskolnikov, 74–82
   and Sonya, 96

Rahv, Philip, 105
Rakitin (BK), 140, 196, 210, 217–20
Raskolnikov, Rodion Romanovich, 53, 60, 61, 200, 221
   and Alyona (moneylender), 79–80, 88–89

   collapse of after the murder, 89–93
   conflict between secular and religious sides of, 58, 67, 71–72, 80–82
   conscientious side of, 63, 71, 90
   conversion of, 70–72, 82, 93, 96, 108–12
   detachment of, 106
   dream of mare of, 85
   dream in prison, 110–12
   and Dunya (sister), 75–76, 77, 79, 81, 86, 109
   extraordinary man, theory of, 65, 66, 77, 88–89
   extraordinary man, need to be an, 74–76, 82, 86, 91, 103, 104, 109, 111
   father of, 77
   and fiancé (landlady's daughter), 80, 81
   foils to and commentators on, 58–72
   fortunate fall of, 67, 113–14
   Grand Inquisitor (*BK*), comparison with, 102
   as imagined human being, 5, 73, 95
   idealized image of, 86–87, 88–89, 91, 112
   inner conflicts of, 71–72, 82–93 *passim*, 102
   inner conflicts, resolution of, 110–11
   Ivan Karamazov, comparison with, 102
   and Lazarus, 53, 67, 69, 70, 101, 102, 111
   and Luzhin, 79
   and Marmeladov, 75, 84, 90
   and modern ideas, receptivity to, 73–74

and mother, xv–xvi, 58, 74–82, 86
and Napoleon, 88–89, 92, 103
and Polenka, 90
and Porfiry Petrovich, 66–68
rage toward family of, 76, 79–80
and Razumikhin, 63–65, 84–85, 86
religious side of 69, 71–72, 80–81, 85, 87–88, 90, 110–11
resurrection of, 57, 114
rhetorical treatment of, 57–58, 87
search for glory of, 75, 88–89, 111–12, 113
self-hatred of, 90–91, 92–93, 104, 105
and Sonya, 69–70, 74, 77, 81, 95–105 *passim*, 106, 108, 111–12, 114
and student he overheard, 58–59, 87
and Svidrigaylov, 62, 74, 95, 106–8
underground man, comparison with, 82, 83, 106
and utilitarian ethics, 87–88
Zossima, Father (*BK*), comparison with, 113
Razumikhin (*CP*), 58, 61, 77, 78, 113
comparison with underground man, 65
as foil to and commentator on Raskolnikov, 63–65
as illustrative rather than mimetic character, 65
rhetoric and mimesis in nineteenth-century fiction, 101
Rimmon-Kenan, Shlomith, xi

Sand, George, 27
self-effacing solution, fictional presentations of, 101–2

Scanlan, James P., 53
Scholes, Robert, 54
Shakespeare's sonnets, poet in, 101
Simmons, Ernest, xi, xv
Simonov ("Notes"), 17, 20, 22
Six Characters in Search of an Author (Pirandello), 55
Sofya Ivanovna (Alyosha's and Ivan's mother), 192–94
Sonya (*CP*, Marmeladov's daughter), 53, 58, 62, 63, 77, 81, 106, 112, 194, 200
anger, fear of, 99–100
bargain of, 98–100, 102, 114
characters similar to in nineteenth-century fiction, 99–100
defenses of, 98–100
and father, 68, 96, 99
favorable presentation of, 68–69, 97
humility of, 96, 98–99, 100, 114
and Katerina Ivanovna, 99–100
letters to Dunya of, 56–57
and Raskolnikov, 68–70, 86, 95–105 *passim*, 112, 114
religious solution of, 69, 97, 100, 101
resurrection of, 114
search for glory of, 100, 101, 114
thematic role of, 68–70, 97
vindication pattern of story of, 114
Smerdyakov (*BK*)
analysis of, 160–61
analysis of by Fetyukovitch (Dmitri's attorney), 179
childhood of, 135
and Dmitri, 161, 164, 172, 179
and Fyodor (father?), 160, 162, 179
and Grigory, 160, 161
guilt feelings of, 178–79
inner conflicts of, 177–78

and Ivan, 159–66 *passim*, 169–79 *passim*
on Ivan, 139–40, 178
suicide of, 178–79
Spilka, Mark, 5, 6
Svidrigaylov (*CP*), 58, 60, 100, 105–8
analysis of Raskolnikov of, 62
detachment of, 106–7
death of Philip, his serf, 62, 107
as *deus ex machina*, 70
and Dunya, 62–63, 75, 76, 107–8
inner conflicts of, 107–8, 113
and Marfa Petrovna (wife), 62, 107
munificence of, 113
and Raskolnikov, 106–8
self-alienation of, 107
self-hatred of, 63, 106, 107–8
transgressions of, 63, 107
unbelief of, 62–63

Terras, Victor, 97, 151, 157

underground man, 3–47
aggressiveness of, 12
childhood of, 6–7, 9, 10
claims of, 19, 39
comparison with Raskolnikov, 82
comparison with Razumikhin (*CP*), 65
compulsiveness of, 6, 46
compliant tendencies and fear of, 12–15, 27, 29
conflicting inner dictates of, 14, 29, 37
contradictory needs of, 12, 19–20, 21, 42
degradation, enjoyment of, 39–41
detachment of, 10–11, 14–15, 19, 30, 45–6
dreams of glory of, 11, 37
as diarist, 33–35

fantasies of, 17, 19–20, 22, 27
on free will versus necessity, 42–46
freedom, affirmation of, 45–46
historical presentation of, 5–6
hopelessness of, 30–31, 38, 41–42
and imaginary interlocutors, 33, 35
inner conflicts of, 9–15, 20, 23, 26, 28, 35–37
laws of nature, dislike of, 44–46
and Liza, 23–31
love, craving for, 12–13, 25, 29, 30
narrator, trustworthy and untrustworthy as, 34–35
oppression of, 6–8
oscillations of, 8, 13–15, 27
paralysis of, 35–38
pride of, 19, 33–36, 39
school years of, 7, 11–13
self-hatred of, 14–15, 29–31, 34, 38–40
self-mockery of, 20
self-understanding, lack of, 34–35
spitefulness of, 8, 13–15
utilitarianism, critique of, 42–46
visit to Simonov, 17, 20
Zverkov, at dinner for, 21–22

Vanity Fair (Thackeray), 101
Vetlovskaya, Valentina, 190–91
Vivas, Eliseo, xi, xii, 190

Wasiolek, Edward, 74, 79, 106
What Is To Be Done? (Chernyshevsky), 4
Wuthering Heights (Emily Brontë), 56

Yefim Petrovitch (BK, Alyosha's benefactor), 136

Zossima, Father (*BK*), 53, 113, 117, 118, 119, 126, 146
    and Alyosha, 191–92, 199–205 *passim*
    and Anfansy (orderly), 128–29
    bargain of, 202
    death of, 216–17
    fortunate fall of, 128–29
    glory, as source of, 200–201
    Grand Inquisitor, comparison with, 203
    happiness of, 208
    irrational guilt, advocacy of, 203–5
    and Ivan, 182–83, 184
    Ivan's arraignment of God answered by, 204
    and Markel (brother), 130
    and Mihail (mysterious visitor), 130
    on responsibility for all, 132, 203–4
    search for glory of, 202, 204–5, 222
    spiritual regeneration, dream of, 132–33
    teachings of, 201–5
Zverkov ("Notes"), 20, 22